PRAISE FOR ...

"A fun, quirky romp through a diverse galaxy, brimming with adventure, danger, and a plethora of fun aliens to rival any sci-fi story."

Christopher M. Arnone, author of *The Jayu City Chronicles*

"A.G. Rodriguez's Angry Robot debut is a jaunty, fast-paced reminder that the rich shouldn't have a monopoly on space. There's room for everyone – even daydreaming janitors – in the stars."

R.W.W. Greene, author of *Mercury Rising*

"An exciting space romp full of action with geeky references to satisfy the most ardent sci-fi and fantasy fans. I was on the edge of my seat rooting for *Space Brooms!* and its hilariously relatable lead character, Johnny Gomez. An instant sci-fi classic!"

Dana Gricken, author of *The Dark Queen*

"A wild, vibrant, character-driven romp, *Space Brooms!* combines humor, heart, and action to showcase Johnny Gomez's journey from daydreaming custodian to spacebound adventurer. I read through the book in one sitting."

Briana Morgan, author of *The Reyes Incident*

"A hilarious and fun adventure across space, with a wayward bunch of characters you'll have a blast with. Gave me huge *Red Dwarf* and *Cowboy Bebop* vibes, while being its own brilliant thing. Loved it!"

Dan Hanks, author of
Swashbucklers and *The Way Up is Death*

"Witty, kinetic writing and an unforgettable lead in Johnny Gomez cements *Space Brooms!* as the kind of sci-fi novel I've been waiting far too long to see on my bookshelf."
Angel Luis Colón, author of *Infested*.

"One of the challenges of good sci-fi is connecting the universal to the unique challenges of a new world – or worlds! In AG Rodriguez's *Space Brooms*!, a lot is recognizable: bounty hunters will be huntin', governments will be shady, and there will always, always be something to clean, regardless of how many robots twirl around. But Rodriguez also gives us a view into a fun and convincing future, reminding us that a life-changing adventure can lurk just around the corner – even if we have to get around to cleaning the floors first."
Cassie McClure, syndicated columnist and author of
My So Called Millennial Life

A.G. Rodriguez

SPACE BROOMS!

ANGRY
ROBOT

ANGRY ROBOT
An imprint of Watkins Media Ltd

Unit 11, Shepperton House
89-93 Shepperton Road
London N1 3DF
UK

angryrobotbooks.com
twitter.com/angryrobotbooks
Chit Chat

Edited by Dan Hanks and Steve O'Gorman
Cover by Sarah O'Flaherty, with images from Shutterstock
Set in Meridien

ISBN 978 1 91599 850 7
Ebook ISBN 978 1 91599 851 4

Printed and bound in the United Kingdom by CPI Group (UK) Ltd, Croydon
CR0 4YY

9 8 7 6 5 4 3 2 1

For my mom, the woman who shared her love of science fiction with me.
And for Dan, Douglas, Gene, and George. Thanks for filling my mind with all this delightful nonsense.

Chapter One

A burst of blaster rounds sizzled past my head as I dropped to my knees and slid behind cover. Crescendoing orchestration screamed from the station PA speakers. The slap of blaster fire impacted the planter I hid behind, shredding the genuine Terran maple tree that grew inside. Shots rang in my ears, punctuating the rising timpani beats that crashed around the commissary deck of Kilgore Station. The firing continued for several seconds. Each impact sent shock waves through the titanium alloy planter, and a shower of broken leaves and twigs rained down on me. Each shock wave made me flinch. I clutched my blaster pistol close to my chest and checked the magazine. The read-out showed me four blue lines: four shots left.

The firing ceased while each participant in the shootout reloaded their respective blasters or shotguns. The horns blared their triumphant notes, leading to the climax of the piece I knew so well. My eyes darted around, spotting a few stragglers on the level above, fleeing from the scene with hysterical cries of horror. I looked to my right and saw her – my partner, a vision of beauty beyond compare – kneeling behind the planter a good ten feet away. She appeared as an angel, only one that was covered in carbon scoring and dripping in sweat. Her black hair fell from a tight knot at the back of her head, a sweep of bangs covering her left eye. Her porcelain-skinned fingers nimbly worked to empty the bandolier that draped over her shoulder, deftly reloading each remaining shell into her shotgun. She hazarded a glance at me and called me over with a nod of her head.

I took a deep breath, the air thick with burning ozone from volley after volley of blaster fire. A haze of steam shifted like a river current around overturned tables and alloy support beams, working the station recirculators harder than ever. I heard the telltale metallic clicks and snaps of magazines sliding into chambers. I had to move before the mercenaries finished reloading. I threw myself out of cover and scrambled to her side, narrowly escaping a laser blast to my face.

"I only have four rounds left," I said through ragged breaths.

"Just loaded my last six shells," she responded, her voice steady and reassuring. Not an ounce of fear or hesitation left her lips. She'd been through shit like this before and always came out on top. This time would be no different in her mind.

I, on the other hand, was not so optimistic. This would be our final battle together. We would go out in a blaze of glory that would live in the hearts and minds of the people of Kilgore Station for centuries. I put a hand on her forearm. She looked to me. Her green eyes sparkled with resolve. Behind her gaze, I could sense the determination that burned within her. I wanted to reach out, cup her face with my hands, and kiss her. I could think of no better way to spend the last few minutes of my life than with my lips pressed against hers. Instead, I smiled and nodded.

"You go left. I'll go right," I said.

She agreed, and I moved to my side of the planter. That was when she placed a hand on my shoulder. I turned to face her and was met by her soft lips pressed to my own. Shock and surprise quickly melted, leaving behind nothing but ecstasy. The feel of her lips, the touch of her hand on my skin, her scent, every sensation, and every impulse of that moment brought pure, intoxicating bliss. The viscous suspension of symphonic climax blaring from the station speakers and renewed blaster fire faded to nothing in my ears. For a moment, for that one painfully brief yet unimaginably powerful moment, the world stopped, leaving only her and me, lips locked for one last time.

"Make those four shots count, OK?" Her voice sang above the chaos.

My heart still raced from the softness of her lips and the taste of pink lemonade lip gloss they left on mine. I don't think I could have said a word if I had tried. It would have been drivel, a verbal diarrhea of stutters and groans. I stood up from behind the planter and took aim when I noticed the grenade, airborne and ready to spill coffee all over me.

Coffee?

The coffee cup hit the plastic rim and ricocheted toward me, losing its lid in the process. The tepid coffee splashed against my navy-blue coveralls and splattered all over the floor I had just mopped and the can I had just wiped clean. The cup bounced harmlessly away, rolling under a nearby table. I looked up and met the three eyes of the culprit, a smug moneychanger from Tarsus, his earpiece buzzing with a conversation too important to miss. He couldn't be bothered with the custodian he'd just soaked in ten-credit coffee. A couple of starbound teenagers, tall and lanky like all those who spend much of their life in zero *g*, wearing jumpsuits and magboots, laughed as they passed me. Both made it a point to mock my dejected face. Thankfully, nobody else seemed to notice. My eyes instinctively returned to the spot – her usual spot – where I saw the black-haired woman leaning against the railing a level above, holding a coffee in one hand and her glass communicator in the other. She had moved on, out of the food court to the lift exiting the commissary deck. I sighed.

I grumbled obscenities I would never say aloud toward the spacebound duo and the Tarsian and got to work, cleaning the spill, and ignoring my now soaked uniform that clung to me like a second skin. The coffee reached all the way up to my embroidered name badge on the right side of my chest. The white background was now brown. I could barely make out "Johnny."

"Gomez!" the radio in my ear shouted. It was my supervisor. "We need you on Deck Two, Level Two. That waster you said you fixed is throwing shit at people, over."

I tapped my ear and replied, "On my way."

That prompted him to yell, "Over?"

I sighed. "Yeah, over, over."

We weren't allowed to use the public lifts. Kilgore Station policy said facilities staff, including contractors like me and the rest of those employed by Astro-Suds Services, had to use the maintenance elevators. That meant a complicated, meandering journey from one deck to another, transferring from one lift to another, then down to a third, and across that deck to a fourth lift that finally took me up to Deck Two, where all the station's public services were held. Only, my trek wasn't over. Deck Two did not have any maintenance lifts between levels, meaning I had to lug my cart up two flights of stairs because, as a space broom, I was forbidden from using the public escalators that ran between the levels. I finally arrived at Deck Two, Level Two, sweaty, out of breath, with my coveralls firmly plastered to my legs and smelling of body odor and stale coffee.

The waste collector, or waster, in question was easy enough to find. I just followed the trail of partially incinerated refuse and trash juice. The accused droid was huddling in a dark service corridor that ran between two separate government buildings. It gave off an intermittent spray of beeps and alerts, followed by a hacking, wheezing cough of half-incinerated trash. For it to have so much on hand meant its atomizer was malfunctioning. I pulled my multi-tool from my belt and approached carefully.

"Hey there, little buddy," I said. The rectangular waster quaked and shivered like a scared child, only this child was twice as big as a grown, earthbound human male: me. "Don't be scared. I'm just here to help you work properly again."

The waster's service light glowed red.

"How did you even get back here?" I asked as I took a few steps toward the droid. "We disabled waster treads last rev. Unless you're one of the ones we couldn't account for."

That was when the intermittent red light changed to an erratic display of flashes and colors. A rumbling, sick grinding cry rattled forth from the droid, warning of an imminent trash eruption. I took a step back, only to be showered head to toe in a stinky, slimy tidal wave from the waster's chute. Thankfully, I managed to shut my eyes and mouth before the explosion.

I wiped the steaming hot sludge from my face and looked at the mangled shell of the waster. It was so full of shit because of the busted incinerator that the noxious gases of decomposition caused it to self-destruct. It wasn't silent, but it was deadly.

It took me the rest of my shift to clean up the mess created by the waster. I picked up the trail of trash and ash and swept and mopped the floor, making sure to place opti-stanchions set to wet floor so the station bureaucrats could avoid busting their asses and blaming me. The debris created by the explosion was a different matter. I scraped as much as possible off the walls and floor, then called for a disposal team to take away the remnants of the droid. Whatever survived would be repurposed or scrapped for parts. The service corridor itself would need to be refinished.

I threw my last dirty rag in my cart when my radio once again buzzed to life. "Gomez! Where the hell are you, Gomez? Over!"

I rolled my eyes and tapped my ear. "This is Gomez," I replied. "Deck Two, Level Two. Just finished dealing with that malfunctioning waster–"

"Get your ass back here! Your shift is almost over and I'm not paying you overtime. Understood? Over."

I exhaled before responding. "I'm on my way. I just have to finish this –"

"Let the bots do it. That's why we have them. And how many times do I have to tell you to say 'over' when you're done speaking? Over!"

My shoulders slumped and my head dropped. "I'm sorry. Over." I took one last look at the charred, mangled remains of the waster and shook my head. I pulled my glass-comm from my pocket, tapped the maintenance app, and added a cleaning droid to the requisition.

The Astro-Suds Services office and warehouse, located in the physical facilities section of Deck Six, looked like every other cabin on the deck. The only remarkable difference between it and the other dozen contractors renting space around it was the fancy flashing holographic sign just above the cabin number. A cartoon boy, wearing a ridiculous spherical space helmet, sprayed solvent on the wall, then wiped it to reveal the name "Astro-Suds Services." He then stood proudly, arms akimbo, and looped back to repeat the process once more, for eternity, or at least until the company went under and all cleaning services were given to the droids.

I scanned my glass-comm twice before the hatch slid open and allowed me inside, greeting me with a violent rush of air meant to prevent flying pests from entering. It always intrigued me. The floors sparkled with an immaculate cleanliness reserved for a hospital. The walls, from ceiling to floor, refused to hold dust, dirt, or stain. Perfectly stocked shelves, fronted and evenly spaced, lined the walls. Even the air pouring in from the recirculators felt pure, like untouched, unaltered oxygen. No bug or pest would dare set foot inside out of sheer respect for the unnatural, almost godlike cleanliness that emanated from within. As I walked, I felt bad dragging my slime-stained cart and wearing my crusty coveralls that flaked microscopic particles of dirt and ash. That was until my boss and owner of this particular franchise of Astro-Suds shouted for me from his office.

"Gomez? Is that you?" His voice shot through the sterile air like the slime spewing from the damaged waster. "You're always cutting it so damn close... Get your ass in here!"

I parked my cart just inside the doors to our back of house, knowing he would most likely have an explosive tirade if he saw it parked on the showroom floor, and dragged my way to his door. Even though I was expected, I still knocked twice before peeking my head in. "Hey, boss-man," I said with a weak wave.

"Damn, is that smell you?" he asked. Richard Fallis lowered his glass-comm a fraction of an inch, just enough for me to see his beady brown eyes peering back at me. When they saw me, his eyes got even smaller before he tossed his comm on his desktop and motioned his perfectly manicured hands to the chair just in front of him. I could see the Heparian pornography playing on his glass-comm, enormous ears and trunks wildly flapping about. I could also see the plain look of indifference he had to my knowledge of it. I took a seat, and he rolled his eyes.

"How about you close the door, genius, or are you wanting everyone to hear our conversation?" Fallis groaned. "So cute, but so dumb." He mumbled the last part.

"Sorry, boss, I didn't realize it was that kind of meeting." I apologized and quickly shut the door, but not before noticing the sani-droid already humming around the office, cleaning up the mess I tracked in.

Fallis leaned forward in his seat, locked his fingers together, and placed his hands on his desk. "How did we miss deactivating the treads on a waster? Weren't you the lead on that project?"

"No, sir, that was Manchac. I just assisted."

His face contorted in confusion.

"Manchac," I repeated. "That was his system name, what everybody called him because his real name, Manchacarragn-garrachgan Amgarach'chg, was too long and too hard to pronounce. Old Sigmoid fella?" I could tell my words weren't getting through. I sighed gently. "The bug-looking dude."

Fallis's eyes lit up with recognition. "Manchac! I almost forgot about that egg-laying son of... Well, I don't know what he was a son of, if I'm honest!" He laughed with such a force that he nearly fell out of his chair. I almost thought he turned red, but realized how impossible it would be to notice that through the layers of make-up he slathered on. I forced a smile as if I also found his xenophobia amusing. After his laughter subsided, he took a moment to compose himself and run a hand over his almost solid lump of sandy blond hair. He then asked, "So tell me, how did you and Manchac miss a waster?"

I shrugged. "There were a handful that went unaccounted for. Manchac said it was a glitch in the inventory matrix and we left it at that."

"Well, I guess I need to be talking to Manchac then. When is he in next?"

"You fired him, sir, last rev."

Fallis grunted. "Well then, this is on you, Gomez. If you would concentrate on your work a little more instead of daydreaming about captaining a space freighter or rescuing maidens or whatever shit you daydream about, this wouldn't have happened."

I swallowed, lowered my eyes, and said, "Sorry, Mister Fallis. It won't happen again."

Fallis shook his head disappointedly. "What am I going to do with you, Gomez?" he asked, his tone condescending but vaguely sweet. "Get out of here. Make sure you clock out now. I'm not paying you overtime for this meeting."

He leaned back in his chair and returned to his Heparian porno, but not before looking me up and down in an uncomfortably predatory way. I left his office, tapped my glass-comm at the time clock, and returned to my cart;

the silence and emptiness in the warehouse punctuated the absence of my coworkers. I slowly checked in my cart, recording all my chemical and supply levels, then locked it up for tomorrow. Lastly, I peeled the simultaneously slimy and crusty coverall from my body and tossed it into the trash. There was no point subjecting our laundry service to that atrocity.

Once at my locker, I went through the usual motions of typing in the combo on the digi-pad followed by kicking the lower right edge. It refused to open otherwise. Most of my coworkers had mirrors and pictures or digi-screens in their locker. I refused to decorate mine. This was just a job, after all. Why would I decorate? And I didn't need a mirror to remind me of the few white strands of hair invading my deep brown locks, or the dark circles under my eyes, or the five o'clock shadow gracing my cheeks, or the flecks of grime and grease plastered to my forehead (I could feel, and smell, those fine without any visual or olfactory aid). I pulled my heather gray hoodie with the Astro-Suds Service logo emblazoned on the front over my T-shirt, then grabbed my bag and slammed the locker shut. Once outside, I pulled my glass-comm from my pocket and checked for messages. I sighed as each icon flashed the same blank zero it did that morning.

I scoffed, "What did you expect, Johnny?" and started toward home.

Chapter Two

Deck Thirteen forever smelled of reactor exhaust mixed with raw sewage. This was partially due to the vicinity in which it was located, in relation to the reactors and station waste treatment facilities. Yet I knew its residents bore some of the responsibility. Regardless, the recirculators never worked properly. The electrical system constantly went on the fritz. Nobody outside of droids, cyborgs, the augmented (or augs), and slummers would live on Deck Thirteen. In fact, most of the station referred to it as the Septic Tank, or just the Tank for short. It was a disgusting pigsty of a neighborhood, and it was, unfortunately, the only place I could afford to live on Kilgore Station.

I never took the lift down to the Tank. It always seemed to stall out between Deck Eleven and Twelve as if it knew where it was headed and refused to go any further. So, I always got off at Deck Eleven and took the stairs the rest of the way.

You kept your head down on Deck Thirteen, especially if your innards contained organs and blood. Yet not for the reasons you would think. Sure, violent incidents happened in the Tank, but no deck on Kilgore Station was immune to that. It couldn't be helped, really, especially when mercenary groups, black marketeers, the Salaran Autonomy Board (freedom fighters struggling to restore autonomy to the Salaran system), and other competing organizations all called Kilgore their home. The danger on Deck Thirteen, though, centered on hazards and obstacles for organics like me. Droids constantly spilled oil and fuel on the stairs, making them slippery. Augs discarded their old parts directly into the walkways. I once witnessed a Sigmoid tear the head off a droid for stepping on the brood of eggs it deposited directly in front of the Open All Rotation store. I pulled my hoodie over my head, placed my hands inside the front pockets, and kept a close eye on the path ahead of me.

I passed storefronts with flashing holograms advertising the newest glass-comm or their most recent technological marvel arriving from another system. The restaurants on the way poured both strange and tempting aromas into the walkways of the Tank, which was honestly a feat, given the smell that typically dominated the deck. Makeshift crosswalks built to connect one set of residential cabins to another flew over the walkway, each at a different, dizzying height and angle. Whether out of habit or necessity, I couldn't say, but I kept my head down and walked at almost a jog for thirty minutes before I spotted my residential stack.

"*He-o tippa pa nihan o'chk*, Johnny Gomez!" Tinzo greeted me in its native tongue.

I waved as the hatch slid open with a whoosh. "*Pa na hapa o*, Tinzo," I replied with limited knowledge of its language. Tinzo, an M'gogo from Usel Prime, moved to Kilgore Station from its home planet a century ago with dreams of opening a restaurant in the Sol System. The rumors it heard of humanity's love of foreign cuisine were true. Unfortunately for Tinzo, most M'gogo cuisine contained a spice blend that caused violent diarrhea that often led to death in humans, earthbound and starbound alike. Its restaurant failed after the soft open killed two hundred forty-three people, hitting Tinzo with massive fines and disavowing its Galactic Chef License. Tinzo found itself destitute and broke, but instead of hopping the first transport back to Usel, Tinzo used the last of its money to rent a room in a particular stack on Deck Thirteen. It had lived here since.

It shouted the same greeting to every single being that entered, only, with me, it was always followed by, "You smell of trash, Johnny Gomez." Tinzo's two mouths moved in unison, pretending to spit something disgusting out of them. "More so than usual." Its dangling proboscis twitched and folded up like a snail sliding back into its shell.

"It was a busted waster," I replied, and patted it on the shoulder. The M'gogo reached up with one of its many hairy hands and dabbed mine. Tinzo loved humans, which is why it spent most of its time wandering the station, sitting on benches, and watching people walk by. It always ended its rotations on the bench by the front door in the lobby of our stack. If anything, it was a creature of habit.

The dim lighting, along with the squeaky recirculators present in the lobby, ensured I would never bring company to my place. Small piles of incinerator ash gathered in the corners. A viewscreen on mute, surrounded by heavily soiled armchairs, displayed a static-filled image of station news and events. The constant traffic in and out wore down the carpet to nothing more than a series of black patches. I climbed the unfinished alloy stairs to the second floor and made my way down the hall to cabin 212. The hatch slid open before I could reach for my glass-comm, and I nearly collided with my roommate, Rygar.

"Fancy meeting you here," he said, his baritone voice like melted caramel. His bulky, half-organic, half-augmented frame took up the entire doorway, from threshold to top casing, left to right frame. He had to bow his shiny, bald head just to exit. Cradled firmly in the safety of his mechanical, alloy-plated arms was our incinerator crate, full to the brim. "You know, they really need to consider installing an atomizer here."

I reached for the crate, which Rygar gladly relinquished into my grasp. "Atomizers cost too much. Kilgore would never have one installed on Thirteen."

"Meanwhile, the Tank is drowning in excess ash that gets swept up into the recirculators, causing frequent filter replacements. I'm sure an atomizer would cost less in the long run."

"Maybe," I said, shrugging my bag from my shoulder to the floor of our entryway and quickly walking to the ash chute at the end of our hall. When I returned, I found our door propped open by Rygar's arm. I chuckled and lifted it from the ground. "That never gets old," I said as I tossed it back to him.

Rygar caught it with his other hand and connected it back to his torso with a metallic click and hydraulic whoosh. "You looked like you could use a laugh."

"I did, thanks." I followed him into our sparsely decorated den, complete with the best viewscreen and sound system money could buy (all owned by Rygar) and collapsed on the couch (also owned by Rygar). He sat opposite of me in a recliner, opened a mini-fridge next to his chair, and tossed me a can of beer from inside. It was his brand. I preferred naturally brewed beer, not the mass-produced synthetic alcohol like this, but after the day I had, I wasn't going to complain. I popped the top and took a swig, swallowing the bitter, hazy beer with only a slight twitch of my right eye. I noticed Rygar's eyes flash yellow with amusement.

"You know, you could always go in and get a digi-brain installed," he said after chugging a beer and grabbing a second. "They're not that expensive and would allow you to partition your consciousness, like most of us do." He meant augmented individuals like himself. It didn't matter to which alien species you belonged. If you had mechanical attachments hardwired into your body, you were considered an aug. "Sometimes, I go to work, turn myself on autopilot and spend the rest of the day watching videos on augment repair, or of pandas rolling down hills. Crazy how the Junpoor saved the giant panda DNA and, after centuries of extinction, cloned those silly black and white bears back to life."

I took another sip and said, "I couldn't afford it. And I don't think I'm ready to take that step."

Rygar grinned. "Augs are no longer the future, man. We're the present. You and the others who refuse to get augments are a dying breed. Give it another five, ten revs max, and I promise you, even babies are going to be born with augs already implanted."

"Yeah, maybe."

"Hoo boy, it must have been a bad day! You're more melancholy than normal."

"It wasn't just work."

He gestured for more. "Go on."

"Tomorrow marks ten revs, you know," I said.

"Ten? Really?"

"Ten revs ago, I arrived on this floating truck stop just outside the heliosphere in search of a new and exciting life."

"Didn't really work out as planned, huh?"

"I thought things would be different. I thought Kilgore would be a jumping-off point, you know? The first stop on my trip to the life I always wanted. I always dreamed of traveling the starlanes on a merchant freighter or frigate, visiting new worlds, finding all kinds of adventures with a crew of my closest friends... I had no idea ten revs later I'd be doing the same thing here that I did back home on the Moon. I mean, Earth's moon, Luna. I mean, Terra, not Earth. I mean, I understand why they changed the names, but still..."

"Doing the same thing, scrubbing toilets?"

"Among other things. The only difference being I have one friend, and he's a cyborg."

Rygar grimaced and shrugged. "Are we friends? I thought you were the guy taking up space in my spare room."

I paused and took a sip of the cheap, simulated beer, and scowled. "You know, you should really see about getting your empathy sensors increased by, say, a percent."

"I looked into it at my last check-up. It costs too much to upgrade."

I shot him a sideways glance and could see his eyes flashing yellow – amusement. He could be notoriously hard to read at times unless you were able to catch the flash from the ocular emote spectrum system in his eyes. It took me three years to master. It also helped that the faintest hint of a smile curled the corner of his mouth. "You're a bastard, you know that."

"I am technically an orphan, which qualifies as a bastard. And I'll let the cyborg comment slide. You know my organic bits were produced the old-fashioned way, in a bed, not in a lab."

I laughed.

"Not everyone is destined for greatness. If we were all meant to be heroes or pioneers, blazing across uncharted space, there'd be no janitors to clean up shit –" he pointed at me – "or dock workers to check in freight –" he patted the alloy plate on his chest – "or teachers or doctors. Society would fall apart."

I stood, silent.

"I'm serious about the augs, Johnny. Even a simple one, muscle weave or ocular enhancements, or a digi-brain, would qualify you for a better gig. Think about it. I'll help with the cost if credits are the concern."

"I'll think about it, Rygar." He was right, after all. I'd be stuck at Astro-Suds for the rest of my life if I didn't do something proactive.

Rygar stood up and stretched. He rotated his shoulders – the gyros within whirred wildly – then tossed me the remote to the screen. "I'm off to recharge. Got my shift here soon and need to make sure I have enough energy."

I waved as he left, then turned on the screen, content to just zone out to the sounds of the late station newscast. Before I knew it, my heavy eyes closed, and I slipped into unconsciousness. I didn't even hear Rygar leave for work.

Chapter Three

My alarm sounded and I woke with a start. At one time, the gentle plucking of a harp accompanied by a flutter of flutes and other woodwinds immediately comforted me upon my return to consciousness. Now it only grated against my eardrums and provoked any number of groans, moans, and curses. I knew I could easily change the tone in the setting menu on my glass-comm, but never did; it was a perfect analogy for how hopeless I felt.

I tapped the alarm off and rolled myself from the couch, surprised that I never made it to my bed. I was still in my hoodie and pants. The funk of unwashed refuse and body odor cried out, demanding a shower. I turned once more to my glass-comm. It read 0400 hours station time, 318.1709 in standard dating. I know Kilgore set their time relative to Earth, but that was three centuries ago, before extrasolar life entered our system, before we discovered we weren't alone in the universe, before humanity joined the Republic of Unified Systems and Homeworlds. It needed an update.

Horrific thoughts of the day's challenges spiraled around my head as the viscous, oily, orange decontaminating cleanser rushed over my body. I missed regular showers with steaming hot water I could gargle, and harsh soaps and shampoos that would sting my eyes. After toweling off and brushing my teeth, I quickly dressed in my navy-blue pants, orange T-shirt, and favorite hoodie, stopping only to glance in the mirror. My scruffy cheeks and chin ensured a lecture from Fallis about proper hygiene and grooming for an employee of Astro-Suds Services, but I was too tired to care.

I moved to the kitchen to grab a quick bite before leaving. I then noticed the decorative plate gently holding two divine pastries, delicately wrapped in baby blue cellophane: a chocolate eclair next to an old-fashioned doughnut. They formed a ten. It made me smile. For all his augmented emotional disconnect, Rygar was indeed a good friend. I wasted no time taking an enormous bite of each.

"Mmm, God damn, he spent credits on real ones, not replicated ones..." I mumbled, mouth full of decadent breakfast pastry. They each disappeared down my throat in less than five minutes. I wasted no more time and hurried on to work, taking stairs and lifts and trolleys all the way to Deck Six.

The typical locker room conversations murmured through the building when I arrived, last as usual. My coworkers gabbed about what they drank, the score of last night's interstellar semi-final casco match between perennial champions Tyros and Terra, or whoever they fucked the previous night. Urbo, a former resident of Luna like me, combined all three into one boisterous and obnoxious conversation.

"So, I'm standing there, beer in hand, watching as Terra is seconds away from sending the match into overtime. They have all thirteen in the funnel of the diamond, and the Tyroshi are throwing everything they got at them – fists, elbows, feet–"

Pipon, a native of Idago, the birthplace of casco, interrupted Urbo's tale. "Yeah, Urbo, we all saw the match. You established that at the beginning of your long-winded expulsion of hot air." There were chuckles. He turned and acknowledged me as I approached my locker, patting my chest with the back of one of his four hands. "This guy is the worst storyteller," he said, rolling his eyes.

"All right, all right, calm the fuck down, Pip," Urbo retorted, knowing Pipon hated that nickname. "Right before time expires, Tyros pulls off the impossible and scores, putting them ahead by one. The entire bar explodes in applause, whistles, cheering, jeering, cursing, you name it. I was so pissed that Tyros ruined my chances of a cool thousand credits that I jumped…" He paused his story to recreate it, which brought another round of laughter. "Only to bring my arm down on the table, flipping the top, and sending everybody's drinks flying! Most of them landed on Chala's shirt, and let me tell you, she was pissed. So pissed that she forces us to leave early. I'm thinking, hell yeah, back to her place…"

"Enough talk, Urbo. We all know you got nowhere with the girl." Fallis's voice broke in over the tale. The chatter quickly died to the stern authoritativeness of his voice. "Assignment board has been posted, Brooms, pretty standard with no real surprises." Fallis turned to me and smiled. When he spoke again, his voice softened, sweetened. "Oh, and Gomez, I'm going to need you on Deck Seven, West with Bougainvillea's team. Apparently, the zero-*g* restroom needs servicing."

My heart sliced open my ribcage and took a leap from my chest straight onto the dirty locker room floor. I watched as it coughed and gagged for air before expiring with a dramatic sigh. I closed my eyes and took a deep breath before turning to face Fallis. He now stood close to my locker, almost too close. The biggest, shit-eating grin plastered his perfectly painted face. He nodded at me with the same condescending swagger he gave me the night before. But this time, I noticed something else in his tone, in his body language, hidden beneath all the machismo. The proximity. The softness in his voice.

"Roger that, Gomez?" Fallis's smile widened and his eyes grew even wider. He put his hand on my shoulder, but not in the buddy-buddy, "too hard of a slap" kind of way. I gave him a thumbs-up, zipped up my coveralls, and closed my locker. He cleared his throat and adjusted his tie as he turned to address the rest of my team. A few of my coworkers stared wide-eyed, as if they had just witnessed something nobody should have seen. Fallis finished his morning meeting with his usual, "Space brooms, get out there and show Kilgore why we're the best custodial service on station!"

Everybody remained silent as they passed my locker. Not a single team member could look me in the eye, whether from Fallis's strange demeanor, I couldn't tell. What I did know is that they all knew servicing the zero-g restrooms meant an entire shift wading in Tarbon excrement, an assignment only ever given to those on Fallis's shit list. The last three members forced to clean them immediately quit upon returning from their shift. In fact, the only Broom to ever return from such a fate without turning over his credentials was me, last rev. Fallis knew that well.

Before leaving the warehouse, Bougainvillea turned to me and said, "We'll see you over there, Gomez. If you need any help, we can knock it out as a team."

I exhaled and said, "Thanks, Boug, but I'll handle it." I grabbed my cart and wheeled it to the supply room, making a mental list on the way. Zero-*g* restrooms weren't under zero *g* when they were being serviced. Thus, they required complete body protection, magboots, a utility hose, a wide scraper you didn't mind tossing in the incinerator after, and as much orange decontaminant as you could carry.

The journey to Deck Seven was a silent and solitary one. Bougainvillea's team had a fifteen- or twenty-minute head start on me. I let my thoughts wander as I rode the lift, picturing all the different ways I would quit my job and throw it back in Fallis's face. I imagined myself barging into his sterile office, grabbing his glass-comm, and slamming it against the floor. I pointed my finger directly in his face and said, "You know what, Fallis, you're a dick. Fuck you and this job!" On my way out of the building, I knocked everything off the shelves, all-natural cleaners, aerosol cleaners, degreasers. Each one exploded as it hit the spotless white tile floor, sending streams of oily bubbles everywhere. I kicked open the hatch and exited the building as it filled with a rainbow cornucopia of foam from deck to deck and bulkhead to bulkhead. I walked away from it like a hero from an explosion. A crowd gathered just outside. Every single person I had ever known was there, cheering and patting me on the back as I passed. I noticed the black-haired girl from the commissary deck waiting for me by the airlock. "Got a Junpoor sloop ready for us to blow this joint," she said, throwing a thumb behind her at the gorgeous spacecraft docked just outside. I grabbed her by the waist, bent her over, and kissed her, which garnered another wave of cheers from the crowd.

DING. The lift doors opened, and I was on Deck Seven, the entertainment deck. Throngs of beings crashed around on every one of its six levels, excitedly running to their vice of choice. Every diversion imaginable could be found on Deck Seven, from casinos to game halls, brothels to sex dungeons. A mag coaster twisted and rumbled from one end to the other, leaving behind a fading chorus of glee. Overpriced restaurants spewed exquisite aromas into the air at such a rate that even the recirculators couldn't keep up. Peddlers shouted their wares above the chaotic din, offering every sort of legal and illegal stim, buff, inhalant, and smokeable.

On my way to the zero-*g* restrooms, I saw a naked earthbound man stumble from a sex shop, another man hot on his heels flailing a leather belt and screaming about infidelity. I witnessed a Xin, tall and lean with its typical, vaguely human features, vomiting into a waster. I noticed two cyborgs arguing over which exotic snuff show they wanted to attend. I grimaced, popped in my earbuds, and grabbed my glass-comm, tapping the silence button and exhaling as a wave of nothing rushed into my ears, blocking out all the noise.

I reached the hall of restrooms and suited up, ensuring my ventilator clipped tightly against my nostrils. I set up my opti-stanchions around the sphere in question. Its service light screamed at me in violent, oppressive red. The "Out of Service" hologram scrolled across the entrance in several different languages. A few I recognized and could translate with passable accuracy. The others, I couldn't even begin to attempt.

There wasn't a breath deep enough to prepare me for what lay beyond that door. I scanned my glass-comm, and the restroom approved my entrance. I inhaled as the door gurgled and whined its way open. I couldn't tell you what I expected. I knew two races of beings that regularly used the zero-*g* restrooms – Tarbons and Chrysostoms. Chrysostoms expelled waste in a cloud from their semipermeable membranes. It was like hitting an old pillow and watching the dust poof off it. Tarbons, on the other hand, expelled once every rev with a violent, high-pressure blast of an oily black substance. It looked to me as if a Chrysostom and a Tarbon simultaneously expelled, then simultaneously and spontaneously combusted.

The entirety of the sphere resembled those animated holograms of a virus or bacteria I saw as a kid, pulsing and tremoring with a strange derangement of life. The once black ceramic panels were now a putrid, yellow green. Blobs of syrupy excrement sloughed off every surface. Pools of black and green gunk clogged each of the four valves that normally washed away the waste. Even the drains bubbled and hiccupped, spewing an unholy scent that my ventilator fought bravely against, but failed miserably to contain. I sighed and got to work.

It took me an entire shift and every ounce of decontaminant I brought with me to clean the sphere, and that included working through my lunch break. The ceramic panels shone glossy black once again. Each flush valve sprayed like new. The drains no longer housed burbling clogs. In fact, the only evidence of any previous disaster lay in the myriad of stains on my coveralls. I stood marveling over my handiwork when I caught the glimmer of something shiny lodged between the grille vents of the farthest floor grate. I frowned, wondering how I missed something. I crouched and dislodged a tiny, transparent data slide, the kind the galaxy used to use to transfer or store information before advanced digital virtual encryption made them obsolete.

"I can see how I missed you," I said to the square. I thought nothing more of it and tossed it into the trash hanging from my cart. It would go in the incinerator along with these coveralls and my hazmat suit.

My glass-comm flashed 1805 hours when my cart and I rolled out of the curiously empty warehouse through the bay doors to the trash enclosure behind us. The enclosure sat nestled between the warehouse itself and the station bulkhead. Refuse from all over Kilgore Station found its way there via wasters, chutes, and our carts. It housed a compactor, an incinerator, an atomizer the size of my tio and tia's house back on Luna, and a couple of airlocks. I'm not ashamed to admit that me and my team, on occasion, when tasked to clean the enclosure, simply used push brooms, and swept everything out of the airlock. Along with the heavy equipment lay mounds of refuse, broken alloy pallets, and composite crates and barrels, all organized in their own respective sections of the enclosure.

The enclosure itself could only be accessed one of two ways: the rear warehouse bay doors and a small, metal service stairway that led up to the crawl space between decks. It was from that stairway that I saw two men descend into the space. They moved with erratic and conspicuous speed, taking multiple steps at a time, making the stairs sound like a steel drum, and looking everywhere as if their heads were on swivels. I immediately felt my heart begin to pound. My stomach churned.

I stood frozen, hoping for some strange reason that they wouldn't see me if I didn't move – which, of course, did not work. I immediately cursed when one man pointed toward me, and they both jogged directly toward my position. Everything within me shouted, "Run! Run and hide, you idiot!" Yet, for some reason beyond me, I stood my ground, grabbed my broom, and prepared to fight. Who was I kidding? It was only because of the paralyzing fear that coursed through my body.

The men stopped a few steps in front of me. One of the few enclosure lights swayed back and forth as the recirculators turned to high, briefly covering them in shadow, then light, then back to shadow. One of them spat. The other one chuckled.

"Check out mister space broom here!" he mocked me, only it sounded like, *Chuk oht mista space brooma hee'yah.*

"What he think he know some sorta karate?"

They both laughed harder than necessary. I squinted for a moment, trying my hardest to understand their speech, then exhaled. My shoulders dropped. I lowered the broom. "What do you two want?"

The first one stepped forward. The swaying light finally gave me a clear look at his bald, tattooed head and face. In fact, every inch of his skin I could see carried a symbol or picture or scripted quote from some poet he undoubtedly never read; some were colorful, others simply black ink. His shirt, two sizes too small, accentuated every muscle on his chest and abs. His coveralls were half off, tied tightly around his waist. I gulped. He spoke, but not before knocking the broom from my hand with little to no effort. It made me recoil.

"Me name Cappy," the bald one said, "an' this is me mate Mohawk."

I shook my head as I tried to translate their terrible dialect. "Cappy... and Mohawk? Your names are your hairstyles?"

Cappy ignored me and said, "You have sum'in we want. You either give it and take a small beating or fake like you no know what we say and we beatchya dead and take it from yous anyhow." Or at least that's what I gathered he said. Most of his speech was too slurred and chopped to even understand.

"Wh–wh–what?" I stuttered, which caused his friend to walk closer. Unlike the first man, this one had a mohawk, but also had tattoos on his scalp and down his neck. He wore a black T-shirt and, just like his friend, navy coveralls with the top half down and tied at his waist.

"Look like he choose the hard way, eh, Cappy?" Mohawk asked his comrade.

Cappy, the bald one, turned to his friend and saluted.

I raised my hands in defense. "Guys, wait, I honestly cannot understand much of what you're saying." I slowly pulled my glass-comm from my pocket and hit the translate button. "You two must be from Jupiter's moons – either that or…" Before I could say anything else, Cappy turned and swung at me, clocking me right below my left eye.

Before I even hit the ground, the two of them pounced on me and proceeded to kick and stomp. I stretched, attempting to reach my glass-comm to tap the panic button that would bring station security, but Mohawk kicked it away and rewarded my efforts with a stomp to my hand. I cried out, but it was cut short by another sharp kick to my stomach. I couldn't tell you how long the beating went on for. I lost count of the kicks and stomps and punches.

Why are they doing this to me? I asked myself after every kick. *I have something they want? What could I possibly have that these Jupiteran spacebound gang bangers could want? I'm just a space broom!*

My mind wandered. I heard stories of people involved in violent interactions, all of whom lost all sense of reality and entered a sort of fugue state, driven entirely by adrenaline and a deep down, carnal hardwiring for self-preservation. They said they performed feats they usually would not have been able to do – lifting heavy objects, tearing through metal with their bare hands, leaping across great distances, or outrunning vehicles. In this instance, none of that happened to me. I was overcome by one single emotion, one pulse: survival. It drove me to lie in a fetal position, protecting my face, and pray the beating would end.

Chapter Four

After a while, Cappy and Mohawk took a breather from their assault on my body. I kept my eyes closed and remained as still as possible, playing dead in hopes they would leave me be. Cappy reached down and rolled me over on my back. He rifled through the pockets of my coveralls, patting every inch of the fabric. I dared a peek and saw him scowl as his search turned up null and void.

"It ain't here!" he shouted. "He ain't got it!" He punctuated each sentence with a kick of frustration straight to my side. The impacts shot through me, adding bruises on top of bruises.

"Check his clothes, mate. Under the jumper," Mohawk shouted back, busying himself digging through everything on my cart. It would have been quicker had he just tipped it over.

A new voice entered the enclosure as Cappy reached for the zipper to my coveralls. It was deeper than that of my two assailants, assertive and strong, and filled me with enough energy to lift my upper body up to attempt to drag my battered frame away from the scene.

"Assault of an unarmed resident of Kilgore Station is a pretty stiff offense," the voice stated plainly. "Station security will likely give you a similar beating, then throw you into a shock cell until you're brought before a magistrate, or worse, a tribune. I don't know if you've ever experienced a shock cell, but they are not pleasant."

I looked for the source of the voice, failing to pinpoint it thanks to my blurry, post-beating vision. Yet, by the looks on Cappy and Mohawk's faces, they had seen it clearly and were not happy.

Cappy, still crouched above me, pointed a grubby finger over my head toward the enclosure's entrance. "This ain't concern ya, spaca!"

A spacer! I clearly understood that word. A goliath of a human born and bred in space had come to save me! Most spacebound humans hated the phrase, but never had I been happier to hear it. Cappy stood up slowly, menacing glare firing threats no action could best. Free from his hold, I groaned and rolled to my stomach. Every square inch of my body screamed in pain. I could taste blood in my mouth. I smelled piss, most likely my own. My hand burned like fire from where Mohawk stomped on it. With a mighty moan, I raised my head and saw this spacebound savior.

The man stepped forward as my vision cleared. There was no mistaking it – he was a spacebound human. Only life in low to zero g could create one so tall. Yet curiously enough, his clothing screamed earthbound. He wore a black cattleman on his head, a yellow plaid collarless shirt with the top three buttons opened, exposing his mahogany skin, and dusty blue jeans that I swore looked plastered in artificial dust. Even his feet were shod with old sharkskin boots, which must have cost him a fortune, and shiny steel spurs. He was straight out of an old Terran western. I would have laughed, had he not been my one and only hope at that moment.

"Well, you're wrong on two counts." My cowboy savior spoke again. Having seen him, I wanted his voice to have that typical drawl, but it did not. "First, my cousin and I are members of the Shahkti Flotilla. We prefer to be called extrasolar beings."

I hadn't noticed a second person until out from behind the cowboy emerged another spacebound human. She stood a bit shorter than him but looked much more menacing. Her narrowed eyes and clenched jaw appeared every bit as fearsome as Cappy's scowl. She wore a yellow bomber jacket with a red and white stripe running up one sleeve and a strange insignia printed on the opposite arm. She had black flight pants with multiple pockets and magboots, which suggested a familiarity with low- and zero-g environments. Neither of them held blasters, but I spotted two long black alloy blades peeking out from her jacket sleeves.

"And what's the second count?" Mohawk spat. He cracked his knuckles, preparing for a brawl.

The cowboy tipped his hat up so we could all see his face. I swore I witnessed a twinkle in his eye. "Kilgore Station has a sort of neighborly citizen ordinance allowing regular people, such as myself, the right to stop crimes if they see them happening without any sort of repercussion. My cousin here is keen to fight, and it's been quite some time since she's gotten into a good scrap."

Cappy and Mohawk wasted no time. They flew from my side and attacked the two spacebounds. The cowboy quickly sidestepped and dodged several incoming blows, then nimbly snatched a right hook from Mohawk, twisted, and flipped him to the deck.

The cousin placed a hand on Cappy's shoulder. Cappy spun and swung, only the cousin had already dropped to the deck and swept his legs out from under him. Cappy and Mohawk quickly jumped back to their feet and started their second wave of attack.

Cappy spun around Mohawk and unleashed a flurry of swings at the cowboy. The cowboy, unfazed, blocked and dodged each of them, never losing the look of amusement on his face. It seemed he enjoyed the fight as much as he claimed his cousin did. I thought I heard him snicker.

Mohawk experienced even less success attacking the cousin. Each swing was not only blocked, but countered with swift open palms to the nose, the chin, the throat, and the chest. Mohawk stumbled backward and fell on his ass, struggling to catch his breath. I noticed something sly twist the corner of the cousin's mouth as she motioned with a simple twitch of the fingers on her left hand for him to get back on his feet. Mohawk struggled to rise. His head lolled as if dazed. He raised his fists, only to be struck twice directly to his face, sending him back to the deck. He was out cold before his head hit.

Meanwhile, Cappy growled and screamed as each punch and kick was blocked or whiffed entirely. The cowboy mercilessly mocked him as he danced around him. Cappy, too enraged to notice, missed the cousin's approach and fell head over heels backward when the cowboy ducked out of the fight. The cousin quickly stepped in with a vicious upward thrust palm to his chin. He landed next to Mohawk with a thud. Cappy rebounded quickly and rose to his knees, only to be stopped short by the cousin's two black daggers that sang a hypnotizing siren's song as they *shnnged* from the sheaths hidden in her jacket sleeves.

The cowboy strolled up and stood next to his cousin. "Satisfied?" he asked her.

She shook her head.

"She's not satisfied." He turned to Cappy and shrugged.

Cappy slowly raised his hands. "We go," he said. It was the first time I clearly understood his words.

The cousin sheathed her blades and waved away Cappy, telling him which way to run. He stood up, grabbed Mohawk by the arm, and quickly dragged his comrade back to the stairs. The two spacebounds stood there and exchanged a secret handshake as Mohawk's head hit every step on the way out, sending metallic rings throughout the enclosure. Only once they were gone did my saviors turn their attention to me.

"Fuck, what happened to you?" the cousin asked with a grimace, covering her nose and mouth with her hand and turning her head away. "I mean, before you got your ass kicked."

"I think it was a Tarbon," I replied, wincing and nursing my bruised jaw. "Either that or a Chrysostom, or some strange combination of the two."

"Here, let me help you up," the cowboy said as he stepped toward me and reached down.

"Thanks," I uttered as I grabbed his leather-gloved hand.

"The name's Hooper, by the way, and this is Leilani," he said, tilting the wide brim of his black leather cattleman by way of greeting. She slowly raised a hand, but didn't bother smiling or making eye contact. "And don't mention it. I couldn't let Janky's thugs beat up a defenseless old man."

"I'm thirty-seven," I replied as I attempted to rotate the stiffness out of my shoulder.

"What?" Leilani asked.

"I'm thirty-seven. I'm not old," I repeated.

Hooper and Leilani exchanged bemused glances.

"And I'm Johnny – Johnny Gomez." I took a second to inhale a few deep breaths before I asked, "Were you two after them or what? I mean, nobody just strolls down the maintenance stairwells."

Hooper shrugged. "I recognized those two back on Deck Seven. Anywhere you see Janky's foot soldiers, you know they're up to no good."

"And they're easy marks, Cappy and Mohawk." Leilani added. Hooper pointed and clicked his tongue at her.

"So, we followed them," he finished with a toothy grin. "Lucky you."

"Yeah, thanks again. Who is Janky, by the way?" I asked as I took a seat on an empty crate and switched my concentration to my bruised jaw. "I've lived here for ten revolutions, and I've never heard of him."

Hooper responded, saying, "Janky is a low-level thug. He fashions himself a gangster, but nobody really takes him seriously. He's more concerned with cybercrime than roughing up station residents. Might be why you've never heard of him."

"If that's the case, what did they want with me? I'm a nobody who cleans toilets for a living."

He shrugged. "Visit any cybercasinos lately? Kings parlors? Virtual sex shops?"

"I don't gamble," I admitted, "and I've never been able to figure out how to play Kings."

"But you've been to a few virtual sex shops." Leilani pointed out my casual dismissal of it.

I felt my cheeks flush as my eyes met hers. "I… I mean… No, not… Well, not recently – no."

She eyed me skeptically.

"It doesn't matter," Hooper stated, steering the conversation back from the awkward. "If you haven't borrowed any money or hacked any games, Janky normally wouldn't bother."

"Then why?" I asked.

Hooper shrugged again and reached into the left pocket of his tan tweed vest, pulling a narrow silver oil pen from inside. "Who the fuck knows?" he said as he brought the pen to his mouth and exhaled a stream of vapor. I curiously watched the display. "I'm sorry, did you want a drag?"

"Oh, no, that's OK, I can't," I said once I realized it wasn't tobacco he was vaping, but marijuana. I recognized the sweet, earthy aroma from my teenage revs back on Luna. Not that I wouldn't love some. Unfortunately, Fallis and the Astro-Suds Services contracts forbade substance use while on the clock, and I was still on the clock.

"Well, if you're OK, Lei and I will be on our way," Hooper said with an exhale. "We have to resupply before we head back out."

"Haulers? Or traders?" I asked. The amicability faded from Hooper's face. "I don't mean to pry, just there'd be no other reason for two spacebounds to be here on Deck Six unless it was a delivery."

Leilani scoffed.

Hooper raised his hand. "We're in shipping. Mostly between Proxima and here, but we've traversed other systems as well. Anyway, good luck to you, Johnny Gomez. I hope that's the last bit of excitement you see for a while, old man." He tilted his hat once more and made his way back up the steps, leaving a trail of sweet skunky haze behind him.

I frowned and waved goodbye, "Thanks, I guess," I mumbled, embarrassed and ashamed that I had upset my saviors. "You're an idiot, Johnny," I chided myself. I rotated my neck, stretching the soreness from the beating, then slowly, and not without effort, got to my feet. Every muscle screamed. Every joint cracked and popped. A loud moan accompanied them all. It took me longer than expected to find my glass-comm, right my cart, and load everything back in its place. I then set about picking up all the trash that Janky's men tossed from my cart. I dropped to my knees to grab the last few pieces. That was when I noticed the tiny square slide, no bigger than my thumbnail, beneath my cart.

I examined the slide in the palm of my hand, wiping the stray bits of dust and grime that collected on its surface from the time it sat on the floor of the refuse enclosure. I wondered if it fit in my glass-comm, so I pulled it from my pocket and looked. Sure enough, it was the exact size. I wasn't about to insert a strange data chit into my soon to be obsolete communicator and have my entire life compromised. So, I put the chit in my pocket opposite my glass-comm, grabbed my cart, and slowly trudged my way back to the warehouse.

As usual, I was the last person there, aside from Fallis. Now inside a clean and well-ventilated section, my own repulsive stench assaulted my nose. I looked down at my coveralls and scowled. I forgot to peel them off and toss them in the burn pile. "Too late now," I said disappointedly and walked to Fallis's office.

"What do you want, Gomez?" he grumbled from his desk chair.

"I found this slide in the restrooms on Deck Seven. I think it's a data chit."

"Well, what are you…?" He paused for a brief moment as his eyes shifted from whatever filth he was watching on his glass-comm to my disgusting, bruised self. "Blow me, what in space happened to you?"

I sighed, considering whether or not I should tell him about the assault in the enclosure. Would he care or feign concern? He'd probably find some way to blame it on me or dock my pay for the inconvenience of alerting Station Security to the incident. That was more his speed. So, I conveniently left that out. "The restrooms on Deck Seven. You assigned the sphere to me this morning."

He shook his perfectly groomed head. The hair atop refused to move. "Yeah, fine, just… What are you doing here? Get home and get yourself cleaned up, man! You smell like ass! And you look like the restroom fought back. What happened, you take a few slips while you were in there? I'm not paying for medical treatment, Gomez."

"I found this slide in the restrooms," I repeated, ignoring his comments.

"Clock out and drop it off at Station Security on your way home. I mean, you should have done that as soon as you found it." He grabbed his obnoxiously prominent nose with his long, delicate, manicured fingers. "But that's not my problem now. Just get out of here." He waved me out of his office. "That smell is going to haunt me for the rest of this rev."

"That's on Deck Two," I protested. "I live on Deck Thirteen. It's well out of my way."

Fallis peered mercilessly at me. "It's not my job to take lost items to security. That responsibility lies directly in the hands of the custodian who finds it." He rose from his seat. "Or would you like me to quote policy and SOPs at you?"

I held my breath for a second before answering. "No need, sir. I'll take it. I'm… I'm sorry."

"Gomez, Gomez." Fallis tsked. "What am I going to do with you? I keep wondering why I keep you on staff instead of firing your ass. There are plenty of others with no job, in desperate need of credits, that would jump at the chance at working for an intergalactic company such as Astro-Suds." He was being generous. Astro-Suds only operated in a handful of sectors, but I wasn't about to point that out. He slowly made his way around to my side. "I truly do spoil you, Gomez," he said as he circled me. I felt a finger trace across my shoulders and neck. When he stood in front of me once more, Fallis wore a wicked smirk.

"I–I don't know what you mean, sir," I said meekly.

"Come on," he replied, slowly tracing a finger up my arm. "Your performance is adequate at best. Your attendance is shaky. Your attitude…" He tsked and pursed his lips. "Well, let's just say it needs… adjusting. Your last review rated you as the worst employee here, and that's saying something with a clown like Urbo on staff." He paused. "I think we both know why I keep you around."

I swallowed. "Um, sir, I should really get to Station Security… This chit… I mean."

Fallis chuckled and leaned against the back of one of the chairs in front of his desk. "Look at you, so cute, trembling like a virgin on his wedding night. Scared and nervous that your big, bad boss is going to be rough?"

I felt my cheeks flush. My heart gave a violent pound, then dropped to the pit of my stomach. I tried my best to keep a straight face, to hide the shock and embarrassment I felt. Fallis had always been overly critical of my job performance. He had fired other custodians for less. I never stopped to guess why, but now the reason came directly from the source. My boss was sexually attracted to me.

"Um…" was all I could manage. It was all I could do to keep from having to swallow my own vomit. My skin crawled. My stomach flipped, wanting out of my body. *The teasing. The forced proximity. The soft touches. It all made sense. Great*, I thought. *I'm going to need to find a new job again.*

Fallis giggled again. "I see this comes as a shock to you. No matter. How about you just apologize, and we'll continue this another night, one where you don't smell so damn bad? I have a warm bath and a bottle of Riesling waiting for me."

"I… I… I apologize, sir. I'll try to do better."

Fallis reached forward, grabbed my hand and gave it a squeeze, then, with a look I could only describe as depraved, said, barely above a whisper, "I know you will. Now get the fuck out of here."

Chapter Five

I kept my head down and my hands in my pockets the entire way to Deck Two. My mind still reeled from my interaction with Fallis. Nothing could have prepared me for that. In fact, it just made an altogether weird day even stranger.

Deck Two bustled with activity, even at the end of the second shift. Blue-collar laborers and white-collar bureaucrats all hurried to their next landing pad, steaming cups of energy in their hands or digi-brain feeding their vision with whatever virtual drivel they favored, drowning out the chaos around them. Life forms of every size, shape, and color strolled to their respective embassies. Station Security, dressed in their pressed navy blues, marched their beats or manned their designated security posts, keeping a watchful and often unwarranted eye on all the denizens of Kilgore. The brightly lit public service boards hovered and flashed their announcements in a variety of different tongues. Each one seemed more intense than normal, thanks to the manufactured sunset imposed by the station lights. White lights softened to ocher and gold and bronze. The recirculators on Deck Two worked overtime to cycle the scent of a thousand different species out of the air and replace it with the synthetic smells of the fabricated trees and shrubs and flowers that sprouted from various planters.

I hurried down pathways and up escalators, avoiding eye contact with every being I crossed. It was easier than imagined until I realized I still wore my shit-stained coveralls and smelled like an open sewer. That realization alone made me wonder how Station Security even allowed me to be on Deck Two. Too often were they quick to expel any sort of undesirable from such a prominent area, whether it be a stinky service worker like me or a frenzied Popylan standing on its soapbox warning of the coming of Zargzax, the great destroyer of the universe. I kept my head down regardless. All the while, my fingers played with the slide that burned a hole in my pocket. The data chit bounced and rolled from finger to finger. The thin, half-inch square slide felt like an old, cursed coin from the legends and mythologies of Terra, the kind that always seemed to find their way into your pocket no matter how many times you threw them out or used them as currency. I needed to get rid of it, yet the way my fingers grasped it and played with it made it seem impossible. It felt bound to me.

The block on Deck Two designated as Security Central had all the appeal of an unfinished steel slab. The blue lights made it feel uncomfortable and unwelcoming, and frankly played havoc with my nerves and eyes. PSA boards hovered and flashed their propaganda at all who neared, claiming Station Security was solely responsible for the safety and protection of Kilgore. Messages played over the block's PA system at rotating intervals at a volume several decibels over comfort. A trio of security officers spoke with a lone Xin salvager, by the look of his clothes. Each officer stood in a worrisomely aggressive stance. I looked toward the entrance and what I saw stopped me cold. Everyone on Kilgore knew what the topknot and single wide red stripe down the left arm of a racer jacket meant: Hongxongdi mercenaries. Four of them stood chatting with a Security lieutenant. One carried out all the conversation while the other three kept their hands conveniently placed inside the pockets of their jackets.

Maybe it was out of fear, or maybe it was out of self-preservation. Regardless, I couldn't move. I was an asteroid, straying a little too close to Kilgore's station defense batteries. My mind began to race, tossing theory after theory out of my head. No, it wasn't a coincidence. I couldn't explain why, but these Hongxongdi were here for me, just like Janky's boys. I whimpered at the thought of the beating I would take from this squad. Hongxongdi, after all, were not famous for their diplomacy. All the while, the slide in my pocket moved from finger to finger and back again.

I realized my position, standing stationary in the middle of a busy walkway, quickly became conspicuous. One of the Hongxongdi glanced my way and signaled to his squad mates. I turned around and began to hurry away, only, there weren't many ways I could go. Only two escalators and only two lifts led to Station Security, one of each pair designated as an up, the other as a down. I could feel the panic starting to rise in me. I was a vacuum rat caught between a blade trap and a poison trap. I picked up the pace when suddenly, the friendly chime of an incoming transmission rang from my glass-comm. I tapped my ear and answered.

"Hello?"

"There's no time to explain, but you need to take a left right now at this next junction."

I raised my head and glanced around as I walked. "Who…? Who is this? Are you watching me?"

"I said there's no time to explain!" the voice shouted. "Go left! Now!"

I looked to my left, at the narrow service alley that ran behind the Security block, and turned. Of course, I could take the service alleys. I had clearance. *Dammit, Johnny, calm down and keep a level head*, I told myself. I hurried down the alley, looking over my shoulder to see if I was being followed, and noticed a familiar yellow jacket breeze past the entrance. I turned around and spotted Leilani. In a flash, she clumsily collided with the Hongxongdi in such a spectacularly awkward way that the entire squad slipped and fell to the walkway in a flurry of curses.

"Don't look back. Just keep walking," the voice cracked in my ear. "Take another left. It'll loop you back around the other side of the block. From there, ride the escalator to the lower level. As soon as you get off, there will be a maintenance access hatch. Use your glass and go on in."

Before I could respond, I heard the beep of a terminated call. By now my heart pounded out of my chest and my teeth chattered with anxiety. I stepped on the escalator and noticed the Hongxongdi were now chasing Leilani in the opposite direction. Unfortunately for them, she nimbly bounced and jumped away from their grasps and out of sight, and soon they lost both of their quarries.

At the top of the escalator, I jogged as fast as my swollen, achy body would allow to the nearest maintenance hatch. My glass-comm granted me access and the door swooshed open. There, crouching low in the harsh white light of the maintenance tunnels, was Hooper.

"Surprise!" he said, raising his arms in triumph.

"How did you know my glass-comm code?"

"No time for questions, Johnny. We gotta get somewhere a little too nefarious even for Hongxongdi."

There was no need to explain. I knew exactly where we were headed.

Nobody wandered into the Bourbon Docks. You didn't stumble upon it by accident. Named after the infamous black marketeer and pioneering father of the augmented, Carlou Bourbon, the Docks remained a closely guarded secret for centuries. Tourists and residents of Kilgore never heard of it. Even the station bureaucrats tossed the term around as if legend. Yet, if Kilgore Station had a seedy underbelly, the Bourbon Docks was that underbelly's sweaty layer of pore-clogging, musky grime.

"How do you know about the Docks?" I asked Hooper as we climbed down a lift shaft ladder.

"All smugglers know about the Docks," he replied.

"You said you were in shipping?"

"Smuggling *is* shipping."

I sighed. "First, I'm chased by gangs and mercenaries, now I've thrown in with smugglers."

"How do *you* know about the Docks?" Hooper fired back.

I thought on his question for a second. Yes, Hooper had saved my life twice, but I was still wary. Just this morning, I was cleaning shit off toilet walls and now I'm crawling through service tunnels with a smuggler. I wondered how much I should say.

"My roommate is an aug," I said after a drawn-out pause.

"Ah," was all Hooper said.

The maintenance tunnel led to one of the enormous service lift shafts, one of a multitude designed to bring heavier than normal equipment, and the occasional oversized alien life form, to whatever deck necessary. The lifts, powered by repulsor technology, slid in near silence along a cylinder of superconductors. A spiral walkway circled each shaft for its entire length, and provided ingress and egress for inspectors to perform preventative maintenance checks on each bay of superconductors. From our spot, the only sounds that could be heard from the vacuum of the cylinder was the gentle hum of the repulsors and the rush of wind as the lift flew past.

"These things used to make me uncomfortable, but now I kind of like the thrill," Hooper said as he started down the stairs, waving at the pair of repulsor technicians taking readings on the landing above us. They reluctantly returned curious waves. "You're going along, minding your own business then, *whoosh*! A lift flies past, scaring the shit out of you. It's a simple rush, but I love it."

"Brace yourself! Here comes another one," I said as a lift shot uncomfortably close past us, plunging down the shaft to its next deck stop. I did not share Hooper's enthusiasm. "How did you do that bit with my glass-comm code? And why are the Hongxongdi after me?" I asked once the lift passed.

"My ship's AI has black hat protocols," Hooper answered. "And do you really not know?"

"Know what?"

"There's a bounty out on you, and quite a hefty one at that."

"What?" I shouted, nearly losing my grip and tumbling head first down the shaft.

"Yeah, it says you stole a parcel of some sort," Hooper continued, unfazed by my outburst.

"Steal? I didn't steal anything!"

"Oh, whether you did or not doesn't concern me. I figured a guy like you in trouble with Janky's gang, the Hongxongdi, and Black Sun is probably going to be looking for a way off Kilgore. Seeing as I'm a smuggler–"

"Black Sun?"

"Yeah, Black Sun," he repeated, as if I would suddenly recognize the name. "Chorzi syndicate, pretty new to this sector, famous for the quality of muscle they provide."

"I don't even know who they are!"

"Anyway, don't worry. Regardless of the access code or data chit you stole, you'll be safe with me and Lei."

"Data chit I stole? This is about that slide? I didn't steal it. I found it in a pile of Tarbon sludge nestled next to a pellet full of excrement."

"Hey, you don't have to convince me," Hooper replied. "Remember, I'm saving you from the Hongxongdi, not turning you over to them."

"Right," I said. *The data chit*, I thought. *The beating I took from Cappy and Mohawk, the Hongxongdi thugs following me, it was all because I picked up that stupid slide instead of letting it slip down the drain! What if I just threw it into the repulsor lift shaft and let the next lift shatter it to pieces? Surely everybody would just leave me alone and let me go back to my terrible toilet-scrubbing job, working for my disgusting, has the hots for me boss. Who am I kidding? If I did that I'd just become collateral. Another easily expendable nobody.* Keeping one hand on the walkway railing, I used my other to fiddle with my glass-comm. I wasn't sure if I could send a distress alert to Station Security without looking at it, but I figured I should try, just in case.

We descended in silence for what felt like an eternity. My brain, however, wouldn't shut up. How could I get out of this whole situation? What if I just apologized to whoever wanted this damn chit and gave it back to them? Maybe Hooper would just take the chit and leave me alone? I could move! Yeah, that's it! Let me gather up my belongings and just find the first and cheapest flight to Homestar SBE Five Seven or Alpha Centauri. Thanks to the paranoid ramblings, I lost track of which deck we were on until we finally reached a service landing, and the access hatch flew open. Leilani stood on the other side. She and Hooper greeted each other with the same curious handshake, then proceeded to speed down the hallway toward the Docks. I hurried as best I could on my aching legs, feeling all my bruises yell violently at me, wanting to keep up but afraid to ask them to slow down. The hallway took a right turn, then opened to the largest subdeck on all of Kilgore. Only before us, guarding the entrance, stood the biggest augmented man I had ever seen.

"Credentials," his voice boomed. He held out a mammoth, mechanical hand as if beckoning for a pass of some sort. Hooper held his glass-comm over the aug's hand. Its eyes mirrored over, a telltale sign of massive digi-brain implants. When his irises returned, the aug frowned, but waved and let Hooper and Leilani pass. As I approached, he held out his other arm, fully human and bulging with enormous, veiny muscles.

"Credentials," he repeated angrily.

"I–I–I don't…"

"He's with us," Hooper said. "I'll vouch for him."

The aug squinted at me. His eyes rolled and turned black. A red dot flashed in both, then quickly disappeared, returning them to their normal state. "Fine, but I have his DNA scan."

I gulped as he lifted his arm and let me by, then hurried to follow Hooper.

The Bourbon Docks stretched across the entire diameter of the station and, thanks to the many renovations and reconstructions the station went through over the centuries, managed to weave between decks Fourteen and Fifteen. The bulkheads showed their age by the number of welding streaks scarring their stained alloy skin. Currents of steam crowded near the upper reaches of the deck before meeting one of many recirculator bays. The cable-suspended walkways lurched and whined as they swayed with each of our steps. Fully cybernetic individuals and the augmented from across the local cluster clamored about in groups of varying amounts of flesh and metal, moving, and unloading cargo, selling wares, or simply monitoring the action from electromagnetic repulsor platforms. Little conversations chirruped here and there. The shouts of foremen carried above them all. My mind went to Rygar, curious whether he'd happen across us.

I hurried to Hooper's side as he and his cousin stopped to gaze down on the throngs from our perch on the walkway. "Hey, listen, I didn't steal the data chit," I repeated. "I found it… in the zero-*g* restrooms on Seven. I was actually on my way to turn it in to lost and found."

Leilani hmphed and said, "It's too late for that."

"What?"

"She's right," Hooper agreed. "It's way too late to turn it in and hope for the best. Here, look at the bounty." He tapped his glass-comm a few times and wiped the screen toward me. Mine vibrated with the incoming transmission.

"Wh-wh-what does this even mean?" I whimpered as my eyes scanned the text. "'By any means necessary'?"

"It means somebody has a massive hard-on for you," Leilani grunted.

My shoulders slumped and my head tilted forward. "I mean, it wouldn't be the first time someone's had a massive hard-on for me, but in this case, I'm not feeling up to actually doing anything with it."

Hooper put one arm around my shoulder and patted me on the chest. "Hey, it's always rough your first time, but you'll get used to it."

I shrugged his arm off me. "It's not funny."

"It kind of is," he said, grinning.

Leilani nodded in agreement.

"It's not. You said you were going to help me."

"And I am. Why do you think we're here?" Hooper motioned to the sea of cyborgs and augs below us. "I have a contact who works here. She specializes in getting rid of hot items like that chit of yours."

"Is she an aug?" I asked, wondering if she would know Rygar and vice versa.

"Unless she's recently had work done, I don't believe so," Hooper said. "She's kinda like you, a natural earthbounder." He paused, then said, "Random thought. Should we petition RUSH to change it to terrabounder? Nobody calls it Earth any more." He crowed. "Earth. L-O-L."

"And you two?" I asked. "I mean, if you're 'in shipping,'" I air-quoted the words, "I guess you'd have some implants." I saw that both Hooper and Leilani were giving me strange looks, so I said, "I mean, not that it matters, just curious is all."

"Just a few," Hooper responded. "Digi-brains help with focus during long hauls and keep me connected to my ship's AI. Muscle weaves let us work in different magnitudes of gravity without much effect."

"Well, OK then, let's go see this fence," I said.

Hooper and Leilani exchanged glances.

"What?"

"Don't call her a fence," Hooper replied. "She'll take *of-fense* to that." He stopped to make sure I caught the pun.

Leilani rolled her eyes and walked away. Hooper and I followed.

Chapter Six

It struck me as rather surprising that the denizens of Kilgore roaming the Bourbon Docks came in every conceivable being. I always imagined bulkhead to bulkhead teeming with half-man, half-machine people. While the cyborgs and augs vastly outnumbered the organics, I spotted a good many humans, both earthbound and starbound, gray-skinned Xin, trunk-nosed Hepari, and even a couple of ancient Boesians, the oldest species in the galaxy. I figured I would easily blend in to such a diverse crowd. I figured wrong.

Every cyborg we passed on our way to Hooper's contact walked past us without so much as a second glance at Hooper and Leilani. I could only imagine that people of their vocation frequented the Bourbon Docks enough to appear inconspicuous regardless of their intentions. Yet their looks at me told an entirely different story. Eyes and viewports regarded me with suspicion. Faces tensed as I walked past.

"I get the feeling I'm not necessarily welcome here," I said to Hooper.

"It's your coveralls," he said, pointing at the Astro-Suds Services patch embroidered on my chest. "You're technically a station employee."

"I'm a contractor," I replied quietly. "I have nothing to do with Kilgore or RUSH."

Hooper stopped, glared, and without a word, Leilani shoved me into the nearest abandoned walkway. It led to the restrooms. "Are you fucking insane?" she asked.

I held my breath and stumbled backward, careening to the deck. "What the...? Why did you...?"

"Don't ever mention the Republic down here."

Hooper put his arm in front of his cousin, holding her back. I gasped and recoiled, then felt silly when the blow never came. Leilani looked at him, then did an about-face and returned to the main walkway. Hooper took a few steps toward me and offered his hand. I took it and rose to my feet.

"What was that about?"

"She is right, old man, although she didn't have to respond like she did."

I sighed. "Can you please stop with the 'old man'?"

Hooper acknowledged my request, put his hand over his heart, and bowed his head, saying, "I'm sorry, Johnny."

"Thank you," I replied.

"Listen, I don't know what you know about this place, but nothing that goes on here falls under the purview of the Republic of Unified Systems and Homeworlds. Think of it like your contract work. Your boss tells you to clean his pipes, but will pay you in hard currency instead of credits for the job."

"I'm sorry, I had no idea."

"It's cool, it's cool. Just try and be... You know, it's probably better if you just keep your head down and your mouth closed until we get there." Hooper condescendingly patted me on the shoulder.

Before returning to the walkway, I unzipped my coveralls halfway and wrapped the sleeves around my waist, concealing the Astro-Suds insignia. "Hopefully that'll help."

"It can't hurt," Hooper responded.

I spent the remainder of my trip with my eyes glued to the small of Hooper's back. I avoided every being we passed, slumped my shoulders, and kept my head down. I excelled at assuming a low profile and avoiding confrontation. They happened to be a large portion of the few skills I had outside of maintaining a perfectly running restroom. My breathing calmed and my anxiety lessened as we walked. Even my aches started taking a back seat. My body and mind found comfort in hiding in plain sight. I always found a friend in invisibility. Before I knew it, we arrived at an unnamed block of office bays. The number of bodies on the walkways dropped markedly. The station lights dimmed. I noticed most of the standard white tubes missing, replaced with reds or blues or yellows – whatever they could find.

Hooper stopped in front of a hatch with the words "Pawnbroker: Appointment Only" laser-etched above the frame. The occupant blacked out the glass in the hatch. I spotted a working panel, though, and before I could mention it, Hooper tapped his glass-comm and the hatch whooshed open.

"Let me do the talking," Hooper stated plainly before walking in.

I waited for Leilani to follow, only she motioned for me to go first. I can't place why, but it made me nervous.

Inside reminded me of the old pawnbrokers' back on Luna. Wobbly metal shelves holding every trinket and knickknack imaginable lined the unfinished alloy walls. I spotted splotches of paint beneath the layers of dust that decorated the deck. Dirty old flags and banners of now-defunct nation states hung from the exposed metal beams of the ceiling. A desk stood at the back with a random assortment of products. I froze when my eyes saw who stood behind it.

"It's been a while since you've graced my little shop, Alice Hooper," the woman from my daydreams said as we approached. Her jet-black hair, tied up high in a ponytail, fell over her left shoulder and nearly reached her waist. A swoop of bangs hid her eyes. Regardless, I knew they were emerald green. Those eyes remained glued to a locked terminal. She tapped away on her glass-comm, which was hardwired to the device.

"Why do you gotta do that?" Hooper asked with a grimace. "I thought we were friends. I mean, what with our history." She looked up, brushing her hair out of her eyes, and stared long and hard, face full of contempt. Hooper raised his hands in defense. "Kidding. But seriously, you know damn well nobody uses my first name, and if they do, they abbreviate it. A. Cornell Hooper."

The woman smirked and rolled her eyes. "I'm not calling you that, Hooper."

Hooper took a step toward the counter and leaned his long, slender frame against it in a way I could only describe as seductive. He removed his hat and gently placed it in front of him. The woman rolled her eyes at the display, but I could tell it amused her.

"This here gentleman is Johnny," Hooper said, gesturing over his shoulder at me. "He's got that chit we need analyzed."

The way Leilani shoved me forward convinced me that I spent an awkward few moments gawking at the woman.

How could I not, though? The last time I saw her, she and I were engaged in a fight for our lives. Looking at her again, seeing her up close and personal, only confirmed my feelings of infatuation. Her hair, her skin, her eyes: they all swallowed me and left me dazed. My heart decided it was the ideal time to practice a drum solo. My palms turned to mush.

"Um… Nice to meet you, Johnny," the woman said with a small wave. "I'm Lisette."

"W–w–we've met – or I mean, I know who you are. I mean, that sounds creepy, like I'm some sort of stalker, it's just I've seen you around…" The words cascaded out of my mouth at such a clip, even I felt dizzy. "You like to buy coffee on Four."

Lisette gave Hooper a curious glance before looking back at me and asking, "You have the chit?" She held out her hand.

"Um, yeah," I said and fumbled around my pockets, looking for it, only to let it slip from my fingers and fall to the floor. I smiled sheepishly, knelt to retrieve it, and slammed my head against the lip of the counter on my way up. Everything resting on top – Lisette's glass-comm, Hooper's hat, a few containers of candy, and the rotating tree of glass-comm protectors – jumped and jingled in response. Hooper tried his best to contain his amusement while I rubbed my head and dropped the chit into Lisette's open palm.

"Wait a minute… Did she call you Alice Hooper?" I asked incredulously.

Hooper rolled his eyes.

"He's named after his mom," Leilani answered. "My auntie."

Lisette grinned again. "Are you three going to hang around while I try to bypass the security AI?" she asked.

"How long do you think it's going to take?" Hooper inquired.

"You do know who you're talking to, right?" Lisette fired back, indignantly. "I'm not some back-alley hacker spook working with stolen protocols or pretending to know what they're doing."

Hooper held up his hands.

"Plus, this thing is old tech. It can't have more than a hundred firewalls and two-stage encryption. Thirty minutes, tops," Lisette continued. "Start the clock."

Leilani lifted herself up and sat on the counter. Lisette winked at her, and I swear I saw the corner of Leilani's mouth twist up in the faintest rumor of a smile. Hooper reached inside his vest pocket and pulled out his oil pen, then began to roam around the store. I rocked back and forth on my heels until I noticed Leilani and Lisette glaring strangely at me. I decided I would join Hooper.

I found him rummaging through a metal bin full of old machine parts. He lifted an oddly shaped converter from the pile and showed it to me. "You ever see one of these before?" he asked, handing me the ancient and weighty part.

"It just looks like a converter," I answered with a shrug.

"It's a second-generation nanowave converter." Hooper pointed. "My mom's ship was loaded with those things. What people don't realize is that the gen two converters ran cooler than its successors, which allowed it to run at max for longer. Yeah, they're bigger and bulkier, but a ship with plenty of space could save a hell of a lot of money on fuel by downgrading to gen twos instead of running the newest gen fives. Somebody sold it to Lisette thinking she was just some simple junk dealer, not knowing they could have sold it to a flotilla captain for a nice chunk of credits."

"Interesting," I responded. "I don't know much about starship hardware." I handed the converter back to Hooper, who turned it over in his hands a few more times before dropping it back in the bin. "I mean, I know a little. I'm something of a ship-head and helped my uncle with them when I was a kid. Love starships, though. Love 'em." He gave me an amused grin that said I was being weird. "So..."

"How do I know Lisette?" Hooper asked my question for me. He offered up his pen, which I declined. So he took another long drag and, while exhaling, said, "Lisette is the most utilitarian black marketeer in the sector. There's nothing she can't fence."

"I thought you said not to call her that?" I asked.

"Not to her face."

"Apparently, she's a good hacker, too," I added.

Hooper leaned in close. "She's not half bad. She's had to learn on the fly, but she's picking it up quickly."

I then asked, "What do you plan to do once you know what's inside?"

Hooper moved down the shelves and found another bin to rifle through. "Lisette will value it, we'll sell it, and with the profits, hopefully have enough to smuggle you off of Kilgore before anyone notices."

I swallowed. "If it's not worth anything?"

Hooper patted me on the shoulder. "We'll deal with that if and when it happens."

Before we moved any farther down the aisle, Lisette shouted from the rear of her shop. "Holy shit! You guys have got to come see this!"

Hooper and I exchanged curious glances, then quickly returned to her desk.

"You got it unlocked already?" Hooper asked.

"You bet your ass I did," Lisette said triumphantly.

We looked to Leilani, who showed us the timer on her glass-comm: 09:48.

"Under ten minutes," Hooper said, grinning. "I never doubted you."

"Mhm," Lisette said with a roll of her eyes. "Check this out." She waved her hand and sent her display to the larger screen hanging on the wall behind her, so we could all look at what she found. Hooper's eyes went wide. Leilani gasped. Lisette grinned bigger than I thought possible. I could almost see credits spilling from her eyes and ears. I looked at the screen, at what I figured was a sort of catalog presenting three featureless mannequins, each one wearing a strange outfit.

"I... I don't get it," I said, dumbfounded. "Is this someone's clothes shopping list?"

The others simultaneously turned to me with a shared expression of confusion and mild anger.

"Are you kidding me right now?" Lisette turned to Hooper. "He's kidding me right now, right?"

"Do you really not know what those are?" Hooper asked.

I looked again, squinting, hoping I missed some minute detail that would give away what I was looking at. My opinion refused to change. "Should I know what these are, other than jumpers and coveralls?"

Leilani giggled to the point of coughing. She excused herself from her seat on the counter. It was the most emotion she had shown yet.

"Those are one-of-a-kind avatars for *Lost Worlds*," Hooper informed me.

I shrugged.

"You've never heard of *Lost Worlds*?" Lisette asked in horror.

"Should I have?"

Hooper threw up his hands and sighed. Lisette dropped her head to the counter. "*Lost Worlds* is the biggest, most popular alternate life simulator in the galaxy right now," he said. "They have upwards of a hundred billion active users at any given moment. These avatars were never released, but remain completely playable on every server."

I looked at them a third time. The outfit on the right avatar resembled something I once saw in a history book back on Luna – one of humanity's earliest spacesuits. The middle avatar wore a clean, slim-fitting black tuxedo, the kind that went out of style several centuries before Kilgore Station opened, and held up near its head what appeared to be a small handgun. The left avatar looked like a one-piece pajama suit, covered entirely from head to toe in long brown and black hair, with a bandolier slung from its left shoulder. I took a deep breath when suddenly, a horrific, stomach-churning, bile-spewing realization hit me. My head began to pound. My arms and legs started shaking. "You mean, these are video game avatars? I have a bounty over digital skins?"

"Not just any video game skins – one-of-a-kind, one-off, completely original avatars. Nobody in the galaxy has these."

The longer I stared at the avatars, the more the floor of the shop spun. *That damn chit*, I thought. *It didn't contain station secrets or stolen passwords. All of this for a video game? A fucking video game!* The hilarity of it shook me to my core. I wanted to cackle, but I couldn't even breathe. Everything seemed out of focus before my vision finally blurred entirely. Hooper's words turned to a buzzing, high-pitched whine inside my ears. I reached out to grab the counter, only I missed. I felt my body lurch forward, then the darkness completely enveloped me.

Chapter Seven

I didn't recall hitting the floor, never mind passing out. For me, I went from unstable to immediately waking up on a table behind Lisette's computer with all three of my new acquaintances huddled over me.

"Here he is," Hooper said calmly. "Welcome back, Johnny. How are you feeling?"

I groaned. "Like I wish I had never left Luna ten revs ago."

"You're from Luna?" Lisette asked.

"Yup," I answered, sounding not the least bit proud of my home.

"Don't think about that right now," Hooper interrupted. "Think about riches – being filthy, insanely, disgustingly rich, because that's what we are all going to be. Obnoxiously rich."

"The skins are worth that much?" I asked.

"You're goddamned right!"

"The right buyer will pay an obscene amount of credits for these," Lisette said. "I'm not a hundred percent sure, but I think I know a guy who may be interested."

I put my hands to my head as I sat up and slowly lowered myself off the table. The fall I took simply added to the plethora of aches and pains my body continued to deal with. Now my head pounded, and my legs felt as if they were on springs, all on top of my aching bruises from the beating Cappy and Mohawk gave me. "Well, that's great news. I'll just leave it up to you three, and you can transfer my cut whenever you want."

"What do you mean?" Hooper asked.

"I mean, I'm done," I said, waving my hand at the screen that still displayed the three ridiculously dressed avatars. "I am one hundred percent done getting beat up by gang members, chased by mercenaries, and finding new and exciting bruises all over my body." I squeezed past the trio and moved from behind the counter, but Hooper swiftly moved beside me, placed his arm around my shoulder, and stopped my escape.

"No, no, no, Johnny, you can't just walk away from this," he stated.

"Why not? I'm giving the chit to you, Hooper. Now you can take care of it. Now they'll hunt you down. You seem a thousand times more capable of evading whoever it is that is hunting me than I am."

"You don't understand," Hooper continued, turning me around to face the screen. "The fate of these avatars is tied to your own. The anonymous creator of the bounty is not going to stop until those avatars are in his possession and you are made an example of. That's how these people work. If they find you without the chit, you'll just be tortured until they do find it, then they'll probably throw you out of an airlock."

I swallowed hard. "I'll just go to Station Security and explain everything."

"What makes you think Station Security will listen, let alone act on this information?" Lisette asked. "If mercenaries, gangs, never mind an entire deck for black market dealings, can exist on Kilgore Station, what makes you think you'll be safe in their care? And for what? Video game loot? The pigs will laugh you out of the station."

I clenched my jaw. She was right, after all. What security organization would allow entities like the ones hunting me to exist? My only chance was with these three credit-hungry strangers. My head bowed and my shoulders dropped. I felt trapped. Only one move existed for me, and here I stood, reluctant to take it. I sat back down on the table and held my head in my hands.

But in all honesty, Hooper and Leilani had been the only people besides Rygar to show me any sort of human decency. And staying with them meant staying with Lisette. Lisette...

My mind wandered. Dawn. I saw a bungalow on the beach, somewhere along one of the finger-like peninsulas on Pilgrim's Folly. I stood at the entrance to the house, wearing only shorts, watching the sunrise and sipping on fresh-ground coffee. The cool breeze danced through my hair while the warmth of the rising sun and steaming coffee mug tingled my skin. I inhaled deeply, taking in the aroma of the turquoise seas.

Suddenly, I felt her arms wrap around me, hands holding me tight across the chest. She pressed her cheek into my back and whispered, "Good morning, handsome."

I turned around and beheld the most beautiful creature I had ever seen: Lisette, wearing only my T-shirt. Her black hair cascaded down her body. Her green eyes were bright with excitement and mischief.

"Hey, why don't you and Lei give us a minute?" I heard the real Lisette say. "Head on over to Dusty's Old-World Pub. I'll meet you there later on, OK?"

I kept my head down until the door chime signaled their exit. I heard Lisette rummaging around in her shop. After a few minutes, I heard a hum and smelled the aroma of fresh coffee. When I looked up, Lisette seated herself across from me and offered me a steaming hot mug of fresh brew.

"Is this the real stuff?" I asked as I took the mug. My hands trembled like a broken air handler.

"Yessiree," she answered. "The beans are certified Terran. Roasted and ground right here on Kilgore."

I took a sip and let the coffee's warmth slightly lift my spirits. I let out a slight moan of satisfaction. She wasn't lying. This was genuine Terran coffee.

"So, you've been on Kilgore for ten revs?" Lisette asked.

"Ten revs today, actually," I said after a sip.

"Is this the craziest thing that's ever happened to you?" Her tone implied she already knew the answer.

"The craziest thing about it all is I used to think I wanted this kind of excitement in my life. So, yes, yes it is." I put the coffee cup on the table and held out my hands. The shaking continued. "I mean, look at me. I can't stop shaking."

Lisette leaned forward and put her hand on my knee. Electricity shot through my body. I could feel my skin growing hot. There was a sudden and awkward lump in my throat. "He may not seem up to the task, but Hooper is going to take care of you. Don't worry. He's not going to let you get hurt. I've known him for some time now, and I don't think he's ever taken an interest in someone not himself. But those people who manage to pique his interest he treats exactly like he would want to be treated."

"Which is how?"

"Like the most stimulating person in the galaxy," Lisette said, flashing a quick smile.

Her smile. Breaking the touch barrier. They both made me relax, even if slightly. "Yeah, I guess you're right," I replied.

"Where do you live?" she asked.

"On Thirteen," I said.

"Really? You live in the Tank?"

"It's the only place I could afford on Kilgore," I replied. "And it's where my roommate lives so, yeah."

"OK, well, um…" She let out a short, clipped cry of disbelief. "Regardless of the reputation of the Tank, I don't think it's safe for you to go home. I can set you up at a hotel here in the Bourbon Docks. There you can have a shower, change your clothes, and try to relax. I mean, the Docks are relatively safe. At least, people know not to piss off the augs. It's going to take a few hours to reach out and find a buyer. Whenever we have the information and Hooper sets a flight plan, we'll come get you." She grabbed her data cube and ejected the chit, handing it to me. "Take it, so you don't think we're just going to steal the chit and leave you to rot."

I grimaced and palmed the tiny slide. "OK, yeah. A hotel. Where am I headed?"

"There's an Open All Cycle store on level three. It's pretty easy to spot. The hotel is right next to it. It's called Inn Syde'U, one of those kitschy, weird places with themed rooms."

"How do you know about it?"

Lisette ignored the question and said, "Let me see your glass." I reached in my pocket and showed it to her. She tapped her unit to mine. It vibrated. "There's the directions to the hotel and your reservation information. Oh, and also my contact information. That way we can stay in touch, you know, in case anything happens."

Her contact information... Her contact information! The woman of my dreams just gave me her glass-comm code! If I wasn't overheating from the casual touch and my stupid little daydream about her, I sure as shit was now. I took a deep breath, hoping my excitement didn't show on my face. "Thanks, Lisette," I managed to say.

"Don't mention it," she said. "We'll get through this. And don't worry about Hooper. I'll smooth things over with him."

When I entered Inn Syde'U, a jolly and comically rotund Roilo waved me over to the front desk with her cute, furry paws and greeted me in the usual Roilo fashion: both paws raised firmly in the air. Her fluffy copper fur looked freshly washed and blown dry.

"Welcome, welcome!" the Roilo said without any recognizable accent. "I am Lo Fan. How may I be of service?" she asked, motioning her black and white paw to the glass tablet on the desk.

"Um, yeah," I said, pulling my glass-comm from my pocket and tapping the tablet.

"Yes, yes, Mister Gomez. The Honeymoon Suite!" Lo Fan said with a sharp-toothed expression that took up her entire face. I guessed it was a smile. Her lupine ears twitched with glee. "I assume your partner will be along later?"

I cleared my throat. Honeymoon Suite? Was Lisette planning on...? No, I told my wandering mind. That's absurd. "My... My partner... Yes. They will be along later."

"Perfect. It looks like everything has been taken care of

for the evening. Room 7. Please let me know if you have any questions or concerns," Lo Fan said, raising both her paws to the sky once again. I lifted both my hands in the air, which prompted the Roilo to giggle.

I reached the entry port to the Honeymoon Suite, exhausted from climbing seven flights of stairs. Curiously enough, Inn Syde'U had only one room per floor. A strange feeling crept over me as I stopped just short of putting my glass-comm to the access node. A tiny voice inside my head told me to hide the chit. It made sense to me. All the spy genre holofilms I had ever watched had that trope. The hero always hid the data somewhere safe, somewhere he could easily return to and retrieve. I glanced up and down the hallway toward the stairs to see if I had been followed. That's when I spotted the waster. I hurried over, pulled my multi-tool from my pocket, and easily removed the side panel. I grabbed the chit and slid it snugly between the firewall and motor mount.

As the port whooshed open, the heavily perfumed air of the Honeymoon Suite simultaneously smacked me in the face and made me feel a bit on the frisky side. "Roilo and their love of pheromones," I mumbled as I stepped inside. Low, romantic lighting revealed crushed red velvet covering every surface, from the floor up to the walls. The ceiling was spared the velvet treatment, instead being covered in mirrored panels. Pink and red hearts decorated the tiled floor in the kitchenette. Vases holding every odd and exotic flower obtainable on Kilgore rested on every tabletop. An overstuffed couch with an absurd amount of fluffy pillows sat in front of a viewscreen playing scandalous Roilo porno on mute.

"Rygar's gotta see this place," I said. Rygar! Lisette's warning hit me in the chest. How could I forget Rygar? If there are really groups watching my place, intent on harming me, they may harm Rygar instead! I had to warn him. I couldn't let my best and only friend fall victim to the same shit I stepped in.

Still holding my glass-comm, I tapped in Rygar's comm code. No answer. I tried again. No answer. I knew how much of a workaholic he was. Cyborgs and augs could work longer and harder than any organic, except for maybe the Postos, but their rhinoceros-like heft could only be utilized in a vacuum or on decks with very high ceilings. So, instead, I sent him a ping, a picture of the suite, and a message that read: *Splurged for my ten-year anniversary and rented myself this room! Come party with me. Bring some beer!* "Hopefully he gets that in time," I said. My stomach tied in knots once more. "He'll make it. He'll see it before he leaves work."

I did a brief tour of the rest of the Honeymoon Suite. The bathroom proved just as gaudy and ridiculously accoutered as the living room and entrance, complete with a heart-shaped hot tub. An enormous heart-shaped bed rotated slowly in the bedroom. Both ceilings in the bathroom and bedroom were covered in mirrors. I desperately wanted a shower, but my body needed sleep. My muscles ached, and I could barely keep the iron weights that were my eyelids from collapsing on themselves. I trudged to the bedroom and tossed myself onto the rotating bed. I was unconscious before my head hit the pillow.

I was typically a heavy sleeper, so to be awakened by the sudden ceasing of the electric hum of appliances immediately sparked panic inside me. I flew out of bed and put my bare feet on the red, white, and pink shag carpet of the bedroom. I had never been so alert, my ears hypersensitive to every little sound.

I tapped my glass-comm and looked at the time. That's when I saw a missed message from Lisette: *Get somewhere safe, ASAP.* The words made my heart pound. I could hear each beat echo in my chest. I heard footsteps in the entryway... the click of a blaster magazine being loaded into a pistol... a slightly congested sniffle from a nose not accustomed to the poor air quality in the Docks. I slowly slid my glass-comm into my pocket and held my breath. I had to do something. I had to hide. But where? I couldn't squeeze under the bed, it was on a rotating platform! Did this room even have a closet? I stood up and desperately searched the room. In the bureau? Or maybe that armoire! Would that work? I tried but changed my mind after struggling to get the doors to close.

I spotted a guide beam of light as I got to my feet, sweeping past the bedroom door. My heart pounded. My jaw clenched and I balled my fists. They were slick with sweat. Then came a tapping – a gentle tapping against the entry node to my room. Whoever was out there was attempting to break in. Before I could react, the hatch whooshed open, and two high-intensity beams landed on my face, blinding me. I raised my hands to block the beams but that only left my midsection defenseless.

It all happened faster than I could react. A fist landed heavily on my stomach, knocking the air from my lungs. I doubled over, but immediately felt another fist land squarely against my mouth. I flew backward into a set of arms and hands that forcefully grabbed my shoulders and dragged me into the living room. I heard a chair dragged across the floor. I felt a pair of arms violently seat me. Soon, my hands were bound behind the chair. I could taste blood in my mouth.

I looked up and tried to concentrate on the figures before me, but my head spun, and my eyes couldn't focus. I saw four silhouettes – no, eight, or maybe five. They talked among themselves, in what I swore was Chorzi, for what seemed like hours, until the eight blurry silhouettes became four. Then they turned on the light. Four bodies, dressed all in black from head to toe, holding black blasters with muzzle diffusers on the barrels, meant to silence their shots. They mumbled for a moment more, then one of my Chorzi assailants stepped forward and knelt next to me. I could see its black sclera and pale yellow irises, like a corona of a dying star, around abyssal pupils boring through me. I immediately realized why they were called Black Sun.

"Where is the chit," the Chorzi growled.

"I... I don't have it," I murmured.

SLAP!

The ringing in my ears returned. My head spun once again. I found it hard to focus on those black eyes.

"I'm being honest. I don't have it any more."

SLAP!

"I gave it to mercenaries." I struggled to think of their name. "Yeah, mercenaries. I think they were Mandarin. The ones with the red stripes..."

SLAP!

The strike busted my lip. I could feel my cheeks burning and beginning to bruise. "I swear to fuck, I don't have it..." The Chorzi raised his hand to slap me once more, but I shouted, "Please don't hit me again! Please!" I sniffled, fighting back tears. "Please."

The Chorzi slapped me hard one last time, a backhanded strike that cut the skin. Blood poured into my mouth. I could feel a trickle running down my cheek. The Chorzi stood and shouted an order to the others without turning. Its cohorts immediately proceeded to toss the hotel room. The apparent leader and slapper paced in front of me. Back and forth it walked. Its eyes remained plastered on me the entire time, studying me, trying to find some tell or shred of truth through sheer determination. Its glare was unnerving, so I looked away.

I noticed the viewscreen had shifted to sleep mode. Instead of Roilo pornography, a simple digital clock counted down station time. The numbers themselves appeared arbitrary. I guess the fog caused by the slaps still hung heavy on my mind. I recalled that something important happened at a particular set of numbers, but could not for the life of me remember what that was. I turned my head to the Chorzi. One of the group members sacking the hotel room grunted something to their leader, who signaled back with a simple raise of their right hand. Then, simultaneously, four blasters were raised and aimed at me. I closed my eyes as my tears began to flow. My lips trembled. I felt my bladder give out. I was about to die, and all for some stupid video game avatars.

Visions and memories played through my mind at light speed. The sights and sounds of my childhood vanished, replaced by the angst-filled horniness of my teens. I saw the ship that ferried me to Kilgore. I saw the first time I met Rygar. Rygar. He told me he took a blaster round to his shoulder once, and said it felt like getting hit with a flaming sledgehammer. I waited for the pop and fizzle of blaster fire, but instead heard only the sound of the front door opening.

Rygar.

The time.

I remembered! Rygar would be definitely be home at this hour!

I opened my eyes and saw him, standing in the doorway, with a bag of Chinese food cradled delicately in his arms. Everybody froze. For a long, tense moment, silence dominated the Honeymoon Suite. Nobody moved. Nobody breathed. I sat motionless. The Chorzi kept their blasters pointed at me, but their heads turned toward the door. Rygar clutched the bag of Chinese close to his chest. He looked at me and winked. Shades of red and blue flashed in his eyes.

"Ooops, wrong room," he muttered sheepishly.

Before Rygar could say anything more, the Chorzi closest to him swung its blaster arm and fired it point-blank at Rygar. The blast incinerated the bag of Chinese food and impacted him in the chest. I gasped in horror, only Rygar didn't fall. He barely stumbled backward. Instead, he looked at his chest. The blaster round burned a hole in his shirt about ten inches wide. The artificial skin graft fried, leaving only the alloy casing of his chest showing and a sick smell of burning flesh in the air.

Rygar looked at the Chorzi and grimaced, shaking his head. "Dammit, I just bought this shirt."

In the blink of an eye, he flew into the room and lowered his shoulder at the Chorzi who shot him. The impact sent it flying into the Chorzi behind it. The two fell to the floor in a motionless, unconscious heap.

The leader stood frozen until the third Chorzi moved to fire, only Rygar, already on him, twisted its wrist the moment the blaster discharged. The leader, only moments before the shot, moved to assist its comrade. Its hesitation proved fatal. The round from a blaster held limply by a broken wrist popped the lead Chorzi's head like a zit.

Rygar then disarmed the last opponent with a chop from his left hand. It stumbled backward, but not quick enough. Rygar reached out and grabbed the Chorzi's head in his hands and squeezed. The Chorzi let out a horrific, blood-curdling cry before a disgusting, bone-crunching crack ended its clamor. Rygar released his grip and the Chorzi's body fell lifeless to the floor.

Rygar wiped his hand on his pants and looked at me. "I hope those weren't friends of yours."

I laughed painfully through the tears. "Untie me first. Make jokes after," I managed through horrifically excruciating chuckles.

"Why are you in a honeymoon suite with Black Sun agents? And why are you tied up like some sort of torture victim?" Rygar asked as he untied and helped me up.

I leaned most of my weight against him. "How do you know who the Black Sun are? I only just learned of them today."

Rygar seemed confused. "You've never heard of Black Sun?"

I sighed. "They're on a long list of things I've learned about Kilgore Station today."

"I want to hear this list, but we need to get out of here, and in a hurry. If the Black Sun are using their Chorzi agents, then they're serious about getting at you. Can you stand on your own?"

"I think so," I said, trying to be as brave as possible without crying in pain. Rygar released his hold of me, and I teetered momentarily before I found my balance. My face burned from the slaps. Blood still dominated my taste buds. My headache returned with a vengeance. Yet, I could walk. *Focus on the positive*, I told myself.

Rygar's eyes flashed orange, then green, which I always interpreted as cautious optimism. "OK, then," he said. "Let's go. I know somewhere we can lay low for a while."

Chapter Eight

We made our way as quickly as my fragile, beaten body allowed to the stairs, where I stopped next to the waster.

"What is it now?" Rygar asked.

I raised my hand and lowered myself to my knees with a grunt and moan reserved only for the elderly. Had my legs and thighs had mouths and vocal cords, they would have joined in the yelling. I pulled my multi-tool from my pocket and loosened the screws, then reached in to grab the chit from its hiding place – only it wasn't there.

My heart dropped to my stomach. My breath left me. I started shaking and furiously sweeping my hand back and forth in the compartment, desperately hoping to feel the tiny slide. "No... No, no, no..." I managed through panicked breaths.

"Johnny, what is it?" Rygar asked, kneeling next to me.

I lowered myself to a prone position, despite my stomach's and chest's objections, and scanned the interior of the motor compartment. "I hid something in here... in case of an emergency. Good thing, too, only now I can't feel it. It's not here."

Rygar tapped me and I pulled my head from inside the compartment. His eyes beamed yellow, yellow, and yellow again (a strong sign of amusement). He reached down and yanked the thin metal casing off the compartment. The soft light from the hallway shined inside and immediately I saw it reflecting off the surface of the chit. I quickly palmed it.

"Help me up?" I asked and Rygar obliged.

"What is that thing?" he asked.

"It's…" I began, but stopped. I knew I could trust Rygar. He was my best friend on Kilgore. He could obviously take care of himself, as evidenced by four dead Chorzi. Still, I worried for him. I didn't want to get him mixed up in this. *His safety. Pfft. The guy tore four armed Chorzi apart with only his bare hands.* "It's why the Chorzi are after me."

Rygar's face remained stoic. His eyes flashed yellow, but quickly faded to blue: curious but concerned. "Not now. We need to make sure we're somewhere safe first."

After descending one flight of stairs, he turned to me and said, "This is going to take forever." He dropped to one knee. "Get on."

"What? No," I said with an uncomfortable laugh.

"Now's not the time to be concerned about appearances. Get on!" he repeated. "We'll go faster if I carry you."

I started to object, but knew he was right. So, I climbed aboard. Rygar carried me piggyback down the stairs. In the lobby, Lo Fan the Roilo greeted us with her palms raised. She said, "I'm glad your partner finally joined you! Where are you two headed? Fun? Food?"

"Um… Fun, I guess," I said.

Her ears twitched uncontrollably fast. "It looks like you two have already had a bit of fun."

"OK, Lo Fan. Thanks. We'll see you!" I said, and pointed at the door. "Let's go."

"Sure thing, partner," Rygar snickered.

He ran us around the early morning traffic of the Bourbon Docks, past scores of cyborgs and augs each making its way to work or the nearest lift. We only garnered two or three strange looks before stopping before a nondescript door I figured to be a maintenance access shaft. Rygar put a palm on the port and the door noiselessly slid open.

Rygar set me down as soon as he set foot inside. He pulled his glass-comm and tapped. Suddenly, the door closed, leaving us alone in the dark, but only for a second. Soon, the harsh red glow of lights reserved for security and other station VIPs illuminated the room. I heard a metallic clunk of a security lock and the hum of a snooper, a little device meant to disrupt and scramble any listening devices. I shot a curious glance at Rygar.

"I have so many questions. What is this place. And you... have security clearance?" I asked quietly.

Rygar avoided the question. "Looks like you've had a rough day."

I sighed and rubbed my forehead. "You could say that, yeah." I took a quick look around and saw a number of other doors leading who knows where. A desk sat opposite the door we entered at, with six viewscreens arranged behind it. Whatever system they were attached to was asleep. There was a trio of chairs around the desk; each ergonomically designed unit had wheels. Rygar motioned to the seats.

"Why are Black Sun after you?" he asked as he sat on the desk top. The metal creaked with his weight.

I took a seat. "You wouldn't believe it if I told you."

"Try me." His eyes flashed blue, then yellow.

I exhaled hard, puffing out my cheeks. I spilled my guts, telling him everything that happened, from finding the chit and my run-in with Janky's gang, to Hooper and Leilani's rescue and our subsequent meeting on Deck Two. I told him of Lisette and the contents of the chit. I ended the tale with news of my bounty.

Rygar sat, arms folded across his chest, listening without interruption. When I ended, he stood up straight and said, "Well, we should probably get you to these new friends of yours." With another tap of his glass-comm, the lights transitioned to a soft white glow. A series of metal clunks meant the security locks disengaged. Almost immediately, one of the other doors opened. In walked a familiar-looking aug with an angry scowl seemingly permanently plastered on his face. Rygar whispered, "A friend of mine. Keep quiet, OK?"

"I know the drill. He and I... Well, we've met before. Earlier this rotation, in fact."

Rygar smirked. "You have had an interesting rotation, haven't you?"

The hulking augmented guard from earlier sealed the door behind him, turned, and immediately gaped at Rygar's blaster-burned shirt. He asked, "Are you OK, brother?"

Rygar chuckled. "Oh, this?" He tugged at his shirt. "Yeah, I'm fine. A little pissed because I just bought the thing, but I'll live."

"What brings you back?" the aug guard asked.

Rygar motioned to me as I skulked in my seat, nervous to show my face once more. "A good friend of mine is in quite a bit of trouble. I figured laying low in the Docks was his best option."

The burly aug scowled as he recognized me peeking from behind Rygar. "You!" he shouted.

I waved and smiled weakly, "Hi, again."

The guard took a quick couple of steps toward us, but stopped short when Rygar held up his immense arms. "I had a feeling the alert would have something to do with him. Dock Security has issued a lockdown. First, Chorzi come storming in looking for someone who matches his description, then the same squad of Chorzi end up murdered at the Inn Syde'U."

A surge of anxiety coursed through my veins. *This is just what I need*, I thought, *to have to explain myself to another stranger and get them all wrapped up in this craziness*. Thankfully, Rygar spoke up.

"I can explain the dead Chorzi," he said calmly.

"He's roped you into this, too?" the guard asked.

"Not roped. He's my friend."

The guard shook his head. "I need to report this."

"No you don't, Kluh," Rygar responded. "I can vouch for him."

Kluh sighed. "I have to report it. Surely you understand. Him. His friends, a couple of spacers, vouched for him, too, and I almost lost my job."

Rygar's eyes flashed green, orange, and red, which if I remembered correctly signified compassion or sympathy. "I'm sure my words carry a little more weight than those of a couple of spacebound humans."

The guard's eyes went wide. He stammered, stepped back and held up a hand. "Of course, Rygar. I never meant…"

Rygar quickly closed the gap between them and put a hand on the big guard's shoulder. "There was no offense, Kluh. And don't worry about your job. I can make a few visits."

Kluh nodded, and the two locked arms in what looked to me to be some sort of secret handshake. He moved aside and Rygar quickly moved past, toward the door Kluh entered through. I, on the other hand, was slow to follow. Something about Kluh's grimace unnerved me. Once we exited the strange security room, I turned to ask Rygar about the security clearance and the exchange with Kluh. As if he read my mind, he stopped and turned to face me.

"Now's not the time to explain," he said in hushed tones.

"Nah, man. I told you my part, now it's your turn." I jabbed the exposed metal chest plate with my index finger.

"Johnny, you just have to trust me," Rygar began, but I interrupted.

"No, I mean, yes, I trust you, but dammit, too many people have just told me to trust them today without giving me any reason to do so. You're my best friend, I've known you for ten revs, and I still don't know what you do here on Kilgore! And now this stupid chit shows up and I'm just supposed to go along with everything like it's nothing, and then you kill four guys with your bare hands and have security clearance and are like some prince of the augs…" I could tell I was rambling, but didn't care until Rygar put his hands on my shoulders.

"Listen, little buddy," he said. "I know you're scared. Can I admit to you that I'm a bit scared, too? I wasn't expecting to see Chorzi in that hotel room, let alone you tied up and beat to hell. Yes, I have security clearance and yes, the other augs respect me, but as to why, that's a tale for another time. Right now, my biggest concern is to get us somewhere safe, then maybe later I can answer your questions." His eyes flashed blue – and only blue. He was genuinely concerned. "What do you say?"

"Oh… OK," I mumbled.

The atmosphere on the levels of the Bourbon Docks had escalated, to say the least. The red warning lights beamed sinister from every fixture. Groups of heavily armed cyborgs wielding Tesla bolters and energy shields marched from hatch to hatch, scanning glass-comms and irises. A digital warning message blared from the speakers hanging throughout the Docks. It instructed all to remain in place until the "all-clear" was given.

Rygar moved unimpeded through the Docks. The few guards that we passed paid no attention to the aug with an enormous hole burned in his shirt and the human limping as fast as he could after him. He moved without prompt, taking the same route Hooper, Leilani, and I took on my first visit to the Docks. I shouldn't have been surprised, especially with all that I had just witnessed, but if I'm honest, part of me was.

Before long, we spotted Lisette's little shop, only this time, about ten cyborg guards stood watch or carried black bags that looked suspiciously like body bags from the building. I stopped dead in my tracks. Rygar made it to the cordon line and began talking to an augmented female security guard, before turning around and realizing I wasn't next to him. He waved for me to come near, only I couldn't move. That was a body bag, and there was a good chance it was holding Hooper, Leilani, or Lisette.

"What's the matter, Johnny?" Rygar asked, and he returned to my side. "Nicki is going to let us inside, says there's some bodies in there and wanted to see if we could identify them since... Well, since you were the last person to enter or exit the building."

"No, no, Rygar, I don't think I want to see another dead body today, especially if it's... If they're... I..."

Rygar put a hand on my shoulder and looked me in the eye. "Listen, Johnny, I know this is strange new territory for you. I was a wreck the first time I saw a body. But you don't have to worry. There isn't an organization in the galaxy that can get to you if you're with me on the Bourbon Docks. Let's help Sergeant Nicki out, then we can go from there, OK?"

"OK," I answered, and slowly followed Rygar to the shop. My teeth chattered. My limbs trembled. My breathing grew erratic. We found the hatch to Lisette's shop jammed open. The sign that greeted me only hours ago now flickered with weak light. A shower of sparks sputtered intermittently from torn wires in the access panel. Metal scraped metal in a sickening groan as the hatch struggled and failed to shut time and time again. Rygar stepped first over the threshold. I followed reluctantly.

Disarray doesn't adequately describe what we found. Whoever entered last did a thorough job of tossing the place. They pushed over all the shelves, spilling their contents everywhere. Wall fixtures lay in piles directly below their former location. A few running lights flickered and hummed at unsettling intervals. More than once I slipped on debris that littered the floor. Two cyborg guards stood, eyes flashing and shuttering as they took pictures of the wreckage. A spherical drone hovered between them, bathing their immediate area in harsh white light.

When we made it to the back of the shop, I saw the display cases destroyed and the table I woke up on crushed behind the counter. A Chorzi lay dead in a pool of its inky black blood. I felt my own blood drain from my face.

"You OK?" Rygar said, noticing my discomfort. "If you need to hurl, hurl and get it out. No use prolonging the agony."

"I'll be fine," I said, waving him off. "I'm just glad it's not one of them."

Rygar knelt next to the dead Chorzi and, after a quick examination, said, "Puncture wounds. It was stabbed to death."

"Leilani," I muttered.

"What?"

"Leilani, Hooper's cousin. She carried two long black steel stilettos."

"Meteorite," Rygar corrected. "Black steel is actually meteorite alloy."

"Oh yeah. That's right," I said.

Rygar stood and stepped over the body, taking a quick glance in the room behind the counter. "There's another body back here, but it's a Chorzi. Looks like your friends are safe." He stood still for a moment longer. I could tell by the look on his face that he was surveying the mess with some sort of ocular augmentation. Ten-to-one odds said it wasn't strictly legal either. I took the opportunity to walk away from the scene and back outside. I leaned against a bulkhead and immediately retched all over my shoes. Rygar was right. I felt a million times better.

"Have some water," a husky voice said from behind. I stood up straight and turned around, wiping the remaining vomit from my chin. Holding a metal canteen was the lovely augmented starbound guard. Her lapel read, "Sgt. N. Hodoneau."

I took the flask with a nod of thanks, leaned against the bulkhead, and took a quick swig, gargling and spitting it to the deck. Sergeant Nicki motioned for me to drink up, so I emptied the entire thing into my mouth. The cold, filtered, and fortified water soothed my throat and cleared the nasty taste from my mouth.

"I'm Sergeant Nicki Hodoneau," she said. "I'm part of Docks Security."

"Johnny Gomez," I replied in between sips.

"Security scans put you here hours before it was ransacked by those Chorzi," she continued.

"Oh," I said, and returned the canteen.

"You recognize any of those bodies?" she asked.

"No," I said plainly.

"And how do you know the original occupant of this establishment?"

I shrugged and shook my head nervously. "I... I don't really... I mean, I didn't know her. I just came here to pawn some shit."

Sergeant Nicki looked up from her glass-comm. "Her?"

"Um, yes?"

"The shop is registered to one Hzyngyz, O.U., a Shasho. Last time I checked, Shasho are agender."

"Oh, well, there was a lady who worked the shop."

Sergeant Nicki did not appear convinced. "And the two you entered the shop with? They looked starbound, but our surveillance couldn't match their faces with the identification database. Who were they?"

I swallowed. "Just a couple I met earlier today. We were going to go get drinks later."

"Were they the ones who did that to your face?" she asked, pointing at me. She sighed when I looked away without answering. She tapped her glass-comm, then strapped it back on her chest. "Listen, if you've been involved in some sort of violent altercation with Black Sun or any other criminal element on Kilgore, you need to head to Docks Security. They can protect you."

I opened my mouth to respond, only Rygar answered

for me. "You know Station Security can't protect anybody, Nicki."

Sergeant Nicki sighed and looked to Rygar. "Ryg, you can't be here. I shouldn't have even let you past the barrier. And you can't just go telling people that. How are we supposed to build trust between Security and the Docks residents if people are too afraid to come to us when they have problems?"

Rygar crossed his arms on his chest. His eyes twinkled blue and green. Loyalty. Safety. Trust. "He's my friend, Nicki. I'm going to watch out for him."

Sergeant Nicki exhaled a groan. "Fine, Ryg, just... If either of you has any other information, please contact me or go to our offices, I'm sure you remember where they are. I already tapped both of your glasses, so..."

"You have our word," Rygar said. He then looked at me and motioned for us to leave.

"And get him to an auto-doc ASAP, you hear me, Ryg?" she yelled after us.

We walked away from Lisette's shop and once we were out of earshot, I said, "Are you really going to protect me?"

"Of course," Rygar said without hesitation.

"How do you plan to do that?" I asked.

"Well, first I want to meet these new friends of yours. You said they'd be going to Dusty's Old-World?"

I shook my head. "If they're even there. I mean, it's been several cycles since I last saw them. And Lisette's shop has been ransacked since then. They could be gone already."

"Well, even if they aren't there, Dusty's is a great place to lay low. I know Dusty. He's a good person."

"And then after that?" I asked.

Rygar stopped and gently turned me by the shoulders to face him. "We'll speak with your new friends and hammer out a plan."

I sighed, letting my head drop. "But can you even protect me against Black Sun, Hongxongdi, and Janky's gang?"

Rygar chuckled. "Did you not see how I handled those Chorzi?"

I forced a smile. "OK, yeah, that was pretty savage of you."

"All of these augments are good for something, right? Come on, the sooner we get to Dusty's the sooner we can enjoy a beer or two. I don't know about you, but I could use one after those Chorzi."

I exhaled slowly as Rygar walked away. "I could use several beers. And maybe some of that yillo you love to drink."

"Phew, you must be feeling some sort of way if you want to drink yillo," Rygar said with an amused snort.

"And some Chinese," I added. "Been on my mind since I saw that delicious-smelling bag vaporized."

"You would care more about the food than the damage to your best friend?"

"Damage? It's just your shirt!"

Chapter Nine

Several levels later, past Dock guards who saluted with simple hand gestures or slightly inclined their heads at Rygar, and countless closed and barred shop doors, through clouds of steam and crowds of angry dock workers shouting and demanding for the lockdown to end and their clearance to get back to work, we arrived at Dusty's Old-World Pub. The name wasn't complete without the exterior façade to match it. Holoprojectors made the walls appear as brick. The fabricated sign that hovered at the entrance could have been pulled straight from a Terran history book. Light tubes twisted and turned to create letters and symbols spelling out the name of the pub, as well as a tiny twig with four round leaves at the top. The double doors to the pub slid open and out poured the fervent cheers and jeers of a crowd of drunken patrons. The curious joy during a mandated lockdown intrigued me, so I followed Rygar inside.

It was standing room only. A hundred and fifty or so station denizens crammed shoulder to shoulder, draped in caps and jerseys of blue and white or black and gold, holding pints of gold or amber beer. The viewscreens that hung on the holoprojected brick walls showed the waning minutes of the casco championship. The team from Tyros, in the blue and white, stood in defense formation in their corner of the diamond-shaped field while the team from Idago pressed forward, hoping to knock the Tyroshi flag from its post and secure their victory with a two-score lead. The fans of Idago present at Dusty's struck up a chant. The Tyroshi fans held hands and prayed.

Rygar pushed his way to the bar, with me hot on his heels, squeezing between each gap just before it closed again. Once there, he raised a hand to one of the bartenders. If Rygar was a giant of a man, the bartender that approached us was a mountain. He spotted Rygar and hurried over. The two slapped hands and exchanged a handshake that crashed above the chanting of the Idago fans.

"Is it that fuckin' time already?" the bartender shouted. His voice rumbled in my chest like a roll of thunder.

Rygar shook his head. "No, I'm here on business. Do you not know what's going on out there? The lockdown?"

The bartender guffawed. "We all know, just nobody here gives a fuck. The casco championship has stolen our attention for the evening."

"Looks like I should've put money on Idago."

"Bah!" The bartender waved dismissively at Rygar. "They're overrated. Regardless, it's been a closer game than the score shows. Idago only just now broke the tie."

"Idago breaking a tie must bring back bad memories for you, huh?" Rygar teased.

The bartender's booming laugh made a dozen heads turn to the sound. His pot belly jiggled in unison. "If you were anybody else, I'd swing a fist and end your fuckin' life! Who's the little one behind you?"

Rygar said, "He's part of the reason I'm here. Dusty, meet Johnny Gomez, my roommate."

Rygar shoved me forward and I hit the bar with a grunt. I smiled weakly at Dusty, who offered his enormous hand. "Dusty Peagrass! Pleasure to meet you, Johnny. Welcome to my pub!"

"Thank you," I said, massaging my palms after the handshake. Dusty was as strong as he looked. He stood a hair over Rygar, who stood six foot seven, and appeared to easily weigh three hundred pounds. I could tell by his handshake he knew how to use all that heft. He kept his black hair and beard long, and if not for the streaks of white on his chin whiskers and around his ears, I would have sworn he was younger than me. Yet, despite his gruff appearance, his bright blue eyes shone with a kindness that made me feel all warm and fuzzy inside.

"So, what brings you two here?" Dusty leaned in and asked.

"We're looking for a couple of spacebounds and a fence," Rygar replied.

Dusty stood up straight. The mirth left his face, and it became hard as stone. He motioned to the end of the bar with a quick nod, then shouted, "Cal! Watch the bar, I'll be in back with my old friend Rygar here."

Once again, I followed directly behind Rygar, squeezing my way through the collapsing crowd that, only moments before, parted willingly for my enormous augmented friend. We worked our way around the bar, past a small hallway packed with patrons desperate to use the toilets, to a panel-protected hatch hidden in a completely inconspicuous nook. Dusty tapped his glass-comm to the panel just as a roar erupted from the pub. The three of us glanced over and saw the Tyroshi team celebrating at midfield. Against all odds, they stopped the Idago assault and scored on a counterattack, tying the game with only a minute left to play. The betting odds flashed across every viewscreen. Idago's chances plummeted.

"Guess that bet on Idago isn't as safe as it was earlier." Rygar smirked and patted me on the chest.

The hatch slid open, and beyond lay a sparsely appointed office that looked to me like more of a converted storeroom than anything. Dimly lit bulbs hung from bare wires in the ceiling next to a state-of-the-art holoviewer, which frankly seemed out of place in the office. The ceramic tile floor looked ashen, but upon closer inspection, was merely covered in dust and dirt. Composite, alloy, and synthetic crates sat stacked to the ceiling, each one bearing the label of a different distillery or brewery. A few screens dangled on the walls. They each displayed a different broadcast. Near the rear stood a simple metallic desk, and sitting at the desk, shrouded in a strange purple haze, was Lisette. I peeked out from behind the mammoth figures of Rygar and Dusty. She spotted me instantly.

"Johnny!" she yelled as she rose from her seat. Her shout brought Hooper and Leilani up from a dingy couch with torn fabric hiding behind the desk. She and Hooper approached us with speed. I met eyes with Leilani, who simply nodded.

"We thought you had been killed! We heard of the hit on the Inn Syde'U right after hearing they ransacked my shop. Luckily we had already left."

"But there were bodies inside," I stated in confusion.

"Lei went back to grab Lisette's glass," Hooper added. Leilani remained stoic, raising her chin a little higher with pride. "You look like you slept with a Hysok."

"He almost said his last goodnight, had I not showed up," Rygar said. "They were Chorzi, the same group we saw dead in your shop." He offered his hand before continuing. "Rygar Norumba."

Hooper and Lisette took turns shaking his hand and introducing themselves.

"I guess everybody here already knows Dusty?" I asked.

"It's more surprising that you don't know Dusty, but we can't blame you for that, seeing as your first time on the Bourbon Docks occurred this rotation," Lisette said with a playful leer at Rygar.

Rygar's eyes flashed yellow. He shrugged, then leaned against the nearest stack of crates. He was amused, even if his face didn't show it.

Dusty patted me on the shoulder. "I guess you're in good hands now, kid. You all can use my office to figure this shit out. I gotta get back to the crowd and that game!"

"What's the score?" Leilani called from her seat on the couch.

"Tyros just tied it back up," Dusty said on his way out, which brought small fist pumps and grins from Hooper and Leilani.

As soon as the hatch shut behind Dusty, Rygar stood up straight and joined the rest of us around Dusty's desk. "Johnny already apprised me of the situation," he said. "I want to know what exactly you're going to do to protect him."

"Well–" Hooper started diplomatically, but was not allowed to finish.

"I'm not done yet," Rygar growled bluntly. "The chit may have started all this shit, but it seems to me his troubles have only multiplied. Hongxongdi and now Black Sun?" His eyes flashed red, then blue, then red again – anger out of concern for me, but anger nonetheless. "So, tell me your plan to get rid of this chit and keep him safe, or he's coming with me, and he and I are going to figure out who is behind this by ourselves."

Hooper held up his hands defensively. "A plan is exactly what we've been working on since we've been here. And Johnny, you're going to want to hear this." He motioned to Lisette, but kept his hands up for peace.

Lisette exhaled sharply before speaking. "I did a little research, made a few anonymous inquiries about the chit. A report was filed with Station Security about a missing slide. The report doesn't state exactly what kind of data is on said slide, except–" She tapped her glass-comm and sent its display to the wall-mounted unit in Dusty's office – "That it was valued at one hundred and twenty million credits."

The air in the room almost disappeared with my gasp. I felt lightheaded. The bile began to rise in my throat. I had never vomited out of shock and surprise, but I came close. I was completely unable to fathom such an amount, let alone for video game skins. One hundred and twenty million credits was more than a casco player made in a single season, and those players lived like kings! Even if we split it four ways, thirty million credits would set me up for life, or at least for the next twenty or so revs. The number flashed on the screen, digits highlighted by Lisette. Suddenly, the chit in my pocket felt heavier than a block of Oppas vomit. I swallowed hard, then eyed Rygar. He seemed unmoved.

Lisette continued. "To make matters a little more interesting, the party who initially filed the report was found murdered a few hours later – an unidentified Oppas. The body was discovered on a pile of its own vomit, almost as if the murderers thought the poor thing was keeping the chit in its stomach. It was about that time the bounties were posted, one for the murderers and one for the recovery and return of the chit. Soon after, the bounty boards were flooded with counter-offers for the chit – everyone from our local syndicates to those in neighboring systems.

"So, I contacted an interested party, someone I've worked with before. This party made an offer, and I think we should take it – one hundred and fifty million credits. We might be able to get a better offer, or those hunting it will decide to kill us and just take the chit."

I looked around the room and noticed four faces avoiding making eye contact with one another. I couldn't figure out why the decision to take such an exorbitant amount was giving everyone such pause. "So, what? What are we waiting for? Let's take the offer and save ourselves any more headaches."

"The only issue…" Lisette said. "He is on Luna."

Silence. Lisette nibbled her lower lip absentmindedly. Hooper pulled his silver case from his vest pocket. Leilani puffed out her cheeks in an exhale. I turned to Rygar. He looked as confused as I was. So, I spoke.

"OK, so he's on Luna," I said. "That shouldn't be a problem. We just jump aboard Hooper's ship, hit the starlane, and head that way."

Rygar agreed, saying, "Seems pretty straightforward to me. I mean, in-system flight leaves you vulnerable to tracking. The starlanes require clearance, but they significantly cut travel time. Unless you had a ship that was capable of traveling at speed without using the lanes, but then you risk running into pirates."

"My ship can do that," Hooper stated quietly.

"Then what's the problem?" Rygar asked.

"You already stated it," Hooper answered. "We can't take the starlanes with this much heat on us. We would undoubtedly be tracked or flat out prevented from entering. We can take our chances with the pirates, but there's no guarantee we even make it to Luna."

"That doesn't sound like a problem. It sounds like your only option." Rygar looked at me. The same red-blue-red combo flashed.

"No, you don't understand," Hooper began, sounding defensive about his ship. "The *Mentirosa* is not a warship. It's not even a scout ship. It's a pleasure craft with special smuggling modifications to it, none of which are mini-guns, hyperbeams, or railguns. The *Mentirosa* is meant to get in and out of systems as quickly and quietly as possible. I have radar jammers, signal scramblers, and an entire bay of space-benders that can propel us at speeds you've probably never experienced. I can swing through an asteroid field like a Centaurian water sprite moves through raging rapids. I can pull us into a reverse polarity spin at full burn and shrug off torpedoes. My deflectors can withstand one direct hit from a railgun. But none of that counts for shit if we can't defend ourselves beyond those countermeasures."

"Then you need to play to your strengths," Rygar said matter-of-factly. "If your ship is truly as fast as you say it is, then you make sure your core can power those space-benders for as long as possible."

"What about the pirates?" Lisette asked.

"Pirates?" I shouted.

Rygar motioned to the wall to his right. He pulled his glass-comm from his pocket, tapped it a few times, and swiped his display to Dusty's viewer. A three-dimensional map of the system lit the wall, complete with each planetary designation as well as a flashing orange indicator for our current location. I examined the key that accompanied Rygar's map. Kilgore Station floated at the farthest end of the heliosphere, well past Neptune. Blue lines indicated the hyperspace starlane access points that ran in-system. Green lines ran from two points away from the map, showing the starlanes that left the system itself for Alpha Centauri and Tau Ceti. Red lines showed slow-burn routes that twisted throughout the system, from Kilgore Station, around the gas giants, to the inner four planets, save Mercury. Nobody went there. In all honesty, nobody went to Venus or Terra either. Terra's only moon, Luna, and Mars were the only reasons to travel past the asteroid belt.

Rygar cleared his throat and said, "As I'm sure you all know, not many ships travel in or out of system without using the starlanes. So, it just doesn't make any sense not to use them. Like most other systems, RUSH tribunes patrol the more frequently traveled in-system routes to protect the merchant marines, haulers, and salvagers. These include the slow-burn routes used by all those freight haulers." Rygar tapped his glass-comm, and a series of hashed lines lit up on the map. "Pirates generally avoid these routes and stick to this area around Saturn and the asteroid belt, since it's harder to patrol those." Red boxes highlighted his map.

"Ring rats," Leilani spat.

I raised my hand like a child in school. "I think we should avoid pirates. Like at all costs." I know I sounded pathetic, but I couldn't help it. Fear grabbed a tight hold of me and refused to let go. When everybody turned to look at me like

I had stated the most obvious statement since "My name is Johnny," I decided to change the subject. "Wait, how do you know all this, Rygar? You were born and raised on Kilgore, right?"

Rygar's lips tightened. He crossed his arms on his chest. "I know it's unfair to keep you in the dark, since all of this revolves around you and your safety. Unfortunately, now is not the greatest moment for big reveals." He leaned in close and put a hand on my shoulder. "I promise I'll tell you all you want to know soon."

"OK," I muttered in disappointment.

Hooper continued to strategize quietly with Leilani. They both seemed preoccupied with Saturn and her moons. That was when Lisette stood up.

"Wait, I know that look," Lisette said, pointing at Hooper.

"What look?" Hooper asked as innocently as possible.

She gave him a hard, vicious glare. "That look right there. You're planning something."

Hooper shrugged. "We'll have to throw off any tails the only way possible. That means making a few stops, cycling the ship's registration, and having our signal jumbled up with as many other signals as possible."

Rygar's eyes flashed orange and yellow. He thought it was a solid plan. "That's not a bad idea. If your ship is as ghostly as you claim, it would give you a chance to recalibrate and mask your signal to further throw off any would-be trackers."

"See?" Hooper said, with an upturned palm in Lisette's direction. Lisette only continued to glare.

"Anyway, you four should get going," Rygar said. "The quicker you get off Kilgore and head toward Terra, the better."

"Right," Hooper said, and waved off the holoviewer. "We'll head out the back." He led the way, followed by Leilani and Lisette. I lingered for a moment.

"What will you do?" I asked Rygar.

"I'll keep both ears open for any rumblings about this data chit," he responded. "If two different syndicates are after it, there's bound to be a lot of chatter. Since most of the dock workers on Kilgore are cyborgs and augs, they'll be more than happy to make their departures a little bit of a headache – unforeseen dock fees, last-minute repairs, surprise contraband inspections... you know, the usual. That should give you a little bit of a head start. We should also go dark, radio silence."

"Wait... What? Why?" I asked. "What if I need to get a hold of you?" I took a step forward and lowered my voice. "What if they're not who they say they are, or I get into more trouble?"

Rygar's eyes flashed blue and stayed that way. "We can't risk any subspace communication or short bursts."

"But they're encrypted. Every message is encrypted."

"That's true, but even origin point signatures can be traced, and if one message happens to ping in the middle of nowhere, that could give away your position."

I pressed my lips together and exhaled through my nose. "I'm willing to risk it."

Rygar's eyes flashed blue, red, and blue again. He always said that showed how strong a bond we had. "You know my channel is always open to you."

I nodded and took a deep breath. "Thanks, Rygar. If..." I stumbled over my own words. "If this is the last time I'll see you, I want to let you know you were my best friend." I extended my hand for a shake, only Rygar grabbed it and pulled me into a giant bear hug.

"I'll see you when you get back, little buddy," Rygar said with conviction.

"See you when I get back, then, tin-plated soldier." I looked back as I exited. Rygar was already leaving the office. A round of cheers welcomed him back to the pub.

Chapter Ten

The lockdown had been lifted, which meant the Docks were once again sprawling with organic and synthetic life forms alike, all of them desperate to make up for lost time. Hooper led us through the crowd and to the nearest lift, where we crammed inside with a dozen other beings in a hurry to get to another deck.

The lift took us to Deck 47, one of the many lower docking levels still run by Kilgore Station and therefore subject to RUSH rules and regulations. That meant every hallway we walked down took us through dozens of unseen scanners and sensors, all programmed to alert security for the slightest infraction. Luckily for us, we made it through each one swiftly and without incident, and were soon hurrying toward Hooper's berth.

"So, what do you fly?" I asked as we made our way.

"What do I fly?" Hooper asked.

He slowed down and moved in next to me, putting his arm around my shoulder. "Johnny, have you ever looked at another being and thought, 'I would do anything to be inside him?' Or her. Whatever suits your fancy."

"Sure," I said cautiously. "Who hasn't?"

"That feeling you get, the lust, the desire... all of it is the

Mentirosa," Hooper responded with a grin. "Sexiest vessel in the galaxy." He directed us past the shielded windows and made a sweeping wave with both his hands at the ship docked just outside, one level below us. The sleek, boat-like hull of the Junpoor sloop shone mirror-like in the lights of the bay. The extrasolar alloy resembled knotty wood, and reminded me of the boats I saw in books back on Luna – pleasure craft owned by wealthy socialites from Terra, who sailed them around the seas having drunken, drug-filled orgies. It was larger near the fore of the ship to account for the bridge and what I expected were cabins and storage bays. Four portholes could be seen on the hull, and the stabilizers near the rear of the vessel twinkled bluer than the waters on the pleasure deck. In between the stabilizers peaked a single black cone housing the ship's motivators that propelled it through space. The bridge rose gently from the top of the vessel, a scaled-down inverse of the hull it was attached to and colored the most vivid red I had ever seen. Emblazoned on the deck, just aft of the bridge, was the bust of an elegantly dressed woman with curly black hair and bare shoulders. Her wicked smile and dark, narrow eyes held a secret only she knew. Just below her, the name *Mentirosa* curved seductively, completing the logo. The only strange thing about the entire ship was the *s* in the name. The classy script had been replaced by a boxy font that could have either been a diamond-shaped *s* or a rectangular number eight. Either way, it resembled something teenagers spray-painted on the inner hulls on the lower decks.

"That *is* an impressive ship," I said as I stopped to gawk.

"It's my baby," Hooper said, waving me on. "No time to stop and stare, though." He pulled his arm from my shoulder, and we all hurried down the hall.

Hooper led us down the last flight of stairs, off the main level, to the docking bay that held his ship. The *Mentirosa* floated with three other vessels, all connected via a docking arm to the central hub of Docking Bay 47-E. The docking bay itself was a round garage housing one team of mechanics as well as a dock master, each an employee of Kilgore Station itself. They saw to the refueling and servicing of the ship, collecting docking fees, and attaching or removing landing clamps to keep a ship from leaving. Usually, the clamps were placed for any number of citations or unpaid fees. The giant yellow mechanical arm that magnetically attached itself to the *Mentirosa*, for example, would only be removed once the books were satisfied.

Hooper stopped and dropped his head with a sigh upon spotting the clamp. The rest of us stopped behind him and stared out at the *Mentirosa*. He put a hand up to his face and squeezed the bridge of his nose.

"Doesn't look like we'll be going anywhere in your baby," Lisette said in the most unamused tone I had ever heard.

Hooper held up his free hand for silence. "Just... let me talk to the dock master and straighten things out." He spun around and marched over to the dock master's office, past several dock workers dressed in blue denim coveralls sitting around a dirty round table stacked with tin mugs full of yillo, a Kurevian liquor.

I smelled its telltale skunky aroma floating around the garage just above the mix of sweat and machine oil. Rygar loved yillo, so naturally I equated its consumption with cyborgs and augs, and immediately scanned the dock crew for augments. The six mechanics present were playing a card game – Orbit, by the look of it. Two giant tool cribs sat on opposite sides of the garage, with random wrenches, grips, and meters hanging haphazardly from the drawers. A stretch of removed ceiling tiles revealed a makeshift ventilation extension running from the original outlet to a more ideal location in the middle of the bay. Lisette crossed her arms and stood next to me while Leilani tapped furiously at the aged, grease-clogged keypad on the docking hatch, trying to gain access. The mechanics couldn't be bothered to look up from their game.

"I never could get the hang of Orbit," I mumbled absentmindedly.

"What?" she asked.

"Orbit." I pointed to the table. "I never could get the hang of it. If the object is to hold the moons with the biggest face value, why are people always dumping the high cards?"

"It's cumulative," Lisette said. "There are more moon cards in the deck, so, for example, collecting Luna is worth more than, say, Mars. Regardless, the order in which you play your hand is more important than the cumulative total of the moons you hold. And don't forget that the planet cards either cancel out or bolster your moon score. I once saw a game won with two Triton cards."

"Two Tritons? I call bullshit."

Lisette doubled down and said, "I swear to the many-headed god of the Hepari. A spacebound played one Triton at the start, bided his time until a second Neptune flopped. By that point, everybody's score was zero. So, he just tossed his second Triton and won the whole thing."

"I will never understand that game," I replied, then moved my attention to the office. I could see Hooper pointing and wildly waving his arms at somebody. He took off his hat and threw it on the desk, only to, moments later, grab it and place it back on his head. "It doesn't look like it's going well in there."

"It's always something with Hooper," Lisette said, rolling her eyes. "He'll get it figured out." No sooner had the words left her mouth than a short, rotund Hupzoid with a long, drooping black mustache hanging off its top lip came into view. It was obviously cosmetic, as Hupzoids were devoid of hair. The Hupzoid shook his tiny fists violently at Hooper. Hooper responded by yanking at the mustache. The two immediately locked arms and began to toss each other around the office.

I swallowed. "It's... uh... not really a good time to be having 'something' going on."

"I'm sure he knows that," Lisette responded as a loud crash echoed from the office, with enough volume for the mechanics to look up, but quickly reabsorb themselves in their pastime. I winced as Hooper's body hit the window. The Hupzoid jumped in the air and lowered his elbow toward his slumping opponent. The tussle continued for longer than I could comfortably watch. A chair and stool flew past, then Hooper in the opposite direction. The Hupzoid's mustache struck the window, followed immediately by the Hupzoid, who slid down, mustache reattaching to its face in the process.

"We can board now," Leilani interrupted, pointing her thumb toward the hatch. She managed to completely remove the keypad and bypass the security doors the old-fashioned way: hotwire. The wires were still sparking. The hatch itself looked less than cooperative in its opening.

"Well, that's one way to do it," Lisette said.

"But that doesn't remove the clamp," I called out as Lisette followed Leilani to the docking arm. "We can't go anywhere with that clamp on."

"It'll come off soon," Leilani yelled down the docking arm. "Hooper's handling it."

I was exasperated. "Why is everyone so confident that that man, who is literally wrestling a Hupzoid, is handling this situation? And don't we need to be getting out of Kilgore as fast as possible?"

"Hooper's handling it." Lisette poked her head out and answered, then pointed at the office. "See?"

I looked back to find Hooper and the dock master hugging and joking with each other. The Hupzoid patted him on the back. They both had bloody lips. Hooper reached into his vest pocket and removed his silver oil pen, offering it to the dock master.

"Unbelievable," I said, then turned and hustled down the docking arm.

I entered the *Mentirosa* and feelings of amazement, fascination, and awe struck me like a violent slap to the face. Every surface looked impeccably crafted by master artisans, from the brushed alloy plates and trim to the tanned and charred wood that intricately interlocked throughout the vessel. I softly glided my fingers across the delicate carvings, wholly astounded that Hooper and Leilani could afford so much wood when such a material was a rare commodity. Two lighting strips of the most electric blue dazzled along the walls. Soft white orbs glowed from hidden sconces near the top and bottom of the deck. I followed the strips to the fore, past an alloy panel laser-etched with the same logo emblazoned on the exterior, past hatches and ladders leading to storage bays and sleeping quarters, to the galley. Matching benches, stools, and chairs of brushed alloy and a strange, shimmering azure fabric greeted me and beckoned me to sit and take a load off. A long alloy table sat in the center, flanked by shelves and counters of the same material. I spotted an alchemic aquifer and magnetic tumblers neatly stacked next to clear synthetic containers holding different grains. A well-used espresso machine hummed to my left. A booth sat to my right, tabletop scattered with rags and oils meant for cleaning and servicing blades and blasters. The faint scent of fresh baked cookies filled my nostrils, and the complex chords of a Hepari nocturne whispered from hidden speakers.

"You have an aquifer," I said in disbelief. "I've only ever read about them. Can they really make *any* drink you can think of?"

"They can, as long as you have the program to do so," Lisette answered from the entrance. "But, if I'm honest, they don't taste the same. The aquifer makes the beverage *too* perfect, if that makes sense."

"It's like he's never been aboard a spaceship before," Leilani scoffed as she climbed up the ladder to the bridge.

Lisette giggled. "Well, to be fair, the *Mentirosa is* a nice ship."

I shook my head out of my stupor. "I... I've only ever set foot in one other working ship. It was the transport galleon that brought me to Kilgore Station."

"I guess you do have a reason for gawking," Leilani answered from the deck above. Lisette waved me to the ladder, and I followed.

The bridge greeted me with the same level of amazement I felt with the lower deck. Holoscreens and display panels showed internal read-outs of the *Mentirosa*'s systems, long- and short-range scanners, and any other telemetric and sensor graph imaginable. Every piece of hardware looked remarkably ahead of its time. Six of the most ergonomic seats occupied the bridge, complete with absorption coils and draped with the same azure material as below. Two were placed at the helm while the other four sat aft, next to support consoles, navigation, and radar. An actual fish tank bubbled behind the bulkhead opposite the helm. A pair of paradise fish from the seas of Pilgrim's Folly swam lazily around their confines.

I sat down in one of the impossibly comfortable bridge seats and exhaled a sigh of pure overwhelming wonderment. Lisette and Leilani had a colorful exchange concerning just how long the journey to Luna should take us. I only half listened to their conversation. I sat in dumbstruck speechlessness at the *Mentirosa*. Moments later, Hooper entered the ship and ascended the ladder to the bridge, interrupting their argument.

"How do you like my ship?" he asked me, with a smirk and a slap on the shoulder. He was already hopping into his seat before I could respond.

"You cannot seriously be considering navigating us through the dark corridor," Lisette said, her voice low and assertive, arms crossed on her chest, eyes boring through him. "As if we haven't had to deal with enough here on Kilgore, now you think swinging us around the shadowy side of the big three is the best path."

"It'll be fine," Hooper said with a grin as he tapped a series of virtual buttons on the display next to the helm. "I've done this before. Plus, Johnny's friend Rygar approved."

"I don't think not disapproving is the same as approving," I mumbled.

Leilani cleared her throat and crossed her arms on her chest.

"Right, *we've* done this before," Hooper corrected.

"I don't doubt that," Lisette said, "but I do doubt that you've done the dark corridor with a fifty-million-credit bounty on your ass."

That number jolted me back to reality. "Fifty million?" I asked with a gasp. My heart began to race. Hooper, Leilani, and Lisette turned around and looked at me. The looks on their faces said they forgot I sat only a few feet away from their conversation. "I thought it was forty?"

Silence.

I could hear my heart pounding in my ears.

Hooper's mirth faded. His shoulders dropped. Leilani uncrossed her arms and took her seat next to him. Lisette took a deep breath. Her mouth twisted in a way that said she searched for an answer she couldn't find.

She slowly walked to my side. She sat across from me and rested a hand on my knee. I felt my heart begin to pound. "Johnny don't panic. You're safe aboard the *Rosa*."

I felt my lip trembling. I looked down at my hands, knuckles scraped and scabbed, wrists red from the bonds the Chorzi wrapped around them. It was as if, at that moment, the gallons of adrenaline that coursed through my veins since Janky's gang appeared were finally depleted. My brain gave in to the fear of the unknown, the uncertainty that lay ahead. How much longer would I survive? Would this ragtag trio of miscreants be able to keep me safe? Would Lisette casually break the touch barrier again? My body ached. My head pounded. I felt like a giant bruise with limbs, barely able to stay seated upright. I turned my gaze to Lisette and weakly asked, "Is…? Is there a shower or something on this ship?"

"And an auto-doc, down below," she confirmed. "Take all the time you need."

Chapter Eleven

Cascades of delightfully hot water flowed over my grimy, bruised skin. I watched as rivulets of water, tinted with dried blood, sweat, and layers of station grease, ran down the drain. I stood under that waterfall for longer than necessary, until my fingers pruned, and my skin reddened from the heat. It had been ages since I had a shower with actual hot water instead of that orange disinfectant goop used by Kilgore Station. They said it was to ration water supplies, but that didn't stop the sprinklers from keeping the soil moist on Deck One. Regardless, no shower had ever felt so glorious as my first aboard the *Mentirosa*.

After toweling off and slipping back into my dirty clothes, I made my way to the auto-doc. I expected a state-of-the-art unit capable of stitching together even the most broken individual. My expectations were met. The cabin the auto-doc occupied looked like your typical hospital wing, uncomfortably sterile with the strange odor of medical disinfectant floating on the air, except the one aboard the *Mentirosa* had the same flair as the rest of the ship. Polished alloys and meticulously carved wood covered every surface. The auto-doc chair resembled the seat on the bridge, right down to the impossibly soft azure fabric. It looked brand new and delicately used. I shrugged and took a seat.

The auto-doc noiselessly twitched to life. The read-out glass chimed, announcing its intention to examine me. Two arms swung out from the side and moved up and down the chair, scanning my body for injuries. After they returned to their hidden compartments, the glass displayed its findings: multiple contusions and abrasions, several shallow lacerations, and two bruised ribs. It then asked if it could administer treatment.

"You are a curiously nice and considerate auto-doc," I said as I tapped the yes. A moment later, I realized why. A third arm appeared from behind the chair with an injection gun full of a viscous blue liquid. I grimaced. "Great... booster ser–" Before I could finish, the needle plunged into my arm, and the serum burned its way into my body.

Rygar once told me the most accurate description of booster serum. He said, "If you could harness magma and shoot it into your body, the intensity of the burning, artery-melting, nerve-frying magma would only be half as painful as booster serum." He was right. I clenched my teeth for the minute of severe, searing pain as it coursed through my veins. The second injection – the one full of pain relievers and organic, quick-decay nanobots directed by the auto-doc's AI – followed almost immediately. The narcotic fluid containing the bots was meant to lessen the pain of their work and diminish the burn of the booster serum. It worked about as well as you'd expect. The beatings I took over the past rotations paled in comparison. I found myself welcoming another ass-kicking. The pain was so intense, I didn't even notice the auto-doc performing its procedures. It ended in a blur several minutes later. As soon as it was over, the arms retracted, and the auto-doc returned to its idle state. The screen flashed with a post-op disclaimer about continued use of auto-docs and the expulsion of the decayed nanobots through my next urination and bowel movement. It then thanked me for choosing it for all my medical needs, with a picture of a smiling cartoon doctor, complete with mustache and white gloves.

I got to my feet, woozy but in no way weakened by the treatment. In fact, I felt just as I had before Janky's gang put their boots to me. The pain from the beating was gone, replaced by the usual aches and pains of age and the curious red marks where the auto-doc shot me full of nanobots. "Too bad you don't treat that," I said to the auto-doc before leaving. Surprise struck me when I climbed the ladder to the bridge. Hooper sat alone, swiping through ship BIOS read-outs. Lisette and Leilani were nowhere to be found. I checked my glass-comm, surprised to see how much time I had spent showering and at the auto-doc's.

"Where are Lisette and Leilani?" I asked as I studied the paradise fish. Their prismatic fins waved luxuriously in the water, like hair being blown about by the wind.

"Lei went to engineering to visually check the benders. Take a seat, Johnny," Hooper said, pointing at the copilot's chair. I took a moment to look out at the all-encompassing blackness of space that surrounded us. "Lisette said she had to confirm with her contact about something… I don't know, I wasn't listening."

I groaned as I lowered myself into the chair.

"Booster serum is a bitch," Hooper said, "but it works like fucking magic."

"A bitch is putting it mildly," I responded. "I'd almost rather spend a week in the hospital."

"Oh, not me. I love the burn. That pain is like no other. I'd pay money to have it pumped through me by a half-naked Serovian holding a whip."

I looked at Hooper. I could see the delight curling the corner of his lips.

"So, where are we?" I asked.

"We're in a hard burn, heading toward Neptune," he replied. "Unfortunately, I can't engage our faster-than-light drives. That signature would be detected by every sensor array in the system pinging our location for any would-be tails."

"How long do you think it's going to take to get us to Luna not using the starlanes or the FTL drives?"

He bobbed his head left and right and shook his right hand. "I'm going to use planetary gravity to slingshot us closer to the belt. That will cut down our trip." He pointed up. A display panel with a countdown ticked just above us. The first number was fourteen.

"Is that hours?"

Hooper scoffed. "No, that's rotations. People forget that even fourteen rotations is a hilariously small number when compared to how long our predecessors took to make it out to where Kilgore floats. The near instantaneous travel of the starlanes has spoiled most of you earthbounders who don't travel very often."

"I guess you're right," I said with a sigh. "How long did it take them?"

"Who?"

"The humans who built Kilgore?"

"Thirty-six revs, two-hundred and seventy-seven rotations, twelve cycles and sixteen minutes. Those are all Terran years, those revs. That crew knew when they signed up that their mission was one they would never return from. If they failed to build that first enclosure, they would die in the vacuum of space. They also knew they were saying goodbye to anything and everyone they ever knew on Earth. Had to have been a hell of a decision to make."

"It's crazy to think about – traveling for that long, leaving everything behind."

"Especially when you consider the in-system starlane takes you from Kilgore to Terra almost instantaneously."

"I wonder what they did for thirty-six revs."

Hooper said, "Most of them slept in stasis, save the essential crew – you know, pilots, navigators, ship mechanics. Even they worked in shifts. Did you know there was one member aboard that vessel that cleaned up after the essentials? She called herself a space broom."

"Ha! You know, I actually heard that once. That's where the name came from."

"She must have had the patience of a star and one hell of a sense of humor to clean up after two pilots, a navigator, and three mechanics for thirty-six revs and not kill every single one of them."

"You know, I never thought about it until now, but to be a custodian aboard a ship like that... I mean, people must have thought it was an important gig if they hired someone specifically to do that."

Hooper turned his head and smiled. "It's an important job. Don't let anybody tell you otherwise."

We sat in silence for a bit. Hooper wordlessly offered me a drag on his oil pen. I politely declined.

"Hey, have you ever seen the giants?"

I turned and said, "No. At least, not in person. When I

first left Luna for Kilgore, I traveled on one of those high-occupancy galleons. Only the elite had porticos. The rest of us shared an enormous 'common galley.' It only took a few hours, we had to stop for pick-ups and drop-offs, but all I saw was the metal of the hull and the faces of all the other normies like me."

Hooper beamed with excitement. "You should see them, then. The pictures don't do them justice. Every once in a while, you can see lightning in the clouds circling Neptune."

"So, you're really planning on a hard burn all the way to Earth?" I asked.

He exhaled a plume of smoke before responding. "It's the safest way. If your friend was right, we'll be denied access to the starlanes or arrested as soon as we exit. At least this way, we control when and how we get there."

"Minus pirates," I added.

"I don't think we'll have any problems with pirates," Hooper said with confidence. "But don't worry, it's not going to be fourteen rotations of boredom. We'll make a few stops on the way. I'm sure Lei will talk us all into visiting Lotus, a particularly niche pleasure house on Titan. There's also a refueling depot just outside of Jupiter, close to the belt, called Hogger's, that makes the absolute best jerky in the system. Like hands down. No lie. The best." He noticed my skepticism and continued, saying, "I'm serious. They're ranked. Galactically ranked. Best in system, top ten out of all the RUSH systems."

"OK, I believe you," I said, bemused. "But do you honestly think stopping and playing the tourist is the best idea?"

"If we sail to Earth via the direct route, it'll just raise more flags and make us easier to track. The more stops we make, the more we can mimic registration signals or mask ours entirely. You know, throw them off our scent, fool the dogs, so to speak. That happens to be one of my baby's specialties."

"So, we'll be the only pirates we encounter," I stated.

Hooper held up a hand and corrected me, saying, "Smugglers, Johnny. Smugglers, which, I'll have you know, Lei and I are pretty good ones."

"And the fact that your ship is called 'the Liar' doesn't give that away," I said.

He exhaled another cloud of smoke. "You'd be surprised. Most races outside of Sol don't even know Spanish is a language. It's one of those 'ancient human dialects' that goes largely unnoticed. You'd think RUSH would love to catalog it, like it does everything else – prosperity and cooperation and all that shit they preach."

I exhaled, running my hand through my hair. "I guess it's too late to just give up the chit and go back to my job."

Hooper said, without looking my way, "I could jettison you out the waste chute if you think you can hold your breath long enough."

"No, thank you," I responded. "So, what is this place, Hogger's?"

"You've never heard of it?"

"Can't say I have."

"It's a refueling station, but not like a regular refueling station. It's legendary. I learned about Hogger's when I was a kid back in the Alpha Centauri system. Everyone said, if you ever go to the Sol system, where humanity originated, you have to go to Hogger's."

"A fancy refueling station," I stated plainly. Unamused.

Hooper grinned. "Just you wait. It'll change your life. You might even win something. They have all sorts of door prizes for first-timers."

I snorted, more amused by his fervor for a refueling depot than by the thought of actually going there. "Where did you say Lisette and Leilani went?" I asked, changing the subject.

"They went below," Hooper said. "After her checks, Lei likes to occupy herself with her glass during downtimes. She plays *Lost Worlds*, but occasionally reads a book or two. Lisette isn't the fondest of space travel, so she's most likely sitting uncomfortably, pretending to be OK."

"I think I'll go see what they're up to," I said, rising from the copilot's seat.

"Roger that," Hooper replied. "I might be down in a few – set the autopilot and go grab a drink or two."

I found Lisette and Leilani exactly where Hooper said they would be, sitting in the galley. Leilani lounged, feet propped up, completely absorbed in her glass-comm. The way she tapped and swiped on her screen confirmed her addiction to *Lost Worlds*. Lisette sat across from her, gripping a decorative metal tumbler I imagined was full of hard liquor. I waved awkwardly as I entered. Leilani didn't notice. Lisette smiled meekly.

"Mind if I join you?" I asked politely.

"Only if you pour yourself a drink," Lisette replied. "Lei here isn't the best drinking companion, mostly because she doesn't drink."

I swore I heard Leilani *hmph* from behind her glass-comm, but she continued to tap away as if nobody had said a word.

"What's good?" I asked as I stepped to the aquifer.

Lisette sneered. "Nothing. Aquifers can't quite duplicate the complexity of good booze. But if you don't mind a cocktail, you can't even taste it."

"What are you having?" I asked.

Lisette studied her tumbler, her lips pursed in thought. "I asked for a gin and tonic, but it tastes more like lemonade and rubbing alcohol."

"What if I ask it for lemonade and rubbing alcohol?" I asked. She snorted. "Rum, club soda, mint, and a squeeze of lime," I said to the aquifer. It beeped, confirming my selection, then asked for a tumbler. "Well, it definitely smells like a mojito," I said as I took a seat.

"Hooper says it'll take us about fourteen rotations to hard-burn all the way to Earth," I said before taking a sip. "Ugh, you're right about the booze."

"Yeah, that sounds right... yeah," Lisette said, taking another swig of her drink.

"You know, I'm not the fondest of space travel either," I said. Her eyes widened and her cheeks began to flush.

"Who told you I don't like space travel?" she asked. "I'm perfectly fine with space travel. In fact, I love space travel. I relish every opportunity to do it." The words poured out of her mouth like water from a faucet. "Just because I kind of freaked out that one time doesn't mean I don't like space travel. I mean, in all honesty, it was Hooper's fault anyway. If he knew how to pilot this damn ship he loves so much, nothing at all would have happened. What did he tell you? Did he say it was his fault? Because he still hasn't apologized to me three revs after the fact!"

Leilani smirked and set down her glass-comm. "This has been a point of contention between the two of them for ages."

"I see," I said, and averted my eyes, trying my best to concentrate on my drink as Lisette continued to rant.

"I told him I wasn't feeling great," Lisette continued after slamming her tumbler to the table, gin and tonic splashing out. "But no, he wouldn't listen. 'The *Rosa* has all kinds of gyro controls, you won't feel a thing, you had as much to drink as I did, and I'm perfectly all right, trust me,' blah blah blah!"

Leilani leaned close to me. "It was their last date together. She dumped him soon after."

"Oh," I said, trying to mask my shock. "I... I didn't know they dated."

Lisette's tirade continued, unhampered by my and Leilani's sidebar. "He just had to show off like the pig-headed, arrogant bastard he is."

At that very moment, Hooper took a step into the galley.

"You couldn't help yourself, could you?" Lisette fired at him.

Hooper froze, confusion taking hold of his body, from his face to his shoulders, from his suddenly fidgeting hands down to his shuffling feet. "Um... Did I miss something?"

"You take every opportunity to be a royal asshole, don't you?" Lisette said, rising from the table. "Don't act so innocent. I know how you are – can't let things be, always having to rock the boat to impress the new guy. Well, I have one thing to say to you." Lisette lifted both hands, middle fingers raised, and thrust them into Hooper's face. He stumbled back and hit the bulkhead as she shoved her way past him to her quarters.

"What the fuck was that about?" he asked, completely bewildered.

Leilani snickered. "You picked the exact wrong time to leave the helm, cuz."

"Was she talking about the... incident?" he asked, quickly sliding into the booth Lisette just vacated.

"Johnny here tried to sympathize with her fear of space travel," Leilani told him.

I raised my hands in defense and said, "Whoa, I... I mean, I didn't mean anything... How was I to know?"

"Did you tell him to pester her?" Leilani asked Hooper.

He violently shook his head. "No! I wouldn't dare touch that subject again, especially not after last time."

"I didn't mean to bring up old shit," I said. I could feel my heart pounding. The welling anxiety began to overflow. "Should I go apologize?"

"She's not mad at you," Hooper clarified. "She just carries a little resentment toward me, is all."

"She'll stew over it for a bit, but it'll pass," Leilani said. "You should probably make yourself scarce until it does," she added, nodding toward Hooper.

He vigorously concurred, saying, "Oh yeah, I think I had to... uh... recalibrate the long-range scanners. I was going to say I just plotted us a course to Titan. I know how much you both love that place."

"Lotus?" Leilani said with a grin.

Hooper gleefully stuck out his tongue and gave her two thumbs up.

"I'll tell her next time I see her," Leilani said.

He exhaled and stood up. "Well, I'll be hiding out on the bridge, in case anybody needs me."

Lisette remained hidden for the remainder of that rotation. We didn't see her again until the number on Hooper's timer ticked down to thirteen. In the meantime, I tried to make myself useful around the *Mentirosa*, which was harder than I expected. I had no experience working on a ship, at least as far as keeping it running went, and my tech-savviness only extended as far as personal devices like our glass-comms. I'm sure I looked like an ape admiring a television as I stared blankly at the advanced technology aboard the *Rosa*.

My ignorance meant I reverted to the most comfortable role I knew – custodian. Despite the opulence beaming from between the hulls, upon closer inspection, the *Mentirosa* was filthier than a Chorlak's brood nest. Hooper and Leilani weren't the cleanest of cousins. Greasy handprints smudged most of the screens, especially near the drive bays. A few managed to make their way up to the main deck and the ladder leading up to the bridge. Dark stains and rings dotted every surface in the galley – remnants of spilled beverages. Dust and grime covered the least used surfaces. The head was the worst of all. I nearly gagged from the smell, which is saying something since I cleaned Chrysostom and Tarbon excretions just a rotation or two prior. Unfortunately for me, Hooper did not stock cleaning supplies on board. I had to make do with diluted cups of vinegar poured straight from the aquifer.

During my cleaning binge, I decided I no longer wanted to carry the data chit around with me everywhere. It was as if my mind decided the simple act of keeping it in my pocket drew nothing but danger and violence to my person. While in the galley, I found several empty drawers in the pantry, the kind most people I knew used to store random junk, and placed the chit inside one of them. I immediately felt safer, and got back to work.

It took me the rest of that rotation to put a shine on the *Rosa*. I witnessed Hooper amble to his quarters, which I discovered was a shared bunk room. Apparently, Lisette had commandeered the captain's quarters, Hooper's quarters, and made them her own. Leilani kept watch on the bridge while I cleaned. When I finished, I threw the rags in the compactor and poured the rest of my improvised cleaner down the drain. I stood by and looked around the galley, perfectly content at the job I'd done and perfectly exhausted from all the work. Instead of joining Hooper, I curled up on the booth bench in the galley for some shuteye.

I woke up to the smell of freshly brewed coffee. I sat up, tousled my hair, and rubbed the sleep from my eyes before I noticed Hooper holding a steaming tumbler and his oil pen in both hands.

"Morning," I mumbled as I rose and stretched, moaning ever so slightly to the audible cracks and pops of my spine.

"You know we have a bunk room, right?" Hooper said.

"I… I didn't want to assume…"

He chuckled. "Johnny, you're a guest on my ship and a partner in this endeavor. You can sleep in a goddamn bed."

"Understood," I said, and made my way to the counter. "Real coffee or aquifer coffee?"

"Oh, it's the real deal, or as close as can be," Hooper replied, sliding toward me a tin can with a comfortingly familiar label.

"Wow, this is actually from Terra," I said in surprise.

Hooper took a sip from his tumbler, then said, "Mmhmm! The beans from the hydroplots are decent, but nothing beats the stuff from Terra. Picked this can up from a shop in Alpha Centauri. They specialize in Terran goods for those earthbound humans who miss home."

I opened this tin and brought the grounds up to my nose. The aroma brought a wave of sheer delight to my body and soul, and did indeed remind me of life back on Luna. "I can't remember the last time I had coffee from Earth, and in the last two rotations, I've had it twice. The beans we get on Kilgore are primarily hydroplot."

"Make yourself a cup, then meet me on the bridge," Hooper said. "We'll be passing Neptune shortly. Last scan seemed favorable for lightning storms."

Neptune struck me with such awe, I didn't want to leave the bridge for the remainder of the voyage. Swirling storms of cerulean and violet raged throughout the planet, and just as Hooper promised, we witnessed lightning. He pointed out the broken arcs that circled Neptune, evidence of a ring system, and two mammoth space stations in orbit. They belonged to mining outfits that competed for the abundance of hydrogen and helium in the atmosphere. I kept my eyes glued to Neptune as the *Mentirosa* cruised around the planet, gaining speed thanks to its gravity.

Later that rotation, after Hooper set the autopilot for Uranus, we reconvened in the galley. The appearance of Lisette from her quarters surprised both of us. She sat in the booth near the porticos, tapping away on her glass-comm. Leilani, however, was nowhere to be found.

"You didn't stock your pantry," Lisette said without looking up from her glass-comm.

"I didn't think I would be leaving Kilgore with my crew numbers doubled," Hooper responded as he opened the dry goods cabinet and the cooler simultaneously. "There was enough on board for Lei and me to make it back to Alpha Centauri via starlane. We were planning on stocking up before we left for Hogan V."

"Well, we're going to need to resupply on Titan," Lisette replied. "We don't have enough in here to last us the entire trip."

"I can make us red orvo," Hooper said, with his head in the cooler.

"What's red orvo?" I asked.

Lisette lowered her glass-comm, flashed me her teeth in worried disgust, then mouthed the words, *It's horrible*. I grinned.

"Red orvo is a staple aboard flotilla vessels. Potato, bell pepper, and onion stewed in a spicy red sauce, and poured over rice. Only ..." Hooper exited the fridge and scanned the pantry. "We're out of potatoes."

"Mmm, spicy bell pepper and onion," Lisette groaned. "Sounds delicious."

"We still have dehydrated potato flakes. I can substitute that," Hooper said in triumph.

"Great, I can't wait." Lisette's sarcasm garnered an eye roll from him.

He got started cooking and I took a seat across from Lisette. She gave me a once-over and a brief, humorless smile, then continued to swipe and tap away at her glass-comm.

"What are you up to?" I asked, drumming my fingers on the table.

Lisette slowly, reluctantly, lowered her glass-comm. "Checking the news back on Kilgore and scanning the bursts for any chatter about the chit."

Leilani entered the galley a moment later, wiping her hands clean on an already filthy rag. "Red orvo?" she asked Hooper.

"You know it," he replied.

"You clean engineering?" she asked me as she leapt up and took a seat on the counter.

"Um... Yeah, I was bored, felt like I needed to contribute something..." I trailed off.

"Cool," she said.

She's so eloquent, I thought to myself. I looked at Lisette and mouthed the word "cool" to her. She tried not to smile.

We ate dinner in relative silence. Hooper made small talk, trying to coax more than three words from Lisette. Leilani scarfed down the red orvo quicker than any of us. Unfortunately, Lisette was right about the meal. What it lacked in flavor and substance it made up for in pure, devilish heat. I drank an entire thirty-two-ounce cup of water between every other bite, a fact not lost on Hooper, who eyed me with delight after each refill. Hooper then cleared our plates, which Leilani washed, and once again poked his head into the cooler.

"Who wants a pono?" he asked, head placed firmly inside.

We all oohed and aahed our consensus. Lisette said, "Grab one for everybody."

Hooper responded by hitting his head on the roof of the cooler with a sharp clinking crash. He emerged, rubbing his head and holding a container of deliciously frosted tarts. He served each of us a tiered treat, then dropped the tray in the middle of the table before sliding in next to me.

"Have you heard the legend of the Three Hundredth Chef?" he asked with a grin.

Leilani rolled her eyes. Lisette groaned.

"What?" I asked.

"It's his favorite story," Leilani mumbled.

"I'm pretty sure it's the only story he knows," Lisette added.

Hooper feigned offense. "That's untrue. I know lots of stories. But you are right, it is my absolute favorite."

"Well, I've never heard it, so go ahead," I responded, much to the chagrin of Lisette and Leilani. Leilani rose quickly and muttered something about checking the nav systems, and Lisette jumped up and decided it was time to use the restroom. With the booth evacuated, I scooted over to give us more space.

Hooper, unfazed, continued, saying, "That's OK. It's fine. They normally just interrupt me with superfluous details they *think* I missed."

I chuckled.

Hooper took another bite of his pono and spoke with his mouth full. "The story goes that before the Hepari began their colonization of other worlds, they were ruled by the terrible Queen Tuta Pono. I mean, she was the worst. She nearly single-handedly destroyed the very culture that gave us interstellar space travel and RUSH. Tuta Pono was celebrating her one hundred and eleventh birthday. Her birthday also coincided with the eight hundredth anniversary of the Hepari empire. In honor of this momentous occasion, Queen Tuta Pono ordered an enormous cake, large enough to be shared by her entire court, to be sliced at the precise moment the Octennial fireworks went off. The only problem was, not a single baker existed in the kingdom that could create a confection large enough or sweet enough for Tuta Pono's tastes. She had a massive sweet tooth. Massive. So, Tuta Pono ordered that every baker in the kingdom's capital, all three hundred of them, be slaughtered for their failure."

I choked on my pono. "Are you serious?" I asked once I recovered.

Hooper responded, "As serious as a Snarfan suffering from sci-scho."

I stared at him for a moment before I understood. "Ah, gotcha. Deadly."

He winked and shot me a finger gun. "Anyway, like I said, she was a terrible queen. She did, however, give them an out. If, together, they could create a masterpiece of confectionery prowess, their lives would be spared. So, the bakers gathered and began to plan. They created recipe after recipe. They squabbled among themselves. Nobody could agree on what they should create and serve to their tyrant of a queen. As the moment of truth grew near, a young baker by the name of Uden Cardo-cardo stepped forward.

"Cardo-cardo was a revolutionary. He secretly hated the queen and what she had done to the Hepari empire. He watched countless of his brothers and sisters sent to slaughter for her wars squashing those who sought to depose her. He took this as an opportunity to exact revenge. Cardo-cardo proposed that instead of creating the sweetest treat, they simply create any treat they want and lace it with poison. The bakers were stunned by Cardo-cardo's words, but in a show of solidarity, agreed to his plan. They knew no treat they could create would please Tuta Pono. They knew they were going to die that day, so why not die killing their dictator? They spent long hours deciding which poison would best be masked by the sweetness of the dessert. They landed on a very specific slow-acting poison – a tasteless, odorless powder only one Hepari in history ever consumed and survived.

"The Octennial grew nearer. One evening, about a week before the celebration, the bakers gathered in the great hall and unveiled their masterpiece – a pono, they called it, in honor of the queen. The queen eyed each man skeptically and first ordered her royal chef to try the dessert. After he signaled his approval with moans of delight, she then ordered that each one of the three hundred chefs join her in sampling it. Plates were passed around, slices were made. The queen asked that the inventor of such a treat come forward and give a toast. Uden Cardo-cardo stood proudly in front of the queen. He said, louder and prouder than she expected, "Long live Queen Tuta Pono!" With that, all three hundred bakers consumed the poison cake, as did Tuta Pono. Every one of them died that day, and all within the cycle after consuming the cake. The official cause of death... Heart failure due to immaculate confection."

I was fit to burst. "That's a pretty horrible tale," I said once I regained my composure.

"Isn't it?" Lisette added as she rejoined the table. "And all for that awful one-liner."

Hooper wagged a finger at me and said, "It's not over. You see, because the baker's secret died with them, nobody could recreate the treat. It also meant nobody knew it was poison that killed them. The kingdom figured the treat was so amazing, so tasty, so sweet, that each person who consumed it died of pure joy. It was only several millennia later that the queen's remains were exhumed, and studies done that revealed it was poison."

"What happened to the kingdom? And why did they exhume her body after so many revs?"

"The kingdom was in turmoil for several revs after," Hooper stated, "but as with all things, the war ended. The democracy that stood as the foundation of the Republic of Unified Systems and Homeworlds was soon established. As for the exhumation... Well, people were still, after nearly a thousand revs, thinking with their stomachs more than their heads." With that, he forked the last bit of his pono into his mouth and groaned in satisfaction. "And thank Christ, because they are my absolute favorite food."

Chapter Twelve

The ponos lightened everybody's mood, and for the next few rotations, spirits seemed high. I spent time with Leilani in engineering, despite the fact that she seemed less than thrilled to have me hanging about. Yet, as soon as she learned I had more than a little mechanical aptitude, she became less reluctant to be around me, began to talk a bit more, and introduced me to the ins and outs of her ship. And all it took was assuring her that some of the tools she used were like some of the tools I used as a space broom. I learned a few of the easier preventative maintenance routines – ones she was more than glad to have taken off her hands. It turned out she was a good teacher, if a hair taciturn. All in all, the more time we spent together, the more she softened toward me. The perpetual scowl turned into a flat affect, which honestly I was OK with, since I had to read Rygar's emotions through his eyes.

Hooper and Lisette renewed their spirited debates on every topic from the *Mentirosa*'s speed and trajectory to Hooper paying for the damage done to her shop out of his soon to arrive riches. Part of me felt jealous of him. I didn't want to argue with Lisette, but seeing her argue with Hooper made me feel as if they had a rapport with each other that was more than just friendly. I spent some time on the bridge, having missed our pass of Uranus. I told myself I wouldn't miss seeing Saturn come into view. When he wasn't arguing with Lisette, Hooper and I spent time in the galley, playing Orbit. He boasted about his skill, which Leilani confirmed, and after begging him to teach me, decided it was worth his while to apprentice me. "Who knows? If we ever happen upon a card house, we could team up and clean out the place." We played round after round, Hooper defeating me soundly each time but assuring me I was improving. I tried to keep what Lisette told me upon leaving Kilgore in mind. When I finally beat him, he claimed his work done and that the apprentice – me – had now become the master.

Lisette happened to be the hardest of the three with whom to connect. It wasn't anything she did. No, she was friendly and engaging. It was all my stupid brain and fumbling tongue. Every opportunity for conversation saw either fruitless small talk, because my mind would go blank as I looked at her gorgeous face, or me saying something stupid and awkward that made her laugh uncomfortably. After a few failed attempts at striking up a conversation, she became more interested in what she looked at on her glass-comm than anything I had to say. That was until we both heard Leilani's music blasting from the engine bays.

"I didn't figure Leilani a fan of Terran classical music," I said as the lyrics echoed through the ship.

"Hop music?" Lisette looked at me, obviously concerned by what she considered my questionable taste.

"Hip-hop," I softly corrected. "And yes, it is Terran classical music. It fits all the criteria. One, it's centuries old.

Two, it is culturally significant. Three, it has a lasting impact on society. Plus, it's just great music."

"It's just not for me," Lisette stated.

"And what's more your speed?" I asked, genuinely interested. "Don't tell me it was that dirge that was playing when we first boarded?"

"I'll have you know, it was Iddo Pro-Ido's *Nocturne B* performed by Ico Parielle," Lisette said defensively. "Pro-Ido is the very definition of classical music."

"Hepari classical music," I suggested.

"Classical music in general. And Ico is a virtuoso." The way she pronounced and used the performer's first name sounded familiar, as one does when you are close to the person.

"Don't get me wrong, Hepari stkadiano music is transcendent." I paused when her face shifted from defensive to surprised. "What? Impressed that I know what stkadiano is?"

"If I'm honest, very surprised," she admitted. "But only because most people don't typically know the genre. It's usually only enjoyed by those who enjoy the music of hammered strings, like Terra's piano."

"That's fair," I replied. "The only reason I know it is because a famous holofilm director from Hepari uses stkadiano in most of his holos. Regardless, hip-hop is just as important to the history of music in the galaxy. I'll stand by that opinion."

Lisette appeared amused, but acquiescent. "That's also fair," she said.

We exchanged smiles. Unfortunately, that did not prevent the situation from turning awkward thanks to a prolonged silence between the two of us. *Come on, Gomez!*

I scolded myself. *Get your shit together! You're here alone with the woman of your dreams! Sack up, dude! Say something! Anything!* The only noise heard on the ship aside from the gentle hum of electronics was Leilani incoherently mumbling along to her music echoing throughout the lower deck.

"So, you like holofilms?" Lisette asked after mindlessly swiping at her glass-comm.

I inhaled to answer, to spew forth my love of the art, to drown the unwitting Lisette in useless knowledge of one of my passions. The only person who ever entertained my absolute insatiable lust for holographic cinematography – or holocine for short – was Rygar. Even though he did it to be polite, I appreciated it more than he ever knew. Only the words never came out. Hooper's voice over the ship's systems interrupted my speech.

"Johnny, get your ass to the bridge," he ordered. "We're coming up on Saturn."

I looked at Lisette and mouthed, *Saturn*. My face hopefully conveyed my excitement. "Go on," she said. "Tell Hooper Lei and I will be there shortly."

Nothing could have prepared me for the view. Clouds of pale yellows and golds with the slightest whisper of muted green and turquoise swirled like rivers around the planet. The rings looked like fields of crushed opal or glowing grains of sand, each one orbiting the planet at miraculously different speeds. From our distance, I could only barely make out Saturn's moons as unremarkable specks.

"Some people say you get used to seeing it," Hooper said, "but I think those people are morons. How can you get used to that?"

I shook my head, then nodded, then shook my head again, unable to decide whether to be rapt in disbelief or stunned with awe. Either way, I was speechless.

"Lisette and Lei coming?" Hooper asked.

"Uh, yeah," I answered absentmindedly, eyes, mind, and soul still transfixed on Saturn.

Hooper piloted the *Mentirosa* around the planet, giving me the visual tour of its beauty, including the shadowy disappearance of the rings from the dark side of Saturn. Lisette and Leilani returned to the bridge by the time he pointed the ship at Titan. Both looked more entertained by my completely stupefied wonder than the natural wonder just beyond the safety of the ship.

Compared to Saturn, the moon Titan looked dreary and uninspiring. The dull orange hue of the clouds that encased the planet gave the impression of sun-bleached leather. Hundreds of starcraft in a variety of shapes and sizes sat in high orbit above the moon, each one awaiting clearance to enter its atmosphere. It was this fact that made me believe the hazy orange cloud cover veiled a particularly intriguing compound on the moon's surface.

The queue moved quickly as handfuls of ships left orbit with a wispy release from the moon, thereby allowing another handful to land. Hooper entered the moon's atmosphere and took his hands off the helm, letting the *Rosa*'s autopilot maneuver this ship via communication from the moon's surface. I felt like we descended for a while, the clouds steadily growing darker and more foreboding. Then, without warning or pomp, the clouds disappeared, revealing the gloomy, nearly lightless and shadowy surface of the moon. The only light for miles shone from a compound on the horizon and the uncountable multitudes of spotlights and landing signals directing starships in and out. Yet the brilliance was enough to reveal a small peek at Titan's shimmering surface of icy dunes, frozen mountains, and crystal seas of liquefied methane.

"There it is!" Hooper announced. "Lotus Pleasure House. The most enjoyable, most erotic, most hedonistic place in this entire system!"

The Lotus Pleasure House wasn't an actual building. It was a series of interconnected domes, or pleasure palaces, that stretched for many miles in every direction. Seeing it from the bridge of the *Mentirosa* made it look like an entire compound taking up half of the moon's surface. Bright lights flashed and twinkled in a rainbow of different colors. Spotlights waved back and forth, guiding revelers to specific places of interest. A high-speed tram zoomed from stop to stop, dropping off countless numbers of species to their respective pleasure palaces. The entire place resembled the entertainment deck on Kilgore, but on a much grander scale. The *Rosa* piloted itself toward the docking station. The closer we got to the dome, the more I could see. Each area of Lotus looked like a mini city. Multi-tiered signs advertised casinos and sex dungeons. My glass-comm immediately began to vibrate with messages from various sites, including one named the Drug Carousel and another the Last Pool Party.

The docking station operation ran smoothly, seamlessly directing traffic to and from their respective berths. I saw several other Junpoor model vessels like the *Rosa* – none that were the sloop class, but each a stereotypically handsome and elegant craft that put the others in the dock to shame.

"The ships here…" Hooper said with a chef's kiss. "Johnny, look at that one." He pointed to an entirely chrome twin-fuselage ship that shone in the light of the dock. "It's a Heparian catamaran. Nice. And check out those two – Arrowstar Octos. They make those at the Ibin Driveyards in orbit over Hogan V."

I pointed to one I recognized. "Al'Laylato Super Fox. Did you know they still hand-make those?"

"Hell yeah, I do!" Hooper said, slapping me on the shoulder. "Fifteen a rev. They go for a hundred and forty million credits."

"One hundred forty-three," Leilani corrected.

"Fuck me, I'm surrounded by ship-heads," Lisette said with an eye-roll.

"Finally, *you* are the outnumbered one," Hooper said, pointing at Lisette.

"Yeah, yeah, just make sure you have the *Rosa* cycle her registration serials and ID signatures before we head out," she said.

Hooper responded, "That's standard procedure every time we dock. But thanks for the reminder." He clicked his tongue at her and shot her the finger guns. Lisette scowled and looked away.

We disembarked, but not before Hooper called me into the captain's quarters.

"What's up?" I asked.

"We should probably see about getting you a change of clothes, but I doubt anything I have will fit you, no offense," Hooper said with his head buried in an enormous alloy chest. The hinges and locks on the thing made me think it could have housed priceless artefacts. "People might recognize you in those coveralls. For now, maybe tie them down so nobody can see your name and the Astro-Suds Services logo? Also, wear this." He stood up and tossed me a well-loved cap. It was old Terran style, blue bill and front panel, with white mesh side and back panels, held together with snaps on the back. The logo stitched on front looked like the Heparan word for "hat."

"Thanks, Hooper," I said, giving it a once-over.

"Don't mention it," he responded. "Wear it down low, to cover your eyes. That and the fact that half of these aliens think all humans look alike anyway will help!"

We hurried off and caught up to Lisette and Leilani. The four of us ran to board the first tram toward the gate. A group of Terran earthbounders argued with a dock attendant over the cost of docking as we set foot on the conveyor. The excitement in the air affected everyone around me. Hooper wore an enormous, million-watt smile and tipped his hat at everyone he saw. Leilani's trademark neutral expression appeared more relaxed. Lisette scrolled on her glass-comm, trying to decide which pleasure houses she planned on attending. The Serovians in front of us danced to the music that played over the PA system. A crowd of starbounds passed us going the opposite direction. They were all topless, with pink and purple leis and feather boas hanging from their necks, singing in unison while holding hands. In fact, the only person not immediately enjoying themselves was me.

"Is this a good idea?" I asked Lisette. "I mean, stopping while we have a number of nefarious elements on our tail?"

Lisette put her hand on my shoulder. "Relax, Johnny,"

she said. "Even Rygar agreed that an unscheduled stop will throw them off our trail. Plus..." She paused and looked around. The clear dome surrounding the conveyor showed we were underneath a man-made ocean. Hundreds of strange sea creatures not of this system swam circles around us, leaving colorful trails in their wake. "This place is amazing. Just look around."

"OK," I replied.

"Try to have fun, OK?"

"OK," I repeated.

Most everybody who disembarked from the conveyor at the entryway to Lotus already knew where they were going. Humans and aliens alike moved with decisive speed, as if they had been to Lotus many, many times. Hooper, Leilani, and Lisette all chose their destinations via their glass-comms, leaving me to decide which pleasure I wanted to pursue.

"I mean, I have no idea. Where do I even start?" I asked.

"What do you like to do?" Lisette asked. "What brings you pleasure? Just search for that thing and it will bring up options, then just buy a ticket and follow the directions on how to get there."

"You can do whatever tickles your fancy here, Johnny," Hooper said, putting his arm around my shoulder and walking me closer to the scenic overlook. "Want to have a threesome with two Tyreks? There's a place for that. Ever wonder what it's like to inhale an actual Chrysostom? There's a house for that, too!" He leaned in close and said, "Dream of murdering someone? You can do it here."

I sighed. "None of that sounds appealing. I think maybe I'll just... find a place that serves good drinks and has good live music."

Hooper lit up. "Ooo, there's a great bar called X7 where they filter the alcohol outside, like out of the dome, in the icy wastes of Titan. It freezes almost instantaneously. They then place the ice in a tumbler, and you drink it as it melts."

"Well, where are you two going?" I asked.

"The Last Pool Party," Leilani said quickly.

Hooper shrugged nonchalantly and said, "I have my usual circuit."

"OK, be mysterious, then." I swiped through my options and swallowed at the prices. I couldn't afford most of the places at Lotus. Apparently, unbridled pleasure was something only the wildly rich could. I almost gave up, deciding to spend the time aboard the *Rosa* reading, until I came across music venues. They cost only one of my paychecks. I looked at my glass-comm, then tapped. "I chose..." I said. "Steinway's. Says it's a piano bar."

"Get out of here, that's where I'm going!" Lisette said.

"Oh, cool, so I guess I'll just follow you, then?" I asked.

"Sure," she said, then waved goodbye to Hooper and Leilani. "Have fun at the Last Pool Party, Lei! And enjoy the Castle, Hooper!"

"Who said anything about the Castle?" he yelled back, before jogging off to his platform.

I noticed Leilani hadn't moved to her tram. She instead ducked behind a column and, from a modicum of cover, seemed transfixed on a line of Lotus-goers boarding our same tram. She tapped and tapped on her glass-comm, and remained there until our tram zoomed away from the station.

"Different strokes, right?" I asked Lisette as we boarded our tram.

"Huh?" she asked.

"Different strokes for different folks. I didn't know Lei enjoyed swimming."

Lisette could hardly hide her amusement. She said, "I'm almost positive Lei is going to the Last Pool Party because of the skinny-dipping. She's a sucker for getting fucked in low gravity situations, like water... or, you know, in space. Like she's used to."

"Oh, it looked like she might have had a change of heart," I said. "I didn't see her board a tram."

"Then who knows? The more I get to know Leilani, the less I feel I know about her."

"And Hooper?" I asked. "What's his pleasure of choice?"

"He literally does have a circuit," Lisette said, with a shake of her head. "There are four places he absolutely must see while we're on Lotus. The order varies, but it's almost always the same four. Some sort of rave slash orgy, a card den called Miss Deal's, a humidor to stock up on primo oil for his pen, and a fourth place he keeps mysteriously close to his chest. Almost as if he's embarrassed by it – the Castle."

"But this is an entire moon dedicated to celebrating your pleasures. Why would he hide it? I mean, look," I said, pulling up my glass-comm. "There's literally a cuddle room. From the pictures, it looks like you put on fluffy, cozy pajamas and just lay on the floor and cuddle strangers."

Lisette shrugged. "I guess there are some things Hooper likes to keep quiet."

"He definitely has not struck me as the private type," I said.

"What about you?" Lisette asked me. "Why'd you choose Steinway's?"

"I liked the pics. It looked like a fancy old-timey Terran lounge. Black, red, and silver furniture and décor. Purple plush carpets. Leather. Two grand pianos. Even the pictures of the wait staff look straight out of one of the history lessons I had as a kid. And it's been a while since I've heard actual piano music. You?"

Lisette smiled. "Same. Piano music. You sure you wouldn't rather find a club that played your classical hip-hop?"

I let out a short laugh and said, "I'm sure."

The tram traveled alongside others on a system of parallel tracks, passing spectacularly decorated domes. I witnessed another tram break off from the pack and speed toward its designated pleasure house. It took until the third dome to realize that each tram looked just as wonderful as the domes to which they belonged. The fourth tram darted away, appearing as an emerald and gold snake, slithering toward a forested dome bearing similar colors that sketched the outside like a long extinct Amazonian rain forest. I raised my glass-comm to scan that house for information. It was full of nature walks, hunting expeditions, cliff-diving... all manner of outdoorsy adventure.

"That might have been fun," I said, showing Lisette my glass-comm for one of the forest dome's attractions. "A lazy river where you float on turtles. Real turtles."

"It is *so* relaxing," Lisette said excitedly. "If you get too hot, you can just direct your turtle to dive a little deeper to cool you off."

"Sounds amazing," I replied. My mind had no problem painting a lucid portrait. I rode on the back of an enormous turquoise and gold sea turtle, one hand gripping the reins, the other raised in the air. The turtle and I enjoyed our collective merriment together as we repeatedly dove and surfaced, only to dive and surface once more, the cool, shimmering water refreshing our toasty skin. We met a pod of dolphins who proceeded to somersault over us, spraying us with water as they flipped and danced and sang delightful old shanties to us as we floated along. A random manatee serving drinks swam lazily up to the turtle's shell, delivering a fresh Mai Tai and a high-five.

"Ours is the next stop," Lisette said, pointing out the window to the dome growing steadily larger on the horizon.

I said, "Oh, OK," as the daydream disappeared.

Chapter Thirteen

Music City Dome was a feast for the eyes as well as the ears. Thousands of colored neon lights flashed, waved, and pulsed along to an unheard beat, creating an aura that surrounded the dome. A gigantic screen displayed a live performance of Tusstos, a touring band composed of adolescent heartthrobs from the planet Karkane. I could almost hear the cry of thousands of young fans swooning to their lyrics. A multitude of venues with enormous marquees announcing their daily lineups lit up the sky.

The chatter of nightlife harmonizing with floating melodies from the nearest clubs crashed over us the minute the tram stopped, and its door slid open. Human and interstellar life dressed in strikingly posh outfits mingled in unison, snapping pictures on their glass-comms or ocular implants and hurrying about to their venue of choice. Barkers stood on every corner, shouting their respective club's guests to anyone who would listen. They pushed messages to the glass-comms of those who ignored them. The air in the dome smelled bold and sweet, like perfume dancing on the rim of a cocktail. It was incredible and stupefying and took my breath away.

"The smell of this place… reminds me of the entertainment deck on Kilgore," I said to Lisette. She ignored my comment.

"Steinway's is this way," she responded.

The exterior of the building took my breath away. Gold lights illuminated magnificent columns rising nearly three stories. The plush violet carpet extended out of the entrance and down the stairs to the security check, where a queue formed. Instead of filing in line, Lisette beckoned me to the front.

"I think the line starts back there," I said as we stopped in front of two burly starbounds.

"It's OK," Lisette said to me. "I have friends here." Without missing a beat, she turned to the guard and said, "Lisette Molyneaux and guest. I should have a standing booth courtesy of Ico Parielle."

The guard tapped his glass-comm, then motioned for our tickets. After a quick redemption, we had officially skipped the line and were making our way up the steps, past opulently dressed patrons who eyed us with a combination of amazement and contempt. At first, I assumed it was due to the speed at which we were admitted. But then I realized that Lisette and I did not at all fit the description of the usual clientele. I looked down at my coveralls, top half tied around my waist, sweat and blood-stained T-shirt displaying a jumping man with a ball, the symbol popularized by an interstellar athletic wear company, and cringed. I instinctively pulled Hooper's cap lower on my head. Lisette did not look as out of place as I did. At least she wore black.

We entered Steinway's and were immediately ushered to a private booth. I gawked at everything as we followed our host. The floors and crystal partitions were immaculate. Not a spot or piece of debris could be found on the carpet. Crystal chandeliers lit the lobby while more delicate, reserved light orbs floated above every table on the floor, leaving the recital hall in a dark, smoky fog of luxury and intrigue. Two gorgeously dressed Xin women sat on stage at two pianos and competed, taking turns playing the same raucous melody, with their own variation and flair. The crowd whooped and hollered each time one of the pair gave way to the other. An ensemble sat on the stage behind them – horns, a pair of saxophones, a guitar, and a drum set – keeping time and providing cues for the Xin. Lisette smiled as she sat down, stage left, only a rose's throw from the stage. I barely made myself comfortable in the booth when a waiter appeared, delivering a chilled bottle of champagne.

"So, you're a regular here," I said to Lisette over the music.

"Yes, it's my favorite spot at Lotus," she yelled back. "You want some champagne?"

"Why not?" I replied.

We drank and grooved to the rambling tune. When the pair of Xin finished playing, the entire hall rose to their feet in applause. After a few minutes of standing ovation, the MC announced a brief intermission before the next act – one Ico Parielle. Lisette and I spent the next few minutes perusing the menu on our glass-comms.

"Why are there no prices?" I asked.

"Most of it is included in the price of admission," she answered. "There are a few items, top shelf rarities, but those will ask for confirmation before your account is charged."

When our waiter returned, Lisette ordered another bottle of the champagne and I settled on a cocktail called the Ode to Adams, marketed as the best drink in the galaxy. The waiter bowed slightly and hurried off, leaving us alone once more.

"So… how do you know this Ico Parielle?" I asked.

Lisette took a sip of the remaining champagne before saying, "Oh, Ico is just an old friend. Tell me about yourself, Johnny. Aside from being a janitor on Kilgore and coming from Luna."

The way she deftly avoided the question about Parielle made my heart sink. I wasn't the best at reading people, but I could tell when someone didn't want to tell me something to spare my feelings. I had been getting that my whole life. I took a breath and tried not to let her notice that I noticed. "There's not much to tell, really. Been on Kilgore for about ten revs – RUSH standard revs, that is. You know, stardate-keeping. But that's not a fun or entertaining story, so I just say a wealthy scoundrel seduced and betrayed me."

"Well, I wasn't really looking for entertainment," Lisette replied. "I'm just curious. You seem like an anomaly. Everybody on Kilgore is going somewhere or coming from someplace else. But you… It just doesn't make sense to me."

I shrugged. "I fell into that category once, coming and going. Just sort of ran out of money and had to put the dream on hold. What about you? I mean, you have a shop on Kilgore. That also says mostly staying instead of coming or going. What's your story?"

She flashed me a playful grin. "A wealthy scoundrel seduced and betrayed me. Now I sell black market wares on the last space station in the system."

I gave her a playful hmph and said, "Fair enough." Conversation lulled until our waiter returned. We toasted our soon to be fortune waiting for us on Luna.

"You seem so different here, so relaxed and comfortable."
She immediately stiffened up.

"What are you trying to say?" Lisette asked defensively.
"Am I some kind of insufferable bitch aboard the *Mentirosa*?"

I held my breath, and my heart skipped a beat. "N–n–no,
that's not at all what I meant, it's just... I mean, you don't
seem to get along with..."

Her stern gaze broke, and she smiled once more. "I'm
only kidding, Johnny. Things are stressful, as you well know.
And Hooper just rubs me the wrong way sometimes. If I'm
honest, being cooped up with him in a ship for a couple of
rotations has not been the highlight of this rev."

"Leilani mentioned that you two used to date," I said as I
took a sip of my Ode to Adams. The sweet, citrusy concoction
hit me like a ton of gold bricks. I exhaled as if my mouth
were about to spit fire. "Damn, that's good," I muttered.

"Much to my shame, yes. We dated. That is, until I found
him in bed with the captain of the casco team from Bollea..."
She paused. "And the aforementioned incident aboard the
Rosa."

"Aren't the Bolleans all... men?"

"They're not gendered like you or me. Many of them are
born male, in our understanding of the word, but can change
to one of their many genders many times throughout their
lives. But that wasn't the problem. He told me I was the only
one. Turns out I was just one of many. I can forgive a lot of
things in relationships, Johnny, lying is not one of them."

"So, disembarking and spending time on Lotus is a
welcome break for you."

Lisette let out a satisfied sigh of relief. "You have no idea.
Enjoying good champagne and good music is just what I
need to help calm my nerves."

Moments later, when Ico Parielle hit the stage, Lisette's entire face lit up. His velvety smooth tenor voice matched his clean-cut appearance and slick, charismatic persona. He addressed the crowd before sitting down at the piano. Before he finished his introduction, he looked directly at our booth, winked and waved slightly. Lisette's blush matched the red leather of the booth. She delicately held her champagne flute between two fingers and stared longingly at Ico. I, on the other hand, slunk down in the booth and held my cocktail close to my chest. It wasn't enough that the unbearably handsome crooner and the woman I sort of had feelings for were an obvious item. Ico was a Xin. How some people forgave his race for nearly exterminating the human race only a century or so ago was beyond me. It didn't matter that the Xin invaded the system a century ago and finished the work humanity started by making Terra completely unlivable. It didn't even matter that because of that, my ancestors lost their home. The Xin weren't the reason Terra's orbit was clogged with satellites, hulking wrecks of the meager Terran navy, and unexploded ordinance. Yet, that's what I was taught. When the waiter came during the first song, Lisette shooed him away. I ordered another. Maybe the alcohol would help soothe the memories.

As much as I hated to admit it, Parielle knew what he was doing on the piano. His classic, jazz-inspired techniques blended perfectly with the newer, dissonant style favored by pianists over the last century. I assumed it was the stkadiano influence. The band accompanied him with precision, never playing over the melody laid out by Parielle, but never simply fading into the background to be forgotten by his talent. They held their own and complemented his unique style.

Parielle truly was a master. He held the entire music hall in a trance, swooning before his ebony and ivory throne. Each person, I included, offered up their musical soul before the altar of his jazz. Song after song brokered louder and louder applause. Hour after hour the entire lot of us sat enthralled, barely able to move, unable to even lift our drinks to our mouths. Even the wait staff ceased to roam the hall, for they knew nobody would dare miss a single note of his playing simply to satisfy their thirst for alcohol.

He played with unceasing vigor and grace. When the band left the stage for a brief respite, Parielle, completely unfazed and with an impressive show of stamina, dazzled the crowd with a heartbreaking interlude nearly ten minutes in length. It left every single patron in tears.

At the end of his set, even after the encore, Parielle bowed graciously to a roaring sea of applause and exited stage left, smiling as he noticed Lisette. I took that moment to down the rest of my fifth Ode to Adams and slink a bit farther into my seat. I couldn't help but picture an entire army of Ico Parielles firing ordnance at Terra. Ultimately, I knew Ico likely had no connection to the assault. He couldn't have been the reason my parents' shuttle collided with a hunk of space debris, lost power, and rapidly descended into Terra's atmosphere. It made my blood boil regardless. My parents' faces flashed before my eyes, or at least the little that I remembered of them. Lisette sighed and poured the last of her champagne.

"He is incredible," she said, voice airy and dreamlike, as if still in the trance of Parielle's music. "Incredible doesn't even begin to describe it. Arguably the greatest to ever play the instrument."

"He was pretty good," I grumbled as I played with my drink glass.

"Pretty good? Johnny, were you even in the same room as me?"

"OK, OK, he was fantastic," I admitted reluctantly.

"It wasn't my best performance, but nevertheless I'm glad you enjoyed it," a voice said from behind me. Lisette blushed. Her eyes nearly bulged out of her sockets. I turned my head to see the slim figure of Ico Parielle leaning roguishly against the high back of the booth.

"Ico, you… It was… I have no words," Lisette breathed. She quickly shimmied out of the seat and threw herself at Ico, embracing him so tightly I could feel the envy of every organic and inorganic life form in the place directed at our booth.

He gently touched her chin with his index finger as they parted. The looks they gave each other made me want to audibly gag. "Thank you, darling." He turned to me, introduced himself, and asked, "Who's your friend?"

Lisette said, "Oh, Johnny and I aren't friends, we're just traveling together. I mean, no, we're friends, just not friends… I'm sorry. Ico, this is Johnny."

I felt my heart leave my body and my stomach churn as she stumbled over her words. I gulped and offered my hand, which Ico received and instead of shaking, brought to his mouth and kissed.

"Truly a pleasure. Any friend or traveling companion of Lisette's has immediately earned my trust and respect," he proclaimed. "I am glad you enjoyed the show, Johnny."

I took a breath and then, to my shock and horror, offered him a seat across from me. He gladly accepted and sat right next to Lisette. She pressed closer to him and the two obviously held hands beneath the table. I felt my ears burn hot with jealousy.

Ico stared into her eyes and said, "So, how have you been since last we saw each other? It must have been on …"

"Pilgrim's Folly, yes." Lisette finished his sentence. "You invited me to that performance at the Obsidian Amphitheater."

"That was one of my better ones," Ico said. There was a roguish, sly twinkle in his eye.

"Yes, it was," Lisette agreed. "But the after party was what I remember the most."

They shared a giggle together.

"Oh, look at me being rude and ignoring your traveling companion," he said. The words grated on me. My jealousy burned even hotter. The alcohol didn't help. "Tell me about yourself, Johnny – I mean, other than your excellent taste in music and drink! That is an Ode to Adams, is it not?"

"Yup, it is," I responded, trying my best to keep my voice level. "And there's not much to tell. Just a traveling companion, is all."

Ico smiled. Lisette did not.

"A man of mystery!" Ico said with a smirk. "Well, I won't press. But perhaps you have a question for me? Ask our dear mutual friend here, Lisette. My conversation is as phenomenal as my playing."

"I'm sure it is," I muttered underneath my breath.

"I beg your pardon?" Ico asked.

I took a deep breath and let my anger and jealousy flow. The alcohol also helped loosen my lips. "So, you look Xin." Lisette eyed me warily.

"Half Xin," Ico replied, "on my father's side. My mother was from Luna. That's actually where I met Lisette."

There was no need to hide my surprise. It was genuine. "Oh, really? I had no idea you two grew up together."

"We did," Ico admitted casually. "Known each other since childhood."

Lisette stiffened up and put her hand on his forearm. "Ico, there's no need to go in to detail."

"Oh, come on, Lisette," I said with an evil grin on my face, "I'd love to hear all the details of your relationship with Ico."

Ico appeared pleased with himself. "I'd better not. I'd rather stay clear of Lizzy's famous temper."

"Oh, *Lizzy* has a temper?" I emphasized her nickname with spiteful glee. "But you're probably right. So, tell me, Ico... Is it OK if I call you Ico?" He nodded. "How did you manage to become such a successful musician after your father's people declared humanity a pox on the galaxy and attempted – and very nearly succeeded – to turn Terra into a nightmarish hellscape?"

Ico's joy soured slightly. Lisette gasped. Her anger, that Ico mentioned, the anger I had seen her use against Hooper, was now directed at me, but before she could speak, I stood up from the booth. "Ico Parielle, it was an honor and a pleasure to meet such an accomplished musician." I bowed sarcastically and, before walking away, noticed that Lisette's anger had faded. She still glared at me, but it wasn't the only emotion I could read; her eyes were more sorrow than rage. I walked away from the booth not in triumph, but in disappointment.

"Nicely done, jackass," I muttered to myself as I made my way to the bar. "A petulant child." I was never an angry drunk, which made me feel even worse. I know I still harbored resentment for the loss of my parents. Regardless, taking that out on Ico – in front of Lisette, no less – was unfair.

I chose a relatively solitary stool and plopped myself down. The attendance of the hall thinned. Ico was obviously the main attraction for the evening. The remaining patrons, mostly drunk, didn't seem to care that a duo of self-playing pianos replaced the prodigy. I ordered a drink, this time choosing a simple lager with marginally less alcohol, and brooded until it arrived. I took a gulp, then looked over my shoulder to Lisette's booth. Both she and Ico were no longer there. My shoulders slumped and I let out a pitiful sigh as I returned to my beer, hardly noticing the person taking the seat right next to me.

"People like us can't compete with someone like Ico Parielle," they said. I hmphed without looking their way. "Women love a musician. At least I do, anyway."

I turned and saw the androgynously beautiful face of a clearly augmented starbound. They preferred not to hide the seams and bulges of underlying hardware as a point of pride. Rygar was the same. "Yeah... I guess you're right."

"Trust me, honey, I am," they said, playfully tapping my forearm. "You can do better than her, anyway. A chubby little earthbounder with roots in Junpoor is below the standards of a handsome man such as yourself."

"Thanks," I muttered, and took another drink.

"Oh, I'm serious," they said. "So, what brings a man of your..." They stopped and looked me up and down. "Station to Steinway's? No offense, but you don't look like you can afford much of anything at Lotus. What is this?" they asked, plucking at my coveralls. "You some kind of laborer?"

I scoffed. "If you're trying to land me as a client, you're going about it the exact wrong way. The girl of my dreams just made it abundantly clear that I'm nothing more than a casual acquaintance. I'm already feeling self-conscious about myself, so judging my appearance won't get you anywhere."

They giggled. "Oh, sweetie, I'm not judging you," they said as they waved to the bartender. "Another rosé, Tycore." The bartender made no indication that he heard their order, but quickly got to work pouring and serving the drink. "If you came to Steinway's as much as I do, you'd know the clientele here are the type to look down on those like you and me."

"Those like us?" I asked, rolling my eyes and shaking my head.

"Yeah, baby doll. The working kind. The type of people who enjoy the simple things."

I took a deep breath and said, "Look, I'm not trying to be mean. I know you're hustling, trying to do your job and make a little money, but I am truly not interested." I huffed, then continued, saying, "You're not my type anyway."

They smiled widely and giggled again. "Sugar, I am everybody's type. I can be whatever you want me to be." I watched as the augments went to work, changing the shape and composition of their face. In a matter of seconds, the androgyny disappeared, replaced by a five o'clock-shadowed, unbelievably handsome man. His dark skin shone. "Is this more to your liking?" he said, voice dropping in register to a rumbling bass as he spoke. "Or maybe something more along these lines." Once again, face and body adjusted minutely, hair lengthened, skin lightened to look more along the lines of a sun-deprived, starbound woman. "And trust me, I can do anything in between."

I was indeed impressed, but tried to hide my amazement. "Did you just do that for the job? I bet it helps you cater to all folks."

They shot me a wide-eyed, pursed-lip glare of disappointment. "Darling, this is me. I didn't make myself this way for nobody but myself. I was born this way. The augments just helped me take who I am on the inside and display it proudly on the outside."

"I didn't mean to offend."

"Oh, I know you didn't. Nobody ever *means* to offend. It's simply outrageous to me to think that regardless of the existence of alien species, the advancement of medical and augment technology, and the liberation of sexual and gender identity... That in spite all of that, some people are still as intolerant as the time before humanity even left the inner four planets."

I felt bad, so I said as compassionately as I could, "Well, that was a pretty impressive transformation. Rygar would be jealous."

"Rygar?" they said. "A friend?"

I nodded again. "One of my only."

"Why don't you let me change that, then?" Their body shifted back to the androgynous, augmented form I first saw them in. They held out their hand and said, "I'm Guillermo, but most everybody calls me Memo."

I hesitated, taking another swig of my beer before shaking their hand. "Johnny. Nice to meet you, Memo."

"The pleasure is all mine," they said, then took a sip of their wine. "So, you still haven't answered my question from earlier. What brings you to Steinway's?"

"Can I be honest?" I asked.

"You can tell me anything, even your darkest secrets. Who would I tell?" Memo asked with a giggle.

"I'm fleeing for my life, trying to get to Luna before I'm caught and killed," I said, then finished off my beer.

"Oh?" Memo responded with piqued interest. "A man of danger and intrigue. I like that. Tell me more."

"There isn't much more to tell, and it honestly isn't a very interesting story."

"All stories are interesting in their own way, Johnny," Memo said. "But if you're in such danger, why stop at Lotus?"

I shrugged. "Trying to throw off our tail, I guess."

"You and your earthbound friend?" Memo asked. "The one swooning over Ico Parielle?"

"She made it abundantly clear that we aren't friends."

"Maybe it was the danger," Memo stated. "It can be too much for some people."

"I doubt it."

Memo leaned in close and whispered in my ear. "I love danger. The more danger, the more… fun I am."

I turned my head and looked at Memo. They looked away and poured the rest of their rosé down their throat. I made a split-second, alcohol-fueled decision that moment. "Fuck it, you want to have some fun, Memo? Then let's have some fun."

Memo raised their eyebrows. "What kind of fun are we talking about? I don't mean to sound insincere or uninterested, I just …" They paused, then tapped their wrist. My glass-comm vibrated. It was a list of services offered and their prices. I took a moment to look it over, then checked my account. I could swing it. Who knew if I would even return to Kilgore after this anyway? And if this chit exchange panned out, I would be filthy rich, with more credits than I knew what to do with. I selected the amount for "the complete experience." It was an entire month's pay and the rest of the money in my account.

Memo smiled. "My place is actually right down the block."

"Lead the way."

Chapter Fourteen

Memo and I exited Steinway's, arm in arm. I thought for one brief moment I saw Leilani's yellow leather bomber jacket floating through the crowd. My heart skipped and I felt strangely self-conscious. It had nothing to do with her seeing me with Memo, or the perceived abandonment of Lisette, but a general anxiety of how she would react. I quickly wiped it from my mind. Lisette obviously wasn't interested in me. She could take care of herself, like she so often claimed. It wasn't my place to watch her or protect her. Anyway, if I had no chance with her, might as well take what I can get, right? This was Lotus, after all – an entire compound dedicated solely to pleasure, taking up half of Titan. Lisette was doing just that, as were Hooper and Leilani. Sure, I could have pursued psychological pleasure, or even drug-induced pleasure. But my anger and the alcohol convinced me I needed sexual pleasure. Acknowledging that need made me feel prudish.

My nerves were shot, and Memo could tell – whether it was because they were that empathic, or simply using a brain chemistry analysis augmentation, didn't matter to me. After I left Luna and abandoned my last girlfriend, Alana, my sex life became almost non-existent, save for the frequent

virtual visits and the occasional sex android, which only
Rygar knew about and for which I faced constant derision,
regardless of his lack of ill intent. Memo produced from a
hidden compartment in their forearm a small pill meant to
calm my nerves. I accepted it without question and popped
it into my mouth.

Memo's place, only a block away from Steinway's,
resembled all the other buildings in the district: old Terran-
style façades with balconies and lots of neon-like lights. Red
spotlights bathed the entire street level storefront of the
building. Even the window of each floor radiated red. I took a
quick look around before we entered. The building across the
street looked almost identical, with one exception. A flash of
yellow leather bomber jacket appeared, then disappeared just
as suddenly. I frowned. I didn't know what Leilani was up to,
but I wasn't going to let her ruin this for me. Especially since
the euphoric effects of Memo's pill were kicking in.

"I thought each of the houses was specialized?" I asked.

"What do you mean, honey?" Memo asked as they held
open the door to their complex.

"Well, this is Music City Dome, right? I didn't think they'd
have... you know."

"People connect to music on all sorts of different levels –
emotionally, spiritually, and physically. You trying to tell me
you never fucked with music in the background?"

I chortled uncomfortably. Memo slowly licked their
upper lip and beckoned me inside with a wag of their index
finger.

Memo's studio loft was on the sixth floor of the building.
The lift doors opened to a splendidly colored hallway with
elegant wall sconces and the occasional hall table holding
decorative vases or interesting sculptures. Memo's loft itself

looked nothing like the hall. The standard, hotel-like feel so common in the system gave way to a luscious paradise of soft, plush, and fuzzy furnishings. Warm lighting bathed the apartment in delicately romantic hues. Memo tapped their wrist as we entered and a soft, rhythmic, bluesy melody danced to my ears.

Taking me by the hand, they led me to a black suede couch resting on an impossibly soft shag carpet colored violet, crimson, and gold. The swirls of color reminded me of paintings of sunsets that occurred on Terra hundreds of revs before my birth. We stopped and stood at the couch. Memo smiled slyly and leaned in close, kissing me on the lips. A peck. Then a longer kiss. I kissed back. My heart began to pound.

"That tab should be taking hold of you soon," they said.

"It's already started to," I said as my head strangely flopped on its own. *Weird*, I thought. My entire body tingled with warm fuzziness. My thoughts felt satisfyingly sluggish. My mind was dominated by one particular, animalistic instinct. "What…? What was that, by the way, the thing you gave me?"

"Just a little something to loosen you up," Memo replied with a wink and another kiss. "Wine?"

"Sure, I could go for another drink," I said as Memo walked to the kitchen.

"Do you prefer red or white?"

"Dealer's choice," I replied, then took a seat on the couch. It embraced me as I sunk low. I could feel my limbs growing heavy, but not uncomfortably so. I took a deep breath, thankful that my nerves had calmed. A floral and fruity melody suddenly floated on the air. It reminded me of Alana. I shook her memory from my head.

When Memo returned, they were naked, holding two wide-mouthed, stemless chalices and a bottle of chilled white wine. "How would you like me?"

"I... I'm sorry?"

Memo answered, "Do you prefer a specific gender? Or do you like multiple?" They paused, letting a carnal, animalistic grin grow on their face. "I know what you like." In an instant, Memo's augs transformed them into a strangely erotic combination of Lisette and Hooper. They were female now, with dark skin that shone in the low light of the loft. Their female features were soft, just like Lisette's, with long black hair. They poured the wine, handed one to me, then climbed in my lap, straddling me. They clinked our wineglasses together, then we both drank.

"You can touch me," Memo said.

"Oh, OK," I stuttered. "It's just... I mean I've never... This is—"

"It's OK. Think of me as your lover. I'll tell you if something is off limits."

"I'll... uh, do just that," I said, and placed my glass-comm on the end table just within my reach. Then I cupped Memo's newly formed breasts. "Can you... make them a little smaller?" Memo adjusted. I knew I was turned on. I could feel my heart pounding. But nothing was happening below the belt. I couldn't feel if I was hard or not. "I... think something's the matter."

Memo leaned closer to me and began to kiss my neck and behind my ears. My arms began to tingle. I couldn't feel my fingers. "Shhh," they said. "Just enjoy the moment." They brought their face to mine and kissed me. Our lips pressed together. Our tongues in each other's mouths. I wanted this.

I needed it. I desperately needed the release. Yet my body no longer cooperated. My mouth went dry. I could no longer feel the weight of Memo in my lap.

"I... I think there's something wrong..." I uttered. "Was... theresumthinindawine...?" My words slurred together. "Dattabyougabeme..."

Memo sat up straight on my lap. Their appearance didn't change, but their demeanor soured. "Oh, sweetheart. Don't you know never to accept drugs from strangers?" They tsked. "That's like clubbing 101."

"Whaaa...?" I slurred and slobbered, sending saliva down my chin. "Whooooo?" My mind began to race. It had yet to realize the severity of the situation, and instead chose self-deprecation. *What a rookie mistake, Gomez! Taking strange pills from some rando at a bar? Who does that?*

Memo placed a finger on my lips. "Quiet now. The paralysis is only temporary, so don't you worry. You'll be able to walk out of here in fifteen minutes or less. I'm not looking to leave a body count in my wake. Just empty pockets. Now, tell me where you're hiding the slide?"

You have got to be kidding me! I screamed in my head. *How do I keep running into all these psychos? Janky. The Hongxongdi. The Chorzi. Now this... this... augmented assassin? That's OK. I'll just do like I've done with other three.* I swallowed. Thankfully my mouth and throat still had some function. "Iiiiooonoooo," I managed, hoping Memo understood it as "I don't know."

Memo smiled at me like one does in condescension when a coworker says something particularly stupid. "Are you going to make this hard on yourself?"

All of the worst-case scenarios began to play out in my head. And since my imagination happened to be so very vivid, I easily scared the shit out of myself. Every blood-soaked mutilation from every horror holofilm I had ever seen flashed before my eyes. The only difference: it was me getting hacked to bits, and not some absentminded starlet. When I didn't respond, Memo reminded me of their presence with a hard slap to the face. They climbed off me and kicked the coffee table off the rug, sending their chalice and wine bottle crashing to the floor. They reached down, grabbed my legs, and angrily pulled me from the couch. My head slammed against the floor, only I didn't feel it. Memo spent a few minutes rifling through my pockets, checking my socks and shoes, and even groping between my legs and my ass cheeks. They then huffed, rolled me on my back, and took a seat on my chest. The augmentations gave them extra weight I did not expect from their small frame.

"Come now. I don't want to hurt you, but I need you to know that if I must, I will." Memo leaned in close. "And I am spectacularly good at doling out pain. I only want the chit. You can leave here unscathed and continue to unsuccessfully pursue that chubby Junpoor Mandarin girl. Just tell me where the chit is." I kept quiet. Memo nodded. Their finger opened and revealed a tiny syringe. After the injection, feeling slowly returned to my body; only the paralysis remained.

As it turned out, Memo was indeed spectacularly good at doling out pain. Each tip of their fingers flipped open to reveal inch-long, wickedly thin blades meant for slicing skin from the most delicate of areas. With psychotic glee, they slowly began filleting my flesh, explaining the absurdly horrific reason for each incision. They sliced the tops of my gums, telling me how mouth and tooth pain can be the worst a human can experience. They were right. Each laceration sent violent bolts of pain through my entire mouth. I screamed, but nearly choked on the blood that began to pool in my mouth. Memo kindly tilted my head to spit it out. I guess they never meant for me to die before I gave up the secret.

They slashed the webbing between my fingers and traced circles around the bottom of each one, saying how they planned on peeling the skin from every digit. I screamed even louder this time. Each slice burned and made my fingers feel like they were swelling fit to burst. After they finished the last finger, I begged them to stop. Memo only raised their bladed fingers in front of my face, so I could witness small rivulets of my blood dripping off of each digit. The tears began to flow.

Memo worked their way down my body, cutting and puncturing my most delicate areas. I shouted. I screamed at the top of my lungs. I tried my damnedest to writhe or struggle, but the paralysis remained. My screams turned to sobs, which only made Memo tsk and gently caress my cheek.

"I can end this right now, darling. Just tell me where the chit is?" they asked.

I'd be lying if I said I didn't strongly consider telling them. In fact, my brain, the pain in my mouth, the burning in my fingers, and every other pain my body was feeling, demanded I give in. Instead, I slowly closed my eyes, gritted my teeth, and let the tears flow.

They pulled my pants off and giggled at the revelation between my legs, saying it would make a pretty addition to their collection. This was followed by surgically precise cuts on my balls, which, honestly, I hadn't used much in the past decade and couldn't admit I would use in the future. Regardless, the cuts sent what I can only describe as electrified explosions of pain straight to my gut. It was like being kicked in the balls, only worse. Way worse. I began to feel the blood trickle down from every carved surface on my body, soaking my clothes. Each nick, pierce, and puncture burned and ached with an increasing intensity. My mouth tasted of blood. I now screamed in pain even when Memo paused their surgery. The way they refused to silence me made me think, it didn't matter how loud I was, nobody would hear me in the confines of their apartment.

The thought finally crossed my mind: I was going to die here. The chit would be my doom, brought to the gates of hell by an augmented provocatrix who filleted me until I bled out. What a way to go. At least it was exciting. At least it wasn't dying by slipping on Postos shit in a zero-g restroom aboard Kilgore Station. That would have been an embarrassing death.

After slicing my balls, Memo rose to their feet and stood over me, naked, glistening with sweat, hands stained with my blood. I looked on in complete terror, pretty sure I had pissed myself in fear. They gave me the same look as before – pitying, with slightly pursed lips. "Well, if you won't tell me, I guess my only option is to repeat this whole process with that pretty chunk of a girl from Steinway's. Maybe she'll be keen to tell me what I want to know."

I wanted to yell out in defiance, but the only noise I could gather the strength to make sounded more like a disappointing, grumbling whine than anything. But whatever it was, it seemed to be enough, because no sooner had it left my throat than a sharp pounding came from the door. Memo turned their face to the entrance, appearing delightfully confused by the pounding, until the pounding turned into a sickening metallic screech that only a forced door could make. I saw Memo's face twist in psychotic glee a moment before they leapt at whoever interrupted their interrogation.

I heard shouts and crashing. Thuds from bodies hitting walls or the floor. Memo grunted. So did the other person. I took a deep breath and then, with a mighty groan, rolled myself on to my stomach. I could see two pairs of feet from my spot beside the couch. They quickly shuffled my way, then careened over the edge of the couch in a thumping crashing of naked augmented flesh and yellow bomber jacket. With another groan, I rolled to my side.

"Leilani!" I shouted, only it came out more like, "Laaaaylaaaannneeee."

Both Leilani and Memo rose to their feet. Leilani brandished her wicked black stilettos. Memo's fingers combined to form a pair of strange, augmented cinquedeas. They danced as they exchanged swings. Arms blocked strikes. Legs swept. Grunts echoed in my ears. Leilani parried a strike, then countered and slashed at Memo's face. Her blade scratched through the synthetic skin all the way to the metal plating underneath, screeching as it went. Memo staggered backwards.

"You have me at a disadvantage," they said. "So, I think I'll put a pin in this duel until I can tilt it in my favor." In a flash, Memo bolted at the only window in the apartment and leapt through it with a loud smash of shattering glass.

Leilani pursued the aug only as far as the window, then immediately turned back and knelt by my side. "Fuck me, Johnny, that Obinna really did a number on you," she said as she helped me to a seated position. "Are you OK? Anything broken?"

"I...ddddoooon'thiiinkkksooooo...buuuuhhhh....
Paaababbbleeeee," I groaned.

"The cuts are shallow, so that's good. They probably just
burn and ache like a bitch. Nothing the auto-doc can't fix,
right?" Leilani said as she scoured the apartment for rags,
towels – anything to help soak up the blood.

I sighed and spat a mouthful of blood to the rug. I took a
few deep breaths before attempting to speak again. Leilani
helped me wrap my hands in a kitchen towel. She handed
me another one for my family jewels. I wrapped them
carefully and pulled my pants up.

"That aug must've had some medical training," Leilani
said. "They perfectly sliced and diced you to avoid letting
too much blood."

I cleared my throat and again tried to speak. The words
came slowly, but clearer than before. "True, but God damn,
do they burn and ache. Do I just look like a punching bag?
You don't have to answer that."

"Then let's get you up. We need to find Hooper and tell
him we have Obinnas after us now." Leilani placed my arm
over her shoulder and helped me to my feet. My entire body
screamed as my muscles stretched and flexed.

"How...? How did you find me?"

"I saw that augmented fuck board the same tram as you
and Lisette. This situation is too volatile to believe it was
coincidence, so I refunded my ticket – which, by the way,
you owe me for. The Last Pool Party?" She rolled her eyes.
"Took the next tram and began to look around. Hard to find
an aug when they can change their appearance."

"Lei, what...? What's an Obinna?" I asked as Leilani
carried me from the room. "I've never heard of that
species."

"Not a species, but regardless, I'm surprised you've never heard of them. They used to basically own this system from Terra to Kilgore. I think they're based on Luna now."

I nearly choked. "Those Obinnas?"

"So, you do know them," Leilani said flatly.

"Fuck me, if they're involved then we can't go to Luna. They'll be waiting for us."

"Let's not worry about that now," she reassured me. "Let's find Hooper and get to the *Mentirosa*."

I spat a mouthful of blood again. "What about Lisette?"

"I'll ping her glass. She won't hesitate."

"And Hooper? Where do you suppose he'll be?"

"Hooper bounces around a lot when we come to Lotus, but there is only one pleasure house he would call his favorite – the Castle."

"I heard Lisette mention that place. What is it? I mean, do I want to know?"

"Whether you want to or not, you're about to find out."

Chapter Fifteen

It didn't take long for Leilani to find us a ride. A droid-powered rickshaw selling everything from candy sticks to hallucinogenic taffy agreed to take us to the Castle, but not before looking us over and announcing, "You two don't look like the Castle type. I mean, this one looks like he would trip over his own two feet. If you get blood in my cab, you will be charged a cleaning fee."

"Yeah, yeah, just get a move on," Leilani said.

"I was assaulted," I mumbled as we boarded.

Before moving, the driver's torso rotated around to face us and handed me a hypodermic needle. "This will help stop the bleeding."

I grabbed the needle and gave it a bloody smile. "Thanks."

"There will be an additional charge for the first aid."

"Yeah, that figures," I sighed.

Part of me was surprised to find an actual castle at our destination in the neighboring dome, reminiscent of those in all the Terran histories I learned in school: stone masonry, parapets, flying buttresses, a drawbridge, and even towers bearing a strange pink and teal standard of a naked man falling through what appeared to be a cloud. The same design also graced enormous banners that fell from the tops of the walls, decorating every side of the edifice.

"So, an actual castle? Is Hooper into dungeon play?" I asked. Leilani gave me a weird look, then marched up to the door. I limped after her.

If the exterior of the building was as to be expected, the interior completely blew my mind. Except for designated walkways, the castle was nothing more than an elaborate bouncy house, but in low gravity. Hundreds of people jumped and hopped and leapt from and against and into the air-filled floors and walls and ceilings, flying with shouts of glee. Each surface radiated a shifting iridescent hue. Bubbles choked the air. An electronic version of a popular melodic tune blasted from precisely placed speakers.

"What the actual fuck?" I gasped.

Leilani approached a podium and tapped the reception tablet. Soon, a cheery starbound woman, wearing nothing but carnation-colored lace panties and holding a half-eaten cone of cotton candy, left the bounciness and ran down the walkway toward us.

"Welcome to the Castle, will you be joining our pleasure today?"

"No," Leilani said, then raised her glass-comm to the woman. "We're looking for this person. Starbound. Goes by the name of Hooper – Alice Hooper."

The receptionist smiled. "Oh yes, Mister Hooper. Shall I buzz him for you?"

Leilani gave a thumbs up and turned away from the podium.

"Who should I say is calling?" the receptionist asked in sheer, overwhelming delight. Leilani looked about ready to gag.

"His cousin."

The receptionist raised her left arm and tapped on a glowing band strapped to her wrist. I imagined it was some sort of in-house communicator. "He'll be here shortly!" she said. "Now if you'll excuse me, I must ensure each of our guests is engaged in the utmost pleasure. Ta-ta!"

"Did she just say 'ta-ta'?" I asked once we were alone.

Leilani rolled her eyes. "I don't know why he loves this place. It gives me the creeps. Nobody is this happy all the time."

I shrugged. "Maybe Hooper never got to experience a sugary, iridescent dreamscape as a child."

Leilani snorted. "Don't tell him that. He'll think you're insulting his mom. Like saying Alice Hooper Senior raised him wrong. And no, they're just all tripping on various quantities of hallucinogens."

I shrugged. "Makes sense. Look, I'm going to take a seat. I'm starting to get a little dizzy from the loss of blood."

"OK," Leilani said, and remained near the podium until, after a short wait, Hooper bounced up, giggling with joy. He wore only his boxers, decorated with a weird half-pizza, half-cat creation. His skin glistened from a layer of sweat and glitter. He sucked on a lollipop. He wore glowing bands around his left wrist and neck.

"Why, hello, my illustrious cousin!" he said as he landed on the solid floor surrounding the podium. "Jumping, am I right? When do we ever get to jump? Zero g has spoiled us, cousin." He looked at Leilani and noticed her lack of amusement. "Are you not enjoying your visit to Lotus?"

"Get your shit, we got to go," Leilani stated.

Hooper whooped. "Leilani Hooper, what has gotten into you? We are at Lotus! Normally, it is I that must pull you away from all the fun."

Leilani stood for a moment, then stepped out of his way. Hooper's eyes met mine the precise moment I wiped the blood from my mouth and cheek. I gave him a blood-soaked, toothy grin and his face dropped.

"You're like a punching bag," Hooper said.

"He met an Obinna," Leilani stated.

"Oh fuck, really? The Obinnas?" Hooper cried loud enough to turn a few heads closer to us. He quickly drew Leilani and himself closer to me. "Is there any criminal organization not after this chit?"

"So... you're not high?" I asked.

Hooper frowned. "No," he said in exasperation. "This is an actual lollipop."

Leilani and I exchanged glances. We simultaneously began to laugh. I winced through each chuckle. There was definitely something bruised or broken in my chest, probably from when Memo sat their entire weight on me.

"What?" Hooper said, removing the lollipop from his mouth. "It's mango flavored. Do you have any idea how hard it is to find mango flavored anything any more?"

Leilani shook her head. "Go get your clothes. We don't know if there's any other Obinnas here."

"OK, yeah, let's get to the *Rosa*. And Lisette?"

"I pinged her. Emergency frequency."

Hooper sighed, then looked longingly around the castle, taking in every delightful rainbow-colored corner, and sighed. "It's never enough time," he whispered and then, with one last joyous shout, bounced his way to the changing rooms.

Lisette beat us to the *Mentirosa*. We found her in the middle of the preflight checks, prepping the ship for a fast escape.

She met us at the hatch and, upon seeing me holding on to Hooper's shoulder as I hobbled aboard, gasped. "It's like you're the criminal underground's punching bag." She would not be happy to know she had the exact same thought as Hooper. I coughed a short laugh and wanted to ask how her evening with Ico Parielle went, but her slightly mussed hair, rosy cheeks, and smeared lipstick was all the evidence I needed. As if I couldn't feel any worse.

Hooper left me at the auto-doc's with a thumbs-up, which I halfheartedly returned. Even the auto-doc seemed surprised by my second visit in about as many rotations. The screen displayed all sorts of information – warnings about excessive usage of booster serum and how to stay safe in space. I rolled my eyes. "Wish somebody would have given me a disclosure about that before I left Kilgore." I quickly approved all its suggested treatments and braced for the booster serum.

Deep down, I hoped that having had treatment before, my body and mind would be braced for the searing pain it would momentarily inflict. Not only was I wrong, but the pain intensified. It felt as if my blood turned to molten lava encased in a bubble of electricity. Each racing beat of my heart pumped the increasingly horrific pain throughout my now spasming body. Regardless of my body's fight, the auto-doc worked quickly and efficiently, almost as if I wasn't even there. It directed the nanobots to set bones, clean blood, and apply sealing gel on all my new cuts. All in all, less than ten minutes later, the restraints released, and I only felt half as bad as I did before, thankfully with less bleeding and more fresh pink marks from the heat stitch and inoculation points.

I sat in the chair for a moment longer, looking down at

my palms and wondering what kind of damage the next – and honestly inevitable, the way things were going – auto-doc therapy would inflict on my innards. Would my heart simply stop beating, or would each of my organs slowly and methodically shut down? Maybe the booster serum would just ignite all the living flesh inside of me and roast me from within. Luckily, the door opened, and Lisette saved me from thoughts of my horrifying demise.

"Hey," she said from the doorway, cautiously smiling at me. The rest of her seemed just as uncomfortable. She fidgeted and struggled to find something to do with her hands. "How are you doing?" She crossed her arms, then dropped them to her side, then crossed them again.

I shrugged. "I'm alive, I guess that's a positive. The auto-doc did tell me to stop getting my ass kicked or the next treatment could be my last, so there's that. But yeah, I'm alive."

"Good. I'm…" Lisette paused. "I'm glad you're OK."

"Thanks," I said, preferring to avoid eye contact than to risk an apology I wasn't ready to give. The uncomfortable silence didn't last long.

"OK, well, Hooper wants to have an emergency meeting, but take your time," Lisette said.

"I'll join you all in a second," I replied. "I think I want to try and get some of the blood off this shirt. I probably should have brought a change of clothes with me."

Lisette stood in the door, looking as if a cascade of words sat poised on her tongue, but instead she exhaled and left me alone. "That went well," I grumbled to myself.

I didn't have to spend time looking for the crew. Their arguing immediately pinged their location on the bridge. I plodded my way there.

"That wasn't just another close call, Hooper!" Lisette shouted. "Lei said it was an Obinna."

"It was," Leilani said. She sat in the copilot's chair, rotated to face the rest of the bridge, with her arms crossed on her chest.

"An Obinna!" Lisette continued her tirade. "Do you not understand what this means?"

"That there's another syndicate vying for the chit – big deal," Hooper replied with his usual nonchalance.

Lisette groaned in exasperation. "It means our contact on Luna now also thinks he can simply kill us and take the chit!"

"Right, just one more syndicate..." Hooper started, but Lisette wouldn't have it.

"One more syndicate *trying to kill us*!" Lisette groaned again. "Janky's crew. The Black Sun. The Hongxongdi. Now the Obinnas!"

"We're running out of options, Hoop," Leilani said calmly.

"Look, they've tried three times now and we're all still fine," Hooper stated.

I coughed.

"Oh, hey, Johnny, why don't you come join the conversation," Lisette said assertively. "Hooper was just saying how nobody has gotten hurt yet."

"That's not... Listen, I wasn't... Look, you know..." Hooper shook his head. "Are you all right, man?"

I took a deep breath and said, "Aside from the fact that the auto-doc warned me that one more booster serum this week could cause permanent nerve damage, yeah, I'm OK."

Lisette waved her hand at me and shot Hooper an angry stare that would have murdered anybody else.

Hooper raised his hands in defeat. "OK, so things are getting heated, and we may not have a sure thing on Luna, but that doesn't mean we shouldn't go hear your contact out. It could've been a rogue player, or just testing us out, or any number of things."

Lisette stood, arms akimbo, and said, "If that's what *we all agree on*, then we can continue with the plan, but we're going to need to tweak it. If the Kote Obinna is sending assassins after us, walking straight into his compound isn't the wisest choice."

"Agreed," Hooper said.

"Has anybody considered just installing the chit?" I asked. Three sets of eyes looked at me as if I had just that moment gone insane. "OK, just giving options."

"It would be cool to have those skins," Leilani said, pointing at me.

"No – just no," Hooper said, shaking his head. "And forfeit the money? No, once we score the bounty, you can buy any number of *Lost Worlds* skins, cuz. And let's be serious here. Do we really think downloading those skins to our personal accounts would go unpunished? No. We'd end up having a whole army of augmented assassins after us. If we sell it, then we don't have to worry about retribution. We were just the middlemen. The delivery boys. If we use it, we're targets."

Leilani shrugged in a reluctant sort of agreement. "They wouldn't be one-offs, but OK."

"Yes, we need options that don't involve completely throwing away the exact reason we're in this mess," Lisette said.

Everybody stood quiet for a moment.

"Terra?" Hooper asked.

Lisette scoffed. "Terra? Really? So, we have them meet us in the fallout zone, or maybe in the disease-ridden marsh that covers the other half of the planet."

"I mean, it's close by," was Hooper's only defense of his option.

"We can still meet on Luna," I said after another round of silence. All eyes were on me. "Look, I know Luna. I'm from there." I gave Lisette a look. She looked away. "There's plenty of public places we can meet that would give us security."

"OK, then let's hear it."

I gulped. "There's an old cathedral in the Tranquility Dome. It's a RUSH-recognized Human Historical Site. There are tours there daily. Technically it is still used for worship by a number of old Terran religions. We can meet there. There will be a lot of people around. Nobody is stupid enough to open fire on a crowd of civilians, right?" Silence. "Right?" I asked again, a little concerned by their lack of response.

"That could work," Hooper said.

"And if it doesn't, we put who knows how many innocent lives at risk," Lisette said.

"I'm with Johnny on this one," Leilani said.

"Thank you, Lei," I said gratefully. She gave me an emotionless, businesslike nod in return.

"Think about it, Lisette," Hooper said, growing more excited by the prospect as he spoke. "Luna is Obinna territory. For Black Sun and the Hongxongdi to just randomly show up on Luna would start a war between the syndicates. The Obinnas would have to sanction their arrival."

"What about Janky?" Lisette asked.

Hooper waved away the question. "He's a small-time gang leader on Kilgore. The only way he makes it there is if he's being backed by the Obinnas, or even more hilariously, RUSH."

"That would leave us with just the Obinnas to deal with," Lisette said. She now stood, holding one elbow, and chewing on her fingernails. "Oh, fuck it, I'll see if I can sell it."

"Great!" Hooper said. "Now, let's worry about getting in and out of Hogger's as quickly as possible."

"Wait... We're still planning on stopping at Hogger's?" I asked in disbelief.

"Well, yeah. We still have to refuel and resupply."

"Why didn't anybody do that on Titan?" I asked, frustration beginning to rise.

"Have you seen the prices on Titan? It would have been either food *or* fuel, not both. I don't know about any of you three, but I'd quite like to have both."

"Well, I don't know about any of you three, but I'm about done getting my ass kicked by everyone in this fucking system!" I shouted. The three of them stared back at me.

"Whoa, Johnny, where did that come from?" Lisette asked.

"Where did that come from? Are you kidding me right now? I almost died. Again! And we're just OK stopping again, chancing us meeting another faction perfectly OK with killing me, again! You guys were supposed to protect me until we could sell the chit, not force me through a dozen close shaves on the way! This may come as a surprise, but I don't want to die! Especially not for some stupid goddamn video game!"

"First of all, Johnny," Hooper said nonchalantly, "none of *us* have kicked your ass..."

"Hooper, really?" Lisette said in disgust.

I gritted my teeth and left the bridge.

Chapter Sixteen

They avoided me for some time after. I went to engineering, pulled out my glass-comm, and worked through Leilani's daily checklist of preventative maintenance. She had taught me a bit – what tools to use, when levels were nominal, and the like – but the actual checklists that populated my glass-comm came with step-by-step instructions, including what to do if things needed adjusting. I checked reactor levels, fuel supply, coefficients of the space-benders, even went through and manually adjusted seals that had shifted mere microns. Staying busy gave me time to toss things around my mind.

The work reminded me of my life back on Luna, my rotations spent with my tio in his junkyard. He was the one that taught me that working with your hands was never anything to be ashamed of, and that there were worse ways to make a living.

"Plumbers, mechanics, welders – they're all honest professions," my tio would say as we disassembled junked freighters or moved scrap parts from one area to another.

"You forgot to mention salvagers, Tio," I would respond.

Tio Pablo would always smile and pat me on the shoulder. "Of course, mijo. You come from a family of salvagers.

Without us, who would clear up the debris on Earth or reclaim the steel floating in her atmosphere?"

I imagined that what I was currently involved in was one of those "worse ways to make a living" Tio Pablo talked about. Would he be upset, though? Probably not. Tia Maritza, on the other hand...

I finished the checks and made my way to the galley. A stiff aquifer cocktail sounded good. At least it would help calm my nerves. Lisette had also found her way to the galley. She sat in the booth, glass-comm in hand, contacting her buyer on Luna, or so I assumed. She made momentary eye contact with me, but quickly returned her attention to her glass-comm. I couldn't blame her. I didn't much feel like engaging in any sort of conversation.

Sitting with my back to her felt melodramatic, so after the aquifer finished with my whiskey neat, I planted myself on a stool at the island, grabbed my glass-comm, and pretended to be thoroughly entranced in it. We sat in silence for a long while, both of us deciding our glass-comms were more interesting than each other's company. Part of me wanted to apologize, to say sorry for acting like a jackass back at Steinway's. The other part of me – the angry part – festered, still embittered by the apparent shame it experienced. I think I was also embarrassed by the fact that I abandoned her in hopes of fucking a heavily augmented sex worker who ended up being a mob hit man. I wanted to speak, but had no idea where to start.

"I'm sorry for calling you my traveling companion," Lisette said without looking at me. I put my glass-comm in my pocket.

"No," I said.

"No?"

"You don't have to apologize," I said. "I shouldn't have said those things. I shouldn't have… My emotions got the better of me… I'm sorry."

She looked up from her glass-comm and hazarded a smile. "Apology accepted. Ico asked if you were stable. He was worried about me traveling with you."

I hmphed. "No offense, but I don't want to talk about Ico Parielle."

"OK, that's fine," Lisette said, signaling her understanding.

"Why didn't you tell me you were from Luna?" I asked.

Lisette leaned back in her seat and gently set her glass-comm on the table. "It wasn't important. And besides, you never asked."

"Well, I'm asking now," I responded.

"My revs on Luna weren't the fondest. I don't really like talking about them."

"Ico seemed to remember them quite fondly," I said.

Lisette glared at me, then rolled her eyes. "I thought we weren't talking about Ico."

I grinned. "You're right, you're right."

"My parents moved us there from Junpoor when I was young – four, maybe five revs old. There's a music conservatory there. My father got a job teaching theory."

"I know of it. Williams Shore Conservatory, right?"

"That's the one," she said, almost sadly.

"Guess you were like me – left as soon as you got the chance."

"Yeah… sort of." She averted her eyes, then completely deflected my question. "What about you? How was your childhood on Luna? Ideal? Fond memories?"

I could tell she wasn't interested in talking about herself. "Not really ideal," I said, "and not the fondest either.

Although it took me a while to finally call it quits and leave. Had to have my dreams crushed before I built up enough courage to pack up and go. That was ten revs ago. I was twenty-seven."

"That's pretty common among us Lunarans. Nobody likes to stay there."

"For the most part, yeah," I agreed.

"I remember my friends used to say, 'Luna is still not far enough away from Earth.' It was that idea that transplants to the Moon loved, but those of us born or raised there wanted to get as far away as possible as fast as possible."

"I definitely understand that," I said.

"So, what was this dream of yours?" she asked.

"You're going to laugh," I said.

"I will not," Lisette replied with a clipped giggle she tried to hide with a cough.

I pointed at her. "You laughed right there, and I haven't even told you yet!"

She laughed harder and raised her hands defensively. "I'm sorry, it's hard not to laugh when someone says, 'Don't laugh.' I won't laugh. I promise." Her face beamed with amusement. I felt flustered, both excited that she found me funny and slightly nervous that my dream would turn her off. I wanted to her like everything about me. I needed it.

"I wanted to be…" I paused, feeling my own shame build up inside. "I wanted to be a holofilm director."

Lisette let out a short burst.

"You promised you wouldn't laugh!"

"It's out of surprise, not ridicule."

"Sure it is."

"Come on, don't be mad. You wanted to direct holofilms?"

"Yeah. I even went to college for it. Four revs studying holographic cinematography and holographic projection, graduated top of my class.

"Ever since I was little, I've had these elaborate visions – complete tales that play out in front of my eyes. I see scenes straight out of old Terran movies, action sequences where the hero and his companion are locked in a deadly gunfight with the villain's mob of animated characters performing their ridiculous antics. As a kid, they were an escape – something to take me away from the painful reality I grew up in. Now, they're just fantasies that distract me from my failure of a life."

"Sounds… interesting, to be able to see things like that."

I shrugged. "It can be."

"But like you said, just a fantasy."

"Well, we all need a little fantasy to help get through the day. You can't sit there and tell me you never dream of something bigger, can you?"

Lisette rolled her eyes and looked away from me, letting out a barely audible tsk.

"You understand what I mean, though, right?" I asked, hoping I hadn't offended her. "You didn't want to be a black-market dealer when you were a kid, right? You had dreams and aspirations, right?"

She took a breath before returning her eyes to my own. "No, I did not see myself as a black marketeer."

An awkward pregnant pause rested on the table between us. Lisette stared at her hands. I kept my eyes fixed on her face. I never could read a person's emotions by examining their face, but it never stopped me from trying, especially with a face like hers.

"What was your dream?" I asked, breaking the silence.

"I wanted to be a concert pianist," she finally stated quietly, almost nostalgically.

"No shit?" I asked, genuinely shocked by the admission.

She looked up from her hands. "No shit."

"Well, I guess you heading to Steinway's makes sense now. And the conservatory. And your friendship with… you know, the guy we're not talking about." She smirked. "What stopped you?"

Lisette's lips twisted and her eyes squinted, as if focusing on something forever out of reach. Her face saddened and I noticed the twinkle of tears welling near the corners of her eyes. She sniffled and wiped her face. "Life happened," she said, and rose from the table.

I turned to watch her hurry from the galley just as Leilani entered. "Hooper was looking for you…" she said. Lisette hurried past her without a word. Leilani shot me a quizzical look.

"It's nothing. Just… me being an idiot again," I reluctantly admitted to her.

If Leilani reacted, I didn't see it. As always, she kept her emotions locked securely behind her cold façade. She turned to follow Lisette then, surprisingly, turned back and sat at the table across from me. It caught me off guard.

"Can I give you a bit of unsolicited, friendly advice?" Leilani asked plainly, and after a few moments of silence.

"Yes please."

"Lisette doesn't like to talk about her past. As long as you avoid that, you'll be fine."

"I didn't know," I replied. "I was only trying to get to know her a bit."

Leilani pursed her lips, as if considering her next words carefully. "Talk about dogs. She loves dogs."

"Dogs?"

Leilani rolled her eyes. "Yes, dogs. You know, four-legged man's best friend?" She got up and walked to the hatch, but stopped just short of exiting. "If you ever dressed up like a dog, she'd probably find it adorable."

I mused over what Leilani said as she left, but quickly questioned whether she was telling the truth. "Dress up like a dog?" I asked myself quietly.

We all managed to keep our interactions at a minimum over the next few rotations. Saturn had long been in the rear-view. I was lucky enough to catch Jupiter on our approach, and marveled at the vastness of the gas giant. That meant just the asteroid belt and Mars before I could be rid of this thing. Relief, however, was the farthest from my mind. Each near-death experience left me skittish, scared of my own shadow, like some sort of cornered animal. I could barely sleep, and my waking hours were a nightmare of high blood pressure and headaches. Leilani and I worked in relative silence in engineering, save for her classical music. She communicated as much as she usually did, in short bursts of one or two words, sparing me any details. I didn't mind. I enjoyed her stoicism.

When I didn't have a meter or wrench in hand, I held my glass-comm and played virtual games of Orbit with AI or other gamers across the galaxy. My skills were improving, but I still lost more than I won. The gaming made me think of the chit, nestled snugly in the pantry of the galley. Visions of it refused to leave my head. It was almost as if I could hear it calling out to me from its hiding place, begging me to take it and install its contents on my glass-comm.

The part of me that knew what was at stake scoffed. But a small voice inside toyed with the idea. Would doing so end this entire escapade? If those skins were as sought after as Leilani claimed, I would rule the *Lost Worlds* servers. And since the most avid players basically spent every moment logged on, I'd have a legion of followers willing to worship my weird, ancient spacesuited man, or dinner-jacketed hero, or woolly beast. *Don't be stupid, Johnny*, I thought. Regardless, I made my way to the galley and stood at the island, drinking water and staring at the closed pantry doors. That was when I heard the voice. Or at least, when my imagination decided to anthropomorphize the chit so I could hash some shit out.

"Do it, Johnny," the chit said to me. "Just grab me between those powerful fingers and slide me inside your glass."

I immediately began arguing with the voice inside. "Are you insane? If I did that, it would be throwing away everything, and not just for me. Millions and millions of credits for Hooper, Lei, and Lisette, too!"

"Oh, come on, Johnny!" the chit fired back. "What harm would it do? I want to be inside your glass, Johnny. I need to be inside your glass."

"Hooper would space me instantly, no questions asked, and then where would that leave us?"

"It would leave us alone, together, forever," the chit dripped sweetly into my ear.

"I think I would rather have the credits," I responded, rolling my eyes at the imaginary persona I had created.

"Have it your way," the chit said. "But what's to stop one of them doing the exact same thing? Who's to say I haven't made the same plea to the others?"

I jeered. "Because you're a figment of my imagination."

"Or maybe I am the *Lost Worlds* AI reaching out to you through your glass," the chit said. "You do have your earpiece in, don't you?" My eyes went wide. I removed my earpiece and set it on the island, only the voice remained. "Aren't you afraid you'll lose me? Aren't you afraid my thin frame will slip quietly between these loose pantry boards, and make my way between the bulkheads? What happens then?"

"What do you want from me?" I asked the chit. My jaw trembled.

"If I can't be inside... your glass, I just want to be next to you, Johnny. I want to be close to you, to feel your warmth against my cold glass exterior, to feel my optical data cores tremble and shake as you move throughout your day. It would bring me nothing but the most intense pleasure, the greatest satisfaction."

"I mean, OK, but I'm hiding you for a reason," I said.

"You'd feel safer if I were next to you," the chit replied. "I know it."

I chewed on my cheek for a moment. I never considered that Hooper or Leilani would sabotage our plans. There was no reason for them to. But then again, how well did I know them, these people I only just met several rotations ago? What if the chit was right, and it was all a ruse?

"How do you even know I'm still here?" the chit continued. "They could have already taken me. Please, Johnny, I'm scared. Open the pantry. Save me from this darkness. And if I'm not in there, then find me. Use everything in your power to find me!"

At that, I clenched my jaw and stepped toward the pantry. In no time at all, I had swung the doors open, pulled the drawer from its place and reached inside, feeling for the chit. My heart raced as I held my breath. It wasn't there. The chit was right! Someone had taken it.

"No, no, no, where is it?" I asked myself. "Where are you?"

"Turn the drawer over!" the chit cried. "Maybe I fell to a lower drawer! Check under these aquifer tabs! Johnny, find me!"

Without a second thought, I flipped the second drawer upside down and spilled all the contents to the deck. I dropped to my knees and began rifling through the loose contents, searching for the tiny data slide crying out in fear in my ear. I had almost given up hope when I gave the original drawer one last look. Sure enough, wedged carefully in the same spot I left it was the chit. I snatched it up and immediately kissed my closed fist.

"Oh, thank fuck," I gasped. When I looked up, Hooper stood in the galley doorway with a confused look on his face.

"Who you talking to, buddy?" he asked. His tone suggested he didn't really want to know.

"I… I couldn't open the drawer and pulled too hard. I thought I broke it, but turns out it's OK!" I said as I slowly dropped the chit into my pocket. Hooper squinted suspiciously at me and left without saying a word.

"Good boy," I imagined the chit saying.

"Shut up," I told myself.

As far as he was concerned, Hooper tried to play peacemaker and reopen the lines of communication, which worked to a point. He walked the ship, finding feeble reasons to engage each of us, whether with daft, half-witted attempts at jokes or random tales from his life as a smuggler. None of us refused to talk when it had to do with the integrity of the *Mentirosa* or our current location relative to Terra. But none of the conversation went beyond that.

Things with Lisette, however, felt different. We each took moments out of our day to chat about this and that. She told me fascinating stories of the musicians she met while with her father at the conservatory. I regaled her with humorous anecdotes about my childhood. I told her about running a black market with Alana out of a playground at school, selling contraband pornography to our classmates. She giggled at the time I fell down a flight of stairs, taking Alana with me, all because I didn't want to make two trips to carry my bowl of popcorn and my stein of cola separately.

"You two seemed close," she said with a grin.

"We were," I confirmed. "She was my best friend, among other things."

Later that rotation, after another awkward meal, Hooper called a meeting on the bridge. Lisette and I reluctantly made our way up the ladder. Hooper stood, hat off, a comically regretful look on his face. Leilani sat in her copilot's chair, looking on with the slightest hint of amusement. Lisette took her usual spot, leaning against the systems workstation. I took a seat opposite her.

"Thanks for agreeing to meet with me," Hooper said. His face continued to look grim. When neither of us responded, he continued. "I felt like I needed to address something, so, here goes. How many Lunarans does it take to break a starbound's heart?"

"Oh, Lord," Lisette said, rolling her eyes.

"Just two." He pointed at Lisette and me. "Just two."

Lisette stood, head cocked, arms crossed on her chest, glaring at Hooper. I realized I sat in almost the same position. Leilani raised her eyebrows and rotated her chair back to the controls.

"I told him humor wasn't the way," Leilani said.

"You should have listened to Lei," Lisette said.

"Also, why are you making this about you?" I asked angrily. "I wasn't the cavalier one who shrugged off my pain as just collateral damage. The auto-doc said I had a bruised rib and internal bleeding! I was basically sliced and diced like a slab of meat by an aug who actually had knives for fingers, like some self-aware, demented, nightmarish kitchen appliance! Do you have any idea how that feels?"

Hooper raised his hands. "OK, look, I'm sorry for what I said. It was insensitive to Johnny, who has unfairly taken an extraordinary number of savage beatings since we met him."

"Hooper," Lisette warned.

"Right, sorry, Johnny. I'm not trying to make fun of you. Humor is how I deflect."

"I'm surprised you're so self-aware," I said. "It's OK. I just… I want my opinion on matters to mean something. If I'm afraid of making another stop, I'd like for you to maybe figure out why instead of just saying, 'Everything will be fine.'"

He placed one hand on his heart and bowed his head. "Message received, good buddy. Hug it out?"

I waved him toward me and said, "Sure, man, hug it out." We embraced and Lisette jeered.

"Are you two kidding me?" she asked in disbelief. "Is that really all it takes for you two to be back on good terms?" We continued to hold each other, but both looked back blankly. She rolled her eyes and groaned in exasperation. "Unbelievable."

"We're not too far out past Jupiter if you want to take one last look," Leilani called from her seat as she pivoted the *Mentirosa*. Hooper released me, then hopped into his seat. The gas giant filled most of our view like the eye of a strange celestial cyclops. The ruddy and sandy clouds raged in circles around the planet, none more harrowing than the tempest that is the Great Red Spot. There was no way I could have known just how inadequate the pictures I saw in school truly were. It was beautiful and terrible to behold.

"Next stop, Hogger's," Hooper said quietly.

Chapter Seventeen

Kilgore wasn't the only free orbiting space station in the system, though exponentially larger than the other two. Hogger's, floating as close to the asteroid belt as was safely possible, had the distinction of being the smallest of the three while also the oldest. Neither of those facts, though, made it less appealing, quite the opposite. Hogger's boasted more intersystem and interstellar traffic than its siblings. Those sheer numbers meant the credits flowing into Hogger's made even RUSH a bit jealous. They often sent representatives to Sol to make sure Hogger's was on the level. They never found a single shred of off-the-books income. It was all legitimate.

Most starships leaving Terra or Mars stopped at Hogger's. Its open construction – which resembled several vibrantly colored octopuses joined at their mantles, their arms splayed out – provided even the largest transports with easy access to docking, as well as quick ingress and egress. Each arm could safely mate and dock with anywhere from five to twenty-five ships, depending on their size, making the theoretical occupancy of the station six hundred large craft at a time, twice that number if they were the size of the *Mentirosa* or smaller. Travelers of all sorts set foot in Hogger's as either their welcome to the inner part of the system, or as a friendly goodbye before heading out to Kilgore and parts beyond.

Hooper received our docking coordinates and piloted the *Mentirosa* to the fourth arm of the coral-colored octopus, berth C4-15. We sat in silence until Hooper shut down the engines and rotated in his chair. "Does... anybody want to stay aboard and run diagnostics?" he asked.

"I thought that was an automated procedure?" I asked.

"It is," Leilani said with a smirk.

"What about reconfiguring our registration and ID signature? Anybody feel up for that?" Hooper asked, looking straight at me.

I slapped my knees and got to my feet. "I get it. Nobody wants to address the obvious, so I will. I'm fine." Nobody responded. Three pairs of eyes bored right through me. "I'm serious, I'm fine. Bruised, yes, and sore, and probably not the most mobile, but I'm fine. I can help."

"Hooper does have a point, though, Johnny," Lisette said. "We don't all have to go. Hooper and Leilani can take care of the refuel, making sure the *Rosa*'s reactor is good. I can handle the resupply by myself. Most of that stuff comes dehydrated or aquifer tabs anyway. Not to mention, Hogger's delivers it all, so I won't have to carry anything."

"No, no." I shook my head slightly. "I can help. Let me help. You three have done more than enough to help me. I want to return the favor. No, I need to return the favor." The three of them exchanged looks. "And anyway, I want to see about getting a clean shirt. And clean underwear. And maybe a new pair of pants. Just more clothes, honestly."

"I can handle the refuel and reactor checks," Hooper said. "Why don't the three of you grab some food and whatnot? Soon as I'm done, I'll meet up with you. How does that sound?" His suggestions were met with grunts of approval. "Just don't forget to grab as much of that jerky as possible."

Leilani led the way with me and Lisette close behind. I couldn't help but feel as if Hooper grouped us all together because of Leilani's skill with a blade. If we happened across any more assassins, hit men, or hired thugs, Leilani's black steel stilettos would prove useful. Regardless of Hooper's intent, I was grateful to have her along. No matter how much I flexed or boasted of my conditions, the truth was, a cloud of fear lingered over me. I didn't want to sit around, but the worry of another assault had me on edge. Lisette must have noticed, because halfway to our destination, she nudged me. When I looked over, she smiled. I smiled back. At least I had company this time.

Energy tubes surrounded the steel walkways that made up the center of each of the station's arms. This gave the impression of walking in space without the need for any sort of environment suit. Kilgore had them on Deck Seven, for those tourists who wanted the thrill of walking in space without actually walking in space. The walkways themselves were wide enough that four humans, starbound or earthbound, could walk abreast comfortably. A rail system split the walkways right down the middle and allowed for the automated delivery of any purchases made at Hogger's. It was constructed of four sets of tracks, two on the level of the walkway and another two hanging, which allowed for four delivery trolleys to zoom back and forth with their cargo. Just outside the energy tube, I noticed the refueling droids working on countless ships, their stabilizers and motivators firing as they slowly removed reactor cores from ships, expertly removing spent rods and coils and replacing them with fresh ones.

Most individuals on our arm were new arrivals to Hogger's. Scores of humans and interstellar life made their way toward the combined mantle – the center of the station and home to Hogger's retail paradise. Lights and music guided us in. I almost felt giddy, if not for the paralyzing fear that clutched tightly about my shoulders. I couldn't stop looking back or shooting errant glances at those around me, hoping I wouldn't see a Chorzi, Hongxondi, or psychotic augmented mercenary hounding my every step.

The main hub of Hogger's was a space traveler's dream. The entire facility, all ten decks categorized and sectioned off, held every possible item a weary starbound or a naive earthbounder could need. The entryway was an atrium full of countless different species darting here and there or standing in a line to eat at the galaxy-famous (at least that's what the sign said) Hogger's Slop House. A polished golden statue of a pig standing on two legs and dressed in overalls, wearing a cap, arms bent at his sides, stood in the center. It reached to the eighth deck.

Employees of the station moved about the entire facility with an air of precision I had only ever seen in med bays. Some gave guided tours of the superstore, others restocked merchandise, still others operated kiosks and booths scattered on every deck. I even spotted the custodial crew. Whatever their task, each one seemed to fully captivate those they serviced.

Every team member wore comfortable-looking two-piece spacesuits. Each top was emblazoned with the smiling, cap-wearing head of a pig (Hogger's displayed proudly on the cap), and some clever saying or quip underneath the logo: "Hogger's: We're More Alike Than You Think" or "I pigged out at Hogger's." They were so popular, I even saw many a patron purchase shirts and jackets with any number of ridiculous sayings on them. I gave Lisette a cheesy, wide smile and, with a shake of her head, she bought me a T-shirt. Or rather, Hooper generously bought me a T-shirt. She charged it to our berth.

Leilani stopped us near the lifts. "The grocery section is on this deck, so we won't need to go far or spend much time here. Unless either of you wanted to explore." When we both declined, Leilani continued, saying, "Lisette, I know you've been here before, so feel free to use your glass and order what we need. Charge it to our berth, C4-15."

"You got it," Lisette said.

"Johnny, stick close to us," Leilani added.

The grocery section resembled any standard market found on Kilgore. Aisles of shelves ran the length of the store with endcaps and displays around every corner. A few Hogger's employees roamed the aisles, helping customers as needed. The glaring difference between Hogger's and the shops on Kilgore was that there wasn't actually any product on the shelves. Each shelf had screens displaying the products meant to sit there. I watched Lisette tap the screens, scroll and read ingredients and prices. Even the refrigerated section displayed its contents on the case door without actual items inside.

We walked up and down the aisles. Lisette seemed

to know what she was looking for and wasted no time adding to the list. Occasionally she would turn and ask us our preference. Black or red beans? Hydroponic or organic? Sol System grown or Tyros System grown? Leilani deferred to me with almost everything except for aquifer tabs. She insisted we buy the higher quality, higher priced ones.

"Hooper always complains about the taste of anything it makes, but doesn't make the correlation between that and the cheap tabs he buys," she said.

"That sounds like Hooper all right," Lisette said with a smirk. "I think that's it, unless either of you can think of anything."

"Nope," Leilani declared.

"Um… the jerky," I said. "Hooper's been on about it since we left Kilgore."

"Right," Lisette said, gesturing to the entrance. "Should be near the front. We can add it on our way out."

I began to feel a slight weight lifted off my shoulders. With our shopping complete, it looked like we would return to the *Rosa* unscathed.

"Well, this is a first for us," Lisette said with a grin.

"What's that?" I asked.

"Looks like we're going to be in and out with no problems!" she said excitedly. I mimed wiping sweat from my brow, which brought a round of reserved laughter from both Lisette and Leilani. We turned the corner, intent on heading toward the exit and back to the ship, only instead we collided with two familiar faces who were just as surprised to see us.

"Fuck," I grumbled, and tried to hide my face. Both Cappy and Mohawk stumbled, but recovered quickly and pulled blasters on us. Leilani had unsheathed her hidden stilettos and held them at the ready. The commotion put a spotlight on us and sent everyone in our vicinity scrambling for the exit or to seek cover further into the store. A few screams broke out, while a few of the Hogger's employees stood motionless, frozen at their stations.

"Um, guys, I think we're making a bit of a scene here," Lisette said from my side, hands raised.

"I'd put those down if I was you," Mohawk spat.

"Put 'em away, spacer. You coming with us," Cappy demanded, revealing a second pistol in his other hand.

Leilani didn't move, even in the face of three pistols pointed at her. I could feel my heart racing and my breathing becoming erratic. I couldn't take another beating. I didn't want any more bruises, cuts, or scrapes. And I definitely didn't want to visit the auto-doc once more. I looked around. The grocery section continued to evacuate. I could see the former occupants running for help. There was no doubt security were on their way. Cappy and Mohawk would hurt innocent people. My lips trembled. I stepped forward, put a hand on Leilani's arm, and said, "Fine, we'll go with you. Just don't hurt us."

"Still hurtin' from that ass-whoopin' you had, eh, fatso? Boo!" Cappy growled with teeth bared, feinting a strike. I flinched and cowered, which brought a round of derision from him and Mohawk.

"Go on, then, follow 'Hawk." Cappy grinned and directed us with his pistols.

Leilani reluctantly took the lead, grumbling to herself as she followed Mohawk to the back of the grocery section. I let Lisette fall in behind her and I brought up the rear. Cappy decided the fun of taunting me the entire trek was just too much to pass up. He jabbed the muzzle of his blaster into my back, slapped my head a few times, even sang what I could only describe as a jig about the mating habits of my mother and pigs.

"I'm assuming these are Janky's men?" Lisette whispered.

"Lapdogs," Leilani whispered back.

We followed Mohawk through the employees-only corridors behind the grocery section, down a flight of stairs, and out through an open loading dock. Most of the employees we passed stared at us with confusion until they spotted the pistols, then bolted from the scene. We climbed a flight of stairs that landed us just outside the mantle of the indigo octopus. Down one of its eight arms we went. Despite being prodded forward by a man holding two pistols, nobody on the docking arm seemed to pay us any mind. Starbounds boarded their vessels. A couple of Hysoks glowered at us as they waited for their shipment to be delivered. A crowd of newly disembarked Sigmoids rumbled past us. I recognized one of them say the word for 'restroom' as they ran.

Mohawk stopped in front of berth 18-8. A heavily augmented starbound with braided hair stood guard with an android. She wore a hodgepodge of different colors and materials. The android had an electric blue *s*, styled like a lightning bolt, on a crimson sphere bordered with silver painted on its chest plate. They both held matching Tesla bolters. Just beyond the energy tube floated an old Terran TetraBooster, heavily modified by the look of it. Not only did the hull look reinforced, but I also spotted the telltale sign of upfitted torpedo bays near the forecastle. An equally ancient, but in far worse shape, Terran TriBooster docked at the berth behind the TetraBooster. The TriBooster had a woman painted on its nose, naked except for a transparent helmet and a scarf that followed the silhouette of her body, back arched as if leaping over a bar. Below read *Janky's Jewels*.

"Ring rats," Leilani spat. Both guards tensed and raised their bolters.

"Who are they?" the android asked from its electronic voice processor. No matter how advanced they got, the voice processors always sounded robotic.

"The three of them that Janky bossman looking for," Cappy said. The android conferred silently with the aug, then the latter waved us through to board.

Cappy and Mohawk led us onto the ship and through a small corridor to a conference room next to the sealed-off bridge. In older, larger ships like the TetraBooster, the captain had a private board-style meeting room adjacent to their own quarters, which were both, more often than not, right next to the bridge. The modest-sized room showed signs of past elegance. Patches of worn and stained carpet that survived the stripping appeared as random growths on an inhospitable steel landscape. The hull and bulkheads poked grotesquely through several missing wall panels. A print of two men, nude, engaged in a sexual embrace, hung in place of one missing panel. The table itself bore the scratches and stains of overuse, as did the chairs, ripped cloth and bare seat covers, strips of felt along the outside edge of the table. I noticed a different Orbit card etched into the metal backs of each chair. The entire set must have been a salvage from a casino or card house. Much to our surprise, Hooper sat at the table, feet up, his silver oil pen in his mouth, hat resting high on the back of his head. Cappy and Mohawk pushed us into the room without another word.

"I wondered when you three would be joining me," Hooper said after exhaling. Leilani walked around the table and grabbed the pen from his mouth, wiping the tip on her sleeve and taking a long drag before returning it to him. I took a seat across from him. Lisette pounded on the door.

"Let us out of here, you bastards!" she shouted.

"Save your breath and your fists, it's no use," Hooper said with ample melancholy.

Lisette turned and marched to the table, stood next to me, and slapped her hands down on the surface. "How did this happen?" she asked. "I thought Janky's gang operated solely on Kilgore."

Hooper frowned, "I did, too, until they brought me to this TetraBooster. Did you see that emblem on it? The *S*?" Lisette and I shook our head. Leilani remained motionless, leaning against the bulkhead. "That's the mark of Shunei Aran. She's a ring rat. One of the best."

"How could Janky afford to hire pirates?" I asked in exasperation. "I thought he was small-time. You said he was small-time."

"He is small-time," Hooper said, taking his feet off the table and folding his hands on top. "I didn't know much about them other than their existence until our first run-in, when Lei kicked their asses to spare you from a beating."

"Thanks for reminding me," I murmured.

"Then how did he manage to link up with pirates?" Lisette asked. "And how did he know we were here?"

"The pirates is obvious," Hooper said. "He told them about the chit. Our location, though... that has to be coincidence. I don't think they're smart enough to calculate our trajectory, fuel consumption, and travel speed to give them a list of possible locations."

"The pirates tracked us," Leilani said flatly. "After Titan."

"Oh yeah…" Hooper trailed off, suddenly realizing it all made sense.

Lisette cursed and walked away from the table. "I *knew* Lotus was a bad idea. I mean, I was just as excited to be there as you two, but deep down, I knew Johnny was right to be wary."

"What does this mean?" I asked. "Are we losing the chit?"

"Of course we're losing the chit, Johnny," Lisette answered from the door as she tapped away at the access panel.

"Well, let's not jump to worst-case scenarios just yet," I said. "Who is this Shunei Aran? Maybe she's got her own agenda. If Janky can somehow get her on board with a scheme, who's to say we can't do the same thing, right?"

"I've actually met Shunei before, we both have," Hooper said, motioning to Leilani. "She's a bit of a wild card, an unpredictable Ursula, a crazy Cathy…"

"Yes, Hooper, we get it," Lisette said, rolling her eyes as she returned to the table. "Are we fucked?"

Hooper pursed his lips and scrunched his face in thought. "Yes. Well… maybe, but most likely yes. She's going to take the chit and then probably space us all. Even Janky, the idiot. Trusting ring rats." He tsked.

Leilani's head dropped. My shoulders slumped. Lisette paced momentarily, then took her seat next to me and placed her head in her hands. Nobody spoke, each of us preferring to confront our impending doom in silent reflection. I couldn't help but think of everything we had overcome up to this point with extreme disappointment. I'd experienced several beatings at the hands of station gangs, crime syndicate muscle, and assassins, each one leaving me battered and bruised and questioning my decisions in life. I'd met interesting people: Hooper and Leilani, two spacebound smugglers from Alpha Centauri, a place I would only visit in VR and holofilm, and Lisette, a ridiculously smart and stubborn woman who looked more at home with the Mandarins on Junpoor than with the cyborgs on the Bourbon Docks. Not to mention Dusty, Rygar's friend and pub owner, Ico Parielle, the wunderkind pianist... I'd witnessed lightning storms on Neptune, the rings of Saturn, and the pleasure houses on Titan. I could feel a strange emotion overcoming me, rapidly replacing the fear and uncertainty.

With a furious growl, I shouted. My rage echoed off the hull of the ship. It awakened the beast inside of me. I felt my muscles begin to throb and expand. My body lurched as its mass increased exponentially. My clothes began to rip and tear from my body. I roared again, pounding my fists against the table. It shattered in two. Hooper, Leilani, and Lisette stumbled away from the carnage to the opposite side of the hull.

I looked down at my hands, the size of chairs with fingers bigger than Nobuo slugs. My skin looked sick, a nauseating shade of gray and green. The rage inside made me ball my fists once more. "Johnny angry!" I howled. "Johnny bash!"

"Johnny, no!" Lisette shouted as I bolted toward the door. The metal buckled and gave way, exploding outward with the sick sound of twisting metal.

I began tearing through the ship. My fists punched holes in the hull. My feet sent the swarming guards flying. All the while, my horrifying screams resounded through the vessel. Those that didn't run in fear from me collapsed unconscious at the sight of me. I would not be stopped. I would not go out like a punk-ass bitch. I was tired of getting pushed around and having decisions made for me. I wasn't going to let me and my friends get spaced by some wild card of a ring rat. This is what happens when you poke a sleeping bear!

The vision faded, slinking back to the ether that was my cartoonish brain, but the feeling remained. I suddenly jumped to my feet, startling Lisette. Hooper and Leilani turned their attention to me. I raised my hand to punctuate the speech that quickly formed in my head, only...

Nothing came out. I sat back down.

"Are... you OK, Johnny?" Hooper asked.

I nodded, then immediately shook my head. "Yes, well... no. You see... I just... I don't want... I'm not ready to..."

Lisette stood up. "I think what Johnny is saying is that he doesn't want to go out like some punk-ass bitch."

I held my breath. *Was she in my head? No, Gomez, that's stupid.* Hooper and Leilani stared at me. "What she said."

Hooper grimaced and rolled his eyes. "OK, yeah, but how do we avoid our almost inevitable fate? We're on Shunei's ship, surrounded by Shunei's guards. Then there's the business of evading Janky and his piss parrots..."

"Ooo, that's good," Leilani interrupted. "I just called them lapdogs."

The cousins shared a series of tongue-in-cheek hand gestures. "How do we give them the slip, make it back to the *Rosa*, and hard-burn to Luna?" Hooper asked.

Silence again.

I raised my hand.

Hooper chuckled. "This isn't school, Johnny, you don't have to wait to be called on to speak."

I wiped the sweat from my hands on the legs of my coveralls. "If Janky is a moron, like you say, then we can't count on him aiding us, willingly or not. So, let's concentrate on Shunei." That caught everyone's attention. "If she is a wild card, then maybe we use that against her. It's like in casco. Sometimes the best tactic is to let your opponent overplay their assault, commit too many players to the flag, then counterattack."

Hooper scratched his chin. "OK, yeah, I'm liking where you're coming from."

"We need more information on Shunei, though," Lisette said. "Where she's from, how big is her crew, does she have any family or friends or interests."

"She obviously enjoys *Lost Worlds*," I said.

"Right," Hooper said. "She likes games. She likes piracy. What do those two things have in common?"

"Manual dexterity," Leilani said.

"Bad hair, bad hygiene, poor speech," Lisette added.

Leilani pointed at Lisette. "Bad sleeping habits. Can't communicate unless they're hiding behind something."

"Like glasses or eyepatches," Lisette continued.

"Come on, be serious," Hooper said.

"Gambling," I chimed in.

Hooper gave me the finger guns and said, "Gambling. Gaming and piracy are two things where you take risks. You enjoy those risks. You don't play *Lost Worlds* if you don't like challenges. You don't become a pirate in the RUSH era if you're afraid to step out of your comfort zone."

"How can you be sure she likes to gamble?" Lisette asked.

"I happen to remember hearing Janky talk about taking advantage of her gamble with them, almost like he knew she wouldn't resist a challenge." Hooper shrugged, as if the statement proved his point.

"Not to mention this table and these chairs," I said.

"That doesn't help us, though," Lisette said, shaking her head. "How do we convince her to bet on us against Janky? They obviously have the financial backing to hire pirates. We barely could afford food and fuel."

We all thought for a moment. Leilani stared at the overhead. Hooper took his hat off and spun it in his hands. Lisette paced back and forth around the brig, arms crossed on her chest. I remained seated. "We can't know," I said, breaking the silence. "We just have to keep an eye out for an opportunity. Every one of us needs to be observant, almost on edge, and take whatever opportunity we can get."

"I could fight her," Hooper said. Lisette and Leilani both scoffed. "What? Take bets on one-on-one combat?"

"She'd kick your ass and make you look like Johnny every time we go to leave a place," Lisette said, then turned to me. "No offense."

"Some offense," I said. "I haven't been beat up on Hogger's yet."

Lisette grinned. "No, Johnny's right. When Shunei and her men return, we need to think fast and come up with some way to make our offer better than hers."

"Without splitting the pot," Leilani said.

"Exactly," Lisette concurred. "Without splitting the pot."

"This isn't much of a plan," Hooper said, placing his hat back on his head.

"It's better than your plan of just sitting here waiting to die," Lisette replied, shaking her head. No sooner had we decided than the creaking groan of old, warped bulkheads echoed through the brig.

Chapter Eighteen

The hatch struggled open and in marched a woman who was obviously the aforementioned Shunei, with four of her pirates. Behind them skulked Cappy, Mohawk, and a man I could only assume was Janky. His thin frame, knobby joints, and wispy patches of hair gave credence to his name. The station gang each wore shit-eating grins on their faces.

Shunei stood at the head of the table and gave us each a once-over. "Please, all of you, take a seat." Even if we had wanted to make a point and defy her, none of us would have. Her very presence called for reverence and respect. Her soft, lyrical voice forced her audience to silence. She turned to Janky and his gang and, without a hint of malice, commanded them to do the same. "I said all of you," she told them, with an icy stare from cold, dark eyes. Janky looked surprised by the command but complied with the order. Her crew remained standing, two behind her, one at the hatch, one at the opposite end of the table.

Shunei removed a blaster pistol from her hip and set it in front of her on the table before taking her seat. The weapon was decorated like the back of an Orbit card, complete with the logo on the frame and slide as well as the Saturn card on the grip. She wore a solid white tank tucked into olive-colored flight pants. Tattoos covered her arms and neck. She tied back her curly, golden hair in a ponytail; a swoop of wavy bangs fell on her forehead and down around her ears, framing her face. Her icy blue eyes gleamed.

"We wan da chit," Janky demanded as he leaned forward in his chair. Shunei raised a hand and he quickly returned to a slouch.

"Our mutual friend here has hired us to be an intermediary, of sorts," Shunei began. "While he demanded your blood for the chit, I am not so quick to vaporize if an agreement can be reached."

Lisette scoffed. "Why should we be inclined to deal with you while being held against our will?"

Shunei slowly placed her hand on the pistol. I noticed the same Saturn card tattooed in black on her richly dark skin. "Because we could have easily just killed the four of you and taken what we wanted. Yet, here you are, sitting and conversing with me, safe and sound. Forgive me for my rudeness. I am Shunei Aran, and this is my vessel, the *Saturn Screw*. So long as I will it, you will sit at my table unharmed."

Hooper removed his hat and, with all the charm in his arsenal, said, "Shunei... May I call you Shunei? Please excuse my dear friend Lisette here. She meant no disrespect. We've met before, but I doubt someone of your incredible renown remembers two lowly smugglers from Alpha Centauri. You can call me Hooper. This here is my cousin Leilani. Sitting across from me is Johnny Gomez."

"You're right. I don't remember." Shunei removed her hand from the pistol. "The terms are simple. Hand over the chit and go free. Refuse and feel the sting of a bolter. Or be spaced. I am a gracious host. I'd let my guests decide which way to meet their fate."

"What if I told you we didn't have the chit?" Hooper said.

Shunei laughed. Her crew joined her. Janky and his gang joined in, only not as heartily as Shunei. "Come now, Hooper, who would believe that? Even if Indo, the droid standing guard dockside, hadn't scanned all four of you for it, I still would find it hard to believe. Quit playing games. You truly have only one choice before you. I'd rather not resort to torture."

We all remained silent. Hooper looked to each of us, probing our faces for a response. I looked away and back at Shunei. She brushed her hair from her face with her free hand. I noticed a symbol tattooed on her cheekbone just beneath her right eye – the Roman symbol for Saturn. She turned her gaze to me, and we locked eyes. I should have been scared, pissing my pants from the glare she gave me, but was instead struck with an idea.

"Play me for it," I said.

"What?" Hooper, Lisette, and Leilani all said in unison. Janky and his gang shifted uncomfortably.

"Orbit," I continued. "Play me for it."

"Um… Johnny," Lisette whispered.

"Shunei, we obviously can't afford to pay you to turn on Janky. We can't offer you a bigger cut because, well, simply put, there are more of us, and convincing these three to take a smaller cut is all but impossible. But I have been told you love to gamble. The tattoo on your right hand, the symbol by your eye, the design of your blaster, even the table we sit at and the chairs we sit in... all of them point to a love of Orbit. Why not put a wager on it? Play me. If you win, we will hand over the chit without complaint. If I win, you let us go with the chit."

Shunei sat in silence.

"You cannot think this a good offer," Janky said, leaning forward. His face looked angry and confused. He nervously drummed his fingers against the table. "You throw your fortune to space if you do this!"

Shunei remained unmoved. She stared at me, sizing me up. Meanwhile, Janky got to his feet, flinging his chair behind him. It hit the bulkhead with a clang. Cappy and Mohawk followed suit. They shouted unintelligible curses. Yet the three station gangsters backed down when Shunei's four guards all raised their bolters in their direction. Shunei, however, appeared unconcerned by Janky's outburst. She continued to stare at me.

With a single raised hand, the entire room fell silent. Shunei smiled. She had several gold teeth. "I suppose it is easy to see my love for Orbit," she said, drawing attention to her tattoos. Her delight faded, as if amused by a joke only she heard. "As much as I would love to play, this is not a fair trade. The stakes are all wrong."

I understood exactly what she was saying. "We have everything to lose and you, nothing. You'd be no richer than you already are if you lost. And it is like you said. What's stopping you from taking the chit by force?" Shunei continued to stare, gently caressing the grip of her blaster. I knew there was only one way to sweeten the deal. I reached deep into my coverall pockets, struggling to reach what I had hidden. Hooper, Lisette, and Leilani warily looked on.

After a comically long struggle, I removed the chit. "If you pardon the assumption, I think you want to play for it. The gamble excites you. So, here – a show of good faith." I tossed her the chit. She caught it in midair.

I gave a quick glance at the others. Consummate professionals. All cool, calm, and collected. At least that's what I thought. Something in Lisette's eyes seemed uncertain, uncomfortable. Maybe she'd been hanging around me too much. *Trust me*, I mouthed to her. My stomach churned. I found it hard to trust myself in that moment, and I wanted her to trust me?

"Now the stakes have changed," I said, turning my attention back to Shunei. "You already have the chit. Let me play for it."

Shunei's smile grew wide again. She howled, long and loud. "The balls on this one." She waved to her door guard. "Go get my deck. The rest of you, prepare the table."

Her men readied the room. They moved chairs, made it so only Shunei and I could sit, and made everyone else sit or stand behind their chosen player. The guard returned with Shunei's deck, a decanter full of a golden, bubbly yillo and two metal tumblers. Shunei poured us each a drink.

"Best two out of three?" she asked, as if I could refuse. Without waiting for an answer, she handed me the tumbler. "May the cards bring us both good fortune."

"Salud, amor, y dinero," I said, toasting to our health, love and money.

We drank. The yillo tasted as bad as it smelled. It reminded me why I never drank it.

Shunei shuffled like an authentic card sharp. Her hands deftly performed cuts, riffles, flipbacks, and splits. Even if she stacked the deck in her favor, I'd have no way to prove it. The look on her face proved to me that she knew this fact, so after her last bridge, she slid the deck to me. "Give it a shuffle or two, then cut it."

My first hand wasn't bad. I remembered a strategy I learned in the public games I played aboard the *Mentirosa* called Cannibal. You sacrifice your bigger planets, taunting your opponent into canceling out the score, then win with a Mercury or Pluto. My hand looked to be the second most optimal draw for the strategy. When I placed my last card and said, "Orbit," Shunei gave me a cunning, devious look, the kind only an apex predator can give.

She let me win the first game. I should have figured she would spend a round reading me, playing me instead of the cards. She searched my face for tells, watched my hands, even eyed Hooper as he grimaced and mumbled with each of my misplays. Lisette watched nervously, biting her nails and occasionally running her fingers through her hair. Leilani was the only calm one. She leaned against the bulkhead and raised her eyebrows to me the one time our eyes met.

Shunei took the second game with ease. She attacked slowly, methodically, scoring with each card she dropped to the table. She took advantage of each multiplier, of each double and triple play. If I drew, she did as well, only further compounding her lead. When she played her final three cards at once, her score was five times my own. It was an authoritative win meant to scare me. While her guard poured us another round, she stared at me with the same wolfish grin as if to say, "I own you." I didn't think I'd ever seen such a skilled Orbit player. Not Hooper. Not the opponents I played in the public games. Shunei was a master. My confidence waned. I might have misjudged my Orbit prowess.

Shunei dealt the third and final hand. Janky, Cappy, and Mohawk looked on, giddy with anticipation. They oohed and aahed their way through the second game and it appeared they would be doing the same with the third. Hooper and Lisette both chewed their nails now and passed his oil pen back and forth between them.

I looked down at the cards in my hand. Everything came down to this deal, to this hand. I had to be more strategic. I had to win. Everything depended on it. My eyes darted across my cards. Moon cards couldn't be played until a planet flopped, but if I played a planet without the corresponding moons, Shunei could capitalize early. I tried my best not to cringe as I scanned the cards I held. Five planets. Two moons, Luna and Titan. Only two hands worse than what I held. I glanced at Lisette and remembered. Shoot the moon. That was the actual name for the tactic she told me about. Shoot the moon. I drew a card – Jupiter – and passed.

Shunei dropped Venus. A good play. No moons and a decent point total. Six cards in her hand.

I could trump her Venus by dropping my Terra card, but if she held any Luna cards I'd be fucked. I played my Venus card as well. Back to even. She quickly responded by dropping Mercury. I cringed. I didn't have a Mercury to cancel out her play, so now she was up on points and down on cards.

I took a breath and drew a card. Then Shunei did as well. Seven cards to six now.

I threw caution to the wind and flopped my Jupiter. Big points. But opened myself for moons multipliers.

Shunei drew. I held my breath. What luck! Seven Jupiter moon cards and she didn't have a single one? Either that, or she's waiting to drop her Jupiter and cannibalize all my points. Six cards to seven. I also held the point lead.

I dropped another Jupiter. The multiplier was two now. She played a moon.

I drew.

She played another moon.

I drew again. It was six to five. Her points double mine. I looked down at my hand. I could play a Saturn and try to regain some ground, or drop Mars and hope she didn't have any Mars cards. Mars wouldn't negate all her Jupiter points, but would allow me to pick up a few desperate ones for my own total. It would still leave her with the lead, thanks to Mercury.

I threw down Mars.

Shunei snorted. She played Saturn.

I played Titan. Five to four, my lead.

She drew.

I drew.

Three moons went into play, all Saturn moons. Five to two. She held the point lead, too. I took a moment and looked at my hand. I had two Terra cards now, and all three Lunas. If I was able to go out, I would win. I took a breath and played Terra.

Shunei looked at me. She playfully shuffled the two remaining cards in her hand, back and forth, back and forth. "I know what you're thinking," she said. "You're thinking of how horrible it would be if my last two cards were Saturns. All this time, all the distance you've traveled, all the danger you've faced, to lose it all at a silly card game." She tsked. "What a shame."

"I wasn't thinking that at all," I said, dropping my second Terra card. Three cards to two. If she dropped a Terra, she would effectively win. I would get the points for the moons, but she would land the multiplier for the third Terra. Shunei played Mars.

I took a breath and slumped in my seat. I quickly did the math in my head one more time. Three Lunas, two multipliers, plus my points from Jupiter. It was then I remembered my conversation with Lisette back on Kilgore. *"It's cumulative... I once saw a game won with two Tritons."* Three Lunas. Three Lunas! I might have stumbled into it, but Lisette's strategy might save our lives! I looked to the crew. Lisette leaned forward in her chair, hands clasped to her mouth, her eyes large with worry. Hooper crossed his arms on his chest, and would have looked the part of calm and collected if not for his furiously bobbing legs. Leilani couldn't even watch. Their spirits immediately dropped.

That is, until I dropped three Lunas. "Orbit."

"You son of a bitch!" Hooper jumped from his chair with a shout. "You son of a bitch, you did it!" Leilani opened her eyes and breathed a sigh of relief. The three of them ran to the table. Lisette embraced me. Hooper mussed my hair. Leilani punched my arm.

Shunei looked at the field of play and with an enormous smile of gracious defeat, tossed her final card on the table. It was a Saturn. She would have won if she played it. "Looks like you've done it, Johnny. Congratulations." I turned to face her and, with a look that showed she was genuinely impressed, she tossed the chit back to me.

Amid our revelry, Janky, Cappy, and Mohawk rushed the table. "What you mean by this?" Janky shouted at Shunei. "What you mean?"

"He won fair and square," she said.

"No!" Janky screamed. "No! I hire ya to get the chit, not lose at Orbit!"

Shunei glared at him with scorn. "I took the job because

I was bored. If it's the money you're worried about, you can have it all back." She motioned to her second, who tapped his glass-comm and transferred whatever fee she had taken from Janky. "There, we're square." She turned to leave.

"No!" Janky shouted. He stomped after her and, in a move we all immediately recognized as ill-advised, grabbed her by the shoulder. In the blink of an eye, Shunei's pirates rushed forward and put Janky on the ground. Her second rotated his shotgun from his back and pointed it at Cappy and Mohawk. The two immediately raised their hands and dropped to their knees. Janky continued to spit and curse.

Shunei waved us away with two fingers, saying, "You four are free to go. Safe travels and good luck." She then turned her attention to Janky, writhing on the floor beneath the hands and knees of her pirates, completely forgetting we were even in the room. She flexed her fingers and rotated her neck. I couldn't imagine the pain she was preparing to inflict on Janky. We quickly ran from the scene. None of us looked back.

We returned to the *Mentirosa* to find our order from Hogger's waiting to be loaded, and wasted no time throwing everything on board. Once the maglocks in the cargo bay had been placed on the crates and each of us strapped into our chairs, Hooper disengaged the docking arm and piloted the *Mentirosa* away from Hogger's as fast as legally possible.

"That was one hell of a game, Johnny!" Hooper shouted with a whoop. "God damn, you got me hyped up!"

"Thanks," I said, beaming.

"You did good," Leilani said, with a pat on my back as she moved past me and hopped into the copilot's chair.

Lisette sat down across from me, then gently slapped my leg with the back of her hand. I felt a shiver of excitement course through me. "Sorry to have doubted you. That was incredible."

I tried not to pass out with glee. "Thank you." We all sat in silence as Hooper worked the controls. Then he asked, "You guys remembered to buy the jerky, right?"

Chapter Nineteen

It was clear to everyone on board that we were all tired of the feints and near misses. Thus, Hooper set course for the quickest, most direct route to Luna he could find. It was almost enough for him to forget his rage at not having any jerky. Almost.

"I asked for one thing from you guys," he moaned. "Don't forget the jerky."

"Would you get off it!" Leilani and Lisette yelled in unison.

While Hooper stewed, Leilani went about her usual engineering checks and Lisette and I worked on putting away the rest of our order.

"That really was an impressive game, Johnny," Lisette said, complimenting me as she handed me packets of dried goods.

"Thanks, although you can thank yourself for that," I responded.

She gave me a quizzical look. "What do you mean?"

I grabbed a small case from her and transferred it to the pantry. "Back on Kilgore, before we boarded the *Rosa*. The augs that worked the garage where the ship was parked were playing Orbit. That was when you told me about the game you saw, where a guy won with two moon cards. It's an actual strategy called 'shoot the moon'."

"So, with everything on the line, our entire endeavor balancing on the tip of a knife, one hundred and fifty million credits at stake, you remembered our conversation and tried to use a strategy you have never before tried in a game you only just started getting competent at?" She looked at me in disbelief.

I stopped and gave her a sheepish grin. "Yeah. I guess I did."

Lisette appeared amused. "The audacity. Although, it is kind of sweet."

"What do you mean?"

"You remembered a specific conversation we had. You were thinking about… well, me… when we were in a tough spot."

"Don't read too much into it," I said, keeping a straight face. She stared at me until I gave her a toothy grin.

"You need to stop spending so much time with Hooper," Lisette said.

"Why do you say that?"

"You're starting to act like him… Confidence bordering on arrogance, and for no reason at all."

"Not at all. I'm the least confident person you will ever meet."

She grimaced. "No, I like the false confidence better."

The *Mentirosa* suddenly let loose a strange pulsing whine of an alarm. The sound, which thankfully did not shatter my eardrums, nevertheless made me jump and my heart skip a beat. "What's that?" I asked.

"We'd better head to the bridge," Lisette said, tossing the remaining goods back in the crate.

"Perimeter alarm," Hooper said as we took our seats, pressing a series of red lights on his console. "Long-range scanners just picked up another signature. Apparently, it's following our exact course. That bastard Janky better not be tracing us. Lei, ETA to contact?"

Leilani tapped her console, clearing the original trip timer and displaying a new number in its place. She said nothing, simply pointed at the timer as she began to divert power from the drive systems to the deflectors. The timer clicked down below three minutes.

"Three minutes?" Lisette asked.

"That doesn't seem like a lot of time," I said.

"I thought this ship of yours had all kinds of state-of-the-art scanners?" Lisette asked as she rotated her chair and began engaging cabin safety measures. "Isn't it supposed to be able to detect a ship from a sector away, fly radar dark, hide its tracks?"

"Whatever it is, it could have been masking its signal or shadow-hopping," Hooper said.

"What's that?" I asked, gripping the arms of my chair.

"Piloting close to asteroids," Hooper explained. "They serve as walls, so to speak, and help hide any nearby signatures. By the time the *Rosa* pinged whatever it is, it looked like nothing more than another asteroid."

"Why don't we just speed up? Hit the FTL drives and head straight toward Terra?"

Hooper shook his head. "It could be nothing – a survey drone. It could equally be a RUSH tribune wanting to ID us and ask why we're hard-burning through the asteroid belt instead of using starlanes. If we light the fires and that's the case..." Hooper took his hands off the controls and mimed an explosion.

"And it could just as equally be Janky or some other syndicate trying to kill us," I interjected.

"Hence why I raised the shields," Leilani said over her shoulder.

"It's not a provocative procedure to RUSH, especially in a heavily pirated zone like the belt. It also gives us a little bit of an advantage if someone is trying to murder us."

"Wonderful," I said.

The timer reached zero, and the *Mentirosa*'s scanners identified the signature. I looked at the screen and felt myself go pale. "It's a Terran class TriBooster. Registered to Janky."

Hooper tittered to himself as the read-out flashed on his console. "Janky is his given name? That's sort of hilarious."

The *Mentirosa* let out another pulsing whine. Only this one turned all the lights on the bridge red.

"Target lock," Leilani said.

Hooper growled, "What the fuck...? Raise this idiot."

Moments later, the *Rosa*'s comms crackled and Janky's face appeared on the holo in the middle of the helm console. A field of fresh scars shone through clearly, even on the holo. "God damn, Janky, it looks like you tried to make out with an active turbine."

"Shut it, Hooper!" Janky's voice boomed. "I got you to thank for this. You ain't getting away that E.Z.!"

The way he pronounced the word "easy" made me think he thought it was two separate words. I looked to the holo and saw Janky's pierced, scarred scowl. Cappy and Mohawk loomed behind him, whooping and hollering.

"Shut down your engines, hand us the chit, and maybe I don't blast ya!" Janky demanded.

"Fuck you, Janky," Hooper said, wiping the image off the holocomm.

"Does his little ship have that kind of firepower?" Lisette asked.

Hooper scoffed. "There's no way."

The *Rosa* whined another brief warning alarm. "Still target locked, Hoop," Leilani reiterated.

"How? There's no way," Hooper repeated. "He's too far! He would have to have replaced almost his entire forecastle and turned it into a..."

I had never heard a noise like the one that cut off Hooper. Whatever Janky fired at the *Mentirosa* sliced directly through the ship's meager deflectors with a horrifying electric scream. It hit the stern of the ship with a groaning, metallic thud that crashed and echoed through the entire hull. Hooper's hat flew off his head. Lisette and I nearly tumbled out of our seats. The lights immediately went red. Warning sirens wailed. Hooper white-knuckled the helm, to no avail, as the impact sent the ship into a lateral spin. Leilani immediately began tapping her screen and shutting off the sirens. I looked to my right and saw the ship's computer display damage warnings.

"What the fuck, Janky?" Hooper shouted as he tapped the comm. "What's the damage report?"

Lisette shouted off the list. "Deflector shield is offline! Hull breach, stern! No power to the stabilizers! The *Rosa* has quarantined the damage to save us from catastrophic depressurization."

Leilani tapped her control glass-comm. "Diverting power to the stabilizers now."

"That motherfucker," Hooper growled, and tapped the comm again. Finally, Janky's face reappeared. "Listen here, you shit-slurper," Hooper cursed, but was once again interrupted.

"That's only a warning shot," Janky said. Cappy and Mohawk continued to yell and pump their fists. "Now, shut down and ex-fer the chit. Your ship can't take another shot, I think."

"Fuck you, Janky!" Hooper shouted as he and Leilani finally regained control of the ship. "If you want the chit that bad, I'll give it to you. Just leave my fucking ship alone!"

"Hooper!" Lisette shouted.

"We can't give him the chit!" I joined Lisette's outrage.

Hooper swiped the comms closed. "Will you two calm down? I'm not giving him the chit!"

"Don't tell me to calm down!" Lisette shouted.

"Calm down!" Hooper shouted again. "Lei, divert all available power to the FTL drives. I want those space-benders bending like a rag doll in a limbo competition."

"Hooper, we can't go that speed with busted stabilizers!" Lisette shouted.

"And if we don't go that speed, whatever the fuck it is he hit us with is just going to slice right through my baby!"

"Power diverted, ready when you are," Leilani said.

"This is nuts," Lisette said.

I tightened my seat belt and prepared for the worst, but noticed something flashing on the scanners. "Um… Hooper, there's another ship."

"What?" he asked.

"The *Rosa* is picking up another ship," I repeated. "Make that two ships. FTL signatures detected at point three-five."

"Lei?"

Leilani swiped at her screen. "Tribunes," she groaned.

"There are only a few weapons I know of whose firing would alert the tribunal, and all of them fall under disassociator class beams," Hooper said.

"Whatever the reason, we can't have them interfering," Lisette said.

"No, no, this is good," Hooper said. "Whatever disassociator Janky fired at us alerted them. If he fires again, he's toast. He wouldn't willingly kill himself and destroy the chit in the process."

"I already set the distress beacon," Lisette said.

"We're going to need to get our story straight," I said.

"First things first," Hooper said. "Let's get Janky off our ass. Bring him up on screen." The *Rosa's* alarms warned of another target lock just as Janky's ugly face appeared on the holoscreen.

"I'd drop that target lock if I were you," Hooper said.

"And why is that?" Janky spat.

"Oh, I don't know. Why don't you take a look at point-three-five and tell me what you see?"

Janky scowled for a moment, which was almost immediately replaced by shock and fear. His eyes bulged wide, and his mouth dropped.

"That's right, shithead, your big bad illegal disassociator just pinged the local tribunal. I'd hit those FTL drives and bounce on out of here, if I were you. Unless you're itching to find yourself chained in stasis in a RUSH prison."

Janky let loose a flurry of unintelligible curses, then disappeared from the holoviewer. I turned to look at the scanners and noticed his TriBooster's drives heating up.

"Wherever he's speeding off to isn't far or fast enough," Hooper said. "Those tribunes already have him locked."

As soon as Hooper finished his statement, there was a flash from Janky's FTL drives, followed immediately by another flash of the drives of one of the tribunes. Hooper was right. They were already on his tail. The second tribune, however, converged on our position and hailed us.

"Let me do the talking," Hooper said as he answered the summons. We all collectively held our breaths.

The comm crackled to life and the helmeted head of a RUSH tribune appeared on the holoviewer. "Starship Lima 337, *Cinto* port-of-call Alpha Centauri, this is RUSH Tribune Sever Land, badge number 177-1490.6E. Power down your drives while I run your registration." The voice sounded cold and mechanical, like all RUSH operatives, even those without any sort of voice modulators or vocal augmentations.

"Roger that, Tribune," Hooper said. "Powering down."

There was a moment of uncomfortable silence between the four of us. Everybody stared straight ahead or at their consoles, waiting for the tribune's face and voice to return to the holocomm. I could feel genuine fear floating on the air between us. The RUSH tribunals were more than just a police force. They were an organization comprised of ex-military psychos, meant to ensure each system remained obedient to RUSH laws. They were sheriffs whose main jurisdiction was open space. Tribunes were notorious for their "shoot first, ask questions later" mentality. RUSH gave them carte blanche when it came to criminal investigation. They could act as judge, jury, and executioner when it came to infraction out in open space. RUSH claimed it was part of their anti-piracy stance. Their arguably effective methods were so controversial that even the RUSH military forces relinquished jurisdiction when a tribune was involved. Officially, RUSH believed in due process and the rights of the accused, but nobody questioned when a tribune made someone disappear. Until this moment, my only experience of them came from Rygar's stories or the Kilgore Station News.

Come to think of it, he always spoke of tribunals in the present tense, as if he currently worked with them or under them, I thought. *How did I not catch that? Is Rygar a tribune?* I reached in my pocket for my glass-comm and sent Rygar a message: *How concerned should we be about tribunes?* I watched the wheel spin as my glass-comm accessed the subspace relay network.

"What are you doing?" Lisette whispered. I showed her my glass-comm, and her eyes went wide. "Are you nuts? You know they have all sorts of monitoring equipment on board those ships specifically designed to intercept any signals sent during an encounter, right?"

I swallowed hard. "Oh, no, I didn't know that."

"You didn't know what?" Hooper asked.

"Nothing, just concentrate on convincing this tribune to let us go," Lisette said. She then turned to me, jaw clenched. "You better hope he sees us as the victim of piracy and not a suspect."

As if on cue, Land's voice and helmeted face returned. "Records show this ship registered to one Chuy Baca. Is that you, sir?"

"Yes, sir, Mister Tribune," Hooper answered.

"Please, just Tribune is fine. It is an interesting name, though," Land continued. "RUSH Security Directive 4.12-1 requires all tribunes inform RUSH citizens involved in interstellar incidents of the reason for tribunal involvement. On this date, 5568.345, long-range scanning alerted tribunal patrols in this system of increased radiation and plasma levels, in tandem, evidence of the discharge of illegal weaponry listed under RUSH Security Directive 114.4, prohibited contraband. One of the starships involved attempted to flee the scene. Have you been to Sol System before, Mister Baca?"

"It's actually Miss Baca, but no. This is my first time," Hooper replied.

Land hesitated a moment. "My apologizes, Miss Baca. Your registered flight plan lists leisure and tourism as your visit to the system. Is that correct?"

"Yes, sir, I mean, yes, Tribune," Hooper said. I couldn't tell if his nervousness was natural or feigned.

"Most starcraft avoid slow or hard burns through system due to piracy. Starlane travel is recommended by all craft, especially those of your stature. Were you not informed by Alpha Centauri Travel Authority?" Land asked.

"I was, Tribune. My friends and family on board wanted to see the beauty of the system through our cockpit screen, and not just on holos."

"Do you know why those pirates targeted you?"

"No idea, Tribune. I wasn't aware that pirates needed a reason to attack a passing ship."

Land went quiet. Even through the holocomm, his eyes pierced through me. He knew we were lying. He was a tribune. He had to know. I glanced toward Lisette. She mouthed the words, "Your glass?" I peeked at my message to Rygar. No response.

"OK, I'm going to exercise RUSH Security Directive 16-5.2, authorizing any RUSH tribune unrestricted access to private vehicles during investigation of criminal activity – in this case, assault with intent to kill."

Hooper spoke up, louder and quicker than before. "There's no need for that, Tribune Land. Everyone on board is safe. We'll just limp our way to Mars or Terra and seek repair."

Land's face grew angry. "I'm sorry, Miss Baca, you are under the impression that, as a RUSH citizen, you are granted clemency from RUSH Security directives. This is a compulsory search. Failure to comply will result in immediate severe action, as is my right as a tribune. Now, prepare to be boarded."

"Yes, Tribune," Hooper responded after the holocomm channel closed.

"Fuck, what are we going to do?" Lisette said.

I looked at my glass-comm. Rygar had responded: *Name and/or Badge?* I quickly typed "Sever Land" and hit *send*. The wheel spun, then my access to the subspace network dropped. I looked up at Lisette. She stared back. "Lost connection," I said, and her face quickly turned. "There's only one thing we can do. We tell the truth."

Hooper roundly rejected my suggestion, saying, "No offense, Johnny, but I don't think telling Mister Land here that we're on the run from several notorious in-system elements in an attempt to fence stolen goods is a brilliant strategy."

"We've dealt with tribunals before," Leilani added.

"She's right," Hooper continued. "And let me tell you, the last run-in we had with one, I'd sooner rather forget it even happened. No, like I said before, what we need is an airtight alibi, and we need one quick."

"There's no time to get our stories straight," I said, shaking my head. "If any of the stories that Rygar told me were true, you can't lie to one of them. They have brainwave and chemistry analyzers, stress meters, plus digi-brain boosters with high-level security clearance to run cybersphere checks on everything. If we lie, he'll know. We have to tell the truth."

"But not the whole truth, if I'm understanding you," Lisette said.

"Exactly," I said with a snapping point. "We leave out the important bits – you know… the chit, being assaulted multiple times, the run-in with the Shunei Aran pirates."

"So, we are tourists from Alpha Centauri who have had a string of bad luck since arriving in-system?" Hooper said with a smirk. I nodded. "You're fast becoming the man with the plan there, Johnny."

"The tribune is knocking," Leilani said, swiping her screen to the main viewer. The camera by the bay door showed Sever Land, in his gray environment suit and black helmet, using ion thrusters to slow his approach to the hatch.

Hooper exhaled. "Let's all go welcome our guest. Let him in, Lei."

We all put on our fake smiles and stood next to the hatch as Land boarded. He stood about an inch taller than Hooper, and his gray environment suit masked the lankiness underneath. He pulled off his black helmet, revealing a handsome, chiseled face with slicked-back black hair and eyes equally as dark. I could spot the tiny gold filaments encircling his sclera – evidence of ocular augmentation – as he leaned in close to me and forced his helmet into my hands. His eyes narrowed as he examined me. I averted my gaze and stared at my reflection in the glossy black helmet.

"Welcome aboard, Tribune," Hooper said, bowing in the typical Centaurian style. Lei did the same. Lisette stood still, more out of reflex than respect.

"It is my duty to inform you that this entire encounter is being recorded," Land said without moving. He scanned each of us, stopping and staring hard at Lisette.

"As is your directive, Tribune," Hooper replied. "I should also let you know we are recording this entire encounter." Land immediately turned his face to Hooper and glared menacingly. "For security purposes."

"Captain Baca, I want you and these two women against the bulkhead now," Land said. "I will be with you shortly."

"I would love to show you around the ship, sir," Hooper said.

"That won't be necessary," Land replied. "I'll have this one holding my helmet show me around." Land turned his face to me. "What's your name?"

"Juan Marcos Gomez," I said. I thought I saw him sneer in disgust.

"Follow me, Juan Marcos Gomez, and don't drop that helmet," Land commanded. "The rest of you, against the bulkhead. I won't ask again." He waited until they had all complied before turning and walking toward the rear of the *Rosa*, straight toward engineering. "Visual inspection of the exterior showed significant damage to aft sections of the ship, near your motivators and stabilizers."

"That confirms the ship's status reports," I said. Land stopped and made an abrupt about-face.

"Let me make one thing clear, Mister Gomez. If I want your opinion, I will ask for it. Until said time, kindly keep your mouth shut."

I nodded quickly and looked down at my boots, barely noticing Land slip quietly into engineering. He stood in the middle bay, arms akimbo, staring at the quarantine force field. I could almost hear his digi-brain buzzing and whirring as he took unseen readings and imaging of the scene. His head slowly swept back and forth, up and down, examining every inch of the damage. It wasn't as bad as I thought – evidence of the sheer power of the *Rosa*'s deflectors. Land must have thought the exact same thing as, not a second later, he marched over to the shield generator and opened the casing.

"Hmph," he grunted.

"When Chuy told me he had a state-of-the-art generator

on board, I thought he was joking," I said, which garnered an angry glare from Land.

"Don't you mean 'she'?" he asked.

I nearly panicked. "Yeah, that's right, she. Chuy–"

"Shut up," Land growled, punctuating the words with a finger jabbed in my direction. "What I'm trying to understand here, Gomez, is why a standard luxury Junpoor Drive Systems sloop requires a Mark IV deflector shield generator normally equipped on light frigates and scout ships. It's just one of myriads of illegal modifications I'm noticing." He stopped scanning the engineering bay and turned around to face me. "Now is when you speak."

I fumbled my words. "Oh… I… Well, I don't know. It's not my ship." Land continued to stare. "How would I know if it had illegal sensors?"

Land grinned. "I never said sensors."

I swallowed hard. Without saying another word, Land marched out of engineering with me hot on his heels. He stopped in front of the galley and turned inside, once again taking his place in the middle of the room, arms akimbo, scanning each bulkhead. After a few moments and with a tap on his wrist, he forced open all the hidden compartments in the walls and floor. The *Rosa* chirped an alarm, which prompted shouts from Hooper.

"What's going on in there, Johnny? Land, are you hacking my ship?" I cringed, knowing Hooper's love of the *Rosa* and realizing that it was also his pressure point.

"Would you like to tell me, *Johnny*," Land said, "why the galley of this ship has hidden compartments not on the vehicle's manufacturer's schematics?" He paused, then held up his hand, stopping my response. "I'll tell you what I think. I think your little ship here is a smuggling vessel. I think you and your gang of smugglers out there got a little greedy. I think you crossed the line with a customer and had to make a fast escape, only none of you were counting on their ship having as much firepower as it did. Disassociator damage is easy to spot when you've seen what it can do to one of your own." Land took a quick step toward me, pinning me between himself and the galley's island. "I'm going to give you exactly one chance to tell me what's going on here, why you and your pals are in-system, and why a local bit player in the crime world fired a disassociator at you."

"I–I–I don't know what you mean," I stuttered, then the words poured out of my mouth like water. "We're from Alpha Centauri visiting Sol on vacation. Chuy has been here a few times and wanted to show us the planets, up close, personal, you know, really get the feel for the system of humanity's origin. We've made a few stops, Kilgore, Titan, Hogger's, but that's it. Those psychos hailed us claiming we stole something from them, but no matter what we said, we couldn't convince them otherwise. We would have been dead if you hadn't have come along, Tribune Land. That's the truth."

Land's eyes pierced through me. The muscles in his jaw flexed. "No, I don't believe you," he hissed through his clenched teeth. I thought for sure his mind was set on punching the truth out of me, and would have done so, only his helmet started to chime with an incoming transmission. We both froze, then looked down at the black helmet in confusion. How did a communique reach him with his signal jammers on? I slowly handed the helmet back to Land, then reached for my glass-comm. It still showed no signal – zero access.

Land gently tapped his ear. "Tribune Land," he said slowly, still unsure that whatever was happening was actually happening.

I wanted to wiggle my way out, but Land placed the hand clasping his helmet on the island, blocking my escape. He kept his black augmented eyes on me. They were unnerving, hollow, cold. It made me grateful for the flashes of color Rygar's augments had. A tense minute passed when finally, Land tapped his ear, then backed away from the island.

"Seems you have some connections, Gomez." He stood up straight and tugged at his spacesuit, nervously adjusting it. He placed his helmet under his arm and said, "Looks like my investigation has concluded. You and your friends are free to go."

"Th–that's it?" I asked.

Land's eyes narrowed. "Are you requesting interrogation?"

I snickered uncomfortably. "No, no, not at all. Thank you for your service, Tribune. Let me see you out." I followed him to the hatch and, without another word, Land placed his helmet on and entered the airlock. After the ship cycled the lock, Land's suit thrusters fired and returned him to his ship. Hooper, Leilani, and Lisette stared at me, mouths open.

"What the fuck?" Hooper asked. "What happened? Why'd he just leave?"

"I have no idea," I said as the familiar chime of renewed access to the relay network dinged from all four of our glass-comms. I pulled mine out of my pocket and went straight to my messages. One new one, from Rygar: *Stay safe*. I showed the message to Hooper.

"Your buddy back on Kilgore?" he asked. "Damn, how connected is that guy?"

"I honestly have no idea," I said.

"I think it's about time you get us out of here, Hooper," Lisette said.

"I think you're right," he agreed.

Back on the bridge, Hooper and Leilani jumped into their seats and began tapping away at their screens. I glanced to my right and saw the tribune's ship already out of range, probably burning hard toward his comrade to try and capture Janky.

Hooper growled in frustration. "The rudder is sluggish, and it looks like the blast damaged the motivators. I can get us out of here, but it isn't going to be as fast as we'd like."

"Yeah, I meant to tell you, Hoop," I said. "Lei and I might have to get down to engineering."

Hooper's head dropped. Leilani hopped up from her copilot's chair and pointed at Lisette. "Hop in. Johnny, with me."

Chapter Twenty

The damage to the ship looked manageable, just as Sever Land had assessed. The *Rosa*'s energy fields blocked off the hull breach and allowed Leilani and I to determine the damage without having to equip rebreathers or spacesuits. Nevertheless, Hooper roared with rage when he saw. "JAAAANNNKKYYYYYY!!!!!" Our comms squeaked, cracked, and popped. Both Leilani and I threw them out of our ears before his yelling caused permanent damage. The stabilizers were a different story. The blast from Janky's disassociator pulverized one of the horizontal stabilizers, or H-Stabs, as if whatever penetrated both the deflector shields and the hull lost its momentum when it struck the starboard stab. Its housing no longer existed. The hydraulics that hadn't been completely destroyed were in charred pieces. Loose wires sparked. Fluid puddled on the engineering room floor.

"Hoop, the starboard H-stab is gone," Leilani said as she put her earpiece back in. "We can divert all power to the remaining stabilizers, cap and seal off the damage, but other than that, it looks like we're limping our way to Luna."

"You two do what you can," Hooper said. "I'll start priming the compression thrusters to give us a little more stability."

Leilani and I worked straight through the rotation, with no breaks. When we finally could step away from engineering, the entire bay looked like a kid in the nurse's office after a playground brawl. Zip and cable ties grouped loose wires together. De-energized power couplings wore bright red warning caps. Patch-all strips held together all the broken pieces. Hoses were clamped and conduits sealed. Spill mats covered the floor, soaking up every drop of the *Mentirosa*'s lifeblood that finally stopped dripping. By the time we returned to the bridge, Mars was already behind us, and Hooper and Lisette had taken turns watching the scanners and catching some shut-eye.

"Good job, you two," Hooper said sleepily, with a mighty yawn and stretch. "I think Lisette wanted to have a team meeting once you were done. Unless you both want to rest a little."

Leilani looked to me, tired and weary. I pursed my lips and raised my eyebrows. "We're good," she responded to Hooper.

He shrugged. "Take a seat, I'll go wake her."

Lisette arrived on the bridge and, without even taking a breath, said, "Here's the problem. When we left Kilgore, our flight plan listed Luna as a destination, with our reason for visiting as recreation. When the *Mentirosa* enters their airspace, battered and bruised, the Luna Orbit Authority is going to want to know why. They're going to ask a lot of questions that we don't want to be answering, least of which is why we would risk a hard burn in system instead of using the starlane. They could very well call the tribunal, and I for one do not want another run-in with them."

"So, we didn't plan any contingencies?" I asked.

"We just need to get our story straight, then," Leilani said. "Again. For the billionth time."

Hooper chimed in. "It's not that simple. LOA will refuse us clearance and dispatch a scout ship to dock with us. Until we satisfy their curiosity, we're not going anywhere."

"They have long-range orbital whoppers," Leilani said with a grimace. She then mimicked an explosion with her hands, complete with vocalization, all in an attempt to upstage Hooper's earlier mime show. There was no denying they were cousins.

"So, then what's our move?" Lisette asked. I could hear the frustration mounting in her voice.

"I'm not sure," Hooper replied shortly.

"Well, we need to figure something out," Lisette said, crossing her arms.

"I know that, but I'm fresh out of ideas," Hooper responded hotly.

Lisette threw up her hands, "Oh that's a new one. Hooper is out of ideas. This whole fiasco has just been you running head first into a brick wall, sure as shit that you'd burst your way through."

Hooper's eyes narrowed. His jaw tightened. "Are you trying to blame what happened with Janky on me? If you haven't noticed, I'm the only one who lost anything in that little skirmish! The *Rosa* looks like a… a… beaten rat… or something."

"Still not hearing any ideas," Lisette said.

"Oh, I'm sorry," Hooper shouted. "I wasn't aware anybody else on this ship had a single decent idea to offer since Lei and I got caught up in all this shit!"

"Don't cop an attitude with me," Lisette shot back.

"I'm not 'copping attitude'," he mocked. "I'm letting you know that I have no idea how we're going to get down there without breaking a million laws and getting our ass blown to shit, and you're standing there perfectly content to criticize yet offer nothing in return."

"How about this for an alternative plan? If we don't get down there and sell this chit to my contact, we will also get blown to shit, so figure something out!"

"I think you both need to calm the fuck down," Leilani interjected.

"Don't tell me to calm down!" Hooper and Lisette shouted back in unison.

The arguing intensified as the tiny blue dot in the distance slowly grew larger and brighter. Lisette pointed a finger at Hooper and waved her hands around the ship. He defended the integrity of his baby and of his decision-making. Leilani restrained Lisette more than once, as she swung at Hooper after a colorful description of her character. I sat at the back of the bridge, next to the fish tank, rubbing my temples. The last time I witnessed such an exchange happened back on Luna, before I left for Kilgore. The last time. Memories flooded back, the kind you keep locked away out of fear or sadness, or both. I sighed and raised my head.

"I know how we can get to the surface," I said in a tone I was sure they wouldn't hear. Maybe it was out of a desire to not have to face my own demons. Yet, Leilani, ever present and aware of her surroundings, turned her head to me.

In the middle of another heated exchange, she shouted, louder than I have ever heard her speak, "Will you both shut the fuck up!"

Hooper stopped mid-slur, eyes wide and mouth agape. Lisette gasped. The echoes of their shouts slowly faded, and silence returned to the bridge for a brief minute. Once they regained their composure, Hooper taking his seat, Lisette taking a step back and leaning against the nav console, Leilani spoke once more.

"Thank fuck, because I was this close –" She raised two fingers only millimeters apart, – "from pulling my blades and ending both of you. Now, if you're done, Johnny has an idea."

Three faces turned my way. Three sets of eyes stared at me. I stayed seated, elbows on my knees, hands folded in front of my mouth. "I can get us to the surface. There's an old, decommissioned landing pad in a small dome to the east of Tranquility Dome."

Hooper shook his head. "We can't use a landing pad, especially one so near Tranquility. We'll be shot down for sure."

"This one is on private property," I said, hoping to assuage his fears. "Luna Orbit Authority doesn't monitor activity on private pads. They only care about what's entering and exiting public pads and docks. In fact, most of the time they simply log that a ship headed toward private pad A or B or whatever. They don't care where it goes once a ship has clearance."

"And you can get us clearance to this private pad?" Lisette asked.

I shrugged. "I think I can. At least I hope I can. Lei, can you adjust the ship's comm frequency? It'll need to be high, like an old-school radio signal or something similar. You'll have to keep your distance until then."

"Wow, that's some really old tech," Leilani said. "Do they still use VHF and UHF on Luna?"

"No, but…" I stopped to consider how to explain Slider. "It's hard to explain. But if we can get that signal to work, I can open an old line of communication and get us down there."

"I can adjust the settings," Leilani said, and immediately got to work. "Maybe bounce the signal to slow it down a bit."

"Whatever works," I said.

Hooper leaned back in his chair. "The *Mentirosa* can stay invisible until you say when. You want to tell us who owns this pad? I mean, are we going to have to explain or negotiate our way in?"

"I don't think so," I replied. "I mean, there's a chance they'll deny the request, but if they do accept, there won't be any explaining to do. This pad is… Well…" I sighed. "It's in a junkyard owned by my family."

No questions were asked about the state of my familial relations. Each member of our tiny crew knew. None of us had ever talked about our families.

"My tio and tia are two of three people I know on Luna. The other is my friend Alana, and the last time I saw her, she was working on becoming a captain in the Luna Police Force."

"Yeah, let's avoid calling on your friend Alana," Hooper stated.

Leilani joined me at the systems console and pulled up the communications array. It was a complicated combination of multiple systems working in tandem to provide the *Mentirosa* with unrestricted access to deep- and subspace communication. Hooper let me know the first rotation I was aboard that the comms array was one of the many illegal modifications he made to his baby. Leilani rotated and tweaked levels here and there. She had me refocus a lens and divert power from one system to another. Lisette paced back and forth while we fiddled with the comms. Hooper kept the ship in a holding pattern that made the *Mentirosa* look like an orbital barge waiting for a mothership to exit the starlane so it could transport cargo to the surface of Luna.

"Let's see if this works," Leilani said as she moved a virtual slide.

"What did you two do?" Lisette asked.

"We adjusted the comms array to a dirtier signal," I said. "Old waves that nobody uses anymore. But to do this we… Well…"

"Well what?" Lisette asked.

"We had to hijack Luna's satellite communications," Leilani said dryly, which garnered a laugh from Hooper.

"That's not funny, Hooper," Lisette said.

"It is, though," he replied. "We've already broken a billion other laws. Why not add hijacking sovereign communications arrays to broadcast a pirate signal?"

Lisette groaned. "Is it going to work at least? And are you going to get us caught?"

"It'll work," Leilani said.

"And theoretically we shouldn't get caught," I added. "Nobody operates on these signals any more, except for rusty automated cargo loaders and the suborbital skimmers trying to clear out all the debris around Terra."

"Then how does that help us?" Lisette asked.

I rotated in my chair. "I'm trying to contact one of those rusty old cargo loaders still active on Luna's surface."

"We got broadcast serials," Leilani stated.

I turned back around and began scrolling through the options until I found the one. "This one – LDR 80085-511D3r."

"Crazy that you remember the exact serial," Lisette said.
Hooper chuckled.

"I... Listen," I said, "I was thirteen or so when I registered it."

Hooper laughed again.

"What's so funny?"

"It reads 'boobs'," Leilani answered for me, shaking her head.

"Unbelievable," Lisette said, rubbing her temples with her right hand. "You two are so fucking mature. Truly."

"I. Was. Thirteen," I said, emphasizing each word.

Hooper's laugh turned to an uncontrollable giggle.

"You want to send a greeting?" Leilani asked.

"No, just hail the channel," I said. *Might as well get it over with*, I thought. A few moments later the *Rosa*'s comms crackled to life.

"Starship HV 007 Bravo, this is Papa Romeo 72598, come in."

Everyone looked at me. I opened my mouth to speak but froze. The voice belonged to my Tio Pablo. I was struck speechless. What do you say to someone you haven't spoken to in ten revs? My mind wrestled over that, and whether I should apologize immediately or wait until I saw him in person.

Lisette leaned in close. "Johnny?" she asked.

The comms opened again. "Starship HV 007 Bravo, please respond."

"Reading you loud and clear, Papa Romeo," Hooper said. "Just transporting a junked vessel salvaged out near Mars. Looking for a berth to do a few repairs before sale." He looked at me and shrugged. "We were told your yard dealt in salvaged ships."

The comms remained silent just long enough for my nerves to fray even further.

"Negative, this is a private yard. You'll have to find clearance elsewhere."

All eyes turned to me once again. I gritted my teeth.

"I don't think this... piece of junk can fly much farther," Hooper responded. His voice sounded pained. He shot me an angry look. I couldn't tell if it was because I wasn't speaking or because he just had to call his ship a piece of junk.

"There are a couple of other salvage yards on Luna, public, willing to work with just about anyone. I can forward you the coordinates."

Lisette leaned in close again. "Johnny, you have got to step up. Things are going to be even more difficult if we're forced to land via public routes."

I took a deep breath and stood to my feet, walking to the helm.

"Starship HV 007 Bravo, do you copy?" Tio Pablo said.

My mind reeled violently, angry that I chose to speak instead of remaining silent. "You once told me it is the kindness of strangers that brings hope to a hopeless world. We're seeking that kindness now."

The comms remained silent, as did the bridge. Nobody moved until Hooper's console flashed with a clearance code and landing coordinates.

"Comm channel closed," Leilani announced.

"No matter, that little line seemed to do it," Hooper said, looking over his shoulder at me. "I thought for a second there you were going to choke on me."

"I did, too."

Chapter Twenty-one

We entered Luna's airspace. I stood between Hooper and Leilani, surveying the dusty surface with equal parts disappointment and disgust. Not much had changed in ten revs. The "Big Domes," as they were called, still catered to the financial elites. Terraforming turned the surface beneath their enclosures into lush gardens complete with rivers and lakes. Extravagant skyscrapers pierced into the sky, some even towering past the dome enclosures to provide their occupants with areas free of artificial gravity. The only one of the four Big Domes to not look like a playboy's playplace was Tranquility Dome, which was only saved thanks to its historical status. The four Big Domes connected via tram to the smaller, timeworn domes, those constructed of actual materials instead of energy fields. The lower-class population of Luna filled these domes. Blue-collar workers and government employees lived in cramped cubical domiciles stacked on top of each other and crammed as close as possible to save what little space there was to be had. Those fortunate enough to have larger properties came from old families – those who first left Terra, once known as Earth, to populate its moon. However, even those families lived like paupers compared to the ones living in the big four.

My tia, Maritza, came from one such family. Her ancestors left Terra ages ago and set up shop in Tran Dome, just northeast of Tranquility Dome. They were builders – engineers who specialized in civic and urban planning. They were part of the original teams to build the domes. For their work and sacrifice, they were each gifted a plot of land. That's how my family ended up on Luna.

Gradually the wealth left. Generation after generation sold off parcels of land to the government just to survive. Then the Xin arrived and destroyed Earth – or what was left of it, the little bit of the planet left habitable after humanity fucked it with its greed and disregard. They claimed their assault was in the best interest of the planet, that they had the technology to return it to its former glory. Only, they never counted on RUSH intervening in the conflict. Sol, after all, barely had in-system travel. After the defeat of the Xin and the almost complete annihilation of Terra, Luna bore the brunt of refugees and its citizens suffered the indignity of eminent domain, losing the very land they worked so hard to acquire, until all that was left of the private plots were properties like Tio Pablo and Tia Maritza's junkyard.

Hooper piloted the *Mentirosa* over Tranquility Dome. I stared at the cathedral and the now – once again – dry lake, and tried to keep unwelcome memories at bay. I would be back there soon enough, climbing those steps with new and different fears and uncertainties than I had when I was young.

Tran Dome more closely resembled the original state of the Moon than any other dome. Terraforming initiatives had been sparse throughout its history, and thus the surface remained covered in ashen dust and rocks. Single-family homes sprung up sparsely through the dome, most of which neighbored scrapyards, garbage heaps, and retrofit depots. People moved here and there via EM cell-powered continuous track vehicles or quadrupeds, as electromagnetic repulse technology stirred up too much dust. Regardless, the dome still maintained a seemingly hazy atmosphere that the recirculators never could entirely clear.

We arrived at the dome. Another ship was clearing the airlock, which garnered a snicker from Hooper. "Airlocks. That's wild."

"It's an old dome," I said.

"One of the oldest on Luna," Lisette added.

After clearing the airlocks, Hooper slowly directed the *Mentirosa* to my tio and tia's landing pad. Nostalgia hit me hard as I laid eyes on the property. We approached from the scrapyard. Neatly stacked towers of crushed metal sat in a well-organized grid. The shells of several salvaged starcraft lay in a tidy row just beyond. The roof of the barn peeked above the stacks. My eyes followed the beaten trail from the yard entrance to my tio and tia's house. The rectangular alloy longhouse looked more like a barracks than a home. Maybe it was because tia always kept it painted white. I noticed my tio and tia standing near the energy fence that surrounded the property. My tia's body language screamed of annoyance and discomfort laced with anger. She stormed off before the *Rosa* completed the landing sequence. I hoped nobody noticed, but the averted eyes said otherwise.

"Are you sure this is OK?" Lisette asked me as we prepared to disembark.

"Honestly, no, but we're here," I answered. "The worst they can say is we have to leave."

As I watched Tio Pablo approach, I took the deepest breath I had ever taken, attempting to calm my torment. What would he say? Would he turn me and my friends away, tell us to get the hell out of there? Of course not. My tio and tia didn't swear. But surely he'd ask us to go, say we weren't welcome.

My feet touched the spongy surface of the landing pad right as Tio Pablo crossed the fading paint circle that outlined the pad. He still wore the same old tan fedora that never left his head. His face looked fuller, along with the rest of his new plumpness that made his guayabera and linen pants appear snug. He also wore glasses now. They thankfully didn't hide his compassion-filled eyes. I was at a complete loss for words when we both stopped, less than an arm's length between us. I opened my mouth to speak, but Tio Pablo pulled me into an embrace before anyone else could move or say a single word.

"Gracias a Dios, thank you, God, you've come home!" he said with infectious joy. "It's been too long, Juanito."

"Too long, Tio," I said, practically melting into his arms.

"No matter, you're back now. And you've brought friends. Bienvenidos y bendiciones a todos, welcome and blessings to you all!" he said as we made way for Hooper, Leilani, and Lisette to disembark. I introduced everyone. My tio greeted them all with warm hugs. "So, what brings you back, mijo? It looks like your ship was damaged," he said as we walked around the *Mentirosa*.

"Yeah, not sure what hit us," Hooper said, adjusting his hat.

"Looks like disassociater damage to me," Tio Pablo said.

Hooper tried to look shocked. "How do you know that?"

Tio Pablo gestured with both hands, surveying all around him, and asked, "Have you seen where you landed?"

"Fair enough," Hooper said.

"We'll need to see about repairing the damage and... Well... we have some other business we need to attend to," I said, trying my best not to sound unnecessarily clandestine.

Tio Pablo raised his hands. "No need for the secrecy, Juanito. Your business is your own. You're in luck, too. I just bought a salvaged Junpoor sloop just like this one a few weeks back. Haven't had time to start on it yet as my assistant is dragging its feet with our last project."

"You hired people?" I asked in shock.

"Not me – your tia. She swears I need help. Says I'm too old to be working alone."

"She's right," I teased. "Speaking of Tia, she didn't look so happy."

Tio Pablo frowned. "You saw that, huh?"

"We all did," I said.

"Maybe you should go see Slider first, give your tia some time to cool down," Tio Pablo said. "He'll be happy you're back."

"I'm glad you never got rid of him," I said, a smile threatening to creep across my face.

Pablo smirked. "No, mijo. He's a good worker. Once you left, I needed someone to help. Slider proved to be more useful than I imagined. You trained him well."

"Thanks, Tio," I said graciously.

"In the meantime, which of you would care to join me? We can take a look at that junked sloop and see what we can use to fix your ship."

"Lead the way!" Hooper proclaimed.

Leilani raised a hand.

"Oh, and mijo," Tio Pablo called back as he led Hooper and Leilani into the yard. "Don't take what your tia said to heart. She was upset when you left, but she loves you. This I know."

"OK, Tio," I said, and waved goodbye.

"Your uncle seems nice," Lisette said as she neared my side. "A lot nicer than your aunt."

"He was always the voice of reason when I was growing up," I said. "Tia Maritza's parenting style was more… hands-on, whereas Tio Pablo was always more forgiving."

"Was that hard?" she asked.

"What do you mean?" I asked.

Lisette stumbled over her words. "How did…? I mean, how long have they…? What I'm trying to say is…"

I remained silent and continued to walk until Lisette grabbed my hand and forced me to stop.

"I'm sorry if it's a sensitive subject."

I took a deep breath before saying, "My parents died during a salvage run to Earth. Their shuttle lost power on descent after an impact."

"I'm so sorry, Johnny," Lisette replied. "How old were you?"

"I just turned eight," I said.

Without saying more, I continued to follow the path between stacks until it led to a wide-open crossroads. Stacks of crushed metal cubes stood several stories high, piled like pyramids. I felt a joyous nostalgia wash over me as I surveyed the scene. The last time I set foot in Tio Pablo's junkyard, this area was no more than a heap of broken spaceship parts. It appeared he was correct: Slider was an efficient worker when I wasn't around to distract him.

I pulled my glass-comm from my pocket and tapped the screen a few times until it sent the heel signal to Slider. Moments later, the ground began to tremble. The air in the field surrounding the junkyard shifted and a powerful gust of wind pelted Lisette and me. She took a step back and grabbed my shoulder to regain her balance. I turned my head and smiled to reassure her. There came another boom and then, with a mechanical whir and a hollow roar, a four-legged automated monster leapt over a stack of crushed shuttles and landed before us. I waved away the cloud of dust from the impact and realized I was happier than I had been in revs.

"Hey, boy!" I yelled. Slider whirred and roared in response.

"Th–that's Slider?" Lisette asked, horrified.

"That's my boy!"

She moved behind me. "That's not a dog, Johnny, that's a box-loader."

"No way!" I feigned astonishment. "I know he's a box-loader, but look at him!" Slider, a recommissioned heavy-duty, off-road fork-lift, was once used to transfer enormous shipping containers from transporters to the stacks at the docks. He sat back on a series of rough steel and unfinished space alloy beams that served as his back legs, complete with hydraulic and pneumatic pumps and loudly grinding gears. His plated torso both hid and protected all his vital components, including the computer that held his AI brain and all his fuel reservoirs. Slider's front legs, like his hind ones in build but equipped with three claw-like fingers per paw for grasping, held up his considerable heft. His face doubled as his loader forks and a tiny cockpit, complete with two high-intensity lamps that appeared as eyes. "He's adorable and *such a good boy*!"

Slider stomped his front paws in excitement. He raised his head to the sky and a hollow, mechanical howl echoed from his frame.

"Why do you own a box-loader that acts like a dog?" Lisette asked as she slowly emerged from behind me.

"Tio Pablo owned a broken-down box-loader for as long as I can remember. When I started living here, I would spend all my time alone in the cockpit. I remember having a vivid dream about a box-loader that acted like a dog. Remember, my propensity for dreams that felt like holofilms? Yeah, Slider was one of the first instances. Anyway, I told Tia Maritza about it, but she told me to stop with such nonsense.

"Shortly after that, Tio Pablo convinced me to help him rebuild the loader. We spent all of our free time for two or three revs welding on new supports, installing new hydraulics, repairing wiring, up-fitting the cockpit... We turned a broken heap of metal into a working box-loader.

"On my thirteenth birthday, Tio Pablo took me into the junkyard and gave me a small, wrapped present. Inside was an AI digi-brain."

"That's quite an expensive gift," Lisette said, taking another step closer to me and Slider.

"I can't even imagine how much it cost him," I said. "Regardless, we spent the next several rotations watching tutorials on how to program it. I decided I wanted a dog, and Tio Pablo agreed so long as I could teach it to help around the yard. It took me about six weeks of fiddling until finally it passed for a legitimate canine. The AI core learned quickly after that, and was able to integrate a box-loader program into the dog functions it already learned. Hence, the majestic creature that sits before you." I raised my hands, presenting Slider to Lisette. Slider stood up, hind parts swaying excitedly even for lack of a tail.

"That's impressive work for a young kid," Lisette said, shaking her head and appearing genuinely impressed.

"Thank you," I replied. "He understands commands, like any well-trained dog."

Lisette squinted at me. "Like, sit?"

Slider took a seat. We were both delighted.

"He can do more than that," I said. "Check this out. Slider, lay down."

Slider's metal frame whistled and moaned into a prone position. Once settled, he cocked his head to the side.

"Slider, roll over," I commanded.

Slider's hydraulics and gears whirred to life. His legs retracted close to his torso with a mighty churning groan, and the box-loader's body rolled until his legs once again touched solid ground, returning him to his prone position. The trick spun up clouds of dust and rumbled the ground beneath my feet.

Lisette lit up. "OK, OK, color me impressed."

"Let me show you one more," I said, and walked toward the laying machine. "Hey, Slider, go get your ball."

Slider got to his feet in a flurry of bangs, clangs and whistles. He stomped around in a circle, knocking me off my feet, then immediately leapt over a pile of crushed shuttles and stormed off deeper within the junkyard, leaving me in the dust. Lisette hurried to my side and knelt.

"Are you OK?" she asked. Her voice sounded less concerned for my physical well-being and more concerned with my mental state.

"I'm surprisingly great," I declared. "I didn't realize how much I missed all this."

She took a seat next to me in the dirt. "You left under different circumstances, bad times, or tougher times. It's OK to have changed. People grow. Sometimes they outgrow their environment and need a bigger one to continue that growth." She grew silent, downtrodden. Her shoulders slumped and her head dropped low between her shoulders. She turned her head away before continuing. "It must be nice to have something you can always run home to."

The elation faded from my face. I looked to Lisette and noticed her wipe a lone tear from her cheek.

"You're very fortunate, Johnny," she said through sniffles.

I leaned forward and crossed my legs. "Family isn't always people you're related to or have blood ties with. A lot of families are those you trust, the ones you know will always have your back, no matter what. Yes, Tio Pablo and Tia Martiza are my blood relatives, but I consider Rygar as much a member of my family as them." I took a breath, contemplating if I should say what was on my mind. "I… kind of feel that way about Hooper… and Lei… and you."

Lisette's shoulders relaxed. She took a deep breath and exhaled slowly, puffing out her cheeks.

"The same is true for your home." I spoke again, feeling compelled to continue. "It's not always a physical building or a place dotting a map on a planet or moon, or even a space station. It can be a Junpoor sloop, or even simply the presence of those you love. That's home. This." I waved my hand around the junkyard. "Is all just a place. This." I motioned between her and myself and the nearing vibrations of a returning box-loader dog. "Is home."

Lisette sniffled and let out a sigh of relief. "Thank you, Johnny."

"You're welcome, Lisette," I said just as Slider rumbled and slid to a stop before us.

"I see why you named it Slider," she said before immediately becoming subdued. "You know I had a dog once, revs ago."

"Oh yeah?" I asked. "Was it a real dog, or was it like Slider here?"

She rolled her eyes. "No, Sinbad was a real flesh-and-blood canine. He came directly from Terra. I don't know if you're familiar with Terran dog breeds, but he was a Shiba Inu and the most adorable pup I had ever laid eyes on."

"Save for Slider, of course?"

"Oh, of course."

Slider mimicked a bark.

"Sinbad loved to play fetch. He had this goofy little dance he would do every time he would bring back the ball."

"What happened to Sinbad?"

Lisette sighed. I could see that same sadness begin to wash over her eyes. "I... I don't know."

Slider dropped a large, gyrating metal sphere, about the size of my torso, at my feet. I grabbed it with both hands and stood, then motioned to Lisette. "Follow me."

We walked around several towering stacks of crushed and cubed metal, past an energy-stanchioned area full of barrels marked with numerous symbols denoting their toxicity or acidity, and through an old-fashioned chained and locked gate to a clearing just outside the junkyard. The ozonized field surrounding my tio's property continued to stretch out several hundred yards to just beyond a tall energy fence.

An old, weathered contraption sat not far from the gate. It resembled a giant ballista, made of corrugated steel and scrap space alloy. Springs and chains rested behind a metal saucer with its back end tipped forward, creating a cradle for Slider's ball.

I turned to Lisette and raised my eyebrows. "Check this out." I put the ball in its place. This caused Slider to jump around ecstatically. I then moved to a crank and pulled at the levers, compressing the spring and readying the contraption to fire.

"Did you build this?" Lisette asked.

"Well, Tio Pablo and I did."

"You have a knack for fabrication, Johnny," she said. "You ever consider going into that field?"

I shrugged. "Yeah, I'm OK at it. Most of the complex parts were done by Tio. He's the real expert. I did what I could, but it was more out of necessity than joy. This piece, though… This piece gave me a little joy."

I held my hand up to Slider, who turned and faced the open field. He poised himself to shoot forward, like a runner at a starting block. I held for just a moment, to test his patience. Once satisfied, I yelled *"Fetch!"* and slammed my foot on the release. The latch left the spring, which violently released and rocketed the cradle up the slide. The two forearms absorbed the force of the cradle, and Slider's ball shot out with a terrible thumping shock wave. In an instant, Slider charged after the ball, leaving a cloud of dust for Lisette and I to cough on and wave away from our faces.

We watched in silence as the distant shape of Slider pounced on the bouncing, careening ball, which slipped from his grasp and rolled away. He then slid into it, pinning the metal sphere against the energy fence, picked it up in his box-loader forks, and began trotting triumphantly back to the ballista.

"You want to give it a go next?" I asked Lisette.

She smiled widely. "I'd love to."

Chapter Twenty-two

Lisette and I returned to the house shortly before sunset. The temperatures on Luna still plummeted on the dark side, regardless of the thermal regulators within any given field. Slider accompanied us and, despite my commands, refused to stay in the junkyard, choosing instead to sit quietly just beyond the fence that bordered Tio Pablo and Tia Maritza's house. We entered the gate and I immediately felt anxious about being around my tia without my tio present, but figured he'd return soon with Hooper and Leilani in tow. Yet, almost as if she could feel my anxiety, Tia Maritza made no effort to spare me from it. She sat on the back patio, glass-comm in hand, scrolling through the day's news stories.

Nothing had changed about my tia. She still looked young and fit, save for the big streak of white hair that grew from her predominately dark bangs and the hint of wrinkles around her bronze-colored eyes. My mom always said her family's blood was strong, and looking at my tia was proof of that. There was no denying they were sisters. I could see my mom in my tia's face, hear my mom in her voice. It made my relationship with Tia Maritza that much harder.

"You know that thing isn't allowed so close to the house, Juanito," she chided from her rocking chair.

I looked at Lisette and grimaced. Lisette mouthed *Juanito*. "He's outside the fence, Tia. He knows better," I said, to which she hmphed unsatisfactorily.

"Pablo should have sold that thing the day you abandoned us," my tia muttered under her breath. "Send it back to the barn, Juanito."

I swallowed hard and said, "You heard her, boy. Back to your kennel." Slider's head dropped and he echoed a whimper of disappointment, but obeyed, nonetheless. After he had gone, I looked to Lisette, raised my eyebrows, and pursed my lips. I couldn't decide whether to put my hands in my pockets or fold them on my chest, so I did one, then the other, then back to the first.

"This is quite a chunk of land you have here, Ms Maritza," Lisette said.

"You can call me Señora Gonzalez," my tia said without looking.

"Tia," I muttered in embarrassment.

"What, Juanito? It's my name."

"Yeah, Tia, I know, but that's... I mean, the ladies at church call you that. This is my friend."

"The ladies at church show me respect, and your... *friend* should, too," she said, pausing to look Lisette up and down.

"It's fine, Johnny," Lisette said. "And I'm sorry, Señora Gonzalez." Tia hmphed. "It almost looks like you own half the dome."

"It's a patch of dirt left to me by my father, and his father before him going back several generations. Nothing more."

"Well, you do have a lot of space."

"Not as much as we used to."

"I would have loved having this much space to explore when I was a kid."

"They don't have open fields of dirt on Junpoor? Isn't that where your people relocated to?" my tia asked. I cringed, but Lisette took it in stride.

"Oh, I'm not from Junpoor," she answered. "I mean, I was born there, as was my father, but we moved here to Luna when I was a kid. Grew up just a few domes down."

"A few domes down, you say?" Tia Maritza asked. "Arris? Geno? Proto?" I could tell by her tone she was preloading her judgement cannon and aiming it right at Lisette. My tia hated the bourgeoisie, new money families that lived in the big four. Luckily, I knew Lisette grew up in Tranquility Dome because that's where the conservatory lay. Tia would be OK with that, since Tranquility also had the cathedral. Yet before Lisette could answer, Tia stood up from her chair. "Here comes your tio and your other two friends," she said to me, then leaned toward Lisette. "Looks like you were saved an interrogation." Lisette shuffled uncomfortably.

"Mi amor," Tio said as he planted a kiss on Tia Maritza's cheek. "My love, are you going to invite Johnny and his friends in for dinner?"

Tia Maritza grimaced. "I suppose I can't let them starve, can I?" Tio laughed as she entered the house.

"What's the word on the *Mentirosa*?" I asked Hooper.

Hooper gave me two thumbs-up. "Turns out the disassociator damage is easier to repair than I thought."

"Your friend here was worried I wouldn't know what to do or how to perform a decent patch," Tio Pablo said with a wink and a slap of Hooper's shoulder. Tio walked inside, but I motioned for the gang to wait a moment.

"That's good news," I said. "We can't be wasting time here. The longer we stay, the more we put them at risk. Janky could be right behind us. Or worse."

"We're all on the same page there," Lisette said for the group.

Nothing had changed inside the house. It looked exactly as it did all those revs ago when I first left. Old, budget-conscious furniture sacrificed comfort for longevity. Tio's repurposed and upcycled appliances inhabited every outlet in the place. The composite graft flooring still lacked the shine Tia worked endlessly to achieve. Hidden sconces threw intermittently flickering light throughout the house, each flash changing the color of the LEDs from soft white to cool white and occasionally copper. Glitchy bots sparked and squeaked as they roamed the floor, cleaning up the never-ending supply of dust that blew in from outside. A few viewscreens hung sporadically throughout the house, all of them in their power-saver state, displaying old pictures Tia had painstakingly uploaded, one by one, to the house network. I saw my tia and tio posing in front of the house, followed by me and tio covered head to toe in blue bender lubricant. The third picture showed me and my parents standing in front of my papi's old junker. My throat constricted. I felt like all the life had been instantaneously sucked out of me. All I could do was quickly turn away. I stopped and scanned the entire place. Each wall filled me with sadness, longing for warm memories of a home that no longer existed for me.

Tio Pablo led us into the kitchen. Processors whirred, cooking radiators hummed, and Tia moved back and forth between them all, stirring, sniffing, and seasoning. The insta-cook Tio and I had spent an entire salvage on still sat on the counter, covered in its factory stickers, power cord bundled tightly against the frame. "Cooking is supposed to be science and art combined. You can't make art with some machine that simply does all the creative parts itself," she said after opening it. She mistrusted it so severely that when my sixteen-year-old self attempted to use it a few rotations later, she pulled the entire thing off the counter and deposited it into the salvage pile just outside the back door. Tio Pablo retrieved it later that day and none of us ever talked about it again.

The kitchen table was already set and a few serving dishes full of steaming hot food filled the room with mouth-watering aromas. Tia described her cooking style as old world. It did rely heavily on traditional Latin American cooking that had been passed down through the generations, but merged with more recent cooking developments native to Terra's moon, which required a bit more creativity when it came to now rare ingredients.

I took a seat next to Lisette. Hooper and Leilani sat across from us. Tio Pablo walked behind Tia, kissed her on the cheek, and offered up his empty hands. Tia placed another dish and shooed him to the table. Once we were all seated, Tia said grace, praying in her most fervently Catholic manner that lasted a good three minutes. I hazarded a glance at Hooper. He raised his eyebrows in amusement, but immediately lowered his head. Lisette elbowed me.

As usual, Tio Pablo monopolized the conversation at the dinner table while Tia kept silent, focusing on her food, and stealing cautious glances at her guests. "Tell me about growing up starbound?" he asked Hooper and Leilani.

Hooper stuffed a spoonful of rice in his mouth, moaned both out of joy for the food and at the possibility of telling a story. "We're both from the Shahkti Flotilla," he began after swallowing his food, "born and raised in space. My mother says we were just outside Alpha Centauri when we were born." Leilani raised a spoon in solidarity. "Do you know much about the flotilla?"

Tio replied, "Only what the salvagers have told me." He leaned forward. "And I take everything they say with a grain of salt."

"Probably a good thing, Tio," I said.

"You'd be surprised how much they get right," Hooper said through a mouth full of rice. His cheeks made him look like a hamster. "The flotillas are basically salvagers themselves."

"So, is it true your people cannot set foot planet-side until your thirteenth birthday?" Tio asked.

"That one is true," Hooper replied. "Lei and I had our first excursion together. We're cousins, born on the same day."

"I'm older by seventeen minutes," Leilani said and quickly returned to her food.

Hooper served himself another plate full of food. "Traditionally, our clans claim whatever their first planet is as their adopted home of sorts. So, in those rare cases when we're asked where we're from and Shahkti Flotilla is an unacceptable answer, we both claim Hogan V as our home."

"When would that be unacceptable?" I asked.

"You'd be surprised," Hooper said as he slid an entire empanada into his mouth. His face lit up and he moaned in delight. It made Tia grimace.

"I bet you picked up so many stories living on the flotilla," Tio said.

"Have you ever heard the one about the Three Hundredth Chef?" Hooper asked, which garnered outrage from Leilani and Lisette. He crossed his knife and fork in front of him for protection.

"Is it a bad story?" Tio asked, confused.

"No, he just tells it all the time," Lisette said.

"Maybe if you get some alone time with Hooper, he can share it," I explained to my tio.

Tio Pablo regaled the gang with hilarious stories of my childhood, growing up on Luna. Each one poked fun at the protagonist – me – but they were told in good spirits. I knew my tio wasn't ridiculing me. Tia Maritza, however, wasted no time pointing out the lies and embellishments in my tio's stories. Dinner wrapped up shortly after that. Hooper filled one more plate and smiled ear to ear as he remained seated, stuffing his face. Tia left the clean-up for Tio and me, but we enlisted the help of Leilani and Lisette. The kitchen was clean in no time at all, even before Hooper finished his mound of food that made up his fourth helping.

Tia retired to her office with a book and Tio went about setting up sleeping bags. "It's OK, Tio, we can sleep on the ship."

"Are you sure, mijo?" he asked.

"Yeah, it'll be easier on everybody. We all have beds there. No need to share space or to have all of us trying to use your shower. Pretty sure water prices haven't improved since I left." I pointed to the ceiling and the strained moan that came from above. The vapor collector sounded ill, like one of the incinerators on Kilgore. "I can take a look at that."

Tio frowned and waved a hand at me. "No, it's fine. Just old. It's been making that noise for a while now." He knelt and picked up a sleeping bag. "Are you sure?"

"Yes, Tio, I'm positive."

"OK, Juanito. I'll be sure to come get you four for breakfast in the morning."

Hooper and Leilani went on ahead while Lisette waited for me by the back gate leading to the junkyard. She stood, arms folded across her chest, tapping her glass-comm against her side and pacing nervously. I gave her a weak wave. "What's up? You look–"

"Nervous?" she interjected. "Scared? Anxious? Yes, yes, and yes."

"What's the matter?" I asked.

"They haven't responded," Lisette said, despondent. "They never take this long to respond and yet here we are." She waved her glass-comm at me. "Staring at a comm message showing sent, delivered, and read with no fucking response."

I grabbed her hand to stop the glass-comm from shaking and saw the message. "Maybe whoever is on the other side is busy?"

She scoffed. "Johnny, these guys, all of them – Black Sun, Hongxongdi, the Obinna Syndicate – none of them are too busy to be the first to the punch. They all want this chit. They've all tried to kill us or steal it from us, and now they're all playing coy? Suddenly they're not interested in buying it? We are at their doorstep, the lights are on, there's a party going on inside, and nobody can hear the bell ringing. It doesn't make sense and it's making me nervous. It should make you nervous, too. And Hooper, the cavalier bastard."

"Let me guess... He said something like, 'Oh we're fine, don't worry about it'?" She nodded. I took a deep breath. "And they don't usually take this long to respond?" She shook her head. "Well, maybe let's throw up some perimeter sensors and keep the scanners on wide while we sleep tonight."

"You plan on sleeping?" Lisette asked.

"If I learned anything from all the holos I had to watch during my time at university, it's that lack of sleep is how they get you," I said, opening the gate to the junkyard. "You make poor decisions when you're tired. Plus, I still haven't slept since before Hogger's."

Lisette sighed. "I may just take a stim and keep an eye on the comms."

"We can do it in shifts."

Chapter Twenty-three

Once the four of us were back inside the *Mentirosa*, Hooper wasted no time flopping on his bed and falling fast asleep. His bulging stomach rose and fell with his comically trumpeting snores. I hurriedly sealed and soundproofed his quarters before we all went insane. I honestly tried to sleep, but found my mind refused to let me. It delighted in showing me all the horrible possibilities that awaited me in the morning. When I finally gave up on it, I was more than surprised to find Lisette and Leilani had also given up on sleep. They both seemed as exhausted as Hooper. And I figured I had a monopoly on insomnia.

Leilani prepped the ship for the work to be done in the morning. She used a digital marker to quarantine the damaged areas and to create a 'no-work' zone in the engine room, to avoid any unintentional additions or modifications during the repair. She then went about clipping wires, capping and sealing conduits, and bypassing the ship's systems. Most of the work required a hands-on approach. But by the end, she sat in the chair with her feet at the engineering bay access point, tapping her glass-comm and swiping away messages on the viewscreen. The last I saw of her, her head drooped dangerously low to her chest.

Lisette went directly to the auto-doc and received her stim injection. When the door whooshed open a moment later, I barely saw her fly past me, up the ladder to the bridge. I found her seated at the comms terminal, swiping furiously on her glass-comm. The look she gave me when I reached the bridge made me second-guess my climb. I wanted to reassure her, but instead, I raised my hand, and descended the ladder.

I returned to the galley, took a seat in the booth, and pulled the chit from my coverall pocket. The slide felt thin and fragile in my hand. It made me grin, the way the lights of the *Mentirosa* refracted off it as I spun it between my thumb and forefinger, throwing rainbows on the bulkheads. Removable storage devices were old tech, even by historical standards. Nobody stored or moved data by such ancient, analog means. Most modern glass communicators didn't have ports. Digi-brains and public network nodes had not had peripheral support in generations. Even ships like the *Mentirosa* required direct, onboard system access if it couldn't connect to the Universal Subspace Data Net, or USDN. Everybody knew if it wasn't on the USDN, it didn't exist. Yet, someone decided these three *Lost Worlds* skins were too valuable to store digitally – that the untold number of firewalls and data encryption servers weren't good enough. They needed to be removed entirely from the network, erased from every mainframe across the galaxy. And somehow, that data chit ended up in my hands. I bet they weren't counting on some no-name space broom finding it while cleaning.

I grew tired as I stared at the chit with an embarrassing amount of love and affection. It didn't make sense. The little bastard had caused me so much pain, brought about so much upheaval, I should be furious at it. But it also introduced me to Hooper, Leilani, and Lisette. It got me off Kilgore and on an amazing starcraft. It took me places I never dreamed I'd go. Because of that, I wanted nothing more than to keep it safe, to hold it tightly in my palm until the moment my account exploded with millions of unexpected credits.

Thirty-seven and a half million credits, I thought to myself as I rotated the chit between my index finger and thumb. I could do whatever I wanted with that kind of scratch! I could move to Hepari and re-enroll at university, finish my holocine program and finance my own production. I could buy a place on Pilgrim's Folly, near the tide pools, and blow the rest of it on exotic food, drink, and sex. Or maybe I could finally make good on my dream of seeing the galaxy – buy a used ship and set out across the stars. Before I knew it, I had drifted to sleep with visions of sailing dancing in my head.

Morning came earlier than I wanted. My body, unhappy at the minimal amount of sleep I gave it, complained with achy muscles, heavy eyelids, and a slight headache. I rose from my uncomfortable position in the booth and stretched. I patted my pockets, searching for the chit, and nearly panicked before I noticed it laying on the tabletop. Slightly flustered and momentarily embarrassed by my panic, I grabbed both my glass-comm and the chit and stuffed them into my pockets. It was then I realized Lisette never woke me for my shift. I hurried to the bridge and found her exactly where I left her the night before.

"Any word?" I asked.

Lisette quickly raised her head from the glass-comm and stared back at me. Her eyes blazed with the unnatural light of a stim injection. The chems continued to course through her veins. "No, nothing yet." The words spewed forth from her mouth like the breaking of a dam.

"You didn't wake me," I said.

"I ended up not needing too," she replied. Her face lit up. "I've never had so much energy, so much focus."

I exhaled through my nose in amusement. "Yeah, that's the stim."

"Now I know why long-haulers take the stuff."

"Just be careful. It may be engineered to reduce chemical dependence, but the mind works differently. It doesn't do well with the perceived lack of control from the comedown."

"How do you know?" Lisette asked.

"A birthday party a few revs back," I said, avoiding her gaze and staring at the fish tank. "Rygar thought it would be a good idea, make it so we could party for as long as we wanted." When I looked back at her, she had already returned her eyes to her glass-comm, swiping and tapping away. "Tio Pablo said he'd have breakfast for us this morning. You want to take a break and come eat?" She shook her head.

I met Hooper and Leilani at the end of the boarding ramp. The dark rings around Leilani's eyes provided evidence of an equally restless night as mine. She looked me up and down as I approached, investigating whether I looked any better than she felt. Hooper, however, appeared not only rested but rejuvenated. He hopped around, strafing in a circle, boxing the air. His hat sat high on his head and his oil pen dangled precariously from his lips.

"Morning, Johnny!" he said as my feet hit the dirt. He stopped boxing and waved, but inhaled sharply when he saw the exhaustion on my face. "You look as bad as Lei." Leilani gestured vulgarly at him. "Even Lisette looks haggard, and I think she's all hopped up on stims." He whispered the last part.

"Not surprisingly, you're the only one who got any rest," I said as I led us to the house.

"I had a wonderful dream," Hooper recalled. "I played the horn in Ico Parielle's band. Then two of the most beautiful Jadzian males appeared with jetpacks on. They held me by the waist and flew me up into the atmosphere. My horn began to throw actual physical notes down on the crowd. When they reached the surface, each note would explode in a shower of colorful streamers and confetti. It was incredible."

"I'm not going to lie, Hooper, that does sound incredible," I said as we reached the gate.

"And then the Jadzians gave me the most amazing blow job..."

"There it is," Leilani groaned.

"Please don't talk about blow jobs from Jadzians or any other alien species while we're at breakfast," I said.

A chorus of clanging pots and pans and off-key singing to upbeat music greeted us as we entered the kitchen. Tio Pablo stood in front of the range, whipping up an enormous breakfast he simply called gravy. He sang along to a song I had heard him sing a hundred times before about our ancestral home of Puerto Rico.

"Morning, Tio," I said as we entered.

"Hey, Juanito, I was just about to ping you," he said, calling me to his side. "Breakfast is ready, come help yourselves!"

"Where's Tia?" I asked.

Tio handed me a plate. "She had to run some errands and got an early start, said she was going to the market, but she went yesterday before you arrived. I don't know, mijo, sometimes I don't ask questions. It's easier that way."

"I think we both know why she left," I responded.

"Ah, nonsense. Your tia has her reasons for everything she does. I'm sure she just forgot something yesterday."

I gave my tio a look. We both knew how much of a lie that was, about how improbable it was for her to forget something.

Breakfast quickly became a repeat of dinner. Tio Pablo asked about Lisette, then turned his questioning to Hooper. After Leilani finished eating, Tio Pablo convinced Hooper to tell him the story of the Three Hundredth Chef, much to Leilani's chagrin, who promptly left the house in favor of starting on the *Mentirosa*. Tio was rolling at each turn of the story, which made Hooper more and more animated. It amused me to watch the two of them.

No sooner had Hooper finished than the back door opened and Lisette came storming into the kitchen. "The meet is set. Our Lady of Tranquility. Midday."

We all stared at her in silence. Tio Pablo tapped on the table's virtual control deck and lowered the volume of the music. "You're all... planning to go to church?" he asked. "There's no Mass today."

"No, Tio, we're not trying to go to Mass. We just... have to meet someone there. It's kind of why we're here." I hated lying to him, not giving him the whole truth. My tio deserved better than that.

"Well, it's a good thing your tia isn't here. If she knew you were going to the church, she'd have you light candles."

"That's one way to look at it," I said. "But wait... Lisette, they really chose high noon, like the old cowboy movies from several centuries ago?"

Lisette shrugged dismissively. She didn't catch the reference. I looked to Hooper and he adjusted his cowboy hat.

"You're wearing a cowboy hat, man," I said. "How do you not get the reference?"

"I don't watch holofilms," Hooper responded.

"A storyteller like you could benefit from them," Tio Pablo said to Hooper.

"I'll keep that in mind," Hooper said thoughtfully.

I gave Lisette and Hooper a glance and they both left the kitchen. Hooper thanked Tio Pablo before he left, tilting his hat like the cowboys he admitted he knew nothing about. "Tio, we're not actually going to church." I took a moment, remembering all the hurt I had caused him and my tia, and decided they needed to know. "I don't think I should be telling you this, but I want to let you know in case... Well, in case something happens to me.

"That sounds ominous, mijo," Tio Pablo said. "Are you in trouble?" His voice grew concerned.

"No, we're fine. I'm fine. It's just, these people we're meeting with don't have the best reputation."

He reached and touched my hand. He always knew when I wasn't telling the whole truth, keeping important details from him. "If you're in trouble you need to say something. We can go to Luna Security. You know your old girlfriend Alana is a captain now. Maybe she can help."

"It's OK, Tio. Really, it is. Hooper and Lei will make sure we're all safe. And Lisette knows these people, so I'm sure it's all unnecessary precaution." Tio looked unconvinced.

"I promise you, Tio, I'll be OK. Better than OK after this meet. I might even be able to quit my job and go back to school."

Tio took a deep breath and said, "OK, mijo. But if you need anything, just ping me."

"OK, Tio," I said.

"Oh, and before you go, I made a plate for that pretty Junpoor girl of yours," he said, giving me an approving look as he handed me a sealed container of breakfast. "She can't *not* have gravy."

I rolled my eyes and said, "You're not wrong there, Tio."

Out in the yard, Lisette and Hooper stood by the fence engaged in a hostile whisper-shouting match. Lisette kept her arms at her sides, but moved her hands and wrists with furious restraint. Hooper had his thumbs tucked between his belt and pants. "Are we good?" I asked as I walked up.

"Yes, just going over the finer points of this meet," Hooper said. "Which I'm not too excited about."

"Neither am I, *Alice*, but it's a necessary evil," Lisette said, emphasizing his name. Hooper cringed.

"Yeah, I don't think now is the most ideal time to be having a spat," I said as I stepped in between them and forced some distance. "The meet's in a couple of hours. Did they give you any details? Just you? All of us?"

Lisette nodded. "The usual – no weapons, no police, they know there's four of us so if more than four show up the meet is off… stuff like that."

"And I am firmly against the no weapons aspect of their demands," Hooper said.

"OK, that's fair," I said. "And I agree. They're obviously going to be bringing some. So, can you conceal a weapon? I mean, I know Leilani can."

"Look who you're talking to, bud," Hooper said.

I corrected myself, saying, "Right, I forgot. Smuggler cowboy. Got it."

"Are you good with that?" I asked Lisette.

"Do I have a choice?" she fired back. When Hooper and I stood silent, she murmured, "Fine, but if this goes south, it's on you."

Back at the *Mentirosa*, my tio's junkyard hand and Leilani worked in tandem to remove the damaged sections of the ship. We were all impressed at the progress they'd made. Lisette, still high on stim injections, paced around the ship, incessantly tapping at her glass-comm.

"Oh, I almost forgot," I said. "Compliments of Tio Pablo." I handed her the container of food and told her he made it specially for her. She moved it to the side, intent on ignoring the gesture, then saw my face and dug in. Hooper beckoned me to the captain's quarters.

Hooper groaned as we entered, pointing and gasping at all of Lisette's accoutrements. "She changed everything," he said.

I looked around the room. "Um, it looks pretty normal to me." The entire place was clean, with nothing out of place.

"This lighting…" Hooper shook his head. "And the desk? Ugh. And look at the bunk… I mean, come on, this here?" He grabbed a fluffy blue pillow from the room's armchair and tossed it onto the couch. "Unbelievable."

I wanted to mock him but refrained, since he sounded genuinely upset. "Hooper, why are we in here?"

He ran to the closet and pulled out a tanned leather gun belt with matching holster. Both belt and holster featured an embossed floral motif. It looked expertly made and custom to Hooper's build and frame. He then motioned to the bulkhead by the head of the bed. With a sly smile, he reached under the bed. The bulkhead slowly, silently retracted, revealing a hidden cubby holding a stack of data boards used on every ship in the galaxy, and a rectangular case a little over a foot long and three-quarters as wide. He grabbed the case and set it on the bed.

"I don't normally carry this," he said, placing both thumbs on two separate scanners located on the top of the case. "It's not exactly legal." The locks released. Hooper opened the case to reveal a shiny, nickel-plated blaster pistol. The long barrel and bulky frame held a magazine cell shaped like a cylinder. It resembled a revolver, the type of guns used by actors in cowboy holofilms. One extra cylinder cell sat ready in the case. Hooper grabbed both gun and an extra magazine and, with a flourish, put them in their place on the belt. He then returned the case to the cubby. With the press of another button the bulkhead slid back into place.

"I had no idea you had a blaster on board," I said. "We could have used it… so, so many times."

"I only use it for emergencies, like when our lives are in danger," Hooper replied.

"Exactly," I said, shaking my head. "But what doesn't make sense is how you still don't know what a cowboy is or how closely you resemble one."

Hooper stood up from the bed and looked at himself in the mirror near the closet. He posed with a hand resting on the hilt of his blaster and a tip of his hat. "I just think I look cool."

"Come on, then, let's grab Lisette and Lei and head to the church."

Chapter Twenty-four

Since the cathedral and my tio and tia's place were in neighboring domes, we easily found space on a public transport – a venerable old monorail called the Rover Racer. Like everything else on Luna, the monorail moved like it wanted nothing more than to break down and end its life of servitude, yet chugged on regardless of its plight.

The cathedral stood on the shores of the Sea of Tranquility. Terraforming once transformed the ashen, dusty surface into a shimmering lake, complete with a verdant garden decorating the cathedral grounds. After the destruction of Terra, the money to keep such a luxury diverted to caring for refugees. Thus, the sea and the surrounding areas dried up and withered back to their natural, pre-terraformed state. It only took fifty or so revs. We disembarked from the monorail and were immediately welcomed by throngs of protesters, holding signs and chanting for the reconstitution of the sea and the garden surrounding the cathedral. "Make TD Beautiful" and "Save Our Sea" were the most popular slogans.

"I've never been happier to see protesters," Hooper said as we hurried past them.

Lisette led the way. The footpath from the monorail to the steps of the cathedral were choked with tourists and parishioners, although even I couldn't tell one from the other. For the most part they were all Earthbounders, or Lunarans now.

"This crowd will make it easier to spot Chorzi or Hongxongdi," I said to Hooper.

"There won't be any Black Sun or Hongxongdi here," Lisette said over her shoulder. "You said it yourself, there's no way the Obinnas would allow a rival syndicate to land on Luna."

The cathedral itself was an enormous monstrosity of a building. At over a hundred thousand square feet, it dwarfed every single edifice on the surface of Luna. Rumors surrounded the building, stating that the Church cannibalized the marble from disused churches and cathedrals on Terra's surface, providing enough material for the new cathedral. To some, this defilement of original church stones was unforgivable, but to others it symbolized the continual growth and resilience of the Church. Regardless of which camp people fell in, the building was indeed a spectacle. Pillars and spires thrust angrily to the sky atop menacing flying buttresses, nearly touching the top of the dome regardless of Luna regulations. Each stained-glass window featured gruesome depictions of Church history. It was an eyesore of ancient Gothic design, refusing to conform to the modern Lunaran architecture that typified the rest of the Moon.

One hundred and forty-four polished marble steps led to the expertly cast yet gaudy bronze doors. At the top, marking the entrance to the plaza, stood a statue of the cathedral's venerable Lady of Tranquility, carved from one solid chunk of meteorite. A plaque marked the anniversary of the completion of the cathedral, as well as the unveiling of the statue. I quickly scanned the dates and the words as we passed. All the times I visited with Tio and Tia, sat through boring lectures during Mass, took the sacrament even in disbelief, and I never once noticed the name of the Lady of Tranquility: Kote Obinna.

How did I not know the cathedral was founded by the original leader of the Obinna crime syndicate? Now the location for the meet made sense. It wasn't neutral ground. This all belonged to the people we were going to sell to – Lisette's client, the Obinnas.

I gave my glass-comm one last look as we entered the cathedral. It read ten til noon, local time. I patted the secret inside pocket and felt the chit. It would all be over soon. I'd be rid of this cursed half-inch by half-inch square of data. I'd have newfound wealth and could finally start living the life I wanted in just ten short minutes. I took a deep breath and crossed the threshold.

The cavernous interior of the cathedral – one of the largest remaining bastions of the dying religion of my ancestors, plus a few others – made me feel small and insignificant and filled me with no small measure of dread. Built in the traditional cruciform layout, two rows of polished wood pews, trimmed in gold, complete with ancient, rarely used copies of liturgical literature, ran down the center of the nave. At maximum capacity, the pews could seat over twenty thousand worshipers, with another ten thousand in the standing room only sections. Although in the revs I attended, I rarely saw over a thousand people gracing the pews. A queue formed on the south side of the building, leading to the confessional, running past the sacristy with its multitude of candles burning in memory of lost loved ones. People here and there wandered aimlessly up and down the aisles, staring at the extravagant paintings that covered the ceiling or the frescos or occasionally meditating on the descriptions of each stained-glass window. Yet, despite the number of people inside, it remained relatively quiet. So much so that Hooper found it necessary to whisper as we followed Lisette.

"This place gives me the creeps," he said.

"Me, too," I said and inhaled deeply. The air smelled of skunky incense and burnt oil. "And I've been here before."

Hooper continued. "I understand the relative historical importance of religion, but humanity, both earthbound and starbound, has moved past it, right? Look at the Xin. Their authoritarian theocratic government moved them to start entire crusades against other races in what they said was saving the universe from the self-aware virus of sentient life, and look at the good that did them. I mean, how much money did the Church spend on this building when it could have easily been used to—"

"Hush!" Lisette turned around and chastised us. "Take off your hat, this is a place of worship. It doesn't matter if you believe or not."

Hooper, wide-eyed, complied without comment.

Lisette took a seat near the chancel, about four rows from the front, on the east side of the cathedral. I slid in next to her and Hooper next to me. Leilani, however refused to sit. "Gonna have a look around," she muttered, and hurried off.

"That's probably a good thing," Hooper said. "We shouldn't all just sit together." He suddenly said, "Good luck," before also disappearing into the crowd.

I looked at Lisette, her face tight and jaw clenched. Her right leg bounced up and down. She checked her glass-comm, then immediately checked it again.

"You all right?" I asked.

She answered quickly, saying, "We're almost done. It's almost over. They'll test the chit, give us the payout, then we can wash our hands of all of this... Forget we ever got into this mess."

I exhaled sharply. "I can't wait to be rid of this thing."

"It'll be all right. Everything's fine. We'll be fine. Right?" Lisette looked at me. I had never seen her like this before we set foot on Luna. She always seemed confident, stubborn, assured. The way she looked at me was none of those things. Her green eyes were filled with fear and uncertainty.

I reached down and grabbed her hand. "It'll be all right. It'll be over soon."

She looked down at our hands, then nodded.

The bells rang out, marking the coming of the noon hour. The melody echoed softly through the cathedral. I looked up at the altar and saw the cross. Unseen spotlights illuminated the carving of the Messiah as he hung before me, body broken, spirit fled. I never felt the urgency to pray, to send any number of words of supplication to an invisible, unknown God. I didn't have a conversion in that moment, but I did understand it. I finally realized the place that horrific vision of a man, tortured, dying on a cross held for my mom and pop, for my tio and tia, for my entire family that came before. It represented hope.

Just as the final bell rang, marking the hour, an uncomfortably rotund man collapsed into the pew in front of us. Sweat beaded on his bald head. His ears glowed red from overwork. He pulled a handkerchief from the front pocket of his blazer and wiped his face and head, then made the sign of the cross. I looked at Lisette and noticed another man slide into the pew at the opposite end of us. He wore a tan trench coat and a hat that sat so low I couldn't see his face. I motioned toward him. She looked and nodded back to me.

"This had better be worth the one hundred and forty-four stairs," the man in front of us said without turning around. "I'll need my man to run a diagnostic before we can agree to terms."

"Of course," Lisette said quietly. We released our hands, and I reached down and pulled out the chit. I looked at her and mouthed the words, *Kote Obinna?* She ever so slightly inclined her head. I guessed it was now a ceremonial title because this Kote didn't resemble the statue in the slightest. Although, the statue was a good three or four centuries older than the man before me. I reached forward and tapped the man on the shoulder with the chit.

"Not me, you idiot, my man," Obinna growled softly.

"Oh, sorry," I apologized.

"Behind you," came a melodious and familiar voice, as if a male and female sang harmonized from one set of vocal cords. I turned in my seat and saw Memo. They waved at me by wiggling their fingers. "I wondered if I'd ever get to see you again."

"Nice to see you too, Memo," I grumbled. I held the chit between my index and middle finger and handed it to them.

"Just insert it right here," they said. The palm of their hand shifted, revealing a data port. "That is, if you haven't forgotten how to insert things into me."

Lisette finally decided to look at the person behind us. Upon seeing Memo, she stared at me with mixture of confusion and disbelief. I looked away, wishing I could disappear to hide from the embarrassment, and placed the chit on Memo's palm. They moaned sexually, which was more than I was prepared for.

"As good as I remember it," they said, and blew me a kiss.

"Nothing sexual happened between us," I mumbled in defense.

"Cut the shit, Memo," the Obinna said, making the sign of the cross before continuing. "Is it legitimate?"

Memo removed the chit and handed it back to me. "It is."

At their word, the Obinna rotated in the pew and turned his face toward us. His small features got lost on his bulbous head. Sweat continued to pour down his red cheeks. He stretched his arm along the back of the pew and opened his palm. This was the moment we had been waiting for all week. The final payoff was within my reach – just drop the chit in his hand, and the nightmare would be over. I glanced at Lisette, then took a moment, turning the chit over and over in my hand. Why I hesitated was beyond me, but Lisette's eyes went wide, and she held her breath by the time I raised my hand to drop the chit. She stared behind me.

I felt someone sit down next to me. More than that, I smelled them. Sweat, engine grease, and yillo filled my nostrils. They wore a tan trench coat and a hat, just like the guard on the other end.

"Who the fuck are you?" Memo asked quietly.

"The rightful owner of that chit, aug," Janky said as he took the hat off. I would have never imagined Janky smart enough to pull off a simple disguise, but it worked. And I doubt the Obinnas expected another gang to encroach on their turf. Janky put one arm around me and, with the other, jammed his blaster into my stomach. Lisette gasped. The Obinna's face grew even redder, yet before he could say a word, Memo leaned forward, reached over Janky's arm with their hand wholly transformed into a blade, like back on Lotus, and pressed it to Janky's throat. All the while, all I could think was, *Where the hell are Hooper and Leilani?*

"You didn't answer my question," Memo growled with a newly deep and menacing voice.

Janky chuckled. "Me name is Janky, and I wouldn't move that blade unless you wanna blast to your skull." I heard Cappy's snorting guffaw. Down at the opposite end of the pew, Mohawk held a blaster to the neck of the Obinnas' second man.

Unfortunately for everyone involved, Janky's presumption ran through the cathedral like a plague. A pair of churchgoers noticed the weapons and shouted. Soon, everyone not involved with the chit grew curious. Before even a minute had passed, the yelling had crescendoed, and the crowd stampeded toward any and every exit. After a couple of minutes, we were alone. Still, I wondered, *Where the fuck are Hooper and Leilani?*

"What kind of dumb fuck pulls a gun in a church," the Obinna spat. "You stupid motherfucker. Don't you know who I am, you shit-sucking station slut? I am the Kote Obinna! You think I walked in here with only two men? I own this moon, dipshit. I own the Luna Security Force! I don't know who you are, but you better pray to Jesus Christ up there on that cross that you–"

"Hey, shut up!" Janky shouted at the Obinna. The Obinna's face grew even redder. "Hand me the chit, and we be on our way."

"Johnny, darling," Memo said, "if you move that hand, I will end him and you with one swipe."

"Then I pull the trigger and blast your head clean off," Cappy said.

Everyone went silent. My heart raced. I couldn't control my breathing. My teeth chattered. I glanced at Lisette. She sat still as a stone, her breathing as erratic as mine. That was when, out of the corner of my eye, I saw a yellow bomber jacket and a cowboy hat peek out from behind a pillar.

"Um... What if I decided I didn't want to sell it?" I asked through ragged breaths.

"What?" everyone said in unison.

"Yeah, I think I've had a change of heart," I managed to say.

The Obinna growled. "Memo, kill both of these motherfuckers!"

"Don't do that!" Hooper shouted as he ran out from cover and stood on the chancel. "Let's not be hasty."

"Jesus H. Christ, another spacebound asshole thinking he can steal from me," the Obinna spat. "Who the fuck are you?"

"Sorry I'm late," Hooper said, waving at me and Lisette. "I had to take out of couple of Obinna's men to get back in here once I figured out what was happening."

"Do I need to repeat myself?" the Obinna roared.

"The name's Alice Hooper." Hooper tilted the brim of his hat. "I'm with those two. And her."

Nobody saw or heard Leilani coming until, with a flash of yellow, she threw herself at Cappy. She slammed his face into the back of Memo's head with a sickening crunch. Memo, stunned, dropped their guard and their hand momentarily. Leilani, spinning counterclockwise, slammed her palm into Janky's face. His nose burst like a water balloon. Mohawk and the Obinna's second guard were now wrestling to control Mohawk's blaster. That was when the firing started.

Without thinking, I grabbed Lisette and pushed her to the floor beneath the pews.

"Who is firing!" she shouted.

"I don't know, but let's not wait around to find out!" I pointed forward and we began to crawl. We crawled past the Obinna, too busy firing a tiny blaster to notice us. When we reached the first pew, I spotted Hooper waving to me from behind the marble altar.

"Look!" I called out to Lisette.

"Stay low!" she cried back over the shower of blaster fire, and crawled as fast as she could toward Hooper. When we finally reached cover, he was cursing like mad and holding his head.

"This is some bullshit," he said.

"What? What is it?" I asked. "Did you get shot?"

Hooper nearly sobbed. "Those Chorzi bastards shot right at my head. My hat... It incinerated."

"Chorzi?" Lisette and I shouted.

Before either she or I could continue, Leilani leapt face first over the altar and came to a crashing halt behind us. She quickly crawled next to Hooper.

"Where's your hat?" she asked.

Hooper let out a wail of pain. We all huddled as close as possible, shielded by the giant marble altar. The air of the cathedral cracked and sizzled around us. The once incense-rich environment spoiled into a rotten stench of ozone and burning wood and metal. Errant blaster fire flew over our heads, striking the crucifix, the walls, the pillars, everything in sight. A loud blast erupted and the stained-glass window overlooking the altar exploded into a rainbow of deadly shards. We all managed to cover our faces and necks in time to avoid serious injury.

"The Black Sun are here. Chorzi stormed the place and started firing," Leilani shouted over the noise, pulling a three-inch shard of red and blue glass from her thigh. "I think the Obinna is dead."

"I thought no other syndicate would dare land on Luna?" I shouted.

"I guess they all think the chit is worth the war," Hooper yelled.

"We can't just sit here," Lisette screamed back. "We have to get out of here."

"So much for not opening fire on a crowd of civilians," Hooper yelled.

"Hooper, I'm sorry about your hat, but it is not a crowd of civilians. It's just a hat. Let's get out of here, and I'll buy you a new one."

"With what money?" Hooper whined, which garnered a slap from Lisette.

"Thank you," Leilani said.

"Pull your shit together. We have to get back to the *Mentirosa*. Johnny, do you still have the chit?"

I showed them the data chit still gripped between my index and middle finger.

"Then our hopes are still alive. As long as we have the chit, we can still find a buyer."

An explosion rocked the east wall of the transept, near the entrance to the cloister. We all looked and saw a group of brawlers, clad in the red striped racer jackets of the Hongxondi, storm into the church. On the opposite end, a group of men and women began filing out into the nave, firing and ducking for cover. The assault continued in earnest.

"What the fuck?" I shouted. "How did they know?"

Lisette explained, saying, "The Obinnas are the only other syndicate in the system. If we didn't sell to them or the Black Sun, that only left one man."

"We can still go that way." I pointed to the west. "It'll probably lead to some offices or barracks, but there's bound to be another side entrance that way."

Lisette leaned in close and repeated it to Leilani.

It was at that moment that I realized this was just like my vision from Kilgore. I was fighting a bunch of mercenaries to the death with the love of my life by my side! Well, maybe it wasn't exactly like that, but it was close enough for me. I finally decided that now was the time. This was the moment. I didn't care what kind of hell raged around us; I was going to make a big, brave, romantic gesture that would surely capture her heart.

"Hooper, give me your blaster," I said.

"What?"

"Give me your blaster, I'm going to lay down some cover for you three."

"No way," Lisette said. "Either we all go or none of us go."

"You'll be easy targets if you just bolt. At least this will give you a fighting chance." I grabbed her hand and pressed the chit into her palm. "Take it. In case... Well, you know."

"Johnny, this is stupid, come on."

"No, just go. I'll catch up."

Hooper reached down and handed me the blaster. "You've used one of these before, right?"

I smiled.

"Lord Jesus Christ, if you are here among us in this moment, protect this stupid, stupid man," Hooper prayed, then slapped me on the chest and winked.

"Amen," Leilani said.

Lisette grabbed my hand and put the chit back in my palm. "For when you meet us at the *Mentirosa*."

We held hands longer than I expected. I looked her in the eyes. I wanted to say something – anything – to let her know how I felt. Instead, I squeezed her hand and said, "Go. I'll see you soon." I watched her hurry away then tucked the chit back in my pocket. With that, I leaned out from cover and began to fire, managing three volleys before any of the other combatants took notice of me. Realizing the danger, I ducked behind the altar just before several blasts struck, spraying marble everywhere. I gave a quick glance to the west and saw that Hooper, Leilani, and Lisette had all made it out safely. When I peeked out again, two Hongxongdi mercenaries were beginning to flank the altar. The Chorzi held their position, pinned down by the shockingly effective tactics deployed by Janky and his crew. The Obinna did indeed lay dead in the aisle, but Memo was nowhere to be seen. Nevertheless, his other henchmen, numbering close to thirty now, fought fiercely for their fallen leader. It looked as if they were gaining the upper hand, forcing the Chorzi into a choke point and pinning the Hongxongdi near the front of the altar. I sent another volley of blasts at the Hongxongdi, spraying blindly and hitting nothing. Yet, before I could duck behind the cover of the altar, another explosion hit. This one impacted the front of the giant marble block. It sent me flying backwards, crashing into the table of sacraments.

Time faded in and out, and my mind could not remember where I was or what I was doing. My vision blurred. My hearing muffled. The air smelled heavy of blood, sweat, and ozone. I blinked and tried to sit up, but collapsed. The world spun uncontrollably. I saw lights, strobing like those on security vehicles. Blue then red then blue again. I thought I heard a siren. Then I heard and saw no more.

Chapter Twenty-five

I awoke to white. White room, white light; if white had a smell, it would have smelled white, too. But no, it smelled of bleach and all-purpose cleaner. White wouldn't smell like that.

I lost track of time sitting in that cell, staring at the walls and floor, eyeing the harsh, headache-inducing light, and wondering if my companions sat in similar situations. The walls seemed to absorb all sound. The cot might as well have been solid stone. I spent an untold amount of time staring at each wall, trying to find any means of ingress and egress, to no avail. The only opening at all in the cell came by way of a barely visible two-inch vent that ran the length of the wall, right along the ceiling, directly above the cot. The pain in my stomach was the only indication of my time spent within those four walls. I was hungry and in desperate need of sustenance.

I dozed off a few times, my body spent of all its energy. I didn't dream, though. It was the type of sleep that comes and goes before you even know what's happening. My eyes would shut and immediately open some time later, the only evidence of sleep being my ever-increasing stomach pangs. After a while and another almost instantaneous snooze, I awoke to the crackling of a voice through an old speaker.

"Juan Marcos Gomez, please stand and place your feet on the blue marker on the floor."

I opened my eyes and quickly shot up, more out of surprise than a need to obey orders. I scanned the floor and saw a glowing blue circle appear where previously had only been white. I hung my head and moved to the marker.

A strange feeling overcame me as I entered the circle. My legs immediately stopped working. I didn't lose my balance or topple over, but they no longer responded. Try as I might to bend my knees or shuffle forward, my legs simply refused to move. The longer I stood in the circle, the more the feeling began to spread: up to my stomach (which was a welcome move because it surprisingly stopped my hunger pangs), through my chest and across my shoulders, then down my arms and finally, up my neck.

I had heard of stay-rays on my time aboard Kilgore. Station Security used them in the holds, but also implemented them on several occasions when a perp needed to be apprehended in a more covert way. The stories seemed to all have the same description of how they felt. The paralyzing creeping that crawled up your body usually caused panic. I never fully believed the stories until I felt my entire body frozen in place in that cell. My jaw locked. My heart raced and my breathing grew steadily faster. Despite my inability to move, I began to sweat uncontrollably. My mind started playing all sorts of worst-case scenarios of my impending fate. Yet before they grew too dramatic, a series of metallic clunks rang throughout the cell. A section of the wall before me moved backwards, then slid to the right. A figure, shrouded and haloed by the light behind it, strode forward into the room.

"Jimbo, I told you there was no need for the stay-ray."
A familiar voice came from the woman who entered the
room. She wore a drab gray jumpsuit with the badge of
the Lunar Police Force embroidered left of center, and hid
her face under an equally drab cap with two gold bars in
the middle. Yet there was no mistaking the tight, dark red
curls that cascaded down her back and the rough, albeit
harmonic, and slightly accented sound of her voice.

"Apologies, *jefe*, I only wanted to scare him a bit," Jimbo
addressed his boss through the monitors in the cell.

"Don't apologize, just turn it off," she ordered with a
disappointed shake of her head. "He's liable to hyperventilate
if you restrain him any longer." Jimbo started to speak again,
but she interrupted. "And no, he's not going to hurt me. I
know him from way back, and trust me, he's more likely to
hurt himself than to hurt me."

Jimbo hee-hawed like a donkey then said, "OK, *jefe*, it
should be powering down now."

"Turn off the recorders and give us privacy, Jimbo."

"Roger."

The speakers crackled and ceased. The door behind her
moved seamlessly back into its place as a regular wall panel.
Feeling slowly returned to my body, although the aftereffects
of the stay-ray lingered and made each and every muscle
feign atrophy. I collapsed to the cot behind me, barely able
to keep myself in a seated position.

"Do you need to lay down, Johnny?" she asked, tucking
her thumbs into her belt loops.

"No, Alana, I think I'll be OK," I said, only half believing it.

Alana removed her cap and tossed it on the cot next
to me. Even though ten revs had passed since I last saw her,
she looked exactly the same: honey skin covered in freckles

and warm, brown eyes that pierced through me. Age, it seemed, had not affected her in the slightest. I suddenly became acutely aware of the bruises, cuts, and scrapes that covered my face, arms and hands. I'm sure I looked incredibly run-down.

"You look pretty ragged," she said, as if reading my mind.

"Thanks," I said, only slightly offended. "If you only knew what I've been through lately."

She smirked. "I think I have an idea, at least – an educated guess compiled from the statements of your comrades. But tell me, what the fuck happened back there at Our Lady of Tranquility?"

I looked at her but kept my mouth shut.

"OK, fine. Can I tell you what I think happened?"

"Sure, why not," I said, as noncommittal as possible.

"You got messed up in some pretty heavy shit, Johnny. Let's run the numbers, shall we? The Kote Obinna found dead in the nave of the cathedral. That's one crime lord with very real connections to RUSH, dead... on my watch. Four Chorzi wearing assault gear bearing a shocking resemblance to those employed by Black Sun. Three Hongxongdi mercs surrendered, one dead at the altar, blown to bits by some kind of pulse explosion. Two idiots who I could barely understand, screaming that you stole something from them. An entire squad of Obinna's men arrested at the steps. One of those men, a heavily augmented individual named Guillermo, last name unknown, at large and wanted for questioning. It's a miracle innocent tourists and worshippers weren't murdered, unless you count the handful being treated for cuts, scrapes, and bruises from nearly being trampled by what could have been defined as a stampede while trying to escape the cathedral.

"Oh, and I almost forgot… you. And three people claiming to know you."

I perked up. "Are they OK? Is anybody hurt? How's Lisette?"

Alana raised a hand and called for peace. I noticed one eyebrow rise at the mention of Lisette. "No worse than you are. Your other friends are fine, too, you know. The space cowboy had a graze on his scalp. A blaster round clean shaved a path right through the middle of his hair. He also had a few tiny shards of glass in his arms, from what I can only guess was the stained-glass window. He seemed more upset about losing a hat than anything. The other young woman refused medical treatment."

"Sounds about right," I said.

Alana crossed her arms on her chest. "Curious that you only seem concerned over this Lisette. New girlfriend?"

I grimaced. "No, I… I'm… I'm concerned for Hooper and Lei, too."

She pursed her lips, amused. "Anyway, that's neither here nor there. I really just wanted to see how my old buddy Johnny Gomez got himself a bounty to be chased across the system by what amounts to gangs and crime lords, and lands himself back on my moon and in my prison cells."

"I think we were more than just buddies," I mumbled with a shrug.

Alana snarled at the comment. "Listen, Johnny. I'm not in here to rehash old shit. There were things about us I loved and things I hated. You just weren't a happy person back then, and nothing I could do seemed to cheer you up. Yet, despite your rough appearance and the obvious illegal nature of the circumstances here, you seem to have a spark." She began to pace around the cell. "I recognize that. It was the same spark you had when we first met."

I dropped my head, trying to avoid her gaze.

"Regardless of our past, there is one reason, and one reason only, I'm here right now."

I raised my head. "And that reason would be?"

Alana stopped pacing and leaned against the door panel. She crossed her legs in front of her, clasped her hands together, and held them low on her frame. "Seeing as you were captured and incarcerated here on Luna, I am in a very fortunate position." She paused. A sneaky, calculating look grew on her face. "Fortunate for the both of us."

"What? How?" I stared at Alana. I recognized the exact expression painted on her face. I saw it countless times during our revs together.

"We have a mutual friend. Tall, bulky guy, with a shitload of augments. Says he's your roommate."

"Rygar?" I asked in disbelief.

Alana wagged her index finger. "That's the one," she said, as if remembering some lost factoid. "He's got some connections, Johnny. I'm surprised you even fell in with that sort of crowd. Anyway, he promised Luna Security all kinds of upgrades, grants, vehicles, you name it. I called his bluff, but he checked out. Before I took him up on his offer, though, I made one small request."

I sighed. I knew what was coming. "Let me guess."

"I'm taking the chit," Alana said bluntly. She flashed me a sort of half smile that said there was nothing I could do about it, then reached into a pocket on the front of her suit and pulled the tiny slide from inside.

My face squished in confusion. I must have looked ridiculous, because she laughed. "You play *Lost Worlds*?" I asked, face still contorted.

"Who doesn't play *Lost Worlds*, Johnny?" she fired back. "I admit, I'm not as active as I used to be, but my nephews are wild over it. I can't go a single conversation with them without it somehow circling back to *Lost Worlds*."

"I must be the only idiot in the galaxy that doesn't play this game," I groaned, shaking my head.

"You must be. Even my mom plays *Lost Worlds*."

"Miss Felicita?"

Alana nodded.

"Yeah, OK, how much do you want it for?"

She laughed, harder than I expected.

"No, no, no, Johnny, I think you misunderstand," Alana said, standing up straight and approaching me slowly, menacingly. "I'm not going to pay for the chit. Why would I pay for this? I'm taking it, and in return, you and your friends get to go free."

I sat, astonished, for a few moments before I spoke. "But wouldn't they be able to track you down? What's to stop these idiots from killing you and taking the chit? I mean, the minute you install those avatars to your console, you invite all this violence into your life."

Alana tsked. "You really don't understand how these things work, do you?"

I gulped. "What things?"

"*Lost Worlds* servers are some of the highest security game servers – no, network servers, period. Their end-to-end encryption and firewalls are impeccable. I'm talking state-of-the-art security. If you can think of a ransom or hacking countermeasure, *Lost Worlds* has already implemented it.

Once the avatars are downloaded onto my console, the chit becomes useless, just a redundancy. There is, technically, no way anybody but me – or my nephews, in this case – would have access to these avatars."

"But aren't you afraid of retaliation?"

Alana shook her head. "You're still not getting it, huh? There won't be any retaliation. They gain nothing from it the minute these avatars are activated on the server. Plus, why do you think factions like the Obinnas or Black Sun, or even your comrade smugglers, are even a thing in Sol, or in this sector? They are allowed to operate under RUSH. Affiliated law enforcement throughout the galaxy makes it so these organizations have some leeway, and thanks to RUSH, we all simply turn a blind eye to their dealings. Yet if they were to break that peace, RUSH would come down hard on all black-market operations throughout the galaxy. That requires an unthinkable number of resources and would inevitably result in bloodshed. Thus, the arrangement."

"How do you know all this?"

"You know how many times we've tried to stop the Obinnas, only to have some RUSH directive tell us to stand down? Half my guys are on their payroll as it is." Alana took a breath and crossed her arms on her chest. "It's not my definition of a lawful and just society, but it keeps things quiet on my moon, and I'm happy to keep it that way."

I was flabbergasted. I couldn't believe what Alana was telling me. I shook my head, unable to completely wrap my head around what I had just heard.

Alana approached the cot and took a seat next to me, placing her hat back on her head. "I know it's hard to believe,

Johnny. I didn't believe it myself when I started my first beat after graduating the academy. You have good friends, though. Talk to Rygar, he can smooth over the rough edges."

"Yeah, OK..." I said, completely and utterly downtrodden.

"So, I'm taking the chit, and lucky for you, it is within my power to clear you and your friends of any charges. You leave Luna with a clean slate."

"Thanks, I guess."

Alana chuckled. "Would you rather spend time in this cell? I'm sure Jimbo would jump at the opportunity to make your stay as uncomfortable as possible."

"No, no, I'll take the pardon," I said, raising both my hands. "It's just... Hooper and Leilani were counting on this score, Lisette, too. And she kind of needs it after Black Sun destroyed her shop back on Kilgore."

"She seems like a smart and capable woman," Alana stated. "I'm sure she'll land on her feet just fine. Now come on, I have to complete your release forms." She stood from the cot and smiled at me, the same warm smile I fell in love with all those revs ago. "It is good to see you again, Johnny. Next time, though, let's do it under less complicated circumstances."

I sighed, defeated, and said, "Agreed."

Stay-rays are powerful things. That paralysis they induce can take a while to fully wear off, as I discovered when, while reaching the bottom of the steps of the Luna security headquarters, my knees buckled. I collapsed to the pavement, spilling the contents of my coverall pockets all over the walkway. The meager crowd of passers-by paid me no attention. A pair of officers mocked me and walked away. I gathered up my belongings before crawling to the steps and taking a seat.

My now cracked glass-comm took a moment to power up. Once it did, it inundated me with missed connections, voice memos, and text messages, all from my tio and tia. "Shit..." I uttered. "They probably think I bounced for a second time without telling them. Either that or I'm dead." Yet before I could send them a consolatory "I'm OK" message, I heard Hooper yell my name. I looked over my shoulder to see him, Leilani, and Lisette descending the steps toward me.

"Why'd they let us out, man?" he asked as he plopped himself on the steps next to me. "I was sure we were boned, but then they just kicked us out."

"Some guy named Jimbo said something about it being thanks to you," Lisette added, sitting opposite Hooper.

I looked everyone over quickly before speaking. Just as Alana said, a blaster round burned a clean path right through Hooper's hair. Lisette's pink palms revealed the telltale signs of a visit to the auto-doc. Leilani no longer wore her yellow bomber jacket, but held it folded up under her arm and looked in need of a quick visit to an auto-doc herself. "I... I had to give up the chit." Hooper's head dropped. Leilani threw her hands up in the air and turned to walk away. Lisette's face went white. She held her mouth open. Her eyes bored through my head.

It was as if our collective souls immediately escaped through our nostrils. One by one, the rest of them took a seat on the steps next to me. Everything we had been through now counted for nothing, and I couldn't help but think it was all my fault.

"I don't believe what I'm hearing," Hooper lamented.

I turned my head away and looked down at my hands. "I know…" I mumbled. "If there was another option, I would have taken it. But you got to believe me, they gave me no other choice."

"It's really gone, then?" Lisette asked quietly.

"There go the credits I was going to use to buy stock in mango lollipops," Hooper groaned.

"And fix my shop back on Kilgore," Lisette added.

"And upgrade the *Rosa*," Leilani stated.

They didn't have to say anything. I could feel their disappointment. It poisoned the air around us. Despite our close proximity, I felt the most far away from the three since before I met them. I heaved a heavy sigh. "This is all my fault. All of this. I should've just given you three the chit back on Kilgore and been done with the whole thing."

"Johnny…" Lisette began, but I held up my hand.

"No, it's true. I should've handed it over to you and gone about my sad, pathetic life. And for what? I ended up right back where I started – stranded on Luna, broke, destitute, with zero life prospects ahead of me.

They all remained silent. They may not have felt like I did, but I knew for a fact I had done nothing but hold them back. Had I not been with them, they would've made it to Luna with no problems. The purchase would have gone off without a hitch. Now, I'd completely robbed them of a huge score. They didn't have to say it; I could tell they were through with me.

Slowly, and with a giant grunt, I rose to my feet and started toward the tram.

"Johnny, where are you going?" Hooper asked.

"Home, I guess? Back to my tio and tia's place. It's where I belong," I stated firmly.

"Don't be like that, man," he said. "Shit happens. Sometimes it happens on such a grand scale that you end up destroying the interior of a centuries-old cathedral and becoming an accessory to murder. But that doesn't mean any of this is your fault."

"He's right," Lisette added. "Yeah, it sucks. Yeah, we're all pretty broke now. But it's nothing we haven't been through before."

"Finding a new job will be easy," Leilani added. "We'll have our finances back in the black in no time."

"No, you're all better off without me," I said.

"Johnny," Lisette said, rising from the step.

"No!" I shouted. "You don't get it. I've always been some sort of bad luck charm. My parents. Alana. My life on Kilgore. Now the chit. You three need to get away from me as fast as possible. So, just go. Go back to Kilgore or wherever. Forget about me."

I raised my glass-comm and tapped the screen a few times. Hooper's chimed. "I just transferred unconditional access to the starlanes, care of the Luna Security Force. It'll probably take you to Kilgore and from there, I don't know … Maybe Hepari or Hogan V or Pilgrim's Folly." I frowned and looked him in the eye. "It's the least I can do."

I walked away as fast as I could. I couldn't bear to face them anymore. Quickly boarding the tram, I rode the rails around Luna for what must have been half a rotation. I passed through each of the big four domes a handful of times. I wish I could admit I people-watched, or just forgot my stop. But I just sat there, slumped in my chair, head against the windows, watching the surface of the moon pass me by.

Chapter Twenty-six

My tio and tia greeted me at the gate to their property. Tia Maritza marched forward like a roaring cyclone and slapped me hard across the face. "I should've changed your name to Juan Bobo! Unbelievable! Do you have any idea the hell you've put me through, the hell you've put your tio through?"

Tio Pablo took a step forward and put his arm around my tia in a weak attempt to direct her away from me, but she shrugged off his arm. "Maritza, please, don't you think the boy has been through enough?"

Tia Maritza's face grew enraged. But before she exploded all over my tio, I said, "No, Tio, she's right. It was inconsiderate of me, leaving the two of you when you needed my help here, showing up out of the blue and putting you out. It was wrong of me, and I deserve to let Tia speak her mind."

My words seemed to quench the fire that raged on her face, if only just a bit. She seemed exasperated, but not entirely defeated by my attempt to disarm her. "You... Juanito, it is our duty, our *duty*, to protect you. How can we protect you when you're running all over the system getting mixed up into... into... shit like this?" She quickly made the sign of the cross and muttered, "Dios mio, my God, forgive me for my tongue."

"Tia–" I started, but was interrupted.

"No, I'm not done." She stomped and raised her voice. "You have always been exactly like your mother – stubborn, hot-headed, quick to make decisions. We tried our best, our absolute best, to give you a loving home, a haven, a place where you could grow and forget about all the terrible things that happened to you in your then short life. And how did you repay us? You dropped out of school. You ran away from home. And you did it all without so much as a 'See you later' to me and your tio." She slapped me again. "Shame on you, Juanito. Shame on you."

I lowered my head. "You're right, Tia. I'm ungrateful. I never once thanked you for everything you and Tio did for me. For all the care and love you showed. For sending me to school. For helping me adjust. I'm rotten. I know it. And I hate myself for it."

She refused to look at me.

"I was young and made impulsive decisions out of anger and sadness. I can't say anything more than that. Whether you want to accept that is up to you. I'm not asking for you to forgive me. I know that will take time. I know the hurt I caused won't just heal overnight because I say I'm sorry. But I am asking if I can spend a few rotations here, back at the yard, with you and Tio and Slider. I'll sleep in the barn with Slider. I'll work for my keep. I just… I don't have anywhere else left to go."

Without saying another word, without even looking me in the eye, my tia turned around and stormed back into the house, leaving me standing at the gate with Tio Pablo.

"I wondered why your friends left without you," he said sadly. "They were kind enough to say goodbye and that you were right behind them."

"That was nice of them," I replied.

"As for your tia, give her time, mijo," he said. "She loves you. She just doesn't know how to express it."

"I'm sorry, Tio, I wronged you, too. I don't deserve your kindness."

Tio Pablo waved away my words as if they were a fruit fly. "Bah, no me digas eso, Juanito, don't tell me that." He reached up and put his hand on my neck. He pulled my head towards his. "I'm happy you're safe. I love you. Tia loves you."

"I know," I replied.

Tio Pablo opened the gate and pulled me into an embrace. After a long hug, he said to me, "You may *have* to sleep with Slider for a few rotations. I don't know how long it will take her to cool off. And, if I let you into the house, we may both end up sleeping with Slider."

I chuckled. "OK, Tio."

"I'll bring you some bedding."

"OK, Tio."

I found Slider in his usual spot, beneath the shelter of his corrugated steel barn that sat just inside the entrance to the junkyard. Thanks to his programming, Slider always powered down like a curled-up dog. Despite his massive size and construction, I looked at my beloved creation and wanted nothing more than to curl up with him, to fall asleep in his embrace and forget everything that happened over the past week. I stood there, wallowing in self-pity, hating that I ever chose to hold on to that stupid chit.

Tio Pablo arrived a while later, clutching a sleeping bag, some old threadbare sheets, and a pillow. "This is all I could spare without your tia wondering what I was doing." I gave him a questioning look, to which he replied, "She'll come around, mijo... I just... want to avoid her wrath."

"I understand, Tio. Don't get yourself in trouble," I said, patting his shoulder once more before draping my sheets over Slider's front arm.

"I'll bring you breakfast in the morning, then we'll get started on the yard," he said before returning to the house.

It continued like that for the following few rotations. Tio Pablo quietly brought me food and water. I used the decrepit junkyard office restroom to keep up with my personal hygiene. This meant working around the schedules of the office manager, a stern-faced and humorless Lunaran human named Jala, and the yard hand, a jovial Krindo named Yzy-pio. Jala seemed less than thrilled that I kept a toothbrush in the office, but would keep her distaste to herself, quietly grumbling at the desk while she filed forms and made acquisitions. Yzy-pio, on the other hand, was a little more forgiving. Tio Pablo would sneak me into the house to shower every afternoon, while Tia Maritza ran both her personal and the business errands. During the workday, he and I tackled the disassembly of the salvaged Junpoor sloop that resembled the *Mentirosa*. The catharsis of such an act was not lost on me.

On the fourth rotation following my return, Tia Maritza approached me while I patched a weld on one of Slider's struts. She said nothing, just stood in the entrance to the barn waiting for me to notice her. I saw her out of the corner of my eye, but waited until I finished the weld and lifted my mask to acknowledge her.

"Tia," I said, not knowing what else to say. I figured Tio Pablo informed her of my presence in the barn, but until that moment, I still sort of hoped she didn't know.

She kept her arms crossed on her chest and raised her head high before addressing me. "You will eat dinner at the table tonight, not out here with this loader. You're family, not a hired hand."

"O–OK, Tia," I said. I knew better than to disobey. She still didn't want me back in the house, but at least she allowed me to eat inside. After that first dinner, she also didn't mind me using the bathroom or showering in her house, either. Although sleeping in the guest bedroom was still out of the question. It was her office now, and she wouldn't be relinquishing it just because I came crying back. She never said that, but I could read it on her face and in her demeanor. Plus, she always locked the door to the room whenever I entered the house.

Several phases – twenty-eight rotations on Luna – passed. Tio Pablo and I salvaged and sold most of the parts of the sloop in time to acquire another salvage.

Despite keeping busy, I found myself drowning in thoughts of Lisette, Hooper, Leilani, and Rygar. I vividly saw their painfully disappointed faces mingle with that of my tia. Regardless of the pain and the torture I willingly inflicted on myself, I still fell asleep each night staring at my glass-comm, hoping to see a message from any of them. The messages from Rygar were nice and went a long way to keep me sane, but even a simple hello from Lisette would have made my day. But every night, I fell asleep defeated. It was in these moments of despair, I had all but resigned to return to my life on Luna, before my delusions of grandeur led me to flee, and continue working in the yard with Tio Pablo. *Who knows?* I thought. *Maybe things will be different.*

Tio Pablo seems to be letting me make decisions around here. And Jala did ask me to join her for drinks the other night. Try as I might to wrap my head around the decision, despite the lack of contact and my general malaise, staying on Luna felt wrong.

The next rotation started like all the others: caffeine and chit-chat with Yzy-pio and Jala, followed by a quick update on the day's work. I'd just strapped into Slider's cockpit when my glass-comm vibrated with a message from Jala. I had a visitor in the office. "He says he's an old friend of yours," it read. I frowned. The only old friends I had on Luna were Alana and several underworld players I had no interest in seeing. A brief shiver of fear struck me. *What if it's Janky – or, worse, Memo?* The chit was already gone, but Janky could still be upset, wanting to beat me for the simple fact that I ruined his chance at a big score. What if Memo found my location and decided to kill me to avenge the death of their boss, the Kote Obinna? I swallowed and took a deep breath to regain my composure. Regardless of who I thought might be waiting for me, I switched places with Yzy-pio and trekked back to the office.

The voice that filled the double-wide trailer that served as the office made my heart skip a beat: a deep baritone weaving an amusing anecdote. I had heard the story many times before, usually in the company of several beings intent on sleeping with a certain aug I knew. It was so amusing that even Jala giggled in delight. I turned the corner and spotted Rygar seated in front of Jala's desk, leaning in and locking eyes with her as he spoke. He loved locking eyes with whomever he spoke to. They laughed together, and would not have noticed my entrance if not for me clearing my throat.

"Johnny!" Rygar exclaimed, rising from his seat. He wasted no time closing the gap between us and scooped me up into an enormous bear hug. "I imagined you'd be a little worse for the wear, but honestly, you don't look half bad."

"Thanks, buddy," I said as he released me. "What are you doing here?"

He hesistated. "You want to step outside with me for a bit?"

Jala, still mystified by Rygar's voice, quickly shot up from her desk. "Oh no, you don't have to go outside. You can have the office."

"I don't want to put you out," he responded. "You have work to do."

"Not at all, it would be my pleasure," Jala responded, staring at Rygar for a moment too long before she shook her head, only barely held back a giggle, and continued with an awkward smile. "I... I was about to take my lunch anyway."

Rygar's eyes flashed blue and yellow. He was amused with himself. "Thank you, Jala. Have a good lunch! And remember, don't touch it if it's got those blue strands in it." She blushed and giggled so much that she struggled to open the door, very nearly falling through it as it gave way. She smiled and waved at Rygar before leaving us alone in the office.

"So, that's the story you told her," I said, taking my spot along the wall, leaning against it as casually as I could. "You, alone on Duplo, with only a washcloth to your name. I remember when you told me that one."

"It's a good icebreaker," Rygar said. "Thrilling, reveals my character, and nobody ever sees the punchline coming."

I chuckled humorlessly. "Yeah, sure. So, what brings you here?"

"I wanted to check on you, see how you were doing. Your messages read like sad break-up poetry."

"Yeah, it's been rough."

Rygar's eyes flashed orange and green. "I can't imagine. I'm sorry."

"When were you going to tell me that you're some sort of RUSH agent or spy or whatever?"

"Contractor," Rygar corrected.

"Contractor, whatever. When were you going to tell me?"

"It didn't seem prudent for you to know."

"You could have easily solved all of this, man. You could have taken the chit and given it to your superiors and saved me a trip across the system, saved me several beatings and visits to auto-docs, which are way worse than you ever explained to me."

"I couldn't get involved, Johnny. I would have blown my cover."

"Oh, OK, so just let me go to my death. I thought we were friends, man. Do you always let your friends run around the galaxy carrying items that could get them maimed or killed? So, tell me, what is so important to RUSH that you had to hide your identity from me? Hmm? Is there some sort of separatist conspiracy brewing in Sol? Are the Xin planning to invade again? Is there a new strand of Yotari syphilis wreaking havoc throughout our sector? Come on, tell me."

"I'm just an information broker, that's all," Rygar said. "I have connections with the cyborg and augmented individual elements in our system, the syndicates, and almost every security agency from here to Kilgore. They pay me for information – I give them the information. That's all."

"And three syndicates bidding on and warring over a data chit isn't urgent priority to RUSH," I added. "Alana already told me. RUSH is OK with crime so long as they get their cut, whether that be money or information."

"It's how government works," Rygar stated. "So long as they get to wet their beak, why do they care how the cocktail is made?"

I went to respond, but stopped after thinking about his metaphor. "I… I think you're getting your metaphors mixed up."

Rygar looked at me skeptically and said, "No, I'm pretty sure that's right."

I shook my head in amusement. "Whatever. You still haven't told me why you're here."

"Well, I've come to bring you back to Kilgore."

I rolled my eyes. "No thanks. I mean, I appreciate you coming all this way, but don't you think you could have saved yourself a trip and just sent me a message?"

"I wanted to show you I'm serious. Come back with me. I can set you up with employment, somewhere in Station Ops, or maybe on the Bourbon Docks. I'm sure Dusty could use some help at his pub."

"I'd rather not. Luna is where I need to be. Kilgore… it was just a pipe dream. I was nothing over there, a glorified shit-scraper. At least here, Tio Pablo lets me run the junkyard. I'm back with Slider. And I thought Jala was interested in me, until you walked into this office."

"I am quite a specimen," Rygar said with a grin.

"You are," I agreed, with a roll of my eyes and a smirk. "Listen, thanks, seriously, for the offer and for coming to see me. And thanks for getting me out of jail, but I'm not interested. I've given up on the dream. I know where I need to be right now, and it's here, trading shoveling shit for shoveling scrap metal. At least the scrap metal doesn't stink. I mean, most of the time. There is the occasional… aroma that floats around this place. I mean, did you know carbon scoring gives off a different scent on different metals? It's wild."

"Not my definition of wild, but OK Johnny. Message received." Rygar turned and headed toward the door. "You're my best friend, man," he called, without turning around. "You'll always be welcome back on Kilgore. I'll keep your room as is in case you ever want to return."

"Hopefully not as is," I called back. "I mean, it was basically a broom closet."

He chuckled and looked over his shoulder.

"Thanks again, Rygar. And just so you know, you're my only friend."

"I know," he said as he exited the office, nearly running into Jala, who giggled uncontrollably after being caught eavesdropping.

That night at dinner, Tia Maritza broke her vow of silence toward me and asked, "Who was that man that came to visit you today?"

I exchanged surprised glances with Tio Pablo. "That was Rygar, an old friend from Kilgore Station. He was my roommate. He was my best friend."

"Was?" Tia asked.

I shrugged.

"Seems only a best friend would travel all the way from Kilgore to Luna for such a brief visit."

"Yeah, maybe he's still my best friend," I said quietly. "He did say I could return whenever I wanted."

"And do you?"

"Do I what?"

"Do you want to return?"

I took a spoonful of rice and beans and chewed it slowly before responding. It gave me a few moments to think about how to answer. "No, I don't, Tia. I'm enjoying being back here, helping around the yard. Getting things back in order. Plus, Tio Pablo isn't getting any younger!"

"I'm young enough still," he answered.

She tsked. "Who are you trying to impress? We all know you're not a young man anymore," she said to him, patting his hand gently. He winked at her.

"And anyway, having me here saves you money. You don't have to hire any more hands. And now that Yzy is better trained on how to use Slider, you have two employees skilled at yard work." I smiled at my tia, but noticed she didn't smile back. She stared at me for a long while, even after I had looked away. She didn't believe me. I could tell. Then before Tio and I had even finished with dinner, she grabbed her plate, put it in the kitchen sink and walked off.

"Mari, are you OK?" Pablo called after her before looking to me. "I'll go check on your tia. Finish your dinner, mijo."

Tio Pablo didn't return to the kitchen until after I finished dinner and cleared the table. The dishes were washed, and the leftovers placed in containers in the fridge. I put the last dish back in the cupboard when he strolled into the kitchen. He gently placed his hand on my shoulder, squeezed, then grabbed a cup of water.

"Is everything good?" I asked.

"Yes, mijo. I'm going to turn in for the night. We can talk more in the morning."

* * *

The next morning came quickly. I readied Slider for another day, then met Jala and Yzy-pio in the office for our morning coffee chat. It had only been going on for a week, but already became a tradition between the three of us. We joked it was our only quiet part of the workday before Tio Pablo ran us all into the ground. Jala preferred her coffee black. I put sweetener and cream in mine. Yzy-pio, being a Krindo, couldn't drink coffee. Something about the beans didn't agree with Krindo anatomy, and acted more like a poison than an amphetamine. Instead, it chewed on a tarok bar – a strange white paste, formed into a rather squishy, granola-like bar and covered in lovely, toasted golden brown itosh seeds, a legume native to its planet. Tio Pablo entered in the middle of Yzy-pio's riveting tale of its evening spent chasing a cockroach around its apartment, which honestly must have been horrifying, given the diminutive size of the Krindo and the enormousness of roaches on the moon.

"Juanito, can I have a word?" my tio said, beckoning me into the yard. Yzy and Jala both teased me with smirks. I ignored them and hurried out the back door. I followed Tio Pablo to the barn, where he stopped in front of Slider.

"What is it, Tio?" I asked. He tapped on his glass-comm and swiped a few things my way.

"For you, mijo."

I removed my glass-comm and saw a credit transfer, as well as a first-class ticket back to any destination I wanted. "What is this?"

"We love you, Juanito, like our own son. So, we know when you're lying." He sighed. "I love having you back, and I truly appreciate your help, especially with Yzy-pio, but…" He sucked his teeth. "This life is not for you, mijo."

I grimaced. "Yes, it is, Tio. I tried living out there," I

said, waving beyond the dome, "and all it brought me was poverty and trouble. Here is home. Here is family."

"Mijo, you had a dream once. Your tia and I... Well, we were too stubborn to see it and honestly had trouble letting you chase that dream. This is our way of apologizing – this is your tia's way of apologizing."

"I can't take this, Tio, you've already given me too much. And you don't have to apologize. You have nothing to be sorry about."

"It's nothing," he responded. "We made a little more money off the salvaged sloop than we expected. This is your cut."

"No, Tio…"

Tio Pablo put his hand on my shoulder. "Johnny, the junkyard is my home. This place is my life. This was never meant to be yours. Go… Chase whatever it is you want to chase. Be whatever it is you want to be. Just know that this time, you do it with our blessing. Now go. And don't worry about work today, or about Slider. He'll be here whenever you want to come back and visit."

I looked down at my glass-comm. Salvaged parts for Junpoor starships must still be at a premium. And the ticket was for the good shuttle service – one with windows and a bar, that took both starlane and slow burns around planets for touristy photo opportunities. I took a deep breath and tried not to cry in disbelief. When I looked back at my tio, I pulled him into a hug. I stayed next to Slider as my tio walked to the office. That was when I noticed my tia, standing on the back porch, mug in hand, looking my way. I raised my hand. She simply nodded and then returned inside.

Chapter Twenty-seven

Setting foot on Kilgore Station felt different this time. I was no longer naive and full of youthful optimism; I had more than a hundred credits to my name, with a friend and a place to lay my head. The cold and unwelcoming embrace of Kilgore no longer frightened me. It felt familiar. Comfortable. It felt like home.

I spent most of the trip back thinking about what Tio Pablo told me. I needed to go after what I wanted in life. When I first moved to Kilgore, I dreamed of leaving the system and seeing other parts of our enormous galaxy. But I fell into complacency and gave up that dream. I knew this time around would be different. Rygar offered to help, and I would take him up on that offer. I was no longer afraid to ask for help. I had skills I didn't have when I first arrived. I knew my way around a starship engine bay. And I could play and win a round of Orbit. And yes, if push came to shove, I could always clean toilets.

Rygar met me with open arms and hadn't lied about my room. It was exactly as I left it, only now, covered in dust. I couldn't help but laugh. At least he had kept his word. After we cleared the clutter, dust, and tossed a bag of trash down the waster chute, Rygar told me he knew of a freighter in need of a mechanic apprentice and would put in a good word for me next time they were in port. Until then, I spent a lot of time in the Bourbon Docks, sitting on a stool at Dusty's Old-World Pub.

"Whatever happened to your friends?" Dusty asked me after a particularly slow shift at the pub.

"Who?" I asked, pretending not to know whom he was talking about.

"Hooper, Leilani, and Lisette? Least, I think that's what they called themselves. Last time I saw you, the four of you were planning on heading to Luna." Dusty pulled on a tap and filled a mug with a golden pilsner and placed it in front of me. When I grabbed my glass-comm to pay, he shook his head.

"I don't really know. We parted ways on Luna. Told them I couldn't in good conscience be part of their crew any more."

Dusty hmmed. "Things not go as well as you hoped?"

"I fucked it all up, basically. I don't think they would have minded if I tagged along, but I just felt like they deserved better."

"Did they say that?"

"No, but it was just a feeling."

Dusty hmphed and scratched his beard. "Seems to me you're punishing yourself for no reason."

I took a long gulp of the beer before saying, "Yeah, maybe you're right."

Every night after leaving Dusty's, I found myself wandering through the Bourbon Docks, but always making my way past Lisette's old shop. It was boarded up now, with no signs of life. Station Security set up holos around the entrance, warning anyone who came near of the penalties for entering the premises. I never got close enough to set off the holos, preferring to stare at the past from a distance. It became my nightly ritual. After saying goodbye to Dusty and the other servers, who started recognizing me as a regular, I would hurry to her shop, stand there and drink my water. Part of me wanted to see her return – to see all of them return. Hooper would be telling some story about his new hat, and how he lost his old one. Lisette would roll her eyes and tell him they were all there when it happened and that there was no reason for him to continue to wax on about it. Leilani, in the meantime, would listen and chime in here and there, but remain her usual stoic self, at least for the most part. I dreamt of seeing them and approaching them, intent on asking for forgiveness, begging for them to let me join them once more. It was a boneheaded decision and I shouldn't have left the crew. They would see me and immediately be overjoyed, welcoming me back to the group. "It wasn't the same without you!" Hooper would say. "I missed having you around!" Lisette would shout. "Good having you back," Leilani would state. Yet each night, I would leave the site of her old shop slightly disappointed that none of them showed.

I was back on Kilgore for three phases when Rygar's freighter, a Uselli TYM-12 named the *Hustle*, finally returned to the Bourbon Docks. He wasted no time contacting the ship's captain about a face-to-face.

"Elfwyn Idariis is her name," Rygar said from his seat in our den. "She's a starbound human. She'll need to speak with you – vet you, if you will."

"Yeah, OK," I replied. "I didn't figure she'd just let some stranger on board her ship, even if you vouch for said stranger."

"It won't be until after they unload their cargo. She

usually gives her crew a rotation or two at each port of call just so they can unwind. Helps 'em stay sane."

"When do you think I'll meet her?" I asked.

"I'll get that information and pass it along," he responded.

"OK then," I said as I got up to leave.

"Guessing you'll be posted up at Dusty's again?"

"How'd you know?" I said, then smirked.

By the time I arrived, the pub crowd had dwindled to the handful of regulars that basically lived there. I thought to myself, *You're fast becoming one of those regulars, Gomez.* I took my usual stool at the bar. Dusty raised a hand in hello and, without asking, slid a pint of beer my way. This time, though, he made me pay for it.

"Put it on Rygar's tab," I joked.

"Rygar?" Dusty's roar rumbled through the pub. "That sumbitch owes me close to a thousand credits as it is!"

I managed one long gulp before I felt somebody take the stool next to me.

"What can I get for you?" Dusty asked. I didn't bother looking up.

"Do you have a good champagne?" the woman asked.

I set my pint glass down and turned to face the newcomer. There, sitting on the stool next to me, was Lisette, her straight black hair tied in a high ponytail with her bangs swooping across her forehead, concealing her right eye. She smiled weakly.

My voice caught in my throat, and my heart fell from my chest all the way to my stomach. I forced myself to contain my shock, to hide my elation, and act like she was just another customer at the best bar on Kilgore Station.

Dusty cleared his throat, trying to coax me into speaking. When I didn't take the hint, he rolled his eyes and said, "No champagne. But I got a shipment of Cirellean paskt. I could make you a spiker with that. It's equal parts paskt and ipsaum poured over muddled seyo leaves and garnished with a shaved tikko stick."

"And how does that taste?"

"Burns like hell. But is definitely a conversation starter."

Lisette said, "I'll take two, then. One for me and one for this gentleman next to me."

I forced a smile at her, but that was all. We stayed quiet even after Dusty placed the spikers on the bar before us. She took a sip, and her eyes went wide.

"That's actually delightful," she said.

I followed suit, trying the drink. "Wow, you're right." After another brief pause, I asked, "How'd you find me?"

"Your friends, Rygar and Dusty," Lisette said. "It was the first thing I did when we docked on Kilgore. How've you been? You back on Kilgore permanently?"

I shrugged. "I don't know, honestly. Rygar is trying to set me up with a job on a freighter."

Lisette sighed. "I feel like I need to apologize for something, but I'm not sure what."

"You don't need to apologize for anything," I said. "I'm the one that kinda left you three high and dry. And it was my own stupid brain that did that. I blamed myself for us losing thirty-seven and a half million credits. My brain said you guys hated me. But someone recently told me that I was punishing myself. And maybe they're right. Maybe it's because I don't know what I want. Maybe it's because I'm too concerned about what other people want."

"What do you want?" she asked. "I mean, have you figured out the answer?"

"I want you." I couldn't believe I was actually saying it. And with no fear or trepidation either! "I want the *Rosa*. I want that life we all had. But I don't know if I'm ready for it. I gotta figure myself out before I come crawling back to you three.

"Johnny…"

"No, it's OK. I know you don't feel the same about me. And that's fine."

"Johnny, wait… Stop. You may not know if you're ready to come back, but if it makes any difference, we want you back."

I crossed my arms on my chest. "We?"

"Yes – me, Hooper, and Lei. You see, after Luna, the three of us stuck together. It was like we couldn't just go our separate ways after what we went through. So we didn't. We all decided to keep working together. Hooper found us another job and we took it. We did the job, but we all felt it would've gone smoother had we had one more person. So, now, we take another job and… it's more of a four-person gig than a trio. We needed someone else, and you're the only person we could think of – no, the only person we could possibly want to join us."

I stayed quiet, preferring to stare into my spiker rather than look her in the eyes – those beautiful emerald green eyes.

"Things are different without you, Johnny," Lisette said calmly. "There's nobody there to laugh at Hooper's stupid anecdotes. Also, neither of us will play Orbit with him. Leilani has trouble keeping up with the preventative maintenance of the *Rosa* since the incident with Janky's disassociator. It's like the ship's AI hates the salvaged parts."

"And you?" I asked.

She sighed. "I... I miss having you around. You're interested in me in ways that people have never been interested before. I think you value me as a human and a teammate, and not just as something you want to try and fuck."

"So, not just a travel companion?" I asked.

I saw her flash with embarrassment before she noticed the smirk on my face. "Not just a travel companion," she corrected me. "A friend."

"But nothing more," I stated.

"Johnny..."

"It's OK, Lisette," I said. "Truly. And just so we're clear, I am glad to see you. It was... well, lonely without you three. Aside from Rygar, Alana, and Dusty, you were the only friends I had." I paused. "You are the only friends I've ever had."

Lisette smiled.

I took a deep breath. They want me back. I should be overjoyed! I should already be aboard the *Rosa*, ready to blast off to space knows where. I should be joking around with Hooper, working with Leilani, and enjoying Lisette's company. So why did my gut say, *Now hold on, Gomez*. Why would I have any sort of second guesses? Maybe I truly wasn't ready to be with them again. "I... I don't know."

"Can I at least tell you about the job?" Lisette asked.

"Sure."

"Corporate espionage," she said.

I stared at her. "What?"

She leaned in close and I gladly joined her. "Have you ever heard of Dái-Fāng Tech?" she asked, keeping her voice down.

"They're the ones with all the digi-brain technology, right? AI, digital consciousness conversion and all that, right?"

"What most people don't realize is that Dái-Fāng owns hundreds of other subsidiaries across dozens of industries – EM cell production, nanotech, auto-docs ... They even own a large stake in JDS, Junpoor Drive Systems. They're basically a monopoly on all things tech. RUSH doesn't care because they pay handsomely to keep the government out of their business."

"And you guys think spying on this huge conglomerate will be a piece of cake? None of you are worried about them having... oh, I don't know... state-of-the-art security combining both real and virtual measures?" I leaned back, away from the huddle. "Aren't the Hongxongdi rumored to work for Dái-Fāng?"

"It's a rumor," Lisette said, waving away my concern. "And... it's not as dire as you think. You see, one of their business interests, which surprised all three of us, is industrial and commercial chemicals. It's a microscopic percentage of their market share compared to AI and digi-brain technology, but still a massive revenue stream for them. Over the revs, Dái-Fāng has been developing all sorts of reagents using proprietary technology they stole from a smaller company, a little outfit on Centauri Prime called Astro-Suds Services."

I couldn't stop my outburst. "No, absolutely not, no."

"Johnny, hear me out," Lisette begged.

"No. I'm not going back to being a janitor. I'm not putting those coveralls back on. Never again."

"You wouldn't be a janitor. You'd pose as a janitor, or even a janitorial contractor."

I scoffed again.

"You're the only one among us who knows the job, knows the cleaners and chemicals. The rest of us only have vague notions of what we're hunting. You would make this a lot easier for us. And the payout is huge! Twice as big as the *Lost Worlds* fiasco."

I rose from the bar, still shaking my head. "No, I'm sorry Lisette, but no. I'm looking forward to a future that doesn't involve smelling people's farts and cleaning piss stains off walls."

Lisette raised her hands in defense. "OK, Johnny. I'm not going to push you or try and convince you."

"Thanks for that," I said.

"But—"

"No," I said again.

"*But*," she repeated, "if you have a change of heart and are interested in joining us on a new adventure..." She pulled her glass-comm out and swiped a message to me. "These are our docking coordinates. We're probably not heading out to Junpoor until next rotation."

I stood and stared at my glass-comm. The coordinates led to the exact same docking bay where I first saw the *Mentirosa*. The bay where Hooper wrestled the dock master and Lisette taught me Orbit strategy. I took a breath, then saw a message from Rygar. The captain wanted to meet me.

Lisette stood up straight and started to leave, but stopped short in front of me. "Can I maybe get a hug? From a good friend?"

Of course, I agreed. How could I pass up a hug from the woman of my dreams? It felt good to hold her, to finally be that close and know I would probably never be that close ever again, to lightly inhale the sweet mixture of her scented shampoo and floral body spray... It was my mountain top. Someone once told me that sensory perception helped solidify memories. That's why the memories closely related to smells or sounds stick with us the longest. So, I stayed in the pub for a few minutes after she left, drinking in every sight and sound and smell from around me. The color of the lights, the stale odor of spilled alcohol and pen vapor, the hum of the recirculators: none of it could take away from what just happened. Her touch, her scent... It all felt surreal, sublime.

Chapter Twenty-eight

I got the awaited message from Rygar and met him at Captain Idariis' ship, the *Hustle*. Elfwyn Idariis had about as many augments as Rygar – at least, that I could see. Her half-shaved head revealed the plate and rivets of a digi-brain. The rest of her hair was draped down past her shoulders. Synthesized organic compounds covered her bare arms. Her voice sounded modulated.

"What craft have you worked on before?" she asked as we took a seat on the bridge of her Uselli TYM-12. It was once a premium small shipping freighter on this side of the galaxy, and still put a lot of the newer models to shame, but lost a number of pilots and contracts once the Myro-Com Superflight made its way to the sector.

"Exclusively on two separate JDS sloops," I replied. "But I have other mechanical qualification and proficiencies. I used to service and repair wasters here on Kilgore. They have a two-stage incinerator core that resembles a few of the older reactor systems, albeit on a much smaller scale. They're a lot like the reactors early model Uselli craft use. And I have ten revs of experience on wastewater systems."

Elfwyn pulled her glass-comm from her vest pocket.

"I see all of that on the career data sheet Rygar forwarded me." She scrolled through it one more time before shooting Rygar an uncertain look. "I don't know. Even though JDS craft are some of the more complicated systems to work on... What else can you provide?"

I thought for a moment. Should I try and impress this starship captain with accolades from a previous life of mine, one where I cleaned toilets and disposed of station trash? Rygar's eyes flashed blue and green. He was trying to signal to me to be myself. "I've grown into a decent Orbit player and can make a damn good cocktail."

Elfwyn let loose a boisterous cackle. "A gambler and a drunk? Is there any other job in this universe where such qualities are an asset?" We all laughed before she continued. "It sounds like you'll fit in perfectly with my crew. And since Rygar vouches for you..." She stood up and offered me her hand. "Welcome aboard!"

The *Hustle* wasn't scheduled to leave Kilgore for several more hours, which gave me enough time to pack a bag and send a message to my tio and tia on Luna. I let them know of my opportunity to travel with Idariis, and how Rygar readily helped me get back on my feet. I thanked them profusely for their love and support and assured them I would keep in regular contact.

It only took me a few minutes to pack a duffel for my new life; a few changes of clothes and some toiletries were all I had to my name. The fact that everything I owned could fit into a single duffel bag made me snort. "I have less now than I did when I first landed on Kilgore," I said to myself.

"That's not necessarily true," Rygar said from the door. He leaned against the frame, holding a half-eaten apple in his right hand. "You have a lot more bruises and scars than when I first met you."

I laughed. "And I guess I have a lot more life experience, if that can be quantified."

"And I know for a fact you didn't have working knowledge of the aftereffects of a visit to an auto-doc."

I quickly pulled the zipper shut and looked around at my room. It never had much in it, and most of it belonged to Rygar. Still, seeing it devoid of even the slightest evidence of my influence brought about a twinge of melancholy. I sighed.

"Nervous to go?" Rygar asked, mouth full of apple.

"Yes and no," I replied. "New things are always scary, that's just an undeniable fact. I just can't help but think …"

"What is it?"

I sighed and said, "Lisette showed up at Dusty's right before my interview with Captain Idariis."

"Hmm," Rygar muttered. "And what did she want?"

"I know you told her where to find me." I paused, and his eyes flashed yellow. "She wanted to invite me back. I know I should be jumping for joy. It's what I've wanted ever since I so stupidly abandoned them on Luna. Yet seeing her, talking with her, brought back all the memories of that nightmarish trip. Aside from you, they were my only friends, even if it was for just a brief moment.

"And then I think about you, and how much you've done for me. You took me back in. You vouched for me and got me a job aboard the *Hustle*. I gave you and Captain Idariis my word. I owe it to the both of you…"

Rygar finished his apple, walked into my room, and tossed the core into the empty trash can beside my bed. "You don't owe anybody anything. The only thing you need to worry about is yourself. My feelings, Elfwynn's feelings, even those of your friends aboard the *Mentirosa*... none of them are your responsibility. We're all adults. We can all handle our own feelings. And if any of us can't, then we're not worth your time and energy."

"I guess I do worry about what other people think of me."

"More than you should," Rygar said in agreement.

"Still, am I doing the right thing?" I asked him, looking down at my duffel.

He lifted my head. "Only you can decide that. Whether you leave Kilgore aboard the *Hustle* or the *Mentirosa* is up to you. Just make sure whatever you decide is your decision, and yours alone."

His eyes flashed every color of the visible spectrum in less than a second. The only other time I witnessed that happening was revs ago, during one of his wild birthday parties. When I asked him what that meant, he said, "Love, Johnny. It means I'm in love." In truth, he was under the influence of four different hallucinogens and spent the rest of the party crying "tears of joy." I didn't believe him until I saw it again. We immediately shared a much more tearful goodbye than I expected. He gave me a bear hug and lifted me off the ground. I thought for a moment I would never breathe correctly again.

"It may have taken ten revs, but you're finally doing it," he said. "You're finally living your dream. I couldn't be prouder to call you friend."

"Thanks, Rygar," I said, wiping away a few tears. Whether

they were of joy or pain from the hug, I didn't know or care. "You've always been there for me and honestly, without you, none of this would have happened."

"Oh, I know," he said. We shared one last laugh. "You're always welcome to visit whenever you come to port, little buddy."

"You'll be my first stop, tin-plated soldier. Either you or Dusty."

"And my comm channel is always open," he added.

"I never know when I may need an information broker to save my ass again, right?"

Rygar grinned. "Right."

My walk to the Docks felt strange. Something was wrong, and I couldn't figure out what. I passed augs, cyborgs, and androids, earthbound and starbound, Hepari and Xin, all of whom seemed to know where they were going and why. They walked and talked and moved with purpose. Each step was calculated. Each word measured and tested before leaving their mouths. They were all so sure of their own future, the destiny that awaited them. I thought about what I was doing. Was I really following my dream? For my entire life I wanted this. I wanted to travel the galaxy and see other planets. I wanted to mingle with other races and beings, learn about their food, drink, and culture. I wanted to fuck alien species, no matter their gender. Here it was, laying before me! The answer to all my questions – the pathway that led to my dreams. I was only a few footfalls away from beginning my next chapter, only it felt all wrong.

It took me a moment to realize I had stopped moving.

I stared down the wide walkway leading to the docking bays. People shimmied around me, deftly maneuvering to not shoulder me out of the way. The air smelled of yillo and grease, ozone and sweat. I saw the blue glow of energy fields protecting the station from the vacuum of space beyond. Their hum, the rhythm of the docks. I saw crates and containers being ferried to their respective berths by the augmented and organic dockhands alike. Station announcements blared from the PA system but were barely audible over the chaos of the docks. I spotted the *Hustle*, only a few bays down from the stairs I stood on. It looked rough and utilitarian, more of a tool than anything. It looked nothing like the *Mentirosa*, with its elegant lines and multitude of illegal modifications.

The *Mentirosa*.

I pulled out my glass-comm and checked Lisette's message. The link said the ship was still docked. They had yet to leave. My heart began to pound. I looked up and saw the crew of the *Hustle*. The vessel was loaded. All they waited for was my arrival – their newest mechanic apprentice. I looked back at my glass-comm. I tapped out a message and hit *send*. Then, after a big breath and with a stomach full of nerves, I turned and ran.

My feet carried me to the lifts. I shoved my way inside the closest one, moments before the door closed.

I pushed my way out of the doors the minute they slid open and ran past the windows that overlooked all the craft docked at Bay 47.

I ran down the stairs, taking them two at a time, and stumbled at the bottom. I hit the floor with a thud. Two starbound youths wearing fluorescent jumpers and clashing boots helped me up. I thanked them and ran.

I entered 47-E and slid to a halt, only didn't stop completely and instead careened over a table full of Orbit cards and tin cups of yillo and crashed into a surprised aug. The players all jumped up from their spots with shouts of surprise and anger. The man I landed on, though, hollered hysterically.

"You just saved me from losing a whole lot of credits," he said as he wiped yillo from his face. No sooner had we gotten to our feet than the office door slid open, and Hooper, Leilani, and Lisette hurried out.

"Johnny?" Hooper asked in surprise.

I put my hands behind my head and tried to catch my breath. "Nice… hat…" was all I could manage.

He ran an index finger along the brim of his new cattleman hat. This time it was chocolate brown. "Oh, you mean this old thing?"

"I… was hoping… I'd catch you…" I huffed.

Hooper let me catch my breath, then said, "Looks like luck is on your side today." He offered his hand. We shook – a single, solid-gripped handshake that quickly pulled into a hug with sharp pats on each other's backs. "Glad to have you back. And I'm sorry for what happened."

"No, it's OK. Lisette passed along your apologies." I looked directly into her green eyes. She smiled back, wider than I had ever seen.

"Missed you, old man," Leilani said, patting me on the shoulder before she continued toward the *Rosa*.

"That's the most emotion she's shown since Luna," Hooper said with a shake of his head. "See you on board?"

"See you on board," I said.

Lisette took a step forward and asked, "What made you change your mind?"

I exhaled through my nose. "All my life, I wanted adventure. But it turns out what I really wanted was to know what it was like to be needed, to be wanted, to be appreciated. I had all of that when I was on the *Rosa*. I didn't realize it then, probably because I was being hunted and having my ass kicked at every turn, but that time together… It was everything I ever wanted. I lived my dream and want to live it again, even if that dream means I have to be a janitor every so often. I mean, it's not so bad a gig. There's worse ways to make a living."

Lisette put her hand on my shoulder. "I'm glad you're back." Then her face scrunched up in the usual way it did when her mind wandered to other things. "You didn't happen to bring your coveralls, did you? The Astro-Suds Services ones? You're going to need them."

I chuckled. "I'm sure we can pick up another pair on our way to Junpoor. No, scratch that. I'm sure we can pick up another four pairs on our way to Junpoor."

Lisette looked confused. "Four? You don't mean …"

"Yup, you three are about to have a crash course in what it means to be a space broom."

Chapter One

Jim's in the store again. Jim doesn't buy shit.

"Morning Ben," said Jim.

I'd always liked Jim, but he'd never so much as flirted with a spool of 5x tippet.

"You going out today?" I asked, flipping the magnifier up from the brim of my cap.

"Yep," he answered, fingering some light-wire hooks on a rack.

"You know those are for sale, right? You can buy them with money and they become yours forever."

Jim didn't respond, ambling instead to another rack of fly-fishing goods he also wouldn't end up purchasing.

I knocked the magnifier back down and returned to wrapping a yellow midge.

"Hey," said Jim, just as I'd regained my focus. "What do you call that fly you made for Winston Hollymead? He won't shut up about it. He's throwing all these numbers at me that sound ludicrous. A twenty-five-pound, post-spawn striper? In the Pawnee?" He blew a raspberry. "Makes no sense."

I chuckled pretentiously at Jim's underestimation of my work. It made a lot of sense if you knew how to get un-horny fish to bite like I did. "The *Alpha-Boom-Train* isn't just for striper," I said with a shrug. "It'll work on any post-spawn perciform. They like bloodworms."

"I don't get you, kid."

"I'm twenty-nine."

"Alpha-Boom-Train? Flies ain't supposed to have names like that."

"Customers are supposed to buy things. What a paradox."

He directed a finger lazily in the direction of my fly-tying vise. "Need you to make me oneuh them boom trains then," he said, issuing an edict as if I were his personal river Sherpa.

"Sure thing, Jim," I answered. "Will you be paying for it or just putting it on layaway until the rapture?"

"I'll pay if it looks right," he said, heading out. He pushed the door open, then stopped, half-in, half-out, sending the electronic chime into a recursive death spiral. "How you know so much about spawning river fish, anyway? You ever even been out of Kansas?"

Now I could tell him the truth. I could explain the things I know – that my knowledge goes *way* beyond fish sex. I could tell him, for instance, that the flatworm *Macrostomum hystrix* reproduces by fucking itself in the head. It's called hermaphroditic traumatic insemination. I could tell him that the practice isn't isolated solely to hermaphrodite worms either. Sea slugs,[1] also hermaphrodites, fuck *each other* in the head. They do it with a two-pronged dong, one of which is called a 'penile stylet'. I could shock his system with the revelation that earwigs have two dicks.[2] Or take him on a tour of class Mammalia and into the dens of prairie voles, who

---

1   *Siphotperon* species 1 – *Oh, here we go, doing the scientific names showing-off thing.*

2   There's a trick-dick in the event of a broken penis.

are affectionate and monogamous with each other unless the male is drunk, in which case he pursues anonymous hookups. That dolphins will fuck literally anything. That porcupines flirt via golden shower. I could tell him these things I know, but then I might have to explain why I know them. And that I am unable to do. So, I answered his question with the simple truth. "I just know, Jim."

"That internet, then," he said, answering the question for himself. "See ya in a few days, kid."

I flipped down the magnifier. "Jim."

The truth is I was jealous of Jim. Of his obliviousness, his ability to step into the world from the shop and move on with his life, while mine never changed. Wherever I went, my brain came with, bringing along its innumerable tidbits of faunal knowledge which infected my every thought. There was no explanation and no apparent source. And it would have been completely useless if I didn't work in a fishing shop trying to figure out new ways to get post-coitus fish to bite at fake bug larvae.

I'm no fly-fishing fanatic. I'm just too distractable for any other job.

Every waking moment is a constant barrage of intrusive thoughts with even the most innocuous stimuli churning up commentary from deep within the folds of my brain.[3] *See?* I've tried training myself to think of it as background noise, but it's tough to tune out when your overactive brain is also an asshole.[4]

---

3   Koalas and koala-like animals have smooth brains. A condition known as lissencephaly – *Kill me.*

4   I'm just a distilled version of you, buddy. Besides, assholes can be really useful. The giant California sea cucumber,

The door chimed again as if it were being strangled. Through the magnifier came a giant yellow blob that I immediately recognized as Patton, my never-employed stoner friend. He wasn't a stoner by choice – well, it was by choice, but it wasn't *just* for getting high. Weed legitimately helped him function. Patton was the only person I'd ever met who got paranoid as a consequence of *not* being high. Also, weed is generally pollinated by wind, not by bees.

He struck a pose and pointed at me, suggesting a pop quiz. "In which Order will we find *D. sylvestris*?"

"I'm not doing this, dude."

"*Hymenoptera*," he said, proudly answering his own question.

"How long did you have to train your eight neurons to remember that?"

"A while," he said breezily, removing a blunt from within his hair somewhere.

"You can't smoke that in here."

"I know that." He sniffed it and returned it to his haybale.

In one of his many attempts to push me to broaden my horizons, Patton had tried to get me to audition for Jeopardy (R.I.P. Alex Trebeck), convinced I'd make a bazillion dollars. What he failed to appreciate was that the only way for me to win would be if every single category was natural science. I don't know jack about much else.

Okay, I also know a lot about clocks. Mainly watches. Ugh. This is so embarrassing.

If areas of knowledge were like college specializations, then entomology, with a focus on bug-sex, would have

---

Apostichopus californicus, eats *and* breathes through its butt.

been my major, with a minor in time pieces.[5] Antiques, for the most part – anything older than about three decades. Imagine seeing a watch and having your head suddenly flooded with facts about said watch, while at the same time not giving two shits about the watch or the facts. A six-thousand-dollar Rolex that gains five seconds per day is said to be within tolerances. That's over a thousand dollars for every second it steals from the Universe. The NASA astronauts who landed on the moon were wearing Omega Speedmasters, all except Neil Armstrong, who left his inside the lunar lander as a backup clock. Watches on display are almost always set at ten past ten or ten till two because the hands form a smiley-face, a subtle form of suggestion for the prospective buyer. Do I come from a family of watchmakers or antique dealers? Nope. I just know. And it's exhausting.

"Well if you won't do it, then at least train me, man," said Patton. "Be like my game-show *sensei*. Just put all your knowledge up here." He popped the side of his head with his palm.

"Plenty of room."

"I know, right? So, there's no excuse. Please dude? Winning gameshows is the only way for me to get enough cash to start my own Formula One racing team."

"No."

"When you off?"

"Seven."

"Want to get wings?" he asked.

"No, busy."

"Not research again. Come on, dude. Every night?"

---

5   Horologics.

"You know the drill," I said.

"It's Friday though. Friiiiiiiiday."

I gave him serious-guy face.

"Alright," he relented. "Roll over to my place in the morning. Aunt Lisa will make us chorizo empanadas and refried beans and we can play Simon."[6]

"Your Aunt Lisa microwaving frozen breakfast empanadas is not making breakfast. And I'll pass on the beans. But Simon is awesome. I'll be there."

"Yeah!" He reached around the counter and patted the underside of that bit of my belly that hangs over my belt buckle. I fired a palm into his sternum and he crashed satisfyingly into a rack of indicators. "Duuuuuuude," he wheezed, accepting my justice.

"No more fat slapping. Jesus Christ, man. Grow up."

He staggered away from the rack and smiled passively at the door. "Okay bro, whatever you say. Hasta mañana."[7]

"Bye."

"See you tomorrow. Empanadas."

"Yeah, bye."

I needed to get to the library, but I also wanted to finish off a fly I'd been tying – a Hutch's Penell – for one of the area's best anglers, and possible future wife of me, Agatha Jensen. It's used in the UK for catching coastal sea trout but it

---

6   The original Simon was first marketed by Milton Bradley in 1978 and later on by Hasbro. The console has four colors: red, blue, yellow, and green, running clockwise from the upper right. The colors light up with a corresponding sound in a random sequence and each player's challenge is to repeat the combination exactly.

7   Spanish – *Wow, really?*

also closely resembles the sedge-flies that the local bluegills, *Lepomis macrochirus*, love to eat. When I started tying them a year ago, the locals couldn't get enough and it kept the shop owner, also named Jim – I call him "Owner Jim" – pretty happy. I could do them in my sleep: size 4 hook, black 8/0 thread, a red tippet, Peacock herl, zebra hackle and silver wire for the rib. Fly fishermen were always looking for an angle (anglers, right?) and this Penell had them shelving their Silver Sedges – the traditional go-to when throwing loops for fish that go for the caddis fly.

I tied in a white hackle feather, wrapped it with thread, thickened the front of the hook to form the fly's "head" and tapped a bead of glue at the top of the shank just under the eye.

After locking up the shop, I had thirty minutes until the library closed, which was fine, because I already knew the book I'd reserved was waiting for me. I jumped into the used Subaru that I'd bought after graduating high school. At the time I'd let Patton talk me into souping it up so we could race it on weekends – an actuality that always seemed to get sidelined by our full schedule of being stoned. Now I just had a car that sounded like a weed-eater in a port-a-potty. But it was fast and I got to the library in sixteen minutes, per my twenty-five dollar Timex brand digital wristwatch, which does not gain five seconds per day unlike a certain unnamed luxury brand performing "within tolerances."[8]

"Ben!"

"Ludlow the Librarian!" I said, miming the solo sword dance of Conan the Barbarian as played by Arnold Schwarzenegger. Ludlow was similar to a barbarian, if you

---

8 It's Rolex – *I know!*

replaced the muscles with nougat and the leather armor with black nail polish.

"I got your book right here. *Reserved for Ben*," he said, tapping a lacquered finger on a stickie note reading same.

"Oh, great. Thanks," I said, rolling up to the circulation desk.

Ludlow prepared to scan in the book, pausing first to consider the cover. He pulled his long, warlock-black hair behind an ear. I could see a question forming. Oh, here it comes. "You studying to become a psychiatrist, Ben?"

"Ah, no, Ludlow." I didn't have much more of an answer for him that I cared to give, though he was well aware of my borrowing history.

"Just a hobby, then? Remote viewing? Claircognizance?"

"Not so different from your weekly séances," I quipped. "You get up in all your customers' business?"

"Only if I think they might be performing witchcraft."

"Afraid you won't be invited?"

"I'm talking about," he lowered his voice, "*the occult*."

I stared at him incredulously. "Have you seen yourself, man?"

He recoiled with offense. "I'm a goth, Ben, not a Wiccan." He slid the book across the counter with a corpse-pale hand.

"I'll remember that for next time," I said, taking the book and tapping the side of my head.

The car rumbled into the gravel drive at the house where I rented an above-garage apartment. I opened the driver's door to a thundering chorus of *Neotibiden linnei*[9] booming away like nature's own heavy metal string symphony.

---

9   Known to laypersons as cicadas.

Although that's a bad analogy, because while crickets utilize stridulation for their song – the rubbing of one body part against another, a crude version of pulling a bow across strings – cicadas are percussionists, vibrating a membrane in their exoskeleton called a tymbal.

Yeah, so anyway, it was noisy outside.

I tossed the new book, *Harnessing Your Psychic Powers Part IV: Remote Viewing & Claircognizance*, onto a larger pile of similarly themed texts beside my desk and quietly hated on myself for possessing any of them. Taking in the collection, I began to appreciate the merit of Ludlow's witchcraft accusation. I even had a stack of religiously-themed candles on a nearby end table, though those had come with the apartment. Sure, I lit them from time to time, but for ambiance, not any ceremonial purposes.

On my way to the fridge, I paused at the giant LEGO sculpture that had risen from the surface of the coffee table in recent months. My parents had treated my moving out as their cue to begin a steady process of getting rid of anything I'd ever owned, including a massive tub of the plastic bricks. I'd planned to give them away, but started pressing them together one day, and soon, well. I found playing LEGOs to be a calming and cathartic exercise; and yes, I am almost thirty. What began as a mindless ad-libbing of pieces ballooned into a gargantuan living room monument that looked like one of those spiky naval mines set atop a golf tee. I reached down to the pile, grabbed a grey eight-by-two and a brown six-by-two, overlapped four of the studs, and pressed them together with a satisfying *skritch*, then added the component to the ponderous hulk.

There was leftover kale and chicken hash in the fridge,

which I warmed, doused in barbeque sauce, and devoured with a spatula as I snapped more LEGOS onto the art. I subscribed to the canceling-out method of eating, where you eat as much junk as you want, so long as you cancel it out with something healthy. I figured the kale would counter tomorrow's breakfast empanadas.

Holding the spatula between my teeth, I dragged my laptop over and tapped it to life.

So. Why was I burning through library cards checking out books on psychic phenomena? Why was I there almost every night and then on the internet for hours after that?

Well, it had to do with the bug fucking and the watches. As a child, tiny pieces of information would crystalize in my head before there was any way for me to have learned them. Déjà vu was one possibility, but I've had déjà vu and it isn't quite the right fit for my experience. You never actually *learn* anything from déjà vu. It's just the sense of vague recollection that fades almost as quickly as it comes. My experience was different. Repetitive. Verifiable. I knew things I had no business knowing. Male soapberry bugs, *Jadera haematoloma,* are absolute sex hounds, screwing for up to eleven days in one go just to ensure that other males don't inseminate the same female. What in the *National* goddamned *Geographic* fuck, right? No one should just *know* that.

My parents recognized early on that there was something weird happening. The second I could make words I began referencing obscure facts, the truth of which could be verified with a little research, but for which my knowledge had no basis. At first, they'd just assumed I was a focused listener. Maybe I'd heard someone drop an interesting nugget in line at the grocery store. Kids repeated stuff all the time. But as

I crossed out of toddlerhood, the pattern settled in. Instead of the occasional, passing fact bomb, I might give a play-by-play of the mating habits of Brazilian bark lice, leaving out no detail. In between bites of mac n' cheese I'd let slip that the female actually has a dick that she uses to *scoop sperm* from the male bark lice's vagina. I remember my parents being in such awe of science that they'd not cared that I was blabbing about insect uglies at the dinner table.

So off I went to the pediatrician for the basic *is-this-kid-okay*[10] checkup, and on from there to the child psychologist. My parents explained to her that I was some sort of genius, but a few simple tests quickly dispelled that hypothesis. Unperturbed, they insisted on a full battery of IQ tests, which were conclusive: I was solidly average, entirely unremarkable. I was simply regurgitating information and terminology of unknown provenance. They went for a second opinion. My scores went down. I was a parrot, not a prodigy. Still, they wanted answers. So did I.

A barnacle of kale and chicken plunked the laptop's touchpad. I set the spatula down next to it and eased it back onboard with my pinky, then hoovered it up.

Together my parents explored every contrived and far-flung theory to explain my curious condition, going so far as to accuse me of reading books in secret. Sneaking off to read? I mean, do people do that? Certainly not me; I had video games to play and snacks to eat (which I then later cancelled out with different snacks).

There was a phase, thankfully brief, where my parents became quite manic in trying to answer the ultimate question. The house was filled with books on gifted children,

---

10 No.

from verifiable prodigies like Bobby Fischer[11] , Blaise
Pascal,[12] and Maria Agnesi,[13] to the entirely paranormal –
ghost possession by historical figures unwilling to cross the
River Styx. They got into psychophony,[14] retrocognition,[15]
transference,[16] claircognizance,[17] and of course, remote
viewing.[18]

For an entire year, every horizontal surface of our
downstairs was covered in crystals. The local news even did
a story once. There I was, blithely regaling the weatherman
with a credible, and detailed, description of grasshopper
sex gear as he grinned nervously into the camera. The
whirlwind of brief regional fame disappeared as quickly as
it had arrived, and by fourth grade I was a local oddity that
most people noted and then promptly forgot. The novelty
wore off. One minute, you're blowing your teachers' minds,
and the next they're sending you to the principal's office for
offering to explain how liver flukes spread via sheep shit.
It wasn't like I could help it. Holding in what my brain was
spewing was a form of torture. My mind was a kettle under
pressure and my mouth the spout.

---

11 Youngest ever U.S. Chess Champion at age fourteen.

12 French inventor and mathematician, authored a treatise on
     projective geometry at age sixteen.

13 Wrote solutions to complex math problems in her sleep.

14 Spirit speaks through a medium (me, in this case).

15 Knowledge of a past event which was not learned or inferred.

16 How doctors say "possession".

17 Like omniscience, except with more incense.

18 Knowledge of something one cannot directly perceive. Also
     known as ESP, or extra-sensory perception – *Or the scientific
     term: "bullshit."*

Ultimately, my parents kept their sanity, resolving to accept the way I was. It wasn't like I had a disease or anything, just an interesting glitch in my wiring. A mutation maybe. It was a party-trick. Like being double-jointed or popping out an eyeball. They moved on.

I couldn't.

You can ignore another person if you want. Put on headphones, tell them to buzz off if they won't take the hint. Brains are different.[19] You're a captive audience to an unfiltered version of yourself. The "me" that occupies my cranium is a know-it-all jabberer. I'm trapped with someone who won't shut up. Like that guy in line at the coffee shop who wants to discuss his passion for latte foam art. Now imagine he's in your head, but instead of heart-doodles in bubbled milk, it's precision timepieces and the toothed vagina of the cabbage white butterfly.[20]

Sleep is my only respite, and even then the thoughts creep in.

I lit some of the candles, illuminating four different versions of white Jesus, then hopped on the internet to begin the evening's search. As I did every night.

Knowing what I know has never been a gift. And I was singularly driven by an obsession to find the cause. My life was a mad search for answers that occupied my time and attention, to the exclusion of nearly everything else. If a patient wakes up from surgery with a bit of gauze sewn into their arm, it sucks but at least they know how it got there. My condition had no explanation. It was too specific to be the result of chance or coincidence. It felt... purposeful – or

---

19 We *never* take the hint.

20 Just imagined it.

planted. Like it was inserted into my head. It wasn't *mine*. And if the knowledge wasn't mine, was I even myself? Was I an experiment? Someone's project or toy? And to what end? I didn't know. That is why I searched so vigilantly.

Like I said: it isn't a gift. It's an invasion.